"It is time for you to hear something very wonderful, but also maybe frightening." Amagyne's eyes held Jude's. "It was revealed twenty-five years ago that there was a child, a very special child, born on September first, nineteen fifty-nine."

"That's when I was born," Jude said.

"When the time was right, this child, a grown woman by then, would come to us at Circle Edge."

"I am the one?"

"Yes, you. You are not an ordinary person, Jude Alta. You were sent to us."

"I was?"

"Yes. You are the Second Guide, the One Who Chooses." Amagyne's eyes continued to hold Jude's. Jude's heart was pounding. Her breathing was suspended.

"You are called the Catalyst," Amagyne said.

Jude's head was buzzing and she felt close to passing out. "You belong with us," Amagyne said. "You are the Catalyst, the one we await . . ."

EDGEWISE

A NOVEL BY CAMARIN GRAE

The Naiad Press, inc.
1989

Printed in the United States of America
First Edition

Edited by Ann Klauda
Cover design by Pat Tong and Bonnie Liss
    (Phoenix Graphics)
Typeset by Sandi Stancil

Library of Congress Cataloging-in-Publication Data

Grae, Camarin.
  Edgewise / by Camarin Grae.
      p.   cm.
    ISBN 0-941483-19-3 : $9.95
    I. Title.
PS3557.R125E4 1989
813.54—dc20   89-33923
                                                            CIP

Books by Camarin Grae

Winged Dancer
Paz
Soul Snatcher
The Secret in the Bird
Edgewise

CHAPTER 1

Jude Alta parked the rented Toyota on the circular drive of the Wright Mansion and walked to the front door. The housekeeper let her in, and Jude climbed the winding staircase to the second floor.

When she entered the bedroom, Rosalie Wright held out her thin hand. "How delightful that you came early. Mrs. Clarkson called you, didn't she?"

"Nobody called," Jude said teasingly. "It came to me in a dream. 'Head west, woman.' " She settled onto the edge of the bed and gently took Rosalie's frail hand in hers.

"You know how I love those mystical experiences." Rosalie's tone dripped with playful sarcasm.

Jude could see the weariness on her friend's lined and wrinkled face and the painful effort in her movements. "I've missed you, Rosalie."

"I love you, Jude."

Jude resisted the urge to cry. She stroked the shiny soft skin of Rosalie's thin arm. "My mom sends her love."

Jude talked about her mother, about Toni, about her life in Chicago. After a while, she took an envelope from her pack. "I brought some photos for you. Here's Zuzu, the calico. She's the devilish one. Loves to chew my plants and sneak out the door."

"Oh, and here's Toni," Rosalie said. "She's so pretty, Jude. She doesn't look like a dyke to me."

Jude leaned back and roared.

Rosalie continued looking at the pictures. "What's so funny?"

"I love you, too, Rosalie."

Rosalie put the photos aside and let her head sink heavily into the pillow. She looked into Jude's eyes. "Thank you," she said, "for all of it, for everything." Her voice was not strong.

One tear escaped Jude's eyes. She stayed with her lifelong friend until she slept.

* * * * *

Before she left the Mansion, Jude sat for a while on the second floor balcony looking out over the Wright Estate and the Lake Valley. To the left was the town, Doray, Colorado, which still in some ways

2

seemed like home though Jude hadn't lived there for twenty-two years. To the right, past the southern bend of Wright Lake, was the Ladies' Farm, and beyond that the highway to Denver and points east.

The Ladies' Farm had always been there as far as Jude knew. She used to have fantasies about "the ladies" when she was a child. Sometimes they were all magical fairies, nymphs and angels flying and dancing in the surrounding hills. Sometimes they were ogres: giant, frightening witches casting evil spells on any mortal who dared approach their lands. Occasionally they were exotic cloistered nuns who secretly came and did good deeds for the people of Doray. That fantasy usually arose when Jude had badly needed a good deed. Jude even remembered times when she prayed to the ladies. But mostly, she thought of them as the other townspeople did, as a reclusive sect of religious women sworn to chastity, simple living, and the tilling of the earth.

Jude's thoughts returned to the wonderful old woman who lay ill and dying in the room down the hall. She let herself cry then.

* * * * *

Traffic was moderately heavy in town; it was late May and the tourist season was beginning. Many of the well-kept, cheerily painted Victorian homes had tasteful signs announcing "Bed and Breakfast" on front lawns or porches. Tulips and daffodils were in bloom.

Jude parked in front of Corbette's Cafe. Late lunchers sat at formica-topped booths and tables. Martha spotted her as soon as Jude stepped inside. A

3

big warm hug followed the "Jude's here!" to Cal who was in the kitchen. The two sisters took the waitresses' booth in the rear of the cafe.

"You look good, real good. You never age." Martha took Jude's hand. "God, it's good to see you! Davey should be here soon. He's growing up so damn fast, Jude."

Cal joined them for a few minutes, rubbed Jude's shoulders affectionately, asked her if she was still playing in the band, and then got back to the kitchen.

"He seems happy," Jude said.

"I try to keep him that way. How's Toni?"

"Fine. Still involved in everything. She's teaching a new seminar this semester, Sociology of Women and Work."

"I admire you two. You're both such reformers."

"I used to be." When Jude frowned, her thick eyebrows nearly touched in the center. "I told you I pretty much gave up my activism."

Martha smiled but looked serious. "I don't want you to become cynical."

Her smile was similar to Jude's though the women didn't resemble each other otherwise. Jude was tall and angular with wide hips and shoulders. Raven black hair gleamed against the shoulders of her thick cotton jacket. Martha was fairer-skinned, with light brown curly hair, a largish nose, and hazel eyes. People often said she seemed to exude energy, like flashing lights.

"I don't think I'm cynical," Jude said. "I just think most of us get too involved in the trivialities of our own lives to put much energy into anything else." She shrugged. "Maybe I *have* become cynical."

4

Martha frowned pensively. "Well, I'll love you no matter what you become. But, you know, sometimes I think there's a part deep inside of you that's very sad."

Jude did not respond.

"Well, anyway, I think you're pretty fine."

"I know." Jude cocked her head. "Why is it that you love me so much? Because Dad doesn't?"

Martha stared at the napkin holder. "Dad loves you."

"Right." Jude glanced around the cafe. "So how's business?"

"Oh, medium good. I'm ready for bigger and better things though. It won't be long." Her face darkened. "Did you see Rosalie?"

"Yes." The corner of Jude's lip quivered minutely. "God, I'm going to miss her."

"I know." Martha laid her hand over Jude's. "Hey, there's the boy! Look who's here, Davey. Say hi to Aunt Jude."

Davey ran up to them and raised a hand to give Jude five. Third graders in Doray were apparently quite cool.

A little later Jude went for a walk to check out the town. Not many changes. She talked with Ethel Emerson in the five-and-ten, picked up some pruning shears for Martha at the hardware store, then went over to Martha and Cal's house to unpack and wait for Martha who said she'd be home by six. They made dinner together. After her glass of after-dinner wine and a few games of slapjack with Davey, Jude left again to go to Rosalie.

CHAPTER 2

The next day, Jude knocked on the familiar door of her former home on the edge of Doray. Her father's wife greeted her cordially and led her to the living room.

"So it's you," he said. Joe Alta was where he could be found every Saturday afternoon, in front of the TV in the old green easy chair.

"Who's winning?" Jude asked.

"You're interested in sports all of a sudden?"

"Not really."

"I didn't think so. Well, sit down, girl. Don't stand there like an oaf." He laughed caustically.

Jude sat. She took a deep breath. "So, how've you been, Dad?"

"Me? Same as always. Thought you said you weren't coming until July."

"I came early, to see Rosalie. She's sick."

"So I heard. Get the girl a drink or something, Sal," he called out. "Your sister likes sports. Sometimes we sit and watch the games together. Sports are a part of life."

"I won a trophy for racquetball." Jude felt a twinge of self-disgust, knowing she was trying to win his approval.

"That's not a real sport."

They were silent for a while. "Davey's turning out to be a pretty neat kid," Jude said.

Her father looked right at her for the first time, his eyes bright. "Ain't he the fella. Smart as a whip. Going places, that one." He scowled at Jude then, his forehead deeply furrowed over his sizable nose. "Doesn't look like you'll be having any kids. Not the marrying kind, isn't that what you said? Well, probably just as well."

Sal brought their drinks. Joe Alta turned back to the baseball game and after ten more minutes, Jude left. The usual rage and hurt and sadness were there. Maybe she'd try again tomorrow.

She walked to the outskirts of town and sat beside the Amica River. Her eyes automatically scanned the bottom for nuggets. She had never seen one, but always looked. Most of the townspeople did too.

7

It had been the hope of finding gold nuggets that originally brought Dorian Wright to this river and that had made Doray a town. When Wright arrived in 1860, the valley was empty except for the wildlife and trees. With his mule, Dupa, at his side Dorian panned the Amica. Finding nothing there, he left the valley and went up into the hills where he struck it rich. The drilling and blasting was still going on at the Wright Mine.

Untouched by the Silver Panic of 1893, Dorian Wright continued to prosper. He laid claim to the northern section of the valley, called Lake Valley, which included the beautiful crescent-shaped Wright Lake. It also included the natural hot water springs which fed the lake and kept it warm. The area was full of mule deer, elk, Rocky Mountain sheep and thick forests of spruce, fir and aspen.

The settlement that grew up in the valley near Dorian Wright's strike was named Doray, after Dorian. Dorian's son, Kendall, built the logging mill and later the furniture factory. Kendall Wright married Rosalie Gish in 1920. They had no children, but as everyone in town knew, to Rosalie Gish Wright, Jude Alta was like her own.

Jude watched the white bubbles along the stony riverbank. Twenty yards away, a young girl watched Jude. The girl's toe played with the drops of water that splashed from time to time, but she didn't take her eyes off Jude. She was slim and freckled and seemed very serious. Slowly she approached Jude.

Lost in thoughts of her father and of Rosalie, Jude didn't notice the girl until she was next to her.

"Hello."

Jude returned the youngster's smile. There was

such a peaceful mature look in those young eyes. "Hello," Jude replied. Neither spoke for a while. "The river is beautiful today," Jude said.

The girl moved closer. "It changes with the sun."

"Yes. And with the weather. You notice things like that, do you?"

"Always." The youngster sat on the rock next to Jude. "You're not like the others," she said.

Jude tilted her head. "What do you mean?"

"Your kwo-ami is very strong."

"My what?"

The girl nodded solemnly. "You're not a tourist here." She said it with great certainty.

"No, I'm not." Jude looked curiously at the unusual child. "What did you mean by my *kwo-ami*?"

"Sometimes we have visitors at Circle Edge. You remind me of some of them, in a way. Could I be mistaken? I don't think so."

Jude shook her head. "I don't quite understand what you're talking about, but I really would like to. Do you think you could be more clear with me?"

The girl knit her brow. "Are you safe?" She looked very seriously into Jude's eyes.

Jude didn't know what to make of the question. "Yes," she answered simply.

"And you love women."

Jude tilted her head. "I do." Who is this child, she wondered.

"Did you come to find us?"

Jude tugged at her lip. "Can I ask *you* a question? Several questions, perhaps. First, will you tell me your name?"

"Miluna."

"Miluna. And where are you from?"

9

"Circle Edge. There." The girl pointed across the river.

"The Ladies' Farm? You live there?"

Miluna nodded. "It's called Circle Edge."

"Have you lived there long?"

"All my life."

"I see." Jude gazed across the river. "What's it like at Circle Edge?"

"I think it would be better if you came," Miluna said softly.

Jude raised her thick eyebrows. "Is that an invitation?"

Miluna hesitated. "I *feel* that it is OK to invite you, but I don't *know* that it is."

Jude smiled. "Some things are hard to *know*. I'd like to come and visit. Do you talk like this with other people you see sitting by the river?"

"Never before."

"Why now?"

"Miluna!" a woman's voice called.

The two looked toward the caller. She was a tall, muscular woman in blue jeans and a full-cut floral-patterned shirt.

Miluna rose and put on her sandals. "We're leaving now. I hope you come. When they see you, they will let you in." She began to walk away, then turned. "What is *your* name?"

"Jude."

Miluna reached into the air as if taking the word into her hand, and placed her hand over her heart rubbing once across her chest. Then she joined the tall woman.

Jude watched them, feeling strangely moved by her interaction with the child. She wondered what it

10

would be like to grow up in a community of all women. She was reminded of her abandoned fantasies of an alternative society, a place where love and connectedness and sharing were the norms rather than the exceptions.

She had always believed that if people would just tap the best that was in them, they held the potential for changing the injustices and imbalances of life. In college, she had majored in sociology and became active in the Women's Movement. She had joined groups, served on committees, marched, demonstrated, dialogued and processed. It all did some good, and it felt good, yet clearly it was not enough. She had watched many pairings and groups and organizations begin and end. There was much internal dissention. *Maybe we need our own space first,* she had thought then, *away from patriarchal institutions.* She had visited lesbian communes but her hopes were quickly dashed. She saw too many women cut off from their deeper selves, their twisted parts sabotaging their hopes and lofty goals.

Some societal progress did take place, Jude knew, but it was slow, and the changes were small and seemed mostly to benefit the already privileged few. *It's so hard,* she thought. *What we're doing just isn't enough.* She grew tired. *Maybe we can't do it. Maybe the energy we need is so submerged that it can't be reached. Maybe God is dead.*

Though Jude had never been particularly religious, she had always felt somewhat attuned to the spiritual part of herself, and would go through periods when she explored — participating in spiritual workshops and gatherings, reading about different religions and sects, experimenting with various methods of getting

11

in touch with her inner being. At times, when she was playing a particularly beautiful piece on her flute, or when suddenly a rainbow appeared over the lake, she would feel filled with something wonderful and powerful and much larger than herself. She often wished that that something was not so ephemeral and mysterious, that she could grasp it and use it to do what sociology and feminism and good intentions seemed unable to accomplish.

Though she didn't consciously give up, as the years passed, she found herself caught up in her own daily living and seemed to have less and less time or energy to work toward change or to seek that *something more* that she was sure was there somewhere. She knew that the oppression and violence and injustices continued to perpetuate themselves, but it all seemed so inalterable. She played her flute, went to her job, enjoyed her lover and her friends. But sometimes she felt only partly alive.

This is how it is, she thought, as she watched Miluna and the tall woman disappear down the road. *I certainly can't change things.*

She had no idea how wrong she was.

CHAPTER 3

Jude sat at the waitresses' booth with her sister. She had been relating her meeting with the child at the river, and speculating about the Ladies' Farm. "I wonder if they're lesbians," she said.

"Everyone says they're celibates. Like nuns. You know, in all these years I've never had a conversation like that with any of those people, adult or child." Martha took a napkin and rubbed a smudge off the salt shaker.

"It makes me very curious," Jude said. "She was strange, but intriguing. I liked her."

"Cal thinks they're pagans."

Jude smiled. "I'm going to go visit them."

"You used to ask me to take you there when you were little. Once when Dad was out hunting, he saw a couple of them in the woods gathering berries. He said they walked like men and dressed like men. He says they're not right. I doubt if they'll let you in."

"Miluna seemed to think they would."

"Well, don't be disappointed if they don't. On second thought, I should probably be more concerned if they *do* let you in." Martha gave a little laugh. "Who knows what goes on in there? I've watched them at night sometimes, from up on the highway. They do these candle things, move around with candles and make patterns." Martha waved her arms in the air and rolled her eyes.

"Yeah, I've seen it too."

"Cal says they have the right to be left alone if that's what they want. I agree. He got so pissed the last time some of the local guys tried to break in."

"It happens every few years, doesn't it?"

"No one's ever succeeded. They're impenetrable."

Jude laughed at the double entendre.

"And then there are the journalists," Martha continued. "That woman from Denver four or five years ago didn't get in either. She came to the cafe afterwards. Said her editor would be pissed because she didn't get a story." Martha sipped her tea then added more sugar.

"Tea-flavored syrup," Jude said. "I guess a lot of people are curious about them."

"I'm so used to them I hardly ever give them a thought."

"Yeah, I think that's how most people around

here feel. Talking with Miluna got me more interested, though."

"Madsen would like to get them out of there. You know those foothills above their part of the valley? He says they would make a perfect beginner's slope. And he'd like to build a lodge where they have their farm and houses."

"I doubt they'll be leaving."

Martha shrugged. "They might have to. Rosalie owns most of their land, you know. It will go up for sale, too, when she . . ." Martha looked at he sister. "I'm sorry."

"It's all right. How are the plans coming?"

Martha leaned forward excitedly. "Madsen's already hired the contractor. He showed me pictures of how the resort will be. It looks fabulous, Jude. Our restaurant's going to be huge."

Jude stared at the speckled green table top. "It'll seem strange having buildings around the lake." She shrugged. "I guess the whole town is going to change when Rosalie's gone."

"It will be like a flower finally coming to full bloom." Martha's eyes shone until she noticed Jude's expression. "What's wrong?"

"When you talk like that I think of vultures."

Martha lowered her eyes. "I'm sorry, Jude. I can see how it seems that way to you."

Jude blinked away tears. "She always loved the peacefulness of the lake."

"Madsen says Wright Lake is more of a gold mine than the Wright Mine." Martha was beaming again. "We're about to drill the first shaft."

Jude smiled. "You hopeless entrepreneur. You really love making money, don't you?"

"It's not the money, really. It's the challenge and the excitement. I love running a business. Making it work. Yeah, making money too. It's hard work, but I love it."

"Don't you worry about the town losing its character when the developers take over the valley?"

"It's going to take on a much better character," Martha said excitedly. "Things can get pretty dull here sometimes, you know, especially in the winter. They're talking about putting in an airstrip now. Can you believe that? People will flock here. Fishing, boating, swimming in the summer, skiing in the winter. The Mansion will make a fabulous luxury hotel." Martha's face glowed. "The town's going to explode, and Cal and I will be a part of it right from the beginning." She stopped suddenly. "Jude, you don't think I'm a vulture, do you?"

Jude smiled wryly. "I think you're a human being."

They were quiet for a while, then Martha spoke. "In some ways I've envied your relationship with Rosalie. That special magic between you two. She took to you from the very beginning. I wonder if part of it was loneliness."

"She missed Kendall terribly. She still does. Maybe I helped fill the gap a little." Jude smiled sadly. "She loves to tell the story of the first time she saw me."

"At the Harvest Festival. You couldn't have been more than three years old."

Jude still had the sad smile. "Rosalie was sitting at the head table and I came up to her with a little bouquet of wildflowers. Ingrid must have given them to me. Rosalie says I walked right into her heart."

16

"Ingrid's too. You used to want to be a gardener just like her when you grew up. Do you remember that?"

Jude nodded.

"They were your second family in a way. Rosalie Wright, the eccentric millionaire dowager, Ingrid Thorensen, the flower woman, and Jude Alta, the most lovable kid in town." Martha smiled warmly at Jude.

"I remember being very happy as a kid." Jude's smile was melancholy. "I thought the world was a wonderful, loving place to be. People seemed so good and kind." She pursed her lips. "Except for Dad. I thought he was the only exception. But I always believed he was good inside." Jude shook her head. "He really could hurt me."

"I know. I never have figured out why Dad was like that with you. Mom and I used to talk about it. She said maybe it was because the two of you were so different. One time I said maybe he's not really your father. Mom didn't like that."

Jude fiddled with her ring. It was silver with a faint engraving of the double women's symbol, a gift from Toni. "There were lots of times when I wished he *wasn't* my father." She looked at Martha. "At least he always loved *you.*"

"I think he loves you, Jude. There's just something . . . I don't know . . ."

"It affected me. I've had my share of trouble from other people — being used, or even worse, being rejected, but I don't think anyone really got to me like Dad did."

Martha shook her head sadly. "I think it helped that Rosalie was so loving toward you."

17

"You had Dad and I had Rosalie." Jude twisted her slice of lemon and watched the juice squirt into her glass. "After Mom and I left Doray I was afraid I'd never see Rosalie again."

"Really?" Martha's thin eyebrows lifted. "Didn't you think you'd ever come here to visit me and Dad?"

"I didn't know. I didn't know how divorces worked."

"Yeah, that's true, you were only eight."

"Are you glad you stayed in Doray?"

Martha nodded. "It was terrible for a while though, missing you and Mom. But I didn't want to leave Dad."

"What a hard choice."

"And I didn't want to leave Doray." Martha looked out the window. Jude's eyes followed her sister's. They watched a woman emerge from the Orange Star Gift Shop across the street. "I begged Mom to stay." Martha chuckled ruefully. "I can still remember what she said. 'Doray's too small for both of us.' Her and Dad."

"She told me that too. You've always loved this town."

"I know. Just think, Jude, if I had left with you and Mom, I never would have met Cal."

"Probably not."

"And there'd be no Davey."

Jude smiled.

"Anyway, yes I'm glad I stayed," Martha said. "I couldn't wait for your visits. A month every summer. Rosalie always made sure she was in Doray during those months."

"We were together a lot."

"One time she gave me a glass elephant," Martha said. "I'd never let you touch it."

"I remember."

"I still have it. How come she never gave *you* gifts?"

Jude raised her brow. "She didn't, did she? I don't know. I never gave it much thought."

"She'd pay for everything when you two went on trips, but she never gave you *things*. Or money."

"She offered to pay my tuition to college."

"That's right. I remember your telling me that. But you had the scholarship to Northwestern and didn't need it."

Jude smiled nostalgically. "She loved my college days. You know, my involvement in all the political things. She got a lot of vicarious satisfaction out of that. She became a feminist too. I loved it. I used to tell her everything that was going on. I think that's when she finally found names for some of her own feelings. Her anger and her hopes."

"She lived through you in some ways."

"I know she didn't like it when I quit graduate school, but she never guilt-tripped me about it."

"How did she handle your religious periods?"

"Oh, she wasn't crazy about them. But I think she respected my need to search."

"You never did find what you were looking for, did you?"

Jude's eyes grew sad. "I suppose not," she said.

"You know, I've been thinking," Martha said. "Maybe what we all heard is wrong." She had a glint in her eye. "Maybe Rosalie's not going to leave everything to the Wright Foundation after all. Maybe she's going to leave her fortune to you." She laughed gaily. "Wouldn't that be something?"

Jude shook her head. "I can't remember how many times she said all that wealth is just too much for one person to handle. Nope, she wants it spread around. She's already given the Foundation millions, and after . . . when she's gone, it will get the rest."

"I know. My guess is she wanted to be sure your attachment to her wasn't based on money. That's why she never gave you any."

"Maybe," Jude said. "I never gave it much thought. She's always been so loving to me. She accepted me as I was, never pressured me about anything. You know, now that I think of it, that's true of all four of you. The four women in my life: Mom, you, Rosalie, and Toni. I feel very lucky to have you all."

Martha took Jude's hand. "It's mutual," she said warmly. "The cafe is filling up but I don't want to stop talking."

"Want me to help out?"

"No, you're on vacation. Go vacate. We'll talk some more later."

* * * * *

Jude drove to the Wright Estate. She sat for two hours beside Rosalie. Most of the time Rosalie was asleep, but occasionally, she looked at Jude, though she did not speak. Jude felt the bond as if it were tangible.

CHAPTER 4

The next morning Jude took Davey for a ride along the mountain roads in Martha's jeep. Davey spotted a deer and Jude stopped the jeep to watch it.

"Grandpa says Grandma Claire used to hunt them."

"Really? I never heard about that," Jude said. "In fact, I thought she was very against hunting."

The deer leapt away. Jude drove them to the upper rim of the canyon, then back down on Lower Gorge Road. The beauty was magnificent. She dropped Davey in front of the house. "Your mom and dad are back from church. Tell them I'll see them later, that I'm going to visit Rosalie."

* * * * *

Inside Rosalie's quiet bedroom, Jude put on an album and Rosalie smiled. "I thought you'd choose that one."

It was Jean-Pierre Rampal's *Sukaro*. They often used to play it in Rosalie's BMW when they went for a drive. Jude pictured Rosalie at the wheel, her elbow hanging out the window, her glistening brown hair blowing in the wind.

"Our mountain music," Jude said.

"You can always count on the mountains." Rosalie smiled sadly and closed her eyes. "Ingrid used to say that. She couldn't imagine living anywhere but in the mountains. She said they gave her a feeling of security." Rosalie shook her head. "And then they killed her."

Jude stared out the window at the snow-capped peaks. "It feels different here with her gone."

"I wanted to let the weeds take over and let things grow wild, but Eleanor wouldn't allow it. She hired some man to do the gardening. But no one can take Ingrid's place. My room always had flowers when Ingrid was here."

"Would you like me to bring some up? The tulips are blooming."

"No. Eleanor brought some and I told her to take them away." They listened to the lyrical sounds of Rampal's flute. "Ingrid believed her positive energy would come back and enter someone who needed it," Rosalie said. "She believed things like that. Silly twit.

22

Once she said it might enter you. I told her that you seemed very full of good energy already. She said everyone can use more."

"I suppose we can."

"I'm frightened, Jude." She grasped Jude's hand. "Death is so big. I never wanted to handle the big things."

"It's hard." Jude felt her throat clenching up like a fist.

"I wanted to do so much more." Rosalie's eyelids flickered. She sank down deeper into the pillow. "At least I started the Foundation. At least I did that."

"Yes, you did. It's important. It helps a lot of people."

Rosalie looked at Jude with heavy-lidded eyes. "I don't think you're afraid of the big things."

"You need to sleep." Jude pulled the sheet up to her friend's chin. "I'll come again soon."

* * * * *

From the Wright Estate, Jude headed north on Clement Road. She pulled off near a ledge and looked at the view, Rosalie's estate on the left, the Ladies' Farm on the right. Her throat was still tight. Her tears made the lake dance blurrily before her eyes.

She continued north on Clement to the turnoff that led to the Ladies' Farm. A half mile later she came to the gate, pulled the jeep over and stopped. She had been this far a number of times over the years. She wondered if she'd get any farther this time.

The gate was heavy iron and secured by a thick chain and padlock. The farm was entirely surrounded

23

by high cliffs and barbed wire fences. The only way in or out was through the gate. "Protecting their virginity," the townspeople used to say. In the past when Jude had gotten to this point, she would sit awhile waiting to see if anyone would come. They never did. And then she'd leave.

Little was visible from the gate. The road curved just beyond it so the buildings were out of view. Jude considered beeping her horn though that seemed rude. Then she saw a rope hanging on the rock to her right. She had never noticed that before and wondered if it had always been there. She gave it a light pull. A melodious bell sounded somewhere inside the compound.

Jude began to feel nervous. *What am I doing here?*

Two or three minutes later, a woman appeared on the other side of the gate. She was of medium height with long straight hair and no makeup. "Yes," she said pleasantly. "May I help you?"

Jude was tempted to say she was looking for the Kaden Mine Tour, the main tourist attraction in the area. "My name is Jude," she said. "Jude Alta. I talked with Miluna yesterday and she thought it might be OK if I came here for a visit. She wasn't sure." Jude didn't want to get Miluna in trouble. "But she thought that maybe it might be OK. I'm really not sure . . . well . . ." She was feeling warmly embarrassed..

"Would you mind waiting just a couple of minutes?" the woman said in her pleasant way. "I'll be right back."

Jude waited nervously. When the woman returned,

24

she unlocked the huge padlock and pulled open the metal gate. "Come with me, please."

Jude waited while the woman relocked the gate, then followed her around the curve. She could see a small building about fifty yards ahead, made of the same stone as the surrounding hills. Rocks blocked her view of anything more. Inside the small building a short hallway led to a square room about the size of a large bedroom, furnished with a couple of sofas, some chairs and a rectangular table.

The woman beckoned Jude to take a seat. "My name is Sarah," she said. "La will be here soon to talk with you. Make yourself comfortable. It won't be long." Sarah poured Jude a glass of water from a carafe. "Spring water. The most delicious in the world."

Jude took the glass and watched Sarah leave. She looked around the room. Paintings hung on all the walls — oils, watercolors, acrylics — the colors ranging from vivid bright to muted and subdued, the themes from elaborate complex designs to a few simple lines that magically brought mountains and trees to the eye. She drank the water. She moved closer to one of the paintings. A person dancing in the hills — Jude couldn't tell if it was female or male — a dancer with huge golden wings.

"I've seen you before."

Jude turned sharply at the sound of the deep voice.

"The feeling is stronger now."

Jude took her in. The hair was white and full and healthy-looking. She suspected it had never known a curling iron or blow dryer. The forehead was high

25

with arching charcoal gray eyebrows over pale blue, bright, incisive eyes. The wrinkled skin was bronzed, the color of Jude's own, the nose long and narrow, lips thin but not severe. Her appearance was unique, yet vaguely familiar.

"You were born in Doray," the woman said, her voice low and sure. A frown creased her brow as she scrutinized Jude. Her eyes looked momentarily pained, or maybe angry, Jude thought.

"Yes." Jude was about to say more, to make the socially appropriate comments, but something stopped her.

"Almost thirty years ago."

Jude nodded. The older woman stood five or six feet from Jude.

"It was in the summer, late summer. Your birth."

"Yes, September first. How do you . . ."

"Miluna was right. It's good that you've come." The woman went to her and Jude felt the warm strong arms embrace her. The woman stepped back and looked at her again. There were tears in her sky blue eyes. "Your life has not been easy. Your spirit must have struggled and been turned by what you found out there."

Jude's eyes were narrowed, puzzled.

The white-haired woman nodded, smiling. "I know. You don't understand. You're like a child raised by wolves then finally coming home."

"I'm not sure who you think I am but —"

"I know who you are." The woman smiled knowingly. "You don't. Not yet. You will. You must meet Amagyne and begin your reading with her. She will tell you."

Jude was feeling uncomfortable and a little

irritated. "I really have no idea what you're talking about. You think I'm somebody you know, but I'm not."

"Sit down, Jude. Jude Alta. A good name but not your true name."

Jude sat on the sofa and the woman sat across from her on a tapestry chair.

"I am La. Blessed and enabled." She took a deep long breath. "When I was very young, I was compelled to explore, to find the whys of the workings of the human soul. My searching got me nowhere though I looked everywhere. The same was true for you, was it not?"

La smiled and the matrix of wrinkles around her eyes curved like arched bows. "I looked at Buddha and Lao-tse and Jesus," she continued, "in all the ways humans knew them. I looked at Zoroaster and Krishna and Confucius. They were all on the edge but none was in the center, each had only part of Kwo-am's truth, and each called her by a different name." She looked pointedly at Jude. "You know her as God."

Jude tilted her head. "Why do you call God by a new name?"

"The name is not important," La said. "What is important is the message. I am the bringer of Kwo-am's messages. Though I did not choose it, I welcomed it."

Jude was beginning to think this strange woman was crazy.

"The richness of your kwo-ami is very apparent to me. Do you sense any of your specialness?"

This was feeling too weird to Jude. "I'm really not understanding you. I thought perhaps I could

27

look around your . . . around Circle Edge and see what . . . have a tour maybe, but uh . . ."

"Relax," La said gently. "Hummmm-mmmmm." Her eyes were closed.

The humming continued. Jude scrutinized the aging woman critically, but then her eyes began to blur. She could feel the vibrations of the humming sounds reaching a place in the back of her head. It felt very good. She let her eyes close and her tension and discomfort began to diminish.

"Hummm-mm-mmm. Mm-mmm."

Jude wasn't sure how many minutes had passed when La began to speak again. "You've noticed that there's cruelty and hate and destruction in the world."

Jude felt relaxed. The statement seemed strange, yet in this context, not surprising somehow. "I've noticed. Deeply embedded in it."

"It has pained you," La said poignantly. "You sought to understand it and change it through reason and education. And you also sought understanding through the spirit. Your search has brought you to an impasse, yet I tell you, Jude, do not give up. It is not hopeless."

"Maybe not," Jude said. "Some change has taken place. It's a struggle."

La smiled warmly at her. "We are on the brink of great changes."

Jude was beginning to feel some discomfort again. "How do you know about me?" she asked. "My age . . . that I was born here?"

"Your neighbors here at Circle Edge are not so isolated as you think. You and I had a mutual friend. Her kwo-ami has joined the pool of life energy. I speak of the woman-of-the-flowers who was called Ingrid Thorensen."

Jude nodded. For some reason she was only a little surprised. "Ingrid never mentioned you."

"When you left Doray in nineteen sixty-seven, you went with your mother to live in Chicago. And that is where you still live?"

"Yes."

"Not alone."

"Do I live alone? No, I live with a friend."

"The friend, she is your lover, is she not?"

"Yes. Ingrid told you about Toni?"

"We have many sources of knowledge. And you are happy in Chicago?"

Jude shrugged. "Yes, sure, I'm happy. I have everything I need — Toni, some good friends, my mother, my music, my job. I work at a travel agency." She wondered why she was going on like this. "I get to take quite a few trips which is the best part of —"

"It's a shallow happiness," La said decidedly.

Jude was looking into the bottomless blue eyes. "It's good enough. I'm basically satisfied."

"You've adjusted."

Jude shrugged again. "And your life here? Is it satisfying?"

A few moments passed before La responded. "We made the journey in nineteen fifty-one," she said, smiling reminiscently. "That was eight years before your birth. It gets more and more satisfying."

"Why did you settle in Doray?" Jude wondered if La would say much more. She remembered Martha's story about a friend who had tried to talk to some of the women when she met them in town, asking questions about the Ladies' Farm. They had been evasive and Martha's friend had learned very little.

"It was written."

"That you come here? Written by whom?"

"The Sage," La answered.

Jude was beginning to feel the uneasiness again. This woman was an interesting character, but not very easy to converse with — similar to other mystical types Jude had met in the past. "And who is the Sage?"

"I am." La crossed her hands over her chest. "La, the Sage. The writing comes through me, through my hand, and through dreams. It wrote that I should set out toward the middle of the land and take with me some Kwo-amians."

"You mean you have dreams that —"

"Seventeen of us came in nineteen fifty-one. Our community has grown since. And there are many others of us scattered everywhere. Soon there will be many more."

Jude was thinking about the dreams and about other people she had heard of who believed their dreams were messages from the supernatural world. She wondered how crazy this woman was. "You don't usually welcome visitors," she said. "Why me?"

"This you will learn from Amagyne when you come for the readings. You have choices to make. Important choices. Will you choose to come?"

Part of Jude wanted to leave this weird place and never give it another thought. Part of her was undeniably intrigued. "I don't know. This is all very puzzling to me. I don't think I belong here."

"You belong. Many will think you do not. Sadly, your friend, Rosalie, is one of these. If she knew of

30

your visit here it would upset her. But yes, Jude Alta, you do belong. You will learn more at the reading."

"What happens at a reading?"

"Your inner space will be touched," La said, "and you will begin to awaken." She rose and placed her hand on Jude's shoulder. "Before you come, go into the mountains. Go alone and look at the sky and let the sky enter you. See what you feel. We'll stop now. Sarah will walk you to the gate."

Jude stood. "I thought I might have a tour, that maybe someone would show me around."

"Come back tomorrow," La said, "in the afternoon."

CHAPTER 5

Myth, wishful thinking, and asininity. Jude was lying on the grass looking at the calm waters of Wright Lake. That was certainly Rosalie's perspective about the supernatural. Because of a fanatically religious mother, Jude suspected, although Rosalie had never said so.

She watched a leaf floating along the surface of the clear water. Some people really *are* receptive to spiritual experiences, she thought, wondering if La was one of them. Ingrid certainly had been. Jude wondered why Ingrid had never told her of her connection with Circle Edge, and just how deep that connection had been. Obviously, despite how close she and Ingrid had been, Jude hadn't known her as well as she thought.

Now it was too late. It had been the winter before last when Rosalie had called with the tragic news. Ingrid had been buried in an avalanche, had been missing for five days before they found her.

Rosalie had cried and so had Jude as they sat together at the funeral service in neighboring Ridge Valley, Ingrid's hometown. Ingrid, like Rosalie, had been part of Jude's life. She had taught Jude about plants and flowers, God's creations. Ingrid used to refer to God as *she* sometimes, Jude realized. Interesting. Ingrid had told her stories, and played ball with her, and taken her on walks and picnics. When Jude was older, she and Ingrid would sit together and have long talks. Jude had confided in her. She was a good friend, Jude thought, and now she's dead. And Rosalie is dying.

Jude went inside. Rosalie was staring at the TV. She squinted at Jude. "What is it? You look upset."

"I was in the garden."

Rosalie nodded knowingly.

"Can I get you anything?"

The old woman shook her head sadly. Her neck looked pathetically thin. "I don't have the energy to read or the appetite to eat. It's all going, Jude. I wish I could say, let's have a steak together, or even a beer. My body doesn't want those things anymore."

Jude switched off the television and pulled the antique wooden chair closer to Rosalie's bed. "Remember the time you and I and Ingrid went berry gathering and I found that little carving?"

33

"A wolf and a rabbit, asleep side by side. Ingrid thought it was an omen, that you were meant to find it."

"I still have it. Do you think it was an omen?"

"I think you might have the power to make peace among battling elements."

Rosalie was interrupted by a fit of coughing. Afterward, she was exhausted. She could not keep her eyes open. "Oh, Jude, I'm good for nothing anymore," she said, and lay quietly.

Jude sat awhile watching her friend sleep, watching her flat, wasted chest go up and down. She took a paper from the pad on Rosalie's dresser and drew a picture of two women on horseback. *You and Me*, she wrote, and left the drawing on Rosalie's belly.

* * * * *

That night, Jude's father and his wife came for dinner at Martha and Cal's. Joe Alta laughed warmly with Martha, asked her questions about the cafe, congratulated her again on her election to the school board, and teased her fondly about the gray hairs he detected among the brown.

Jude, feeling like an outsider, turned to Cal. They talked about camping and Jude's recent trip to Mexico. She was relieved when her father left and she and Martha could talk. Their conversations always came back to Martha's dream — the new restaurant she and Cal would manage and someday own, the changes that would take place in Doray. Jude didn't tell Martha she had been to Circle Edge. As close as she was to her sister, it was Toni she wanted to talk

34

with. And yet something stopped her from calling
Toni.

* * * * *

The next day, a little after noon, Jude drove up
into the mountains, driving farther and higher until
she had left all signs of human life behind. Then,
taking her pack, she left the jeep and the road and
hiked even deeper into the mountains. She pulled
herself up a steep ridge and sat. She had never been
to this spot before. In every direction were jagged
fir-covered hills and beyond them bare rock peaks
with strips of snow. The sky was clear and bright,
the air cool and the sun pleasantly warm on her skin.

La's face appeared. Wrinkled, warm, and knowing.
Her eyes, blue like the sky. It seemed to Jude as if
she had seen this face many times before, as if she'd
known her for years. And her words came back. *I
know who you are. You don't. Not yet. You are rich
in kwo-ami. You're like a child raised by wolves then
finally coming home.*

What's that supposed to mean, Jude thought. Toni
would dismiss it as mystical nonsense. She wished
Toni were with her now. She felt as if something
weird was happening to her, some irresistible pull
toward that strange place and whatever it
represented. Toni would scoff at it, she knew.

Jude looked at the sky and felt absorbed by the
vast unendingness of it. She felt light-headed. What's
happening to me? I should have called Toni, she
thought.

Just thinking of Toni helped. *God, I love that
woman.* Jude took the canteen from her pack and

35

drank some water. She pictured Toni's full lower lip, the sometimes pouty lip that melted Jude. She pictured her intense eyes and the little group of three freckles on her temple. She wanted to kiss her there. She wanted to hold her and be held.

They had been together four years and four months now, and Jude never tired of kissing Toni and holding her. She could still remember the very first kiss. It hadn't been an explosion exactly; more like a soft, powerful warming of her, inside and out.

They had met at a Chicago Gay and Lesbian Band concert. Jude played the flute. Toni was in the audience. After the performance, Toni had come up to her.

"Beautiful music."

Jude felt the attraction immediately. She couldn't take her eyes off this deep-voiced, bronze-skinned woman. They spoke for a few minutes, then other people crowded around and Toni was gone. Over the next week or two, Jude thought of her frequently. She wondered if she'd ever see her again and how it would be the second time. Then one night there she was, in Found & Out, Jude's favorite women's bar. Toni was leaning on a stool, deep in conversation with a very young, curly-headed fashion dyke. Jude had never been troubled by shyness, but suddenly she felt awkward, squirmy. She could actually feel her heart pounding. Toni spotted her and smiled. Jude's heart raced even more. Toni approached her.

"Jude Alta, the music-maker. I'm Toni Dilano. Do you remember, we spoke at the band concert?"

"Yes, I remember." Jude was afraid she was staring dumbly.

"I know *your* name because I asked around. Does that seem forward?"

"Yes, but uh . . . I like forward." Jude was trying to be calm and casual. "And I like to dance. How about you?" She smiled invitingly.

Toni held out her hand and they walked together to the little dance area. Jude remembered that first touch as well as she remembered the first kiss which came three hours later. They had left the bar and gone to Jude's apartment for coffee. The talk and laughter came so easily, especially the laughter. Jude's sense of humor was a salient part of her, but Toni fed it so perfectly that Jude felt wittier that evening than she ever had before. The attraction grew stronger as the evening progressed.

"Why haven't we ever met before?"

"Maybe we were saving it."

They sat on the sofa in Jude's living room, talking quietly, joking less. Music played, but Jude wasn't paying any attention. Toni moved her fingers gently along the sides of Jude's neck, sweetly stroking her. When their lips softly, warmly touched, Jude knew this was what the songs meant.

The move from the sofa to the bedroom seemed Jude's doing, but she wasn't sure, the two of them seemed so synchronized. She loved touching Toni's face, soft little barely touching strokes. Clothed but barefoot, they stretched out on the bed side by side, and Jude could not get enough of the delightful touching. Each caress warmed and chilled her and filled her with anticipation of what was to come. Slowly, savoring the movements, Jude undid the buttons of Toni's olive green shirt one by one. She rested her head between the sweet, small breasts, content for a while just to lie that way, and then she began to move her head, very slightly, back and forth, caressing the soft, smooth skin with her face and lips. *What a wonderful woman you are,* she said without speaking. Toni's strong arousing fingers stroked Jude's back as Jude's tongue traced moist circles around the peach-colored nipple, erect now under her touches. Her mouth drew the nipple slowly in and she could feel Toni's responsive tremors.

The unrushed lovemaking intensified, gradually becoming more driven and passionate. For Jude it was the most intense, gratifying lovemaking she had ever experienced.

In another month, between silly playful times at the zoo and along the lakefront and everywhere they went and between far-into-the-night talks and lovemaking, they declared to themselves and each other that they were very much in love. Jude wondered how she had ever thought she'd been in love before. This was different. More. More than even those songs and romantic stories and all that foolish propaganda promised. She never thought she would feel this taken, this connected, with another human being.

Six weeks later, they moved in together. The feelings continued to grow even when they thought they could grow no more.

* * * * *

Jude leaned back on a rock looking at the sky. If Toni were here now, Jude knew what she would say. *Cultists. Mystics. Stay away.* Jude often inhibited

38

herself from telling Toni about her spiritual feelings and ideas.

My rejection of religion is logically and compassionately derived, Toni would say. Toni saw herself as so clear-headed and reasonable, believing that if something couldn't be measured or logically inferred, then it didn't exist.

Jude knew there was more. There had to be.

It's a shallow happiness, La had said. *I know who you are. You don't. You must meet Amagyne and begin the readings with her. She will tell you.* Jude started to feel dizzy again. Maybe I'm coming down with a cold, she thought. *Your spirit was turned by what you found out there.* Why am I even thinking about this? Why am I up here looking at the sky? The blueness took her in. La's sky-like eyes drew her irresistibly.

CHAPTER 6

Jude pulled the rope and listened to the melodious clang of the bell. She felt more curious than nervous as she waited. She would go for the *reading*, she had decided. No harm in that.

It was Miluna who arrived with the key. "La said you would come," she declared happily, releasing the lock. She looked at Jude with intense admiration. Taking Jude by the hand she led her past the stone building where Jude had been with La two days before. They continued down the road and around the curve, passing a circle of small wooden A-frame

40

structures. "Those are the sleeping huts," Miluna said.

They turned off the road onto a tree-lined path which curved to follow the river. Jude found the beauty of the place breathtaking. They walked along the river for another five hundred yards. It seemed oddly familiar to Jude, the curve of the path, the mountains in the background. At the end of the path was a large stone building.

"This is the Dome," Miluna said. "Amagyne is inside."

When they entered the building, Jude's gaze was immediately drawn upward by the majestic mountains visible through the glass convex roof. Miluna waited patiently while Jude stared, then urged her gently onward through a sunlit hallway which led to a large open area of plants and trees and soft chairs and little round tables.

The open area was actually a room, enclosed by walls and a ceiling, yet it seemed more outdoors than in. In its center was a circular pond draped with huge plants. Miluna took Jude to the pond's edge and asked if she would like to touch the water.

Jude bent and scooped up a warm-cool handful and watched it trickle away.

"The warmth of it comes from fires deep down in the earth."

The words were not from Miluna's sweet young voice. This voice sounded like velvet and was soft like the water. Jude turned and looked into the woman's eyes and could not look away. *Could one see to the center of the universe through the eyes of a human being?* What a strange thought, but so it seemed to Jude as she felt herself pulled into the deep, dark, sparkling depth of the almond-shaped eyes of the magnificent woman who introduced herself as Amagyne.

"Will you sit with me, Jude?"

Jude moved mechanically, lowering herself onto the white bench beside the pond, staring without self-consciousness at the tall, lithe figure who moved without seeming to touch the floor and who spoke of the messages water sends, words Jude barely heard. How many minutes passed she did not know, so caught up was she in the image before her.

The eyes were the most magnetic feature, but each of the other features captivated Jude as well. The nose was perfectly sculpted, with flared nostrils. The olive skin, smooth and clear, was cut by high cheek bones and dark arching brows. The black hair fell silk-like to the shoulders, with a hint of meandering curl.

Amagyne offered Jude a flower and as Jude took it their fingers touched, Amagyne's skin even more velvety than her voice.

"I thought you would come sooner." A pitcher of ice water sat on the table next to the bench. Amagyne poured them each a glass. "From the earth," she said.

Jude drank. "I grew up near here."

"Yes."

"I thought you were nuns . . . or witches."

Amagyne nodded, her hair brushing against the soft fabric of her tunic. Just then a small, brightly-colored bird landed on her shoulder. "Dia," Amagyne said, turning her face to the little bird. She gave the bird an air kiss that sent a shiver along Jude's spine.

"She always come to me when there is a stranger," Amagyne said, a wide smile framing her milk-white teeth. They both watched Dia fly up into a tree branch. "But you are no stranger," Amagyne said. "Here, give me your hands."

Jude reached for her.

"Yes, good hands, strong and large."

Jude looked at their entwined fingers. "Similar to your own," she said.

"We are sisters." A beam of bright sunlight rested on Amagyne's shoulder. "But you have been in the outer world all your life." Sadness darkened her face for a moment, then lifted. "Do you know of Kwo-amity?"

Their hands came apart and Jude felt the loss. She finished her glass of spring water. "When I met La the other day, she talked about Kwo-am. She said it's the name you use for God. I would assume Kwo-amity is the name of your religion." Jude's heart was pounding wildly and she was surprised she could speak so normally.

"Through La, we have been given a fuller understanding of the Creator than was known to earlier religions. Kwo-amity is the final step. It links all the religions together and reflects the truth about humankind's true purpose and destiny."

Jude watched Amagyne's mouth as she spoke, fascinated by the movement of the lips and by the clear ring of the sounds which came from them.

"Before the beginning," Amagyne said slowly, "there was only one anything, a force. We call her Kwo-am."

Jude's head felt pleasantly light.

"Coming from everywhere, flying freely, timeless.

43

Kwo-am. Always there. The creator of life, movement, growth, love. The generator of all form."

Somehow the words seemed like gifts, and Jude felt immensely fortunate to be hearing them. The late afternoon sun, low in the sky, sent slivered rays through the glass ceiling over Amagyne who seemed to draw them magnetically.

"But then another force arose," Amagyne said. "A counterforce. We call him Zetka, though, like Kwo-am, he too is known by other names. Zetka, the enemy of life, the perverter of all form, the generator of destruction, cruelty, hate, pain and death."

Jude could almost feel the negative energy the word inspired. More evil even than *devil*. "Zetka," she said aloud. The name sounded like a curse, felt harsh and bitter in her mouth.

"And the struggle began," Amagyne continued. "Kwo-am–Zetka. Force–counterforce. Move–counter-move. Kwo-am created and Zetka responded, doing what he could to infiltrate what Kwo-am made. Each had a great influence on what has come to be." Amagyne looked caringly at Jude for a long time. "Are my words reaching a good place inside you?"

"Yes," Jude said in a breathy whisper. "I like the feelings I get listening to you talk."

"The reading goes well."

The image of Amagyne, enveloped now in brilliant sunlight, shone so bright it made Jude squint. It seemed that Amagyne herself was the sun, the brightness emanating from her.

Amagyne stood. "Come."

Without the slightest hesitation, Jude rose and walked with Amagyne back through the hallway and outside. A group of women was at the river. Several seemed to stare with awe at Amagyne as she and Jude passed. The women waved and Amagyne returned the greeting.

Amagyne led Jude around the Dome and along the river toward the mountains. Jude wondered if they were going somewhere to make love. That seemed to be the natural thing to do now.

After a few minutes they came to a clearing. In the distance was a high rocky hillside. As they drew closer Jude could see that the cliff had a vertical crevice about eight feet high and a yard wide. Amagyne entered the crevice and Jude followed. They walked along a rock-walled corridor on a path of mosaic tile. As they went deeper into the tunnel the air became crisp and cool.

Amagyne had taken a torch from somewhere and its bouncing light lit their way. At the end of the passage, they came to a large high hall. There was no door. The walls were of a bamboo-like material and bent inward. There seemed to be no angles, only curves. The hall opened into a vast garden. They were outside again in a rock-surrounded valley with flowers and trees everywhere. A waterfall trickled down smooth stone and into a stream. Amagyne walked softly along the wooden path past tile-lined pools surrounded by walls of fern and flowers. They entered one of the circular enclosures formed of living walls. Contour benches sprouted around the perimeter of the pool, padded with what appeared to be moss. Two of the benches faced each other.

Amagyne took off her soft moccasin-like shoes and slid into one of the benches, bidding Jude to take the other. Jude removed her hiking boots and sank into

45

the deep, soft, mossy fabric which molded to the contours of her body and embraced her. She felt snug and secure, as if she and Amagyne had come home and would soon melt into each other and become one.

They sat quietly listening to the gently falling water, eating fruit and nuts from the bowl nearby. The light was fading and an orange, golden glow covered them and the water and the trees. Jude felt content. She had little awareness of the passage of time, and may have even dozed as darkness grew around her. The air had cooled but the embracing moss kept her warm.

"Human beings evolved with the potential to do what no other of Kwo-am's creatures ever could," Amagyne said. "Eliminate Zetka's power over them." Her voice seemed a natural part of the water and greenness and flowers around them. "The rest of creation was set, controlled by the laws of physics and nature."

Jude nodded, listening intently to the words that seemed so saturated with meaning.

"But humans are different. *We* have the potential for change within ourselves. *We* have the capacity to expel Zetka from our hearts."

The waning sun caught the folds of Amagyne's white flowing tunic and she appeared to be clothed in billowy clouds.

"And, hence, we have the power to bring forth Kwo-world." Amagyne's face and eyes were glowing. "A world of zetkap-free people, kwo-omnis. A world free of cruelty, hate and violence, founded on respect and caring, one for another, and for ourselves. Kwo-world is Kwo-am's dream," Amagyne said, looking at Jude. "It is my dream."

46

"I know the dream," Jude replied. "Do you think it's really possible?"

"Kwo-am has given us the necessary powers. It is up to us."

Their eyes were locked, the air buzzing with the energy between them.

"For us to use our potential, we need Kwo-am's guidance. She has made herself known in many ways, to different people in different cultures in different ages. Some chosen ones, the early Sages, took steps to move things forward. There were successes but also many failures. The counterforce was powerful. There were many distortions of the truths Kwo-am revealed through the Sages. But some of her message did get through. Zoroaster heard some, and Mohammed. Siddhartha, and Jesus of Nazareth, and Tianuma of the Bowesos in Marigua heard. But the perversions and distortions and hypocrisy were great."

Jude nodded knowingly.

"Now, in our time, the situation has grown alarmingly dangerous. Our era is called the Time of Danger. The prophet, Tianuma, predicted many centuries ago that Kwo-am would make herself known more directly than ever before in a time of great technology and danger to the earth." Amagyne looked pointedly at Jude. "That time is now."

Jude was blinking rapidly. Amagyne reached over and took her hand. Jude felt electric energy in the touch.

"You're cold," Amagyne said. "Come. Let us bathe in the warm pool."

Amagyne stood and with a few smooth movements her clothes lay on the lounge. Jude stared at her perfect body, the living statue of a goddess. She

47

couldn't tell if the sensations in her stomach and groin were erotic or something else. Amagyne went to the pool's edge, sat a moment, then slipped down into the dark water.

Jude removed her clothes and followed Amagyne, barely aware of her own movements. The water was very warm. She realized how chilly the air had become.

"These ponds are fed by natural springs, hot waters from beneath the earth," Amagyne said.

"It feels wonderful."

"The water is sweet and delicious." Amagyne carried a drop of it with her finger to the full lips of her open mouth. She moved her tongue slowly across her lips. "When I'm away from Circle Edge, I take some of the spring water with me. There has never been a single day in my thirty-five years that I haven't had a drink of it."

Pushing with her hands, Jude moved slowly about in the shallow pond. There were several smooth seats molded in different shapes beneath the surface. She found one whose contours felt exactly right for her. Amagyne was opposite her. The warm, soothing water came up to their necks.

"Is there something special about the water?" Jude asked.

"Some say it has the power to release bound kwo-ami. That the kwo-ami from the dead seeps into the earth and finds water and permeates it. Those who die very rich in kwo-ami will be reborn full of their original kwo-ami. Those whose will-to-Kwo-am is very strong can bathe in the kwo-ami-rich water or drink it and be permeated by its energy. It has allowed me to remain zetkap free. I am a kwo-omni."

48

"And everyone who drinks it becomes a kwo-omni?"

"No. Everyone who bathes in it, though, or drinks it can feel the freeing up of the kwo-ami they have within themselves."

Jude closed her eyes and tried to feel it. "It is very calming."

They remained quietly under the stars for a long time. The water warmed Jude deeply. When Amagyne began to speak, Jude realized she'd been dozing.

"Our Sage was born over seven decades ago. When she was a very young woman, the Creator, Kwo-am, came to her." Amagyne raised her hands, letting rivulets of warm water spill through her fingers. "Like the other Sages before her, La was chosen. It all became clear to her after she found the carving of the leopard and deer, predator and prey, lying peacefully side by side."

Jude's eyes widened. "I found a carving once."

Amagyne smiled at Jude and nodded. "La found hers in a cave. Afterwards, the new truths were revealed to her. She learned of the competing forces of kwo-ami and zetkap, and of her part in what was to come. She was to share the truth with others who could hear it, and prepare the world for the Coming of the Guides and for the Ceremony of Emergence."

"She told me that she dreams," Jude said hazily. "She said she's blessed and enabled."

"Yes, that she is. Some of what she learns she writes in the *Fruit of She,* a book only La is permitted to view. The words are written *through* her, but they come from Kwo-am."

"*The Fruit of She,*" Jude repeated. Her toes found

an inlet of very warm water. She let it stream over her foot.

"La is told in dreams how much to share with other Kwo-amians and when. Also, through the dreams, new revealments come. Most of them she shares with us. Some, the Mysteries, can be known only by La. She thinks that the Mysteries are settlements, compromises between Kwo-am and Zetka, though she does not know this for sure."

"They must have made lots of compromises," Jude said, thinking of how most everything seemed to be a mix of positive and negative.

"Yes. Both forces are immensely powerful. If it were not for the threat of the other, either one could take over the universe entirely. Each fears the possible results of the other's intervention. If Kwo-am were fully free to act, she could override human choice and directly instill in all humans a profusion of pure kwo-ami."

Jude nodded, trying to imagine what the world would be like then.

"But Zetka has a parallel power. If he were free to act, he could override human choice and directly infect us with immense amounts of pure zetkap."

Jude cringed in spite of herself, not wanting to think of that.

"That is why the world has always been such a mix of good and evil," Amagyne continued. "For if either Kwo-am or Zetka were to begin this direct overriding of human will, the other would respond by doing the same. Neither would be sure of victory. Since the risk is so great, neither has been willing to act with full force."

"Hmm, balance of power," Jude said, pensively.

"Yes, exactly." Amagyne smiled warmly at Jude. "Neither will intervene with full power for each knows it is possible to lose all."

For a brief moment Jude found herself wondering if Amagyne really believed all this — that God spoke to La, that He was a She and Her name was Kwo-am — but the thought slipped away as Amagyne continued.

"Both Kwo-am and Zetka have acted upon human beings over the millennia, but in milder ways. Kwo-am by instilling kwo-ami into humans at birth and by giving us her truths through the Sages, Zetka by instilling zetkap and making us doubt or deny Kwo-am's messages. This is how it has been since the beginning of human life. But with the dawn of the nuclear age, Kwo-am has felt impelled to begin more forceful interventions. The power of Zetka has become so established that evolutionary change to a better world may be impossible."

"Nuclear destruction?" Jude said.

"It is very likely, maybe inevitable, unless something changes the course of the world. So Kwo-am conceived her plan and has begun to work. For each move she makes, Zetka makes a countermove. Yet she must proceed. And so she has entered more directly than ever before into human life. Not only does she communicate, through La, with those who will hear, but she has sent two representatives, two guides, through whom the New Page and the Withering of Zetka will begin."

Jude was beginning to feel overwhelmed by all the words.

"Zetka places many obstacles in the path of this plan," Amagyne said. "Skepticism being the main one.

51

He keeps people clinging to the old ideas, closing their minds to Kwo-am's most recent and most urgent messages." Amagyne looked caringly at Jude. "You are growing weary."

"But I want to hear more," Jude said quickly. "About the representatives and the New Page and all that."

Amagyne nodded. "All that I have told you, we have learned through La's revealments. Nearly forty years ago, La's dreams told her to gather the Kwo-amians and come to the middle of the land and find the place in the mountains by the crescent-shaped lake where the hot springs flow. When she and the others arrived here, La knew this was the place."

"Doray," Jude said. Her mind was feeling hazy.

"Yes. Right here. Soon we will spread around the lake."

Jude cocked her head. "Oh? Wright Lake?"

"La says it will be. We call it Crescent Lake. Its waters are very special. We are to encompass the whole Lake Valley."

Jude thought of Martha, but immediately the thoughts slid away.

"Soon after the first Kwo-amians settled here, La revealed that Kwo-am would send a child, called the One Who is Formed, and this would be the First Guide." Amagyne closed her eyes. "I was born three years later, in nineteen fifty-four."

"You?" Jude tried to sit up but the effort seemed too much.

"Kwo-amians came from around the country for my birth. There was much celebration. La explained how the women must nurture and prepare me for my ascent into the role I must play."

"You were sent by Kwo-am? You're her representative?"

"Yes."

Though still spellbound, Jude was finding this hard to swallow. "So, what do you guide? I mean, what does it mean?" Raising the questions made her feel uneasy.

Amagyne smiled at her, watching her closely. "We must go slowly," she said in her soothing way. "Another time we will talk some more. I think this is enough for now."

Jude realized she was exhausted. They left the pool and dried themselves with towels from a stack on a nearby table, then they lay on hammocks under soft comforters. Amagyne's revelations spun around in Jude's head. Soon she fell asleep. She dreamed of walking in the woods and of the sounds of singing voices, of being in a special place where everything was peaceful and loving. She slept until Amagyne gently roused her.

"Come," she said, "It is time for you to leave."

They walked together to the gate. "Return tomorrow. There will be an Avowal Ritual," Amagyne said as they were parting. "Come at noon." She hugged Jude and the hug kept Jude warm the whole way home.

CHAPTER 7

Jude's sleep that night was filled with dreams of magic and bewitchment, and Amagyne was in them all. In the morning she felt as if she had a hangover. She sat drinking coffee at the breakfast table with Cal and Martha until they and Davey had to leave for the day and Jude was alone with her thoughts.

Good versus evil, prophetic dreams, mysteries, automatic writing, special representatives from God. How tempted she was just to write it all off as made up or delusional. She put her cup in the dishwasher and went to the back porch to sit. Time of Danger.

They're right about that, she thought. The names are unimportant, Amagyne had said. The messages La receives are the truth.

Jude tried to discount the significance of the feelings she'd had while listening to Amagyne, to laugh off what she had heard as just one more mythology, but her head remained fuzzy and aching. Images came of Kwo-am and Zetka battling over the future of the world. *Move–countermove.*

* * * * *

It was nearly noon when she arrived at Circle Edge to witness the Avowal Ritual. Curiosity, she told herself, was all that had brought her here again. The sun was bright, though occasionally partly hidden by thick white cumulus clouds.

Amagyne led her through the grounds to the Dome and down a stairway to a cellar where it was nearly pitch dark. Before entering they were given amber-colored robes. Jude sensed more than saw the others gathered in the eerie room. As her eyes adjusted, she could see the circle of women sitting on benches around the large chamber, all cloaked in identical amber robes. Torches provided the only light.

Jude and Amagyne sat. It was deathly quiet in the huge room. At last a single low note came from a bassoon. It grew until it filled the air and was joined by other low and rumbling sounds — a bass, tom-toms.

A door opened. All eyes turned to watch as three figures entered. They were wearing floor-length black cloaks, bordered in red; hoods covered their heads. Led by a torch-carrying woman in an amber robe, the three moved to the center of the room, the music playing ominously, its volume rising and rising until it became almost deafening. Then suddenly the sound stopped. The silence was startling.

An amber-robed figure stood with raised arms. "To invoke Kwo-am to purge, purify, wash clear, absolve and cleanse," the strong voice said. "For this we gather."

Jude recognized the speaker. It was La.

"Purge and purify," a chorus of low, sonorous voices chanted.

One by one, La asked the three in black, the avowers, if they sought the purification, calling out their names, and each, in turn, answered that she did. Notes of the bassoon punctuated their words. Each avower acknowledged that zetkap had pulled her and that she had written down her zetkap-inspired thoughts. La took a red sheet of paper from each of them, and burned them with the torch.

As the flame died out, the room suddenly was full of movement. Robed women moved about in a heavy, foot-pounding dance, chanting loudly. It took Jude a while to make out the words, ". . . out of her . . . zetkap, be gone . . . zetkap, out . . . zetkap out of her!"

Amagyne was on her feet with the rest and Jude, too, picking up the beat, the pounding feet, the chanting. The three hooded women stood with arms crossed over their chests, hands fisted, heads bent as the chant went on. Soon a deep rumbling sound replaced the chant. A hundred larynxes were humming and the room seemed to vibrate.

"We are sending our kwo-ami energy to push the avowers' zetkap into the farthest tips of their bodies," Amagyne whispered loudly, her lips almost touching Jude's ear.

La had taken hold of the left hand of one of the avowers. She pricked the woman's thumb with a thin knife and a small drop of blood formed. "Zetkap," La said, as someone leaned forward with a small cup of water and the drop of blood was dripped into the cup.

"Captured," the woman said.

The piercing was repeated with the two other avowers. Then someone pulled the cloth off a table in the center of the room, revealing a black wire cage. Many flaming torches cast light on the three jumping, fluttering birds within the cage. La poured the cup of bloodied water into a trough in the cage. The birds ran to it, drinking rapidly. A thick silence hung over the room as all present stared expectantly at the birds while they drank their fill, then staggered to the edges of the cage.

"The shrikes will die now," Amagyne whispered.

Everyone waited soundlessly. The birds' movements became slower and more sluggish, until one after another, they fell and lay motionless.

La looked at the avowers. "Come. Your zetkap has been purged."

As these words were spoken, a ray of bright blinding light appeared from above and fell on the trio in black. The three raised their arms and their faces high into the air. Their hoods fell from their heads. Suddenly many hands began clutching at their cloaks, pulling and tearing. The black cloth gave, falling off in shreds around them, revealing the whiteness beneath. The avowers, cloaked now in

57

milky robes, stood tall, eyes glistening in the stream of bright glowing light.

Two women picked up the cage and began to walk slowly toward the door. A woman with a torch followed, leading La and the three who had been purged. The rest of the women went also, Jude and Amagyne among them. The procession ascended the stairs and poured forth into the outside air where the amber robes glimmered in the bright sunlight. Jude blinked and shaded her eyes.

The congregation formed a circle around the cage in which the three birds lay motionless. La was helped onto a chair. Her arms raised once more, her clear voice broke the silence. "Out of evil comes good as we concentrate the spirit of Kwo-am and bring it forth. Let us begin."

Jude's hand was taken by the woman next to her. Amagyne took the other. "We will bring the birds back to life," Amagyne said to Jude.

All the women had joined hands.

"Into ourselves we go to touch our purest parts and bring forth our strongest kwo-ami." La had come down from the chair and was standing near the three avowers, holding hands with them.

"We are to immerse ourselves in loving thoughts now," Amagyne whispered.

All eyes were closed. A deep humming moved through the group. Jude felt the energy, and thoughts began to come to her. She thought of Toni and the feeling she got when they held each other. She thought of the soft fur of the cats. She thought of her mother, always drinking tea and persevering and being there for her. She thought of Rosalie and the depth of their bond. She felt the warm sun on her shoulders and more thoughts came. The time she'd lost her wallet and it was returned in the mail. The beauty of the mountains, the rush of the surf along a beach. She thought of the many times Gresh had needed to talk and sometimes cry and Jude being there for her and the times it had been the other way around. She thought of Pam and how lucky she was to have a friendship she knew would last forever. She thought of Davey's birth and Martha and Cal's joy. She thought of the many little ways she'd been given to and gave to others in her life. The thoughts went on and on.

As the humming continued and the thoughts continued, Jude felt something she had never felt before, and she felt Amagyne's hand in hers on one side and the hand of a stranger whom she loved on the other.

The thoughts came one upon the other and the feeling grew until it was interrupted by a bustling and cheering. The humming had stopped. People were looking into the cage. The birds were on their feet, stretching their wings and rippling their feathers.

"And the shrike shall be reborn," La intoned. "And go forth to become a sparrow, full of the spirit of Kwo-am."

The three avowers in their pure white gowns approached the cage. One of them undid the latch and threw the cover back. All eyes watched as the birds, one by one, emerged from the cage, flapped their wings, and took off into the blue sky. They became little specks in the distance and when they disappeared entirely, the cheer that arose was deafening.

Dancing followed, and music and food. The three

59

avowers danced until they collapsed and lay on the grass in a state of blissful exhaustion, their eyes glazed. Jude, too, danced madly with the others, feeling joyful and alive.

After the dancing, Amagyne took Jude to a building called Circle House and sat near the open windows in a sitting room.

Jude looked out at the mountains. "You know what part I liked best? When we all held hands and thought about things to bring the kwo-ami out. Something happened to me then. I felt something very . . . powerful and . . . I don't know, it's like I actually felt the energy. I sensed the energy that was there."

"That we all brought forth."

"Yes, I mean I really felt it. It was when I had my eyes closed. I felt your hand and the other woman's and I felt that . . . glowing kind of feeling, very rich and . . . deep. Filling. I've never felt anything like that before."

Amagyne nodded. "I feel it every time. Yes, it is powerful."

"The three who were . . . you know, the avowers, they seemed so happy afterwards. So free."

"They were transported to a state of pure ecstasy," Amagyne said. "We call it Monama."

Jude's lips moved soundlessly to form the word.

"Monama was the first and ultimate idea," Amagyne said. "Perfect rapture. It was from this idea that the need for existence arose. Kwo-am conceived of Monama and that is what inspired her to penetrate the vast void and generate form, and ultimately, life."

Jude nodded pensively. She was still feeling high

from the ritual. "I wonder if that's what I felt. Monama."

"Maybe so. Close, at least."

"The avowers' negative energy, their zetkap . . . it was captured in the drops of blood, right? Wasn't that the idea?"

"Yes. The energy that was associated with what they had written on the red sheets that La burned. The zetkap that had pushed them into whatever it was that they wrote on those sheets was mobilized and concentrated by the ritual, and it was removed from them."

"In the blood."

"Yes, and given to the shrikes."

"Tell me about them. I never heard of shrikes. Are they found in this area?"

"They are found all over the world. The shrike is Zetka's symbol. The Bowesos of South America had a ritual very much like ours, also using shrikes. The shrike is Zetka incarnate. It's an aggressive, predatory creature. With that hooked bill that you saw, it kills insects and birds and little mammals. After killing them, the shrike impales its victims on sharp thorns."

Jude made a face. "A fitting symbol," she said. "So they drank the blood with the zetkap in it, and that killed them."

"Yes, they became saturated enough with evil to extinguish the life Kwo-am had given them. But out of evil we can generate good. And we did. The shrikes were reborn."

"To become sparrows."

"Yes."

"Literally? I mean, when they flew off, they still

looked like they did in the first place. Are they supposed to literally change into sparrows?"

"Perhaps. There is room for individual interpretations."

"I don't believe they were really dead either."

"It was symbolic," Amagyne said.

Jude raised her eyebrows. "Do the others know that?"

"Yes. The water the birds drank contained a sedative."

"I see." Jude was quiet for a while, thinking. "It was very moving, the whole ritual. Very powerful. Much of it is symbolic, isn't it?"

"Yes it is."

"I liked it." Jude felt filled with loving feelings. For Amagyne, for the women of Circle Edge, for the world. "I've been to other religious and spiritual rituals, lots of them, but I never felt before what I felt here today." Jude took a deep breath. "I still feel the afterglow." She laughed. Her cheeks felt warm. "I felt communicated with, personally, by something out there, or in here, something bigger than just me. I felt the energy. It left me feeling so good . . . so full of . . . of love." She looked tenderly at Amagyne.

Amagyne laughed. "It's a wonderfully satisfying feeling."

"Yes, but more than that. To tell the truth, I felt kind of . . . stunned, or . . . overcome. I don't know . . . Even now, just talking about it, I can kind of feel it again. I like it a lot." She smiled lovingly at Amagyne. "I want more."

"It is always there."

"And my mind felt kind of fuzzy and floaty, but in a very positive way."

"I know the feeling well."

Again Jude shook her head. "But all that stuff you told me, about God — Kwo-am — intervening the way you said . . . I don't know . . ."

"Such things are not easy to know."

"God revealing things through La, that's kind of hard for me to . . ."

"You've been long in the outer world. There are many false ideas for you to overcome."

"I was trained as a social scientist," Jude offered.

"There is some truth in that training, but we speak now of another realm."

"That's true," Jude said. "Tell me more about it, Amagyne. I need to hear more." She took a deep breath and smiled dreamily. She felt herself floating closer to Amagyne.

Amagyne crossed her long legs, leaned back comfortably. She told Jude again the true story of the beginning, the battles between the two forces, and the compromises that resulted. She gave many examples. When she mentioned predation, Jude thought of Toni's cat, Alice B, stalking a mouse, slapping it with her paws, shaking it and snapping its neck. "Kwo-am wouldn't have made creatures that had to kill others to survive."

"Never," said Amagyne. "But she could not prevent Zetka's countermoves. She created reproduction, allowing the creatures to make more like themselves. The many births let life go on despite Zetka. Yet Zetka had influence there as well. He evolved two distinct sexes in most animal forms, one of each needed to procreate. Kwo-am would have been happy with just one, generator of both seed and egg."

63

Amagyne's black eyes, angry now, drew Jude in. "Divisiveness resulted. Battles between males for use of females."

"It all could have been done much differently," Jude said.

"Had there been no counterforce, it certainly could have. And yet, as Kwo-am looked over what she had made in the pre-human world, despite Zetka's influence, she surely must have felt great waves of Monama. Seeing her oceans move, mountains rise, the greenery and the flowers, the birth of new creatures, the seasons, the sunshine, the growth."

"Beautiful. Powerful." Jude pictured the primordial scene.

"But Kwo-am did not wish to be alone. The animals she had created were not capable of experiencing Monama, and Kwo-am longed for someone who could. So again she acted, creating a new form of being, step by step, letting it evolve."

"Humans," Jude said.

"When it came to them, to us, Zetka's countermove was immensely strong. Kwo-am's and Zetka's wills battled more than at any previous time. Although neither won decisively, in a sense, Kwo-am did win."

Amagyne told Jude of the three important abilities Kwo-am had given to human beings: the power for conceptual thought, the capacity to feel compassion, and most important, the power to choose. "Unlike any other creatures," she explained, "humans alone were given the capacity to evaluate and make choices. And humans alone among all the creatures are able to affect the flow of zetkap and kwo-ami within themselves."

"Choose who we become," Jude said.

"Yes, though it is not easy to choose the way of Kwo-am, to transcend narrow self-interest and overcome the influence of zetkap. But the reward is great." Amagyne looked pointedly at Jude. "For those who succeed are open to experience more than just monam, more than just the everyday pleasures and joys of life. They are open to pure Monama, complete rapturous joy and ecstasy."

Jude was listening intently.

"Zetka imparts enough of his malignant energy into the human soul," Amagyne continued, "that the kwo-ami within us is distorted and adulterated. The battle to free it is difficult."

Jude nodded. "Yes, extremely difficult."

"But it *is* possible," Amagyne said encouragingly. "People do succeed to various extents. Now, however, in our time, we have been given the opportunity to defeat Zetka *totally*. If we succeed, we will bring forth Kwo-world."

Jude nodded tentatively, trying to feel Amagyne's optimism.

"Kwo-world," Amagyne concluded, "where the joy of Monama — that feeling that you felt a little glimmer of — is more than a fleeting moment known to only a few."

Jude sat quietly, pondering her words. After awhile, she stood. "I want to leave now, but I definitely want to come back."

"We will welcome you." Amagyne stood also and took Jude's hand in hers. Jude felt tingling up and down her spine and in her groin. "When you come next time, perhaps you will spend the night."

65

CHAPTER 8

Amagyne walked Jude to the gate and said goodbye. It was nearly four o'clock when Jude arrived at Martha's house and phoned Toni.

She talked with Toni about Rosalie and Martha and the cats and their Chicago friends and Toni's research and the flat tire Toni had on the way to Gresh's house and how the town of Doray and Jude's father were the same as always. But she did not talk of Circle Edge or Kwo-amity, and Jude did not mention the strange feeling she had that the love she shared with Toni was in jeopardy.

When she hung up, Jude felt a heaviness in her chest. Perhaps it was guilt. Toni sounded so normal, as if nothing had changed.

Jude sat for a long time by the dead telephone. Finally she mobilized herself and called the Mansion. Rosalie was doing better, Eleanor told her. It would be a good time to visit.

* * * * *

Rosalie was out on the balcony, her legs covered with a blanket. "How I love the sun." Her voice sounded stronger. "The sun is life."

Jude kissed her cheek and handed her a bright yellow tulip. "Toni says hello."

"I was thinking about her," Rosalie said. "And about your friend, Gresh. About the time she came here with you."

"Gresh enjoyed the visit. She still talks about it."

"Remember what she said about the Estate? Her friend . . . what was her name?"

"Leslie."

"Yes, Gresh said the Estate would be the perfect location for Leslie's spa. For the Feminist Fund, wasn't it? Yes, build a spa for the rich old ladies — I didn't take that personally — so they can grow healthy and at the same time help the Women's Movement grow."

"They both have dreams — Leslie and Gresh."

Rosalie lay the tulip across her lap. "Do you believe in dreams, Jude?"

Jude smiled to herself. "Sure, some of them. Some people think they get messages from the gods through dreams."

67

"Some people think the moon is green cheese," Rosalie said testily. She looked out over the land and across the river. "When you were a child you used to dream of a *special place,* do you remember? A place where you would play in warm water and listen to music, and sometimes dance."

"My woods dreams." Jude felt the memory drift over her. The dreams were vague but she could fuzzily recall how she would wake up in the woods after a post-picnic nap and tell Ingrid what she had dreamed. Jude smiled at Rosalie. "You're feeling better today, aren't you? I'm glad."

"Maybe there's some life left in me yet."

They chatted pleasantly for another hour. Jude left feeling very happy that Rosalie seemed to be improving.

* * * * *

That evening Jude told Martha she had been to Circle Edge.

"So they actually let you in." Martha heaped sugar into her coffee. "Well, tell me about it, I'm dying to hear."

"They've got a beautiful setup. There are hot spring pools all over the place and the buildings are fabulous. You feel like you're outdoors and indoors at the same time." Jude described the various buildings she had seen and the layout of the compound.

"What about the women?" Martha asked. "What are they like?"

"Very kind. Very nice."

"Did you learn about their religion?"

"A little."

"So is it weird or what? Are *they* weird? Come on, tell me. What are you covering up?"

"I'm not covering up anything. I found them intriguing."

"Really? In what way? Case studies? Interesting sociological phenomena?"

"No. Not like that." Jude squirmed uncomfortably. "I'm going back. I'm going to spend the night there."

Martha scrutinized her. "Are you planning to write a story about them? Sell it to the *Denver Post*?"

Jude laughed. "No."

Martha looked serious. "You're still searching, aren't you, Jude? It's their religion that intrigues you."

Jude did not answer.

"Is it Christian?"

"They speak of Jesus, but no, it's not specifically Christian. From what they say, it links all the religions together."

Martha nodded. "Go on."

Jude hesitated. She didn't think Martha would hear it with an open mind. "They talk about our spiritual energy and ways to free it. They have rituals. It's all very positive."

"Hm-m. It's strange, isn't it?" Martha said. "They've always been so secretive and yet they invite you to come and learn all about them. So why are they interested in you all of a sudden, that's what I want to know. What do they want from you?"

"I don't know what you mean."

"I think they sent that one to the river to get you."

"Oh, really?" Jude was incredulous.

"I've been thinking about it ever since you talked about that weird little kid. I think she was there to recruit you."

"Martha, that's silly. It's not like that."

"I've read about how those cults work."

"It's not a cult." Jude wished they weren't having this conversation. "It's a community. They have some religious beliefs that tie them together."

"Did they let you in because you're a lesbian?"

"I don't know," Jude said. "Martha, it's nothing to worry about. You sound worried. It's innocent. It's no big deal. I find it interesting and I want to learn more about it, that's all."

"Well, I hope you know what you're doing."

* * * * *

The next evening, Jude arrived at Circle Edge with a small overnight bag. When Amagyne came to her and touched her shoulder, Jude's throat constricted. They walked past the sleeping huts to Ambrosia, a stone building fifty yards off the road. A flagstone path led to the entrance.

Inside Ambrosia, groups of women came and went. Amagyne led Jude through double doors to a dining hall which reminded Jude of a Japanese restaurant subdivided into sections by paper walls. It had a simple, clean but cozy look and feel. In the back were long tables of fresh sliced vegetables and fruits and platters of bread. The choice of hot dishes was written neatly on a blackboard. Through a window behind a wall Jude could see women cooking.

Jude and Amagyne got their meals and took them to one of the sectioned-off areas, joining another woman whom Amagyne introduced as Ella.

"You're a Kwo-amian, aren't you?" Ella asked. "You seem to be, but I could be wrong."

"I'm just learning about it," Jude said. "How about you? Have you been here long?"

"Ten years last month. It's hard to believe I spent the first twenty-three years of my life in the outer world. I learned about Kwo-amity directly from Amagyne. I met her at a coffeehouse in Seattle."

Ella looked lovingly at Amagyne. "That was sure the first day of the rest of my life. She told me about La and the revealments and the community here. It struck such a chord I knew it was right for me. Is that happening with you?"

Jude added more creamy dressing to her salad. "It's hard for me to accept everything I'm learning. There's so much that's new to me, but yes, it is striking a chord."

"I thought so. I know what you mean about the new stuff. It's like when Jesus was on earth preaching to people. A lot of them couldn't accept it. That's Zetka at work, fostering the doubt. But you'll overcome it, I'm sure. I can feel your kwo-ami. It's very strong. Mine was pretty weak when I first got here. I'm kwo-z now. I started out as zet-kwo. It took a while to get here. I was kwo-zet for over two years. My competitiveness was so ingrained in me. I was in the Olympics in seventy-four so you can imagine what I had to overcome."

Jude nodded, only partially understanding.

"It took lots of rituals, and the stretching talks helped, of course, and the stories from *The Words*, and just being here at Circle Edge."

"What's zet-kwo and kwo-z and all that about?" Jude asked Ella.

"Ah, the Ascent. Amagyne hasn't told you about that yet." She cut her quiche into little squares as she talked. "Well, there's like steps. Some people get all the way to kwo-z. OK, let me start from the beginning." Ella forked one of the squares into her mouth. "When we're born, we all have some kwo-ami in us and some zetkap. Some say everyone's born with the same amount of each, that we all start out equal. Others think males are born with more zetkap — you know, all that male aggressiveness. Anyway, depending on how your life goes once you're born, your kwo-ami blooms and grows or it's stifled by zetkap and gets submerged. So there ends up being different amounts of kwo-ami and zetkap in everyone. Some people end up just loaded with zetkap. Men mostly, but some women too. We call them zet-k's — full of zetkap with just a little kwo-ami. They're the worst. If you ever met one, you'd feel it. Very bad vibes. Then next is zet-kwos. More zetkap than kwo-ami, but enough kwo-ami to prevent them from being real monsters. That's what I was when I came."

"How did you know?" Jude asked.

"La told me. Then there's the next step, the kwo-zets. A lot of basically good people fall there. More kwo-ami than zetkap, but some fairly serious shortcomings. The next is kwo-z. Still some remnants of zetkap, but not much. Quite a few of us here are kwo-z's."

"Does it end up being like a status thing?" Jude asked, "like a hierarchy with the kwo-z's better thought of than the ones with more zetkap?"

"Absolutely not. Nobody knows anybody else's step, for one thing, unless you tell her yourself. Nobody asks. I always talk about it. Some people do, some don't. The final step in the Ascent is kwo-omni. There's only one kwo-omni in the whole world so far and she was born that way. You're sitting next to her."

Jude glanced at Amagyne.

After dinner, Amagyne and Jude went upstairs to the rec room. Various activities were going on — card games, board games, Ping-Pong, clusters of women talking. Heads turned when Amagyne entered. A woman beckoned her over. Jude was introduced and she felt immediately welcome in their circle.

It was about eleven o'clock when Amagyne suggested sleep and Jude realized how tired she was. Amagyne walked with her to the sleeping hut named Sky Palace. Inside the wooden structure were roomy cubicles with slanted ceilings. Some had single beds, some double; some several beds, some only one. Each had a dresser or chest of drawers, a mirror, a small table, a telephone, and one or two soft easy chairs of various styles. Some had TVs. Each had paintings on the walls and table lamps of polished wood.

"There's an empty room down the hall," Amagyne said. "A single. I think you'll be comfortable there."

Jude knew Amagyne would be leaving her then, and she felt a little sad.

"If you rise early, feel free to wander around. If you sleep late, there is breakfast all morning. Sleep peacefully, Jude."

Jude's sleep was not unpeaceful and yet it was full of dreams. Women of all colors and shapes floated over mountains. They wore long glistening robes of different colors, very bright colors. Like rainbows they arched above the earth beckoning Jude, pulling her to them. She was dressed in a wide cape of brilliant magenta. She raised her arms and began to rise upward, floating above the ground. Straight above her was Amagyne. *Monama*, Amagyne said. Jude felt her whole body tingling, but something stopped her ascent, a tight tugging on her ankles. She looked down but could not see what was holding her back. *We are your true sisters*, the voices called from above. Amagyne's voice stood out from the others. *Come*, she called gently.

* * * * *

After Jude's breakfast with Amagyne, Miluna, and a woman named Honore, Amagyne took Jude to the print shop. All five of the presses were running, each surrounded by sound-absorbing walls. Blank sheet of white or pale blue or buff-colored paper were pulled into the machines while rollers turned, and out came the sheets covered with words and pictures.

"I never knew this was here," Jude said. "We used to wonder how you managed financially. People thought you probably lived very frugally."

"The print shop makes a small profit. It's always busy. And so is the lamp plant. We'll go there next." Amagyne was examining a flyer. "Circle Edge Printing does jobs for places around the country," she said. "Mostly women's organizations. Newsletters, pamphlets. We're hoping to get a web press and begin doing books."

The tour of the print shop lasted over two hours. Jude spoke to the women working at the various jobs and they explained what they were doing and why. "Does everyone at Circle Edge get to work here?" Jude asked.

"Everyone who wants to gets a chance," answered a woman in an orange apron. "I spend most mornings here. In a month or two I'll probably take a break, do something else."

From the print shop they went to the lamp plant, and to the stables, and then to the mine.

"Gold," Amagyne said. "A vein very near the surface."

"I'll be damned!" marveled Jude.

After lunch, Amagyne took Jude to a room in Circle House with sofas and Circle Edge lamps and soft chairs around its perimeter. Paintings and tapestries hung on the walls and there was a beautiful four-foot high bronze statue of a dancer with broad, outstretched wings.

A stretching talk was about to begin. The two participants, Centra and Rose, agreed to allow Amagyne and Jude to observe. Joyce, who was there to witness, took a seat near Jude and Amagyne along the curved wall.

"May Kwo-am be present for our work," Centra began. She sat across from Rose, a small round table between them.

"May the kwo-ami within us be brought forth," Rose said.

They raised their arms, palms facing inward, eyes

closed, and so remained for a minute or more. Then, looking directly at Rose, Centra began.

"I'm feeling sad and hurt by your withdrawal from me. At Ambrosia yesterday, when you passed right by and said nothing to me, I knew I had to ask you for a stretching talk. I'm afraid you don't like me anymore, that I did something to lose your friendship. You've been cold and distant for some time now and it's very upsetting to me." Centra paused.

"You're feeling hurt," Rose said, "because I've been unfriendly to you. Afraid you might lose my friendship."

"Yes. I think it has to do with my relationship with Terra but every time I've tried to talk with you about it, you cut me off. I think maybe you still feel . . . that you still have very strong feelings for Terra even though you told me that you are over her. I want us to talk about it."

Rose nodded sadly and reflected back the essence of what Centra had said. As Jude listened she was aware of Amagyne's eyes on her.

Rose and Centra talked for a long time, each expressing her feelings and her thoughts, each letting the other know she was understanding what was being expressed. After nearly an hour, Rose said she realized it was ridiculous to blame Centra.

"I don't want to lose your friendship any more than you want to lose mine," she said. Centra reached across the table. Rose took her hand and held it lovingly. "I'm sorry I put you through this," she said. "I think I can stop."

"It isn't easy."

"I feel strong kwo-ami with our hands together like this."

"I do too. You're very dear to me."

Hands joined, they raised their arms toward the ceiling. Their eyes were closed. Nearly a minute passed and then they lowered their arms and stood.

Centra's face was glowing. "Thank you for witnessing," she said to Joyce. "Do you want to give us any observation thoughts?"

Joyce shook her head. "Not needed," she said, smiling.

Rose too was smiling. "It was a good stretch, I think. A good start. What do you think, Amagyne?"

"A good start," Amagyne confirmed.

"That's one of the hardest things, don't you think?" Joyce said when Centra and Rose were gone. "Dealing with unrequited love."

"And yet a part of life that not even Kwo-am would try to take away," Amagyne said. She looked at Jude. "The stretching talk you witnessed was one of many that take place here. In this one, Centra made the invitation. Rose could have refused and sometimes people do. It's always by choice. When refusals do take place, it's usually only a matter of time."

"And this is how conflicts are resolved at Circle Edge?" Jude was staring at the painting hanging to Amagyne's left.

"One of the ways." Amagyne followed Jude's eyes. "That is Kwo-am," she said.

The painting was of a tall black woman with fiery red hair. She was mounted on a white rhinoceros. "Kwo-am has a human form?"

"She has many forms. There are many different representations of Kwo-am. She comes to La in numerous ways, often animals, sometimes flowers, or people. Sometimes La describes the vision to an artist who captures it. That one is Kwo-am, too, the swan." Amagyne pointed across the room at a tapestry. "And that one, the old woman with the bent back."

"I must go," Joyce said. She took Jude's hand. "You seem very comfortable here. It's good to have you with us and I hope I get to know you well."

* * * * *

La had called a meeting that night. Women came from all the different buildings dressed in all their different ways. They emerged in groups and singly, some with lighted torches, all moving toward the area called the Amit, a saucer-shaped clearing flat in the center and rising in a gentle slope around the edges, the east end bordered by the steep cliffs of the surrounding mountains. Jude was among the women walking there.

When all were gathered, La began. She stood near the center of the Amit, illuminated by torches burning on either side of her, women sitting all around her on the flat ground and up the slopes. "We are on the verge, sisters. The time is nearly upon us." Her clear and resonant voice sent chills up Jude's spine. "We will begin with a full singing of the *Coming of the Catalyst*."

Applause rang through the valley. A flute began to play, and then another, then several more. The sounds raised goosebumps over Jude's skin.

"*She is here!*" one low voice sang out in rich pure notes.

78

"*The Catalyst exists. Of woman she was born. Woman just,*" a chorus sang in three-part harmony. Flutes played.

"*She is there,*" the first voice rang again.

"*The Catalyst is alive,*" many voices sang, and then from another section of the Amit, "*They think her one of them. They are wrong.*" Flutes came in, picking up the melody.

The song continued:

She is there. Of all races was she born. We will wait for her to come. She will rise.

She is there. Kwo-ami bursts from her. Onto arid ground it flows. Seems to dry.

She is there. Her kwo-ami cloaked by pain. From the zetkap of the world. She'll transcend.

She will come. To our gate to make her choice. When the time to rise is right. She must choose.

Jude was overwhelmed by the beautiful blend of sounds and the feeling of joy that filled the valley. The final words, *She must choose*, reverberated inside her as the flutes played the closing melody.

There was a long peaceful silence, and then La rose again. "I would like us to do the Story of the Beginning. It is apt tonight that we look back since we come now so close to the Time of Emergence when all goes forward."

Berryfire, a round blonde woman, stood. "I would like to begin it." Two women with torches came to stand on either side of her.

"There was a time when there was nothing,"

Berryfire began, "just unformed energy, rushing, moving, flowing, nothing clinging together — no molecules, no matter, no rocks or sky."

"The time of chaos," a voice chanted.

All eyes were on Berryfire. "And then Kwo-am generated form."

"The universe," came the chorus.

The recitation continued and Jude heard again the story Amagyne had told her.

"The compromise is our world," La said. "And the hope is the coming of the Second Guide to join the First. Then can we emerge from Zetka's hold."

"Monama. The beginning and until now," Berryfire ended.

Flutes played softly, then a period of quiet came over the congregation. Jude felt deep peacefulness. She looked at Amagyne sitting next to her on the hill, and the sense of peaceful happiness grew.

Women had begun to stand. They were lighting candles and forming a long, wide line. At its head a black woman dressed in a cape of feathers carried a torch. A slow steady drum beat began, its rhythm gradually picked up by other instruments, flutes and castanets, marimbas, cymbals and bongo drums. The line of women began to dance, led by the caped woman, her thick wild hair lurching from side to side. Hundreds of women, Jude and Amagyne among them, moved in a snake-like pattern, gliding around the Amit, up and down the slopes, candles forming bright lines and curves as the dance went on.

When at last the dance ended and the candles were blown out, Jude felt unutterably happy. On the walk back toward the gate she saw one of the musicians, Sharon, and asked if she might try her flute.

The sounds Jude made, rich and pure, wafted sensually over the grounds and valley, and many women stopped to listen. She played the melody of the *Coming of the Catalyst.*

"You are truly gifted," Amagyne said.

"That's the best I've ever played." Jude took in deep breaths of the cool night air. "What does the song mean?" she asked. "Who is the Catalyst?"

"She is the one we all await," Amagyne replied. "The Second Guide, the One Who Chooses. She lives now in the outer world, but our hope is that soon she will choose to join us."

Jude returned the flute to Sharon and thanked her. "The Catalyst isn't a Kwo-amian?"

"Not yet," Amagyne said. "The time is near for her to rise and come forth."

They had reached Jude's sleeping hut and Jude gathered her belongings. "Do you know who the Catalyst is?" she asked. "Are you in contact with her? How will she know to come? And what about being born of woman only? That's symbolic, right? And there was something about different races. Is she —"

"So many questions," Amagyne interrupted, laughing. "The answers will be yours in time. I think you truly want to know, and so you shall."

They walked to the gate and Miluna undid the lock. "We will speak again soon," Amagyne said.

Miluna pulled the heavy gate back. When Jude hugged her goodbye, she could feel Miluna's affection for her. "I'll be back some day," she said.

Amagyne's embrace enveloped her. Jude felt the

81

moss surrounding her, the warmth of the pools, the rising of the flute music, and tingling up and down her spine. She looked into Amagyne's bottomless eyes. "I'll miss you." She looked away. "All of you."

"Go with Kwo-am." Amagyne put her palm to her chest.

* * * * *

Everyone was asleep when Jude got to Martha's house. Her own sleep was filled again with dreams of Amagyne and of peaceful waters. She slept late and when she arose the house was empty.

She found Martha at the cafe tending the cash register.

"You got away from them."

Jude smiled. "I got home late last night. You were all asleep."

"I heard you come in."

"You weren't worried about me I hope."

"A little. Big sister's prerogative. So are you going to keep me in suspense? What happened? You look all right. Did they feed you well?"

"Yes, the food was delicious."

"Did they preach to you?"

Jude laughed. "No."

"Did you join up? Are you going to start selling flowers in airports?"

Jude rolled her eyes, then told Martha about the gardens, the horses, the print shop, the beautiful lamps the women made, the warm openness of the women, and the music and dancing. But she said very little about Kwo-amity. Martha did not ask if Jude intended to return there.

82

After breakfast, Jude went to the Mansion. Rosalie's face was pale and she was too weak for conversation. Jude sat with her, watching her shallow breathing and cursing death.

Jude spent her final two days in Doray with Martha and Cal, and with Rosalie. She saw her father one more time. They spoke mostly of Davey and of fishing. Jude resisted the temptation to hug him goodbye.

On the last night, she went to say goodbye to Rosalie. Rosalie was feeling better again, sitting up and looking almost as well as she had the other day on the balcony. "I'll call you soon," Jude said when it was time to go.

"I'm glad you came." Tears glistened on Rosalie's cheeks. "It meant a lot to me, my Jude."

"I'll be back soon," Jude said. "Don't do anything foolish while I'm gone." The words caught in her throat. She bent and laid her head on Rosalie's chest. "Call me anytime, day or night." She clutched Rosalie's hand. "I don't want to say goodbye."

"Don't worry. This isn't goodbye. Not yet."

"I love you so." Jude fought tears.

When she left the Mansion, Jude's throat was sore, her pain like boulders in her chest. She let herself cry then.

CHAPTER 9

The plane arrived in Chicago late Sunday afternoon. As Jude embraced Toni she thought of how it had felt to embrace Amagyne. The feeling was different, yet in some ways the same.

When they arrived at their apartment in Lakeview, Toni got them wine. "So tell me more about this women's farm. After all these years, you finally got in."

Jude sipped her wine. "They're Kwo-amians. It's a religion. I'm afraid you'll make fun of it."

Toni laughed. "I probably will, but you're used to

that." They were sitting very close on the sofa in the living room. One of the cats, Zuzu, was sprawled across Jude's lap. "Come on," Toni said, "I want to hear about the Kowamians."

"Kwo-amians," Jude corrected, "from Kwo-am. That's what they call God." She proceeded to tell Toni about Kwo-am and Zetka, their struggle and compromises, and about La, and the Time of Danger. Her explanations and descriptions were occasionally interrupted by quips from Toni.

"I knew you'd make fun," Jude objected at one point. "Where was I?"

"Humans, our potential to defeat the devil."

"You make it sound so silly."

"I'm just listening, hon." Toni rubbed Jude's back affectionately.

Jude was silent a moment. "Maybe if you just think of it symbolically, that might help."

"OK," Toni said, "so these two symbols have metaphoric battles over who's in charge. Identification with the good symbol is the route to ecstatic oneness with the universe, called Moaning."

"Monama." Jude giggled. "Well, it makes sense when you hear it from them. Maybe you have to be there."

Toni chuckled. "Are they dykes?"

"They're women-loving-women," Jude said, grinning broadly.

"Good. Do they have orgies?"

"Sleaze."

"Is Kwo-am a dyke?"

"Do you want to hear more about it or not?" Jude pouted.

Toni drew Jude's protruding lip into her mouth,

kissing her softly. Then she sat back. "OK, I won't say another word until you're finished."

For the next twenty minutes Jude described the physical setting at Circle Edge, the people, the ceremonies and rituals, the concepts of the religion. What she did not mention was the intensity of her response to Amagyne.

"It sounds idyllic," Toni said. "A cozy lesbian commune. It also sounds a little weird. Some of it."

"The religious part."

"Don't you think so?"

"I don't think you have to literally believe everything they believe to be enchanted by it, by the atmosphere and the way of life."

"Beats the shit out of an el ride to the Loop or a stroll through Uptown."

Jude laughed. "But you know, I kind of got into the ideas too. Maybe God — or the creator or spiritual force, or whatever you want to call it — maybe he or she *does* communicate through La. Why not? La wouldn't be the first prophet we've heard about. I do admit it's hard to believe it's happening in our lifetime. But who knows? I'm not ready to completely rule it out. And what La says she's learned through these revelations makes sense, to me at least. Why is there pain and death and oppression? Maybe there *is* an evil force that generates and promotes them. Why is God manifesting herself so directly now? Maybe it is because evil is taking over and there's a strong possibility of our blowing up the earth. And the way they talk about how everything began makes sense too. For one thing, it integrates what we know about evolution. There's a certain logic to their ideas, Toni, don't you think?"

"Rational mysticism," Toni said. She shook her head. "Jude, I think you're just looking for some magical explanation for why things are as they are. And some magical solution."

"Maybe," Jude acknowledged. "But I can't deny that there's a certain beauty and power to what the Kwo-amians believe and the rituals they have. They seem truly content, really peaceful inside themselves."

Toni scrutinized her. "Is that the appeal, hon? Do you think that if you could find a form of spirituality that really suits you, you'd feel happier in that deep down place that's so sad sometimes?"

Jude felt the sadness. It was not difficult to tap. "I guess."

Toni put her arms around Jude and held her tenderly. "It sounds like it was a wonderful vacation for you. Change of scene. Visit to another world."

"I'm glad I'm home."

"You're happy, aren't you? With me? With our life together?"

"I'm very happy with you. I missed you."

Toni cradled Jude and stroked her cheek. "Zuzu and Alice B looked for you every night."

"They were lonely for me."

"So was I."

"We belong together."

"That's right. We're a team, girl."

"Did I ever tell you how superbly sexy you are?"

"Once or twice."

"Can I put my hand on your twat?"

"I suppose."

"Mm-m, warm."

"Getting warmer."

"Your jeans are in the way."

"Easily remedied. Have I ever shown you our bedroom?"

"I'd like to see it."

Jude melted into the familiar curves and smells and textures of Toni's body. Their lovemaking was sometimes very mellow and slow, but this time their kisses were immediately deep and passionate, their touches grasping and needy. They probed and caressed each other, the movements strong and fast. Toni took Jude's nipple into her warm mouth, sucking vigorously, while Jude's eager fingers explored the inner cave of Toni's cunt. Toni peaked with a crooning moan. Jude's excitement grew as Toni slid downward along her body. When Toni's tongue found Jude's clit and she licked and sucked Jude to a powerful climax, Jude felt herself burst with love and fullness.

Neither was ready to stop. They shifted positions, Toni's knees now up, her legs spread. The taste of Toni was nectar, and Jude almost came again when she felt Toni's spasms. Their sounds of delight blended in mutual gratified harmony.

* * * * *

The next day, Jude returned to work at Yvonne's Travel. She met Toni at Giordano's in Evanston for dinner. Neither spoke of Circle Edge or Kwo-amity or anything connected with them.

Each shared the highlights of her day and life felt to Jude very much as it had before.

Pam Holtz was sitting on the porch when they got home. Jude gave her a warm hug. They had been each other's first lover and their friendship was strong and important. "I've been missing you, cutie," Jude said.

Pam handed her a rose. "Welcome home."

The evening of conversation with Pam and Toni was comfortably enjoyable to Jude.

"I'm very happy," she told Toni later that night. "I have a good life, don't I?"

"We sure do."

* * * * *

Two more days went by with Jude barely giving Circle Edge or Amagyne or La's revealments a thought. She felt content. On Wednesday she had dinner with her mother.

They talked while they ate, then Claire dealt out the rummy cards.

"I visited the Ladies' Farm while I was in Doray," Jude said.

Claire's barely discernible eyebrows lifted. "You mean you went inside?"

"Yes, it's beautiful in there. A lot different from what we always thought." Jude described the Dome and the other buildings and talked about lounging in the warm pools. "I learned about their religion, too," she said.

"Are they like the Amish?"

"No." Jude picked up a card. "But their beliefs aren't that different from most religions. I liked what they said, actually. I was even sort of getting into it for a while."

"I'm glad you enjoyed yourself," Claire said. "And what about Rosalie, Jude? You still haven't talked about her."

89

"She's not going to live much longer, Mom." Jude's eyes teared. "I asked her nurse to call me again if it seems close. I want to see her at least one more time." Jude laid down her rummy. She took a deep breath. "I guess Doray is really going to change when Rosalie dies. Martha's thrilled."

"But you aren't, are you? You like it small and quiet."

"I guess. But I'm happy for Martha."

"Martha says most of Rosalie's fortune will go to charity." Claire shuffled the cards. "I thought she might leave it to you."

Jude laughed at that.

"Well, she has no one else. She loves you more than anyone."

* * * * *

When Jude got home that night, Toni was writing in the study. Jude greeted her, then got her flute. She played plaintively, feeling tremendously sad and not knowing why. After a while Toni came to her. They cuddled on the foam sofa which opened to make a very comfortable bed, and talked about their days. Jude did not mention the sadness, the empty spot inside. She seldom did, although Toni always seemed to know.

They watched the news on TV. "The world is a mess," Jude said.

"Yep. But there are certain enjoyable parts to it nonetheless." Toni looked lovingly at her.

"What's it all about, Toni?"

Toni held her tight. "This," she said.

"I love you so," Jude responded, allowing herself to sink into the embrace.

* * * * *

Saturday night Jude and Toni went to the *Feminist Fund Fund-Raiser Dance and Talent Show,* emceed by their friend Grace Greshow, better known as Gresh — a tall, self-assured, forty-year-old woman, with short wavy hair, clear-framed glasses, and a sizable belly at which she always poked fun. She had been a part of Jude's life since they'd both volunteered at a women's hotline years ago. A committed feminist, Gresh had continued to work diligently for women's rights even after many people drifted away from the cause. For a living, she worked at a nursery and plant store. Many of Jude's friends and acquaintances were at the dance. Jude danced until her muscles ached.

After the dance, a group went to a restaurant for coffee.

"I'd guess we raised close to a thousand tonight," Gresh said. The women were seated at a big circular booth in Ricky's on Broadway. "Every little bit helps."

"When are you going to find that wealthy benefactor for your Fund?" Pam asked teasingly.

"I'm still looking," Gresh said. "Know any likely candidates?"

"Sorry," Pam said, "rich people don't associate with me."

"So tell me about Colorado," Gresh said to Jude. "How's your sister? And Mrs. Wright, is she doing any better?"

"Rosalie talked about you," Jude said, "about your idea to turn the Estate into a spa?"

Gresh's eyebrows lifted. "Is she interested?"

Jude shook her head. "I'm afraid not."

"Too bad." Gresh took a spoonful of her matzo ball soup. "So Toni tells me you got involved with some esoteric lesbian religion."

Jude laughed. "I wouldn't characterize it as a lesbian religion. Some of the women are straight. I also wouldn't say I exactly got involved in it."

"Toni never gets anything right."

Toni looked across the table. "Are you gossiping about me?"

"Of course, my love."

* * * * *

That night before she fell asleep, Jude thought about what La had said. *A shallow happiness.* Was there something more, she wondered. My life is fine. Why can't I just feel content? She slept then, and dreamed.

The air was cool. She felt warm water caressing her. There were torches all around and music filled the air. She floated upward for a long, long time. It felt good, dreamy and safe. Then she was on a mountain peak playing the *Coming of the Catalyst* on her flute, and she felt a rising in her heart, a blissful, ecstatic sense of contentment and peace filling every part of her. Amagyne appeared. Jude felt captivated and drawn to her. Amagyne reached out and Jude reached back, stretching her arm as far as it would go. She couldn't reach far enough. Amagyne was slipping away. Jude ran but Amagyne receded farther and farther away from her.

Jude awoke sweating, her breathing rapid. She was tempted to wake Toni, but did not. It took her a long time to fall asleep again.

CHAPTER 10

One cloudy Saturday afternoon in mid-June, Jude was alone in the apartment. Her flute student had left and Toni was out with a friend. Nearly two weeks had passed since her return from Colorado and she had slipped comfortably back into her life, rarely thinking of her adventure at Circle Edge.

She had just begun playing a snappy Mozart cantata on her flute when the phone rang. At the sound of the smooth voice, Jude's heart fluttered absurdly against her ribs.

"I'm in Chicago," Amagyne said.

Jude had to sit. Her legs felt shaky.

Forty-five minutes later, Jude squeezed her Mazda into a parking place a half a block away from the address Amagyne had given her, on Albion Street in Rogers Park. The building was a red brick three-flat. She rang the third-floor bell, got buzzed in, and walked up the two flights of stairs. Amagyne was at the door.

Jude almost gasped at her beauty. She wore a deep maroon shirt and gray pants. A silver chain sparkled on the olive skin of her neck. Her wavy hair shone and light glinted from her white teeth as she smiled in welcome.

They sat on futons in a candlelit living room scented with incense, and drank water that Amagyne had brought from Circle Edge.

"You have been back in the outer world for fifteen days now," Amagyne said. "How is it feeling?"

"I readjusted quickly," Jude said, not looking at Amagyne.

"And Kwo-amity? Does it still speak to you?"

Jude hesitated. "Yes," she said. "Much of it does." She paused again. "But I don't really accept the basic premises, Amagyne. I just can't believe that God is speaking to La. And, of course, everything else is based on that. I wish I could believe it. I wish Kwo-world were a possibility." She felt a dip of fear that her admission would alienate Amagyne and she would never see her again. Almost immediately she knew that this would not happen.

"I am not surprised to hear your doubts," Amagyne said. "You have lived long in the outer

95

world, and you can easily get drawn back in. The forces of Zetka want very much to retain their hold on you."

"Maybe so," Jude said.

"You spoke to me before of having a sense that something is missing for you. Do you still feel this way?"

The sadness immediately came over Jude. "I suppose I always will."

"Perhaps, perhaps not. Do you remember how you felt during the Avowal Ritual, and how you felt after you played the *Coming of the Catalyst* on your flute?"

Jude nodded. Tears came to her eyes.

"Very powerful feelings," Amagyne said. "You felt Kwo-am's presence."

"Yes," Jude said, "I certainly felt something. But it seems so unreal now."

"It is not. We have choices about what realities we live."

Jude narrowed her eyes. "Toni made fun of Kwo-amity."

"Yes. And after awhile, I would guess that you even joined her and did the same."

Jude hung her head. "I don't know why." She looked at Amagyne. "Somehow, back here it all seems . . . I don't know . . . like just a fantasy. Not believable. Kwo-am, Zetka, battling for our . . . our souls. It just seems like make-believe."

"Part of you knows it is very real," Amagyne said. "You felt it. Perhaps you can let it in again."

Suddenly Jude was overwhelmed with feeling. Her shoulders began to shake, and Amagyne held her as she cried. "I think I'm feeling some of it now," Jude said. "How can that be? When I'm with you I . . . I feel confused."

"There's a battle inside you."

Jude clung to her. "I don't feel that empty feeling right now. I don't feel the sadness."

"You are opening again. I will help you."

"Yes. I need you to."

"I will remind you of what you know." Amagyne moved a pillow behind Jude and told her to let herself relax, close her eyes if she wanted. Jude leaned back, her feet stretched out on the futon. Amagyne took her hand. "Kwo-am made our world," she began. She spoke then of Kwo-am and Zetka, of the moves and countermoves, of the Guides, and of Monama and the hope and possibility of a new and better world.

Jude listened raptly to every word. "Zetka is pulling me, I know it," she said angrily. "I have to fight it, don't I?"

"It is difficult."

Jude began to cry again. "Toni's ridicule hurts. And then my own doubt grows. What she says seems so logical. And then it takes over, the fear and doubt and skepticism."

Amagyne held her. "Yet inside you know."

Jude felt engulfed in the soothing arms. "Oh, yes, I do. It feels so true."

"Because it is. It resonates within you."

"Yes. I feel it, Amagyne. I wish I could be part of it. I don't want Zetka to win."

"Good," Amagyne said. She smiled then. "Miluna misses you. She's grown fond of you very quickly. She senses things in people."

Amagyne talked more about Circle Edge. The more

she said, the more drawn in Jude felt. "It seems like I'm supposed to believe what you say to me about Kwo-amity. Even though it's hard to believe."

"Kwo-am wants you to believe. She has a plan, and you are part of it. This is your calling. Of course it is hard to believe, especially when you are away from Circle Edge. Yet, I know you can defeat that zetkap in you that makes you doubt. You're doing it right now. And you will continue, for there are more revealments that you have yet to learn. Like the fact that Kwo-am speaks through La, these new revealments cannot be explained by rational evidence or the laws of nature."

Jude was blinking rapidly. "They're miracles, aren't they?"

"Yes, sometimes called miracles. Kwo-am has the power to sidestep the laws of nature. She is not bound by them, for she created them and is free to alter them if she chooses."

"Yes," Jude said, "if she created everything, then —"

"Do you truly believe she did, that she is as I've told you?"

"Yes," Jude said, nodding. "Deep inside of me I do."

Amagyne smiled. "I am glad. We will talk some more soon. There will be a Rite of Entrance here tomorrow, for a Chicagoan named Nancy. I would like you to come. Afterwards we will talk some more."

* * * * *

Toni was annoyed. "Come on, Jude, it's obvious

what they're doing. They know you're a live one and they're in hot pursuit."

"I like being courted," Jude said lightly. She added sliced zucchini to the mix of vegetables in the wok.

"So do male black widow spiders."

"It's just a little ritual, like confirmation or communion. You were confirmed, weren't you?"

"When I was too young to know any better."

"Consider me an amateur anthropologist, Toni. An observer of the strange rites of a strange sect. Do you want to come along?"

"No way. Don't put any tofu in there, OK?"

"If you quit trying to control me, then I'll leave out the tofu. Deal?"

"Does it feel like I'm trying to control you?" Toni came to Jude's side.

"A little."

"I'm sorry."

"I forgive you. Don't worry about me doing a little spiritual exploring, OK?"

"OK." Toni had her hands around Jude's waist.

"There's nothing to worry about. They're nice women. They're not going to hurt me." Jude felt a twinge of dark fear as she said those words and she couldn't imagine why.

* * * * *

When she arrived at the Rogers Park apartment, Jude was introduced to the dozen or so women present, and then to each new arrival. Everyone seemed friendly and Jude felt very welcome. They sat

99

on futons and pillows in the large, oak-floored living room.

By eight o'clock, twenty-five people had arrived. Around their necks the Kwo-amians draped deep purple scarves with designs embroidered on them — animals, or the women's symbol or double women's symbol. One scarf had a dancer with huge wings; another, flowers around a sheaf of wheat.

There was one other non-Kwo-amian observer present besides Jude, and one additional woman without a scarf; Nancy, dressed in a short-sleeved white shirt and white cotton pants.

Candles burned. The room smelled pleasantly of jasmine incense. One woman had a flute, another a xylophone. Amagyne took Nancy, the initiate, to sit with her in the center of the room on a futon covered with a deep purple cloth. On Nancy's other side sat a woman named Janette. The Kwo-amians gathered around them. Jude and the other observer went to the side of the room as Amagyne had told them. Amagyne signaled the musicians who began to play soft music. She handed Nancy a crystal goblet.

"Water from deep within the earth." Nancy drank the water. Women hummed as the music continued. "We are here to welcome Nancy Parker into our midst," Amagyne said. "She has found one among us who wishes to be her soul-sister."

Janette put her hand on Nancy's shoulder. "We have spoken and opened our hearts to each other. I will be with her as she wants and needs my presence in her life."

"Be with her joyfully," several women said.

"Nancy chooses to be with us and to tell us tonight what is in her heart," Amagyne said.

"Let her speak," several women responded.

Nancy sat up straight in the center of the futon. She held a card in her hand. Jude could see that her hand was trembling. Nancy glanced at the card. "I accept Kwo-am," she began, "the creator, the spirit of love." Her voice was clear though it had a barely noticeable quaver. "I sense her presence, I welcome her."

"She is with you," several Kwo-amians said. The flute and xylophone played softly in the background.

Nancy looked again at her card. "I accept the words of Kwo-am brought to us through La, the Sage, blessed and enabled."

"The words which are truth," responded several women sitting near Jude.

"I accept the kwo-ami in me for it is my nature. My worth came to me with my birth." Nancy's voice was stronger.

"You are worthy," many women replied.

"I choose to treasure and nurture my kwo-ami and do what I can to make it grow." She took a deep breath then went on. "I also accept the zetkap in me for it is my nature which I choose to understand and tame."

"It is a struggle."

"I accept the struggle, force and counterforce within me." Nancy was no longer using the card.

"And in us all."

"I seek growth and ascent. I seek to understand myself and others, to understand and not condemn. I accept my feelings."

"You are who you are and so are we all," many voices said.

"I seek growth and ascent," Nancy repeated. Her

face seemed to glow, the flickering candlelight highlighting her cheeks and forehead. Her soul-sister touched her leg affectionately.

"Do you feel Kwo-am's presence?" Amagyne asked.

"I feel it." The card now lay at Nancy's side. Her clenched hands pressed her chest. Her eyes were tightly closed.

"And welcome her?" Amagyne asked.

"I do."

"She is with you and in you. We join our kwo-ami with yours," Amagyne said.

The music stopped. A deep humming filled the room. Everyone's eyes were closed. Jude closed hers too. The humming continued for several minutes and then the flute began to play. Several more minutes passed and suddenly it was silent.

All eyes were on Nancy. Amagyne draped a long purple scarf over Nancy's neck.

"You are of us," the roomful of women shouted as one.

"I welcome you," Nancy declared happily.

"We welcome you, Nancy Parker," they all said.

People stood and moved toward Nancy. Nancy and her soul-sister and Amagyne stood also. Amagyne was the first to embrace Nancy. "May Monama be yours," she said. Nancy's soul-sister hugged her next. Then one by one, each woman came to her, embracing her and wishing her Monama.

Nancy seemed elevated, glowing. Jude felt it too, the unity, the hope, the love.

Refreshments were brought in and the room buzzed with conversation. From her place near the doorway, Jude watched as one woman after the next sought out Nancy to speak with her. Nancy was flushed and vibrant. Jude knew how Nancy must be feeling and that it must be very powerful. She could feel some of it herself.

Soon Amagyne came to Jude. "You are touched by the ritual."

"Oh, yes. It was very moving, very beautiful." Jude's eyes brimmed with tears.

"Nancy is twenty-five years old today. She wanted her entrance to be on her birthday. 'A quarter century in the dark, the rest of my life full of light,' is what she said. She is very happy."

"I know. She seems to be glowing."

"You are learning more and more about the ways of Kwo-amity. There are still many things for you to learn. I sense that you are ready tonight to hear more."

Jude took the last bite of raw cauliflower from her plate. "I do feel ready."

"Let's go to the porch," Amagyne said, "and talk there."

Like the living room, the enclosed porch was lit with candles. It contained several soft chairs and a small table with a pitcher of water and two glasses. The evening was mild, the open windows on the porch letting in a breeze.

Amagyne poured them water. "There's something important that happened many years ago. A miracle. I want to tell you about it."

Jude drank. She was feeling nervous. "All right."

"I have told you that I am the First Guide. Lorn, my mother, was nineteen when she became pregnant. She was living at Circle Edge and was never away from it during the time when she conceived me. She never was with any man."

"What do you mean?" Jude frowned deeply.

"La has revealed that this would happen, that one of the Firstcomers would have a child —"

"And you're telling me that —"

"— who would be born of woman only."

Jude's eyes were wide. "You're saying you had no father?"

"That is the miracle. Look inside yourself and see if you can find room for this truth."

Jude was shaking her head. "Oh, come on." She blinked her eyes, feeling dizzy. "Maybe Lorn had a lover no one knew about."

"She never left Circle Edge before my birth. I was born three years after she arrived there."

"Some man from Doray maybe."

"She was never with any man, Jude. I was born of woman only. La revealed that this would be."

Jude took another sip of the crystal water. "So Kwo-am . . . you came from Kwo-am then? Is that what you mean? She sent you. Created you through a miracle. Like Jesus. Is that what you're saying?" Jude watched Amagyne's solemn nod, then stared unblinking at her.

"It was because the Time of Danger had come," Amagyne said. "Kwo-am brought me forth to open other's eyes, as many as I can." Amagyne looked deeply into Jude's eyes.

Jude was taking deep short breaths.

"There will be a ceremony, the Ceremony of Emergence. I will participate in that ceremony and from it will begin the New Page, the beginning of the Withering of Zetka."

Although Jude felt herself being irresistibly drawn in, she could not accept what Amagyne was telling her. "I know you are very special," she said. "I knew it from the first moment I saw you, but this is too much, Amagyne. It's almost laughable. Like you're making this up, copying what's already come before, trying to be another messiah. It frightens me, makes me feel a little sick." Jude turned her head away. "I don't like it."

"Miracles truly do happen," Amagyne said gently. "Jesus was part of it, of Kwo-am's plan. And so am I."

Jude shook her head. She found herself laughing through tears. "You know what's weird? I really would like to believe it. I don't even know if I believe the Jesus story. Lots of people don't. Maybe he was just a mortal."

"Neither of us is," Amagyne said. "You would like to believe what I have told you. Don't try to force yourself, Jude, but don't close yourself to it either. Let it be. It will enter you if you just let it be."

Jude nodded.

"I was born kwo-omni," Amagyne said. "My mission is to bring the truth to others so that we may proceed."

"And I am one you are to bring along."

"That you are. But of course you have doubts, Jude. That is part of it too. There are forces which do not want you with us."

"Just letting it be," Jude said.

"That's right." Amagyne took some sheets of red paper from the table and handed them to Jude. "When you leave now and return to the outer world, I want you to write your doubts on this paper. Write them all down, all the zetkap-inspired doubts that are welling up in you. Come here tomorrow at noon. Bring the paper with you. We will go to a house in the country."

Jude nodded numbly.

* * * * *

Jude did not tell Toni about Amagyne being born of woman only. She told her about the Rite of Entrance and said she found it interesting and moving, but she did not mention the miracle.

"My anthropologist," Toni said. "Doing a field study." She was stretched out on the foam sofa-bed reading the newspaper.

Jude did not tell her that she would call in sick at Yvonne's Travel the next day to go with Amagyne into the country.

"It *is* a cult, you know," Toni said, tossing the paper aside. "I need cuddles."

"I suppose, depending on your definition." Jude lay next to her.

"Are you sure you want to be friends with these women?"

"Anthropologists have to befriend the natives," Jude said, blowing softly in Toni's ear.

"Don't you find them kind of silly?" Toni giggled. "That tickles."

"Does it turn you on?"

Toni grabbed her and kissed her deeply.

CHAPTER 11

During the drive, Amagyne went over the steps of the Avowal Ritual, telling Jude what she was supposed to do and say, then practicing with her. Jude felt a little nervous.

It was almost two o'clock when they arrived at their destination near Hammond, Indiana. The house was large and old with a peaked roof, a huge front porch, and a balcony that extended half way around the second floor. No one seemed to be there. Amagyne led Jude to a small bedroom off the kitchen and gave her a white silk robe and a thin black floor-length cloak to wear over it. She pulled the hood of the cloak down over most of Jude's face. Jude held the folded piece of red paper on which she had written, that morning, everything she could think of that was interfering with her fully accepting the truths of Kwo-amity.

Dressed in an amber robe, Amagyne took Jude to a wooden stairway which led down to the basement. Jude could hear low eerie music. The basement was dimly lit by several torches and many candles. Jude saw the outlines of several dozen people, dressed in amber, all looking at her and Amagyne as they entered the room.

A woman holding a torch led Jude and Amagyne to their places on a foot high platform at the back of the room. On the platform was a square object covered with a black cloth. The shrike, Jude thought.

The music from the bassoon grew louder and louder, blocking any thoughts from Jude's mind. Then suddenly it was quiet. Jude's ears rang.

Amagyne raised her arms. "We call upon Kwo-am to purge, purify, wash clear, absolve and cleanse." Her voice rang like a crystal bell. The ritual proceeded. When the red paper caught fire, Jude watched her written doubts go up in flame. Dancing heavily, the women chanted, "Zetkap, be gone." Then came the humming, and then the sharp prick of Jude's thumb. After the shrike drank the bloodied water and fell, Amagyne declared that Jude's zetkap had been purged. At that moment, from a high corner across the room a blinding beam of light shone on Jude and then grasping hands tore at her black cloak until it was shredded away.

Outside, the women formed a circle of amber around the cage. Jude stared at the motionless shrike, knowing it would soon arise. She looked around at the faces, recognizing many from the night before.

The humming began and the thoughts came easily to Jude, good thoughts, pleasant images, loving feelings. She felt her scalp tingling; she felt the warmth of Amagyne's hand and the hand of the woman on her other side. As the humming continued, Jude began to feel lightness. She felt herself floating weightlessly, and then soaring effortlessly through space. Transcending. Moving outward, inward, everywhere at once. She had left the earth. There was bright light, a soft warm breeze, music surrounding her. The feeling was of awe. Ecstasy. Jude was lost in it.

She was in the presence of God. Kwo-am.

Her body, consciousness, the surrounding world — everything had melted away except the consuming, gratifying exaltation of divine contact. Tears rippled down her cheeks. Monama! Her head fell back limply, eyes rolling. She was shaking uncontrollably. Time passed, maybe eons, filled with golden light and glorious music, the blissful, incomparable joy of Kwo-am's presence.

When Jude was brought back by the sounds of cheering and applause, she was not the same.

Her trembling continued. Her breathing came in gasps. Dimly she realized she was standing on the ground, surrounded by people in robes, the sun vibrantly bright. In front of her was a cage with a bird jumping and fluttering its wings. With tremulous fingers, Jude unlatched the door. She squeezed

Amagyne's hand tightly as she watched the reborn shrike take to the sky. *A sparrow now,* Jude thought, sure that it was true.

Amagyne was the first to embrace her. Jude felt them merging, their souls connecting, being one. Other women hugged her then and congratulated her. Jude kept blinking her eyes. Her vision was hazy, her head spinning.

"I was with her," she murmured through dry lips.

"Yes," said Amagyne.

"I saw God. Kwo-am. It happened. It happened to *me.*" Tears of joy undulated in little rivulets down her cheeks.

When the dancing began, Jude moved as in a trance. She kept blinking. Her breathing still was rapid.

"You felt it very powerfully, didn't you?" Janette said, looking into Jude's glazed eyes.

"I was with her," Jude repeated.

There was food and more dancing. Gradually Jude became calmer. Her pounding heart slowed. She was returning to normal, yet she would never be the same. She could not stop smiling.

The party was still going strong when Amagyne asked Jude to come with her into the house so they might talk. Jude felt a deep calm, a sense of solid, anchored peacefulness. She sat in a canvas chair across from Amagyne in the living room of the old house. A pot of tea was on the table.

"You reached Monama," Amagyne said. "I thought that you might. You let Kwo-am fully in."

"I was in her presence," Jude said.

"Yes. If the New Page comes, what you have now

experienced will be there for many who never dreamed of it."

Amagyne poured tea for both of them and waited while Jude sipped. When Jude set the cup aside, Amagyne spoke.

"It is time for you to hear something very wonderful, but also maybe frightening." Amagyne's eyes held Jude's. "It was revealed to La twenty-five years ago that there was a child, a very special child, born on September first, nineteen fifty-nine."

"That's when I was born," Jude said.

"When the time was right, La learned, this child, a grown woman by then, would come to us at Circle Edge."

"I am the one?"

"Yes, you. You are not an ordinary person, Jude Alta. You were sent to us."

"I was?"

"Yes. You are the Second Guide, the One Who Chooses." Amagyne's eyes continued to hold Jude's. Jude's heart was pounding. Her breathing was suspended.

"You are called the Catalyst," Amagyne said. "Kwo-am sent you."

Jude tried to clear her head. The words of the song came back to her. *Born of woman only, of all races. She must choose.* No, she thought, it can't be me. "How could it be?" Her voice was weak.

"It was revealed," Amagyne replied.

Jude was quivering. "But . . . how . . . no, it couldn't be me. The song says the Catalyst was born of woman only." Jude's head was swimming crazily.

"Yes," Amagyne replied. "The man you call your father . . ."

111

Jude felt her heart pounding madly against her ribs. She looked into Amagyne's eyes trying to find strength in them. The eyes looked calm.

"Joseph Alta did not beget you."

Jude's breathing had become audible. Her jaw was slack.

"You are not his," Amagyne declared. "So it was revealed."

Jude's head was buzzing and she felt close to passing out.

"You belong with us," Amagyne said. "You are the Catalyst, the one we await. You are one of us."

Jude was nodding dumbly. "I'm from Kwo-am. Like you." The feelings of awe and exaltation returned. She could see the glorious light. "That's who I am. I am nothing like my father."

"You are nothing like Joseph Alta," Amagyne said with her velvet voice.

Jude pulled herself up in the cushioned chair and sat on the edge of the seat. "He's not my father." She watched Amagyne's hair slowly shaking back and forth against her shoulders. "My conception was like yours, that's what you're saying."

"That is what I'm saying."

Jude sighed audibly. She listened to the music coming from outside. She looked at her body, felt the flesh. "I'm not human."

"You are fully human," Amagyne said.

"What you are telling me just can't be, Amagyne. It's impossible. And yet . . . Kwo-am came to me today. She let me know her. Maybe . . ." Jude thought of the red paper and what she had written. She thought of the limitlessness of divine power. Sent by Kwo-am, she thought. Me. Slowly she began to smile.

"Welcome, Jude," Amagyne said.

Jude was feeling floaty and warm. She nodded. "Yes, I do belong with you."

"You do. Your time has come. Your life in the outer world has finally ended, and your true calling begins."

Jude thought of Toni. Tears immediately stung her eyes. But then she looked again at Amagyne. "I have a calling. My life is at Circle Edge."

"Yes, dear Jude."

Jude took Amagyne's hand. "And if it's true, if I come, what happens then? If I'm the Second Guide and you're the First Guide, what are we supposed to do? What does it mean?"

"You and I, the Guides, will preside at the Ceremony of Emergence. Together we can begin the New Page, the beginning of the Withering of Zetka. That is what it means. It means everything. It means Kwo-world. First the Kwo-amians will change, those who witness the Ceremony, becoming kwo-omnis. They will go forth and spread the power of Kwo-am to others. There will be great changes. Immense changes."

"And you and I will do it."

Amagyne was watching Jude closely. "I know there is much for you to absorb. You are doing well with it now, but I know it will be hard to pull your spirit from the outer world. Yet I have no doubt that you will do it. You have been chosen, and you must choose. If you triumph at the Enactment of the Scourges of Zetka, then the Ceremony of Emergence can take place, and the New Page can begin."

113

Jude was nodding rapidly.

"If you choose not to be of us, then the New Page may never begin and the world will continue on its present course."

Jude shivered. She took the afghan Amagyne offered her and put it around her shoulders.

"It's frightening to you."

"I . . . I don't think I want that kind of power. I'm not right for it."

"You are perfect for it," Amagyne said, "but you must choose."

"The One Who Chooses." Jude pushed quivering fingers through her hair.

"You belong with us, at Circle Edge. Your first choice is to choose to come and stay with us, to make Circle Edge your home."

"But my life," Jude said painfully. "I have a life in Chicago. There's Toni." She felt a terrible heaviness in her stomach. "There are my friends. My job."

"That is your past. If you bring on the New Page, then Monama is the future."

"Monama," Jude repeated, and the feelings came. She closed her eyes, remembering the ecstasy.

"The truth touches you. Kwo-am has touched you."

"I can't deny it," Jude said, and she knew there was no way that she could.

CHAPTER 12

Toni and Gresh arrived at the apartment with a huge bag of Chinese food. Gresh had also brought a dozen yellow daffodils from the shop where she worked. *She's a kwo-z,* Jude thought. Generous and loving. *I will miss her terribly.*

They ate and chatted around the kitchen table. Cartons were spread around them, chopsticks clicked. It was so familiar to Jude, so comfortable. *My past,* she thought, wondering if she would really leave.

After Gresh left to go to a Lesbian Task Force

115

meeting, Jude remained at the table, staring at the remnants of the food.

"What's the matter, hon?" Toni asked.

Jude didn't look up. "I didn't go to work today," she said. "I went to a ritual. An Avowal Ritual. I was the avower."

Toni rolled her eyes. "Jude, I thought —"

"I felt the presence of Kwo-am, Toni. Something very powerful happened to me."

Toni stared at her, speechless. "Let's go in the living room and talk," she said at last.

They settled onto the sofa and Jude tried to describe what she had felt. "It's hard to find the right words. Exalted. Ecstatic. Transcendent. I've never felt anything close to it in my life, Toni. She was there, with me, in me and all around me."

"The goddess."

"Kwo-am, yes." Jude sighed deeply. She was staring into space, remembering. "Then afterwards Amagyne and I had a long talk. Now this is where it gets a little weird." Jude squirmed on the sofa, looking everywhere but at Toni. "They see me as someone special."

"What do you mean?"

Jude looked at her. "Well, to wither Zetka's power, two human guides are needed. One of them was born Kwo-amian. That's Amagyne." Jude looked away again.

"Yeah, go on."

"I don't think I'm explaining any of this right. Somehow when I talk to you about it, it sounds . . ."

"Dumb?"

"No. Like . . . I don't know. It's hard to explain it unless you've experienced . . . I don't think I'm being convincing enough. I don't think you're receptive."

"But you *are* receptive."

"I am one of them. I've been chosen."

"Oh, shit, Jude. Those psychos are brainwashing you."

Jude looked tearfully at Toni. "That makes me feel so sad. I want you to be a part of it with me, Toni."

"Tell me the rest," Toni said flatly.

Jude folded her hands in front of her. "The two guides perform the Ceremony of Emergence and afterwards . . . well, the Ceremony sets off like a chain reaction. People start becoming kwo-omnis — that means they're zetkap-free. The kwo-omnis go out in the world and spread their kwo-ami, and zetkap diminishes until ultimately it vanishes from earth." Jude looked at Toni.

"Is that all?"

Jude stared at her lover angrily. "I'm the Second Guide. Don't you dare laugh."

"It's not funny," Toni said.

"You think I'm just an ordinary nobody."

"On the contrary," Toni said somberly. "I think you're the extraordinary center of my life, but I also think you're in trouble."

"I'm the Second Guide. The Catalyst. Amagyne and I are going to do the Ceremony of Emergence and after that everything will change."

"Jude, please! You're not actually believing this?"

"I was born of woman only," Jude blurted.

Toni sank into the sofa, head back, her eyes tightly closed. Then she clutched Jude's hand. "Jude, don't say things like that."

117

"That person who married my mother is not my father."

"Jude." Toni stroked Jude's arm caringly. "Jude, what's happening to you? How can it be happening? You can't believe this stuff. I know you can't."

"It frightens me too. To be chosen by Kwo-am. My birth, a miracle! It's overwhelming when I think of what it means. Kwo-am chose me, Toni. I've been chosen to help wipe out all the things that we hate so much, all the evil, the vile and violent and cruel things that make life so hard and painful for so many people."

Toni said nothing. Her jaw was tight, her eyes narrow slits.

"What are you thinking?" Jude finally asked.

"I think they hypnotize you, or something close to it. I think they twisted your mind."

Jude shook her head sadly. "The only way for you to understand is to come with me and be a part of it, experience it for yourself. If you could feel what I felt, you'd know it's the truth."

"Jude," Toni said angrily, "you don't get to truth about things like that — things outside yourself — by way of *feelings*. You're deluding yourself. Or they're deluding you. Look at it objectively for a minute. Some strange, half-crazed old woman has dreams about the creation of the universe and good and evil personified in some primitive goddess and devil, and you enter her delusion? That's not being a very good anthropologist. You believe it when they say you never had a father? Where's the data, Jude? It doesn't make sense at all. Where's the proof?"

Jude listened, tight-lipped.

Toni sighed. "Everything they've told you is all

based on this self-proclaimed prophet's dreams, right?"

"Kwo-am speaks through her."

"Oh, shit!" Toni folded her arms. "You are not Jude. They did something to you. I think they drugged you."

Jude felt painfully sad. "I wish you could open your heart. There's so much more to existence than you know, Toni."

"Maybe so, but what you're talking about isn't the answer. This La claims to have these dreams and a bunch of mush-brains believe she'd got a direct line to some new deity and you buy it!"

"I told you, Toni. Kwo-am is not a new deity. She's *the* deity. Just the name is new. She's the same deity everyone talks about, only they had a lot of misinformation. Call her God, if you prefer. She's showing us a way to save ourselves, to save the world. And I'm to play a major part in it, only it's a terrible struggle for me because my kwo-ami's been diluted by living so long in the outer world."

"Instead of on a mental ward," Toni snapped. "So Joe's not your father. That's the only good news you've told me. But Jesus Christ, Jude. They're not very original, are they? Use your head, hon. Don't let them do this to you."

Jude sighed. She sat quietly for a while, staring at the floor. Finally she looked at Toni. Although Toni still seemed angry, she also appeared very vulnerable. Jude reached out and took her hand. "It's frightening to you. I understand that."

Toni did not respond.

"Come here, I want to kiss your freckles," Jude said lovingly.

119

"I don't let fanatics kiss me."

Suddenly Amagyne came to Jude's mind, her lips pressed to Jude's own. Jude felt a heavy thud in her stomach. "Will you come with me, Toni? Live at Circle Edge with me? I need you with me." She tried to lighten her tone. "You'd love it there. You said it sounded like a little utopia."

"I'm worried about you, Jude. I don't know what to do."

"Let's move to Colorado."

Toni shook her head. "You're losing it."

"You've always liked Colorado. The old ways are no good, Toni. The outer world is a haven of zetkap."

"You sound like a Moonie."

"How about a stretch talk?" Jude said.

"Psychobabble."

"You talk, I'll listen. Pause from time to time and let me tell you what I hear."

Toni folded her arms.

"Come on, try it. Talk about your feelings and thoughts."

"I feel frustrated," Toni said. "Worried about you. Frightened."

"Go on."

"Aren't you going to tell me you hear me say I feel frustrated and frightened?"

"Not yet. Say more."

"You're Jude and yet you're not. I'm afraid they're doing something to you that's making you not you anymore." Toni reached for Jude's hand. "I feel you slipping away. I'm very worried. It's so unbelievable that partly I think you're just putting me on. But partly I know you mean it. I want Jude back. I hate this bullshit."

Her hand clasping Toni's, Jude spoke. "It really worries you that I'm believing some new things . . . beliefs that seem threatening to you. You want me the way I was."

"Yes, goddamn it! That's exactly what I want. I love you, Jude. When you talk about this Kwo-am business, I feel like I'm losing you." Toni's eyes were wet.

Jude felt her own eyes tearing. "You don't want to lose me." The words caught in her throat. They reached out to each other simultaneously and clung tightly together. "Oh, I don't want to lose you either, Toni. I love you more than anything." Their tears mixed.

"Jude, my love," Toni said. "Maybe you're especially vulnerable right now, with Rosalie so ill, and . . . and maybe you're bored with your job, or maybe we need to go out more. Maybe there's just too much stress for you to handle right now and that's why all the Kwo-amity stuff hooked you."

"Maybe." Jude's cheek was pressed snugly against Toni's neck.

"You can see it's foolish, can't you?"

"Maybe it is."

"Maybe you need to add something to your life. Let's think about that, Jude. Maybe what you have doesn't feel like enough somehow. Maybe you ought to get more involved with some women's issues. Maybe the Feminist Fund. Or think about a new career. Or maybe we need to go on a trip together."

"Maybe," Jude said.

"Let some time go by, will you, Jude? Put all this Kwo-amity stuff on hold for a while, can you do that?"

"I think I could. Yes, maybe I should. It feels good to hold you."

"We belong together."

They clung to each other.

CHAPTER 13

When she went to sleep that night, Jude was not sure what she would do. By morning, she had no doubt. In between, she had a dream.

She was in warm water, feeling soothed and safe. The music came, the same song, the *Coming of the Catalyst.* It surrounded her and she became the music and it came from her, from her flute. She floated to the mountain top feeling the blissful ecstasy, Amagyne gliding next to her. She saw Amagyne's outstretched hand and she grasped it, felt its strength. But then she felt it slipping away until only their fingertips touched. And then she was falling rapidly, the charred fragments of earth advancing to meet her, and Amagyne far, far away. As she was about to hit the ground she awoke, her heart pounding madly.

"I'm giving my notice today," she said at breakfast. "I'm quitting my job." She looked at Toni. "I can't pretend I don't believe, Toni. Even for you. I'm going back to Circle Edge."

Toni pushed her cereal aside. Her lips moved but no words emerged.

"What I've learned, and what it means, is bigger and truer and more important than anything on earth," Jude said.

Toni looked ill.

"I have to go back and I have to fulfill the Ceremony of Emergence."

"Oh, Jude, that is such garbage."

"I can't let my love for you stop me. You'll come some day too."

Toni's face was lined with tension. "Jude, whatever they did to you, it's not too late. We'll work on it. I'll help you try to understand and . . . get over it. Would you consider seeing a therapist?"

"I know your kwo-ami is very strong."

"Jude, just don't rush into it, OK? Talk it over with people. This is a big decision, right? So you shouldn't rush into it."

"I'm giving a week's notice at Yvonne's."

"Jude, I want a stretch talk."

Jude smiled.

"OK? You listen, OK?" Toni leaned forward. "Jude, I feel frightened. I'm worried that you're blinded by something I don't understand and that *you* don't understand. I want you to agree to wait. To take some time, maybe a few months, at least, to think it over some more, talk to friends, and maybe a therapist."

Jude looked caringly across the table into Toni's eyes. "My decision frightens you. You want me to wait and to talk with people about it."

"Yes. Will you?" Toni asked urgently.

Jude took a deep breath and let it out. "I'll talk to people, Toni, to friends. I'd be happy to talk about it. But I can't wait. I'm leaving a week from Friday."

"Will you talk with a therapist too? Someone who can be more objective? How about Hannah Jones? Everyone says she's good. Will you make an appointment with her?"

"There's no need for that, Toni."

"Will you do it for me?"

Jude looked lovingly at her lover. "All right."

* * * * *

That evening Pam opened the front door for Jude when she got home. "So I hear you're a junior goddess."

Jude chuckled. "Hi, Pam." She hung her jacket on a hook. "Hi, Toni."

Pam lit a cigarette. She beckoned Jude into the living room and pointed to a chair. Jude sat. Pam perched on the arm of the sofa.

"Toni tells me these Kwo-amians have been filling your head with a lot of ideas that most people would find hard to believe. But I know that you're a bright, reasonable woman, Jude. And I've never known you to be particularly gullible. But from what I hear,

125

you're claiming to believe some pretty far out things."

"No more *far out* than other religious ideas," Jude said. "But of course they're going to sound unbelievable to you and Toni. Or to anyone who denies God."

"Your *spirituality* never crossed over the edge before," Pam said. "If people want to believe in a Supreme Being, I have no problem with that. Or goddesses, or spiritual energy, or whatever. I never gave you any flack before, did I? But now you've tumbled right into the middle of the kook fringe, Jude. You quit your job, right? You're talking about leaving Chicago and moving in with a group of cultists. You go too far, Jude. I have to challenge you."

Jude shrugged. "OK, challenge."

"Try to keep an open mind, OK?"

"OK," Jude said.

"Good. All right, now, as intelligent, reasonable people, we don't generally believe strange and unusual things without any proof or evidence just because someone says they're true, do we? You'd need more than just someone's word to believe something like that, wouldn't you, Jude?" Jude nodded. "Well, what do you have from this La person and this Amagyne person other than just their words?"

"My feelings, Pam," Jude said earnestly. "My own experience. I know it's hard for you to believe, but I experienced a communion, a connecting with Kwo-am. She came to me. I felt it."

Pam drew on her cigarette. "How do you know that feeling wasn't because you were pulled in by the Kwo-amians' appeals to you and by the ceremonial

126

ritual business? Maybe you felt what you did because of that and because you *wanted* to feel like you were communing with a god figure."

"It was real."

"Yes, the feeling was. But that doesn't mean it was based on anything real. You're not being logical, Jude."

Jude shook her head. "I don't really care if I'm being logical or not. I know what I felt and what I feel."

Pam turned to Toni who was sitting on the piano bench. "You got any coffee?"

Toni left. Pam sat down on the sofa, stretching her legs, then sat upright. "OK, how about this? The feelings you get may be valid grounds for you to pay attention, to investigate further, to look for supporting evidence. So you listen to what these cultists have to say. You ask questions. You're open, but you don't suspend your mind, all right? You look for things they say that contradict known facts of reality."

"I suppose that would be a reasonable thing to do."

"Good. Now, you know it takes a human sperm and a human ovum to produce a new human being. Right?"

"It usually does," Jude said. "But Amagyne was conceived without a father. And so was I. I believe this, Pam. I don't expect you to at this point."

Pam's upper lip curled. "Isn't that something. You really get off on that idea, don't you, Jude? That you're some kind of goddess yourself. Really, what kind of adolescent fantasy are you trying to satisfy? I can't believe you could be so easily conned. What

127

could possibly make you believe that you had no father?"

"Amagyne told me. La predicted it. It was revealed to La by Kwo-am. Kwo-am is God."

"I see. Is it possible that La and Amagyne could be lying, do you think? Or mistaken?"

"They're not."

"How do you know that?"

"Because of how I feel when they talk to me about it. Because I experienced Kwo-am personally."

Toni handed them each a cup of coffee. Pam blew in hers, took a sip, then set it on the cube table to her right. "Because you get these *feelings*, you're willing to believe things counter to all scientific data."

"You're neglecting the central data, Pam." Jude sipped her coffee.

"Oh? And what's the central data?"

"Kwo-am. The force who created the universe and who certainly could create a baby without the help of a penis."

Pam shook her head in frustration.

"Our science is too narrow, Pam. Kwo-am is bigger than the laws of nature. Why does just about everybody but my lover and my best friend realize there's a supernatural being? You atheists are so damn closed-minded. Kwo-am created what is, Pam; she can do what she wants with it."

"I'd be happy to believe that if there were any evidence," Pam snapped.

"Come to Circle Edge," Jude retorted.

"Fuck Circle Edge," Pam hissed.

Jude reached over to Pam and put her hand on her knee. "You're upset because you're worried about

128

me. That's what's really going on. You think the Kwo-amians are manipulating me."

There were tears in Pam's eyes. "Yes," she said. "That's what I think. I don't want you to run off to Colorado and turn into some sappy weirdo who isn't the Jude I love anymore."

Jude reached for her and cried with her. "What's happening scares me too, but Pam, I feel the truth in it. God is acting directly in my life. She's chosen me. How can I say no? I *have* to follow it through." She rubbed Pam's knee. "I wish you were open to it." She glanced at Toni. "Both of you. I don't want you to hurt or worry. Pam, it doesn't mean I'm crazy or brainwashed because I'm open to God." Their arms were wrapped around each other.

"I don't want to lose you, Jude. None of us do. Do you know what you're putting Toni through? I wish you'd just listen to reason."

Jude wiped away tears. "There's something else going on in me, Pam, that I have to listen to. I'm sorry it frightens you. I certainly don't want to cause you any pain."

Pam dug a handkerchief from her pants pocket. "I believe that," she said, looking into Jude's eyes. "You just don't know what you're getting into. You're mixed up with some very strange people, Jude. They're taking over your life."

Toni put a hand on each of their shoulders. "Maybe it will end up all right," she said. "Logic isn't going to do it, Pam."

Pam shook her head. "Well, I refuse to beg," she said, "but I haven't given up yet."

* * * * *

129

Over the next few days Toni, Pam and Gresh, assisted by other friends, continued trying to persuade Jude that she was misguided. They talked to her about what she would be leaving behind — her life in Chicago, Toni, her friends, playing in the band. They tried ridicule, reason, accusations that she was on a ego-trip. Gresh said she thought Jude's attraction to the religion stemmed from her frustration with all the pain and oppression in the patriarchal world. "But you can't change it by magic," Gresh told her.

Becka Acuna, Toni's former lover, took another stance. "I think she should go. What's the harm? Let her get it out of her system."

It was Monday evening. Jude was at her mother's. Toni had gone out to dinner with Gresh and Dagney Green, a friend of Gresh's whom Toni had never met before. After dinner, they had gone to visit Becka at her apartment on Wellington Avenue.

Toni disagreed with Becka. "Those people have tremendous power over her. I think the more time she spends with them, the more sucked in she'll get."

"She'll get fed up with it," Becka insisted. "She'll play messiah for a while, then laugh in their faces."

"That's psychologically naive," Gresh said. "She's had a conversion experience. She accepts what they tell her as truth. She's hooked."

"I think she's hooked on Amagyne," Becka said.

There was a period of silence. Toni chewed her lip. Becka, sitting next to her, placed a hand comfortingly on Toni's knee.

"Amagyne is quite a charismatic woman. Also very beautiful." This was the first contribution Dagney had made. Dagney had recently moved her publishing

130

business from Kansas to Chicago and had become good friends with Gresh. A tall, large-boned woman, she had a low, powerful voice, and an aura of great self-assurance.

All eyes turned to her. "You've seen her?" Toni asked.

"Once. Briefly." Dagney leaned back, her hands behind her head. "It was at a women's dance in Indianapolis. I danced with her and then sat with her and her friends awhile. I didn't stay long. They started talking spiritual crap. From what I understand, this Amagyne goes around and talks up the religion, gets a lot of converts."

Toni leaned toward Dagney. "What else do you know about her?"

"She did a workshop at last year's Michigan Festival," Dagney said. "A friend of mine went. She said Amagyne impressed the hell out of her — that she's very dynamic, very alluring. My friend, Beth, was intrigued enough to get on their mailing list, was even thinking of joining a group here in Chicago." Dagney smiled. "I was satisfied with a dance."

"How widespread is this religion?" Gresh asked.

"Apparently they have little congregations all over the country," Dagney said. "Covens, I call them. Beth pulled out when she heard some rumors about the leader, La, the so-called Sage. Some friend of Beth in New York apparently had some inside information on La. She told Beth and it turned Beth off. I don't know what the scoop was. If Beth told me, I've forgotten."

"Beth lives here? In Chicago?" Toni asked.

"Mm-hm. Would you like to meet her?"

131

"I sure would."

"I'll arrange it," Dagney said.

* * * * *

Toni met Beth the following night. Beth was a petite, dark-haired woman in her early fifties, who was more than happy to talk about La. They were sitting in the living room of Dagney's house in Evanston.

"A crazy, I'd say. A real psych case." Beth's index finger tapped her temple. "Now her sidekick, Amagyne, is another story altogether. She seemed very fine to me." Beth raised her eyebrows and smiled lasciviously. "But Maggie — that's my friend in New York — she knew about the other one, La. She used to call herself Lavender, then changed it to La. Maggie knew her pretty well, and had the definite impression that La was screwy. She heard voices, did automatic writing, claimed to be a prophet. There was even some talk that she was hospitalized at Bellevue."

"Jude needs to hear this," Toni said.

"She once went out on the ocean on a small boat all by herself," Beth continued. "Her friends gave her up for dead but she came back claiming that the goddess had spoken to her."

"How did Maggie come to know so much about her?" Dagney asked.

"I'm not sure. I don't know if she ever said. Anyway, after Maggie told me these things, I lost all interest in Kwo-amity. I think it was really Amagyne I was interested in." Beth paused, smiling. "Now if *she* came knocking at my door, my interest in Kwo-amity might suddenly be rekindled." She laughed heartily.

"Is Maggie still in New York?" Toni asked.

"Yes. I visited her last summer. She's a doctor. She's got a great apartment in Manhattan."

"She's not planning a trip to Chicago in the next few days by any chance?" Toni poured wine into her own and Dagney's glass.

Beth shook her head. "Not that I know of."

"I'd like Jude to hear it from the horse's mouth."

"I'm going to New York the end of July," Dagney said. "Maybe I'll look the horse up."

"Hey, you really should," Beth said. "I think you two would like each other."

* * * * *

Toni arranged for Beth to talk with Jude, who was agreeable to hearing anything anyone wanted to say to her. She listened patiently.

"Everyone's entitled to her opinion," Jude said when Beth was finished. "Some people just aren't ready to hear the truth. So instead they call her crazy and dismiss her."

"She sounds pretty crazy to me," Beth said.

Unruffled, Jude shrugged.

* * * * *

On Thursday, Jude went for her appointment with Hannah Jones. She freely told the psychologist about Kwo-amity and Circle Edge and about Toni's worries

133

about her. Dr. Jones listened, then questioned Jude. She asked her about her attraction to Amagyne. Jude didn't deny it. She raised the possibility that Jude might be feeling a need to be a part of something bigger than her ordinary world, to feel more needed or important or special. Jude said she didn't know about that but would give it some thought. The therapist suggested they arrange another appointment, but Jude said she was leaving the next day for Colorado.

* * * * *

At the airport, a grim-faced Toni embraced Jude. Jude looked into her lover's red-rimmed eyes, then touched her cheek. "I'll miss you."

Toni didn't speak.

"We'll be together soon," Jude said hopefully.

CHAPTER 14

Jude took the glass from the bedside table and guided the straw between Rosalie's cracked, dry lips.

"Water," Rosalie said, feebly. "I guess I've had all the beer I'm going to drink."

Jude stroked her hair. "It's spring water, full of good spirits."

"I'll need them."

Jude's throat was so constricted it felt as if the edges were glued together.

"It's easier for me to leave this earth knowing you're still on it," Rosalie said in a faltering voice. "I can't imagine that I could ever have loved my own flesh and blood child more than I love you."

Jude had to lean close to hear the words. A tear slipped down her cheek onto Rosalie's flowered pajama top.

"You made the last third of my life . . . you made it worth living."

Rosalie slept then. Jude stayed with her, listening to her breathe, until Mrs. Clarkson came.

Honore was waiting outside. She had picked Jude up at the Denver airport and Jude had asked her to stop at the Estate before going on to Circle Edge.

When Jude and Honore arrived at the entrance to Circle Edge the gate was wide open and a crowd was waiting. At the sight of Jude, a loud cheering rose from the women and they began to sing, *She has come! The Catalyst has come! She is here.*

Delighted, surprised, overwhelmed, and somewhat embarrassed, Jude walked into their midst. Amagyne took her hand. Music played. Children danced around them.

"The Catalyst has come," Amagyne said, kissing Jude lovingly on each cheek.

"We welcome you," La said. She pulled Jude to her breast in a warm embrace. "Come, let us walk to the Amit."

The welcoming ceremony for Jude was lavish and jubilant. There were even fireworks (Miluna's idea, Jude learned). She wondered later what the Dorayites had thought about the fireworks, and wondered if Martha had seen them. Different women spoke briefly at the welcoming ceremony, each saying what the coming of the Catalyst meant to her. Jude felt light-headed and excited. She held hands with the others when circles formed, accepted the candles that were passed from one woman to the next until they reached her.

At one point hundreds of pairs of women, hands linked together above their heads, formed an arched pathway for Jude to pass through.

After the ceremony, everyone ate and drank and sang by torchlight under the moon. The entire Edge orchestra was there and the dancing went on for hours.

When Jude finally collapsed in her bed in Sky Palace it took her a long time to fall asleep. She glowed with happiness and excitement. She was home. Her new life had begun.

* * * * *

In the days that followed, Jude learned more and more about Kwo-amity and about life at Circle Edge. She worked and played and talked with many people. Some were awed by her, and stared or became tongue-tied in her presence. Some asked to touch her hand. Many, many women told Jude how grateful they were that she had come.

She and Honore grew close. They had long talks, sharing with each other the experiences and events that had made up their lives. Jude felt sure they would remain friends forever.

Honore was twenty-seven years old, Jude learned. She had lived at Circle Edge for the past four years. "I was raised Catholic, but when I became a feminist I realized how limited Catholicism is, not to mention sexist and patriarchal. I went through an angry period. Then I learned about the goddess, nature, our

137

oneness with it. I read Starhawk and listened to Z. Budapest. I joined a coven and was content with my new way of experiencing spirituality. But then when I heard about Kwo-amity, I got confused again. I was drawn to it, yet I wasn't sure. But the more I learned, the truer it seemed. One truth, tying all other versions together. I love the clarity of it. It leaves very little unanswered. It seems complete. Not for one minute have I regretted my decision to come here."

"Did you leave anyone behind?" Jude asked.

"Yes. Friends, family. But not like you, Jude. There was no Toni in my life. I think that's the hardest part for you." Jude agreed that it was. "It will work out," Honore predicted. "With the changes that are coming, many things that now seem impossible will happen. Toni will be swept up in them too. You'll see."

* * * * *

Jude began reading the *Words of Kwo-Am* which Honore had given to her. The book contained La's revealments and also stories, parables written by La from visions and inspirations that had come to her from Kwo-am. There were references to events from the Bible.

Jude talked with other Kwo-amians about her reactions to what she read. They had many stimulating discussions and even a few arguments. Through each parable, Jude learned more about the meaning of Kwo-amity. The stories were of people's lives and struggles — falling and rising again, making mistakes and learning from them. Stories of pulling

138

away, then coming back. Stories of fighting and fear, then resolution and peace. The stories seemed full of wisdom.

Jude thought about them as she rode on horseback through the hills with Ella and Honore. The stories came to mind as she worked in the orchard with Starla and Joyce and played card games with Miluna and Berryfire and Rose. Some of the stories seemed to be directed specifically at her.

Jude's phone conversations with Toni were strained. At first Toni tried to argue about Kwo-amity, but Jude would not argue back, saying only that she understood how Toni felt. Toni gave up and tried, instead, to make Jude homesick. But that didn't work either. Their conversations then became clumsy and faltering. Toni did not want to hear about Jude's enchantment with her new life. Jude did not want to hear Toni's objections. Each time they talked Jude would feel guilty and sad. She wished it could be some other way. Talking with Honore about her feelings helped, but the pain remained.

Each day Jude visited Rosalie, and each day she thought about going to see Martha to explain what was happening. Finally on the eighth day after her arrival at Circle Edge, Jude went in the early evening to her sister's home.

Martha was surprised and delighted to see her, then very upset when she learned why Jude had come to Colorado, and that she was staying at Circle Edge.

"Have you joined them? Are you one of them now?"

"Yes," Jude said. "I'm studying Kwo-amity and soon I'll have my Rite of Entrance. I will then be a Kwo-amian."

Martha shook her head. "I always wished you lived closer to me."

Jude smiled. "And now I do."

"Physically," Martha said. "I've heard that people who are in cults go around in a daze."

Jude clucked her tongue.

"That they don't let you sleep enough, or eat enough protein, or ever be alone with your own thoughts."

"It's not like that at Circle Edge."

"That you have to chant or pray all the time so there's no room in your mind for any other thoughts."

"I don't chant or pray."

"You don't?"

Jude shook her head.

"You don't seem to be in a daze."

"My mind's as clear as a bell. I'm happy, Martha. I'm still me, only happier."

Jude did not tell her sister that she was the Catalyst, the Second Guide who would help bring about the New Page. She did not tell her she was born of woman only.

"I heard they don't let you maintain contact with your family."

Jude shook her head. "Not true of the Kwo-amians."

"That they want you to bond only with them."

"There will be no interference with my bond with you."

"So you can visit me whenever you want?"

"Of course. I make my own choices, Martie."

Martha looked askance at her. "Will you stay for dinner tonight?"

140

"I'd like that."

Martha smiled then, a little relieved it seemed. She hugged Jude tightly. "It's great having you here."

* * * * *

One of the things Jude most enjoyed at Circle Edge was basking in one of the warm pools at the Inner Garden with one or two others and talking about how the world would be after the Ceremony of Emergence took place and the Withering of Zetka began. But even more than that she enjoyed the long, leisurely hours she spent with Amagyne. They told each other about their pasts, frequently laughing, sometimes crying together.

"I feel as if I've always known you," Jude said several times, and Amagyne would nod.

Amagyne told Jude about her many trips away from Circle Edge when she was growing up. "La took me from coast to coast. She was always teaching me. Wherever we went, I was learning — about the ways of the world and about the Kwo-amian understandings of things."

"I bet she was quite a teacher."

"The best. I had others as well. When I was a child, we didn't yet have the school at Circle Edge, but I had many teachers here. I was always good at math."

"Really? I wouldn't have thought that," Jude said. "I'd have guessed you didn't like math."

"Why is that?"

"I don't know. Maybe because I didn't."

Amagyne smiled. "I feel our similarities, too."

141

Jude had a strong urge to invite Amagyne to her sleeping hut. This was not the first time she felt the craving. "I've never been with another woman since I met Toni."

"I imagine you never really wanted to be."

Jude did not respond. She knew Amagyne had several lovers but that there was no soul partner who shared her life. She wondered if there ever would be.

* * * * *

On July eighth, two weeks after her return to Circle Edge, La declared that Jude was ready for her Rite of Entrance. Jude was amused with herself for her eagerness about getting that purple scarf, the symbol of her full acceptance as a Kwo-amian.

Everyone was welcome to attend Rites of Entrance. Honore's prediction that there would be a big crowd was correct. On the morning of the rite, as Jude sat on a bench in the center of the Amit, with La on one side and Honore on the other, the mass of faces around them seemed endless. The women nearer the center all had their purple scarves draped over their necks. On the periphery was a scattering of non-Kwo-amians.

Jude felt a twinge of stage fright, but mostly she felt excited happiness. She was dressed in white sweat pants and a white T-shirt. Music played softly and the rite began. La handed Jude the crystal goblet filled with cool spring water, saying the words Jude had heard many times before: "Water from deep within the earth."

Jude drank until the glass was empty, while the huge audience of witnesses hummed and the music played softly.

"We gather here to welcome Jude Alta into our midst," La said. "She has found one among us who wishes to be her soul-sister."

Honore placed her hand on Jude's shoulder. "We have spoken together and opened our hearts to each other," she said, looking warmly at Jude. "I will be with Jude as she wants and needs my presence in her life."

When it was her turn to speak, Jude did not need the card which was stuffed in the little back pocket of her pants. She had memorized the words. "I accept Kwo-am, the creator, the spirit of love. I sense her presence, I welcome her."

"She is with you," Honore and several other Kwo-amians said in unison.

Soft strains of music played as Jude continued her recitation. Her stage fright had disappeared. When she finished and La draped the purple scarf over her neck, Jude felt filled to capacity.

"You are of us," hundreds of voices proclaimed, and the women came forward, one by one embracing Jude and wishing her Monama.

Jude was breathless. She touched the scarf periodically and each time felt a tingling thrill. She could not imagine feeling happier.

* * * * *

The next day Amagyne left Circle Edge to travel

and spread the news about the Catalyst. Jude felt the emptiness the moment they said goodbye. Honore seemed to sense her feelings and invited Jude to talk.

"I'm very attracted to Amagyne," Jude said. "Sometimes I wonder if she's the main reason that I chose to be here."

"She's part of it," Honore said, "but far from all."

The following day, on her way back from Rosalie's, Jude went to visit Joe Alta. The conversation was not pleasant.

"I bet you don't own a dress," he said at one point.

Jude did not reply. It seemed they really had nothing to say to each other.

No blood connects us, she thought angrily, yet happily. She felt very free when she said goodbye to him.

A few days after Amagyne's departure, Jude finished her evening shift at the print shop and was in one of the pools with Starla.

"After the Emergence, older male children and even men will be allowed at Circle Edge," Starla said. "They'll all be kwo-omnis. Wow, that's hard to imagine." She handed Jude some grapes. "There have been a few Edgers who gave birth to males, you know, while they were living here. Most of them leave right away instead of staying until the child reaches age two. A couple of them were so angry that they even left Kwo-amity. I'm glad that's all going to change."

"You seem so sure, Starla."

"I feel the certainty. In here." She laid her hand on her chest. "Of course, I can't really know for

144

sure." She looked at Jude. "Are you frightened of the Scourges?"

Jude hesitated. "Somewhat."

"No one knows exactly what it will be like, only that it'll be very trying for you." Starla raised one leg out of the pool into the cool night air. "La knows, but says it's not time to speak of it yet. A few Edgers do know about it, the ones who've been helping prepare it. But they're not to talk about it."

Jude felt a slight twinge of fear each time the subject of the Scourges came up. "I'll do my best," she said.

"If you don't triumph, we will love you no less, you know."

"I know."

"I'm so glad it's happening in my lifetime," Starla said dreamily. "I can already feel the waves of kwo-ami spreading over me." She seemed not to have a trace of doubt. "After the Ceremony, Janice and I will go to San Francisco for our part in spreading the kwo-ami. I wonder how it will feel to be a kwo-omni. It makes me dizzy thinking of it. No zetkap left in me at all. And to know that every time I speak of Kwo-amity and what it means, those who hear the words will be open to them, and let them in. La says it won't take long for it to spread throughout the world."

* * * * *

Every day Jude drank spring water from the tank at Ambrosia where it was kept chilled. She also exercised daily under the direction of Joyce, who was a health aide. Their sessions became more and more

145

vigorous as time went on. "To prepare you," La had said. Jude ate well and was feeling strong and fit.

From their first meeting, Jude had felt close to Amagyne's mother, Lorn. She was a gentle, soft-spoken woman in her mid-fifties, skin tawny brown from her African forebears. She and Jude took walks and spoke of Amagyne and the bonds each felt to her, and of the miracle of Amagyne's birth and of Jude's.

"Amagyne had many mothers to love her," Lorn said, "I being one of the foremost and La the other. She is my blood, but belongs to everyone."

Lorn and La were the best of friends, Jude discovered, often spending long periods together. Jude was glad they had each other.

The only circumstances preventing Jude's complete happiness were Rosalie's continuing decline, which made Jude feel utterly helpless, and the pain she felt about Toni — pain from missing her, guilt about moving away from her, sadness that Toni remained in the dark.

She talked with Toni frequently, calling her nearly every day. Neither could bend to fit what the other needed. Jude would not give up the "nonsense" and "come back home where you belong." Toni would not entertain the possibility that it was not nonsense at all. She was, however, considering a visit, which pleased Jude very much.

Near the end of July, Amagyne returned. She had gone to sixteen states and spoken to thousands of women. "They are very excited," she said, "very eager." Many of the women planned to come to Circle Edge for the Ceremony of Emergence.

The night of Amagyne's return, she and Jude

stayed up late talking, occasionally touching. Jude felt her whole soul fill with joy from their contact.

A few days later, at the Amit, La announced that she'd had the dream everyone awaited. "The Enactment of the Scourges of Zetka is to begin at sunrise tomorrow."

Jude got a sinking feeling in the pit of her stomach.

"Jude Alta, your true name has come to me," La said.

Jude rose from the midst of the crowd.

"By this name you shall be known from the moment of your triumph and ever after. Hear the name, for it comes from Kwo-am and is your true identity."

La looked at Jude with such intensity that Jude felt it reaching to her core.

"Laki-Seone!" said the Sage.

"La-kee-say-own," Jude repeated.

"Laki-Seone, the name that will be yours if you take on the Scourges of the Evil One and do not fall."

"She shall not fall!" voices chanted.

Jude made herself stand straight and tall.

* * * * *

That evening, Jude went to visit Rosalie and afterwards stopped at Martha's house. She told her sister there was to be a special event the next day. Martha clearly did not want to hear about it, so they spoke of other things. They embraced warmly when Jude left.

From her room at Sky Palace that night, Jude

147

called her mother and they had a pleasant talk. Then, just before going to bed, she phoned Toni. She told her the Scourges would begin in the morning. Toni said she hoped Jude survived them. Jude laughed and told her not to worry.

CHAPTER 15

It was still pitch dark the next morning when Jude woke to the rapping at her door. Her sleep had been peaceful. She was feeling confident. She showered and dressed and went to Ambrosia where La and Amagyne were waiting. A wonderful breakfast of all her favorite foods was served. Jude ate heartily. The food was delicious except for the orange juice, which tasted odd. La insisted she drink it, saying it contained a potion that would help her with the Scourges.

"How are you feeling?" La asked.

"Good. Strong."

"It is almost time. We must be in the Dome before the sun begins to show."

Jude nodded, feeling scared but ready. She followed Amagyne and La outside. Hundreds of women were there in the darkness, lining the path that led to the Dome. Some threw flower petals as Jude passed. Some gave the sign of Kwo-am, a palm placed on the chest, chin high, eyes straight ahead. As the trio neared the Dome, sounds of a single flute from somewhere in the crowd reached Jude's ears. It was playing the *Coming of the Catalyst*.

Inside the Dome, they passed the glass-roofed garden and went down the long corridor. The back room they entered was about nine feet by nine, dimly lit, its floor covered with a quilted cushiony material. Black draperies covered three of the walls. In the center of the room was a circular platform three feet high and three feet in diameter. There was one small window, covered with a black curtain. Two ropes with wooden rings at their ends hung from opposite walls.

"May Kwo-am be with you and augment your courage," La said.

Amagyne asked Jude to remove her clothes. When she was naked, La and Amagyne helped her onto the platform.

"When the sun rises, the Enactment of the Scourges of Zetka begins." La took one of the hanging rings and pulled it over to Jude.

"When the sun rises a second time, it is over." Amagyne handed Jude the other ring.

Jude stood then with her arms outstretched at her sides, each hand grasping a wooden ring.

La was standing barefoot on the padded floor in

front of Jude. "The rings represent humankind," she said solemnly. "We are in your hands. Sunrise to sunrise represents the history of life on earth. This Kwo-am has revealed to me. Your mind will be assaulted during that time by horrible images of what Zetka has wrought since life began."

Jude breathed deeply through her nose.

"And it will enter you. If you can hold onto the rings — to humankind — throughout all the time of life on earth, then you will have triumphed and the Ceremony of Emergence can take place. The Withering of Zetka will begin."

Amagyne's smooth fingers touched Jude's foot and the feel of it gave Jude courage.

"If you let go of one or both of the rings, then we know it was not yet meant to be," Amagyne said.

Jude swallowed. "I'll hold on," she promised.

"You will do what you can," Amagyne said. "I feel your kwo-ami filling this room and it is very powerful." Looking up at her, she held Jude's eyes and Jude felt her great love.

La spoke. "Kwo-am moves us toward the New Page through you, the Catalyst. You are now to experience the raw reality of Zetka's power. Kwo-am hopes your will to fight Zetka will be so strong that when the Enactment of the Scourges is over, you will be fully ready to fulfill the Ceremony of Emergence. Zetka hopes that you will not be able to bear what he will inflict on you, that you will fall and the New Page will not be. Move and countermove. You are in the middle."

Jude's chin was high. "I will do my best," she said.

151

Amagyne touched her foot once more, then left the room.

La stood at the door. "Kwo-am is with you."

"And with us all," Jude said, her voice faltering slightly.

La closed the door. A few seconds later, the weak light illuminating the little room disappeared. Jude stood naked in total blackness, holding the rings that were humankind, feeling the closeness of the room and the importance of her mission. Her eyes were drawn upward and to the right where the window was. The curtains were open now. She could see stars in the black night.

Several minutes passed. She continued staring at the stars. Her head began to feel strange. The stars seemed to be moving. She blinked repeatedly, but the movement only increased. The sky became alive with their darting and swirling. They were moving in every direction at once, leaving comet trails. The colors grew brighter and brighter, reds, deep purples, bright blues and greens, all swirling in crazy patterns, coming closer and closer to the window.

Then the room was swarming with them. Thousands of stars flying wildly in the confines of the tiny room. Then they came together, merging, coalescing into two huge forms that undulated threateningly in front of Jude. The mass took on shapes. Huge animals. Dinosaurs. They were vividly clear, right there in the room with her.

Jude stared wide-eyed as the huge sharp teeth of the Tyrannosaurus Rex penetrated the neck of the plant-eating brontosaurus. She heard a voice. *Devour.* She looked for the speaker but could see nothing but blackness. *Devour each other,* the voice said. A male voice. The dinosaurs disappeared. There was movement to her right. A mass of crabs scampering across the wall, overtaking fleeing baby turtles, grabbing them, pulling them to pieces. To her left a lion pursued a deer, downed it, ripped off chunks of its flesh, gnawed on bones. More animals began coming from above her, in front of her, from everywhere, insects eating insects, mammals eating mammals. Killing, ripping, gnawing. And the voice was there, that fiendish voice describing each scene.

Jude closed her eyes. *The hyenas nip repeatedly at the zebra's ankles. It's down. The pack descends, its leader sinking incisors into the neck, and blood oozes red over the predator's jowls.* Jude turned in every direction to see where the voice was coming from. Foxes filled the room, tearing off chickens' heads, anteaters lapped up ants, birds snapped fish from the sea and insects from the ground. Creatures swarmed menacingly all around her. Snakes' jaws unhinged to take in rodents. Jude's head was spinning as predators attacked and victims fell, emitting little yips of pain or long, howling death screams. The sounds pierced Jude's ears and tore at her brain.

A huge bear lumbered across Jude's vision. It was downed by a spear. *Man has entered the picture,* the voice said, *prehistoric killers, killing for meat, killing to avoid being killed themselves, killing for the thrill of the kill.* A band of wolves pursued a mountain goat, then a band of Neanderthals pursued a moose. The kill. Flesh torn from bone, or cut with primitive tools.

Man turning the spear against man. Jude felt a sharp blade pierce her back, just below her shoulder. She screamed and tried to pull away. A woman was

153

thrown down and raped before her eyes. Jude experienced the horror of the violation in her own body. She was gasping for air, her breathing a low rumble in her throat. A group of early humanoids, furs draped over their shoulders, were on the move, leaving the old ones behind to die. Jude suffered the panic of those who were abandoned.

A youth with a shriveled arm, stoned, scorned, laughed at. All the rejections Jude had ever felt came tenfold upon her. She cried out, writhing on the platform, holding the rings in trembling hands. Girl babies born and drowned. Caves giving way to huts, nomads settling and tilling the earth. Tribe invading tribe, stealing, burning, raping. Flames scorched Jude's flesh, rough hands and penises violated her. She felt blood dripping down her legs.

The onslaught of hideous images was relentless, and so was the voice. Jude talked aloud. "It's not real. I'm just imagining it. I'm in a room. I'm safe." She realized she was gripping the rings with all her strength. She made herself relax. I'll never last this way, she thought. Already the muscles of her arms were sore. She slid her right hand through the ring to rest it.

Huts became houses. There were castles. Walls went up. Towns sprouted before her eyes. Warriors came, trampling peasants under horses' hooves. Jude's bones cracked and she moaned aloud. Masses of soldiers attacked other masses leaving bleeding wounded and dead scattered on the fields. Clubs smashed skulls. Jude's head was split wide. Spears pierced flesh. She bled, grimacing and groaning.

Ragged and haggard people beat on smaller ones using leather and wood. Unshaven, dirty men lay atop women pumping roughly. She felt helpless, defenseless.

On the streets, beggars groveled for crumbs. Droves of poor appeared, thin, in rags, and the rich few with armed guards working the poor and taxing them. She could see huge houses and castles with cells beneath the ground. *For those who steal or will not pay or speak too haughtily,* the voice said. There were chains and spikes and wheels of torture in the cells.

A screaming man was pushed into a body-size iron chamber with spikes on the door at the level of the man's eyes and guts. The man was Jude. The door started to close, the spikes coming closer and closer. Jude's screams echoed in the room. Spasms shook her legs.

"Arrgh!" she screamed. "It's not true!" But she knew it was. A sword lowered with a whish, severing a head which landed with a thud and rolled bleeding on the dusty ground. The face was hers. Guillotines did the same to one after another, men in black carrying away dripping baskets filled with heads. Jude closed her eyes but the images were still there. A row of bodies dangled from gallows in the center of town. Choking, Jude felt her tongue swell and protrude.

That virulent voice went on mercilessly in Jude's head. Dark-skinned men and women were roped, chained, dragged, caged, sold. Jude felt their desperate rage and humiliation. Slaves with bent backs under masters' whips and boots. The whips cut gashes in her skin, the kicks bruised her flesh.

Some of the images came and went quickly, hellish flashes. Others were prolonged scenes of diabolical depravity and corruption. Jude watched

155

children wrenched from mothers' arms, whole peoples dominated by outside conquerors and subjected to merciless oppression.

She saw valiant people squelched because they were the wrong color, harmless people tortured because they were the wrong religion. Scene followed scene, each impacting on Jude as if she were there and it were happening to her.

She was terrified, appalled, filled with horror. She had known, but never like this. The impact was visceral. She was limp and weak, nauseated. She teetered on the platform, her foot nearly slipping off the edge. She caught herself with the tight reflexive hold she maintained on the rings. Her clenched fingers were the only hope.

During an endless onslaught of torture, Jude came so close to fainting that she was sure she could not stand another minute. Clamping her eyes shut, she hummed loudly to fill her head with a buzz instead of the malevolent voice that never stopped. . . . *using sharp pieces of glass to remove the clitoris* . . . She could not stop the words. . . . *sold by their parents or kidnapped to become brothel slaves* . . . There can't be any more, Jude thought. . . . *skinned alive . . . tongues cut out . . . penises cut off and shoved in their mouths . .*

Sweat was pouring from Jude's forehead. She saw and felt the evil whether her eyes were open or closed. . . . *slivers of bamboo pounded under his fingernails* . . . Is this our history? *His* story, she thought, but no sooner did she think it than she witnessed a heinous act of cruelty by a woman.

Jude had no idea how much time had passed. It

156

must have been most of the day, she thought. She looked up at the window but saw only blackness there. Perhaps ten hours had passed, or perhaps six or maybe only three. There was no way she could tell.

All Jude's muscles were sore. She shifted positions, ran in place, moved her head around and around. She had slipped her hands through the rings again, letting them carry the weight of her arms.

. . . *twelve year old girl raped repeatedly over a period of two days by five men* . . . The image of the child burned into Jude's heart. Herself as a child. "She asked for it," they said . . .

* * * * *

The vigil that had begun when the sun first rose continued outside the Dome. Hundreds of women were there, most silent, some humming. Flute music played continuously.

* * * * *

. . . *Armenian slaughter* . . .
Jude's head hung limply.
. . . *African slaves* . . .
Her eyes rolled.
. . . *and the Crusades continued* . . .
Jude was on the edge of unconsciousness.
. . . *thousands burned as witches* . . .
Her wrists were held by the rings, but if she slipped one more inch, her right hand would slide out. And it would be over. Her eyes blinked open just

as the weight of her body was pulling her hand from the ring. She bent her fingers, catching the ring with her fingertips.

Cattle cars, camps, the smell of burning flesh.

A taste of bile rose in Jude's mouth. Her lips and throat were raspy dry.

. . . *ten million corpses* . . .

This was more than she could bear. She had been horrified by pictures of concentration camps, but now she was there. Her body was one of those tossed upon the pile of hundreds of others. She clamped her eyes shut and filled her mind with a silent scream. Or had she screamed aloud? The room was full of screams.

The images and words continued. As Jude saw mushroom-shaped clouds, people with skin dripping from their bodies, she felt something touch her foot. She screamed.

"It is I, Jude, Amagyne."

The images stopped abruptly. Everything was quiet. Total silence in total blackness. "Are you really there?" Jude croaked.

"Yes. Don't speak." Amagyne's voice was like a caress.

There was some light in the room now, dim, but enough for Jude to see Amagyne's silhouette. Amagyne helped Jude down and wrapped a soft robe around her. "It's half over," Amagyne said. "You're doing it. You are very brave." She walked Jude through the corridor and to a washroom.

Jude barely noticed her aching muscles. Memories of the images, sounds, and sensations that had assaulted her for the last twelve hours kept repeating themselves in her head. Amagyne massaged her limbs.

She had her do some exercises then drink some spring water and orange juice and lie for a little while on a cot. Jude was not able to rest. The images were there in her mind. Mutilation. Torture. Humiliation. Rape. Deception. Theft. Betrayal. Starvation. Bombs. Crematoria.

CHAPTER 16

Dagney was seated at a window booth at Triest's in Greenwich Village with Maggie Richards, a self-assured, middle-aged woman, wearing a tweed blazer.

Maggie ordered a glass of white wine. "Beth told me you were interested in the Kwo-amians. I haven't kept up with them in years."

Dagney leaned back. "They're making some waves in Chicago. There's a woman there who seems to be losing her lover to the swamis."

"Hm-m. So Kwo-amity is still growing. Amagyne must be doing a good job."

"According to Beth, you think La, the guru of this group, is a psych case."

Maggie frowned. "That's putting it strongly." Her drink arrived and she took a small sip. "Tell me more about the convert you're worried about."

"Jude Alta. Apparently she was born in the town next to where the swamis live. She goes there for a visit and comes back convinced that the swamis have the way to truth and bliss and that she's to be some big mover in it. The Catalyst. She's supposed to help make the world safe for purity and goodness." Dagney noticed Maggie's expression. "What's the matter?"

Maggie took a large gulp of wine. She cleared her throat. "Where is she now? Jude Alta. Is she there? At Circle Edge?"

"Yes. You look worried. What is it?"

Maggie inhaled deeply. "When so much time went by, I thought La had changed her mind." She shook her head. "I used to get all the news I could about them, but then so many years passed . . ." She was looking into space. "I should have told people."

Dagney moved her head trying to draw Maggie's eyes to hers. "Told them what?"

"I've never talked about this to anyone but my lover. Not the real story." She ran her hand through her graying hair. "I should have. I should have told everyone." She was looking past Dagney. "I think I wanted to believe it wasn't true. That it was my distortion. I even thought maybe Zetka was driving me. It didn't fit so I think I just wanted to believe it

161

wouldn't happen." She looked at Dagney. "If I were Jude Alta I'd be very careful."

"You think she's in danger?" Dagney lit a cigarette, very curious now.

Maggie stared at the table. "I was one of the first," she said. "I met La just after I graduated high school. I was fascinated by her. She seemed very calm and wise. I, on the contrary, was frantic and foolish at that time, having no idea who I was or what I was supposed to do with my life. Six months after I met her I moved to Colorado with her. I was one of the Firstcomers. I stayed for thirteen years."

"I see," Dagney said slowly. "So you were part of it."

"Yes. I never talk about it to anyone."

"You became disillusioned, I assume."

"I believed everything La said — that Kwo-am communicated with her, that zetkap could be overcome, that the potential to live truly loving lives was in us all. All of it. I believed Amagyne's mother conceived sans spermatozoa."

Maggie had twisted her paper napkin into a narrow rope. "I was happy there . . ." Her eyes took on a blank glaze. "For the first few years I did construction work, masonry and carpentry. I loved feeling a part of something meaningful, and just being with women." She sighed. "I still think of them sometimes."

"I'm sure you do," Dagney said. "Thirteen years is a big piece of your life."

"When I was twenty-one I went to college and after that to medical school. I planned always to remain at Circle Edge. I learned a great deal there, about closeness, acceptance, dealing with conflicts. It's been a part of me ever since." Maggie sighed. "But it's Lorn I need to tell you about. It was what I learned from Lorn that —"

"She's Amagyne's mother, right?"

"Yes. She and I were the youngest Firstcomers and we were good friends from the beginning." Maggie frowned. "She didn't tell me until after he'd died that she'd had a lover . . . a man."

"You don't say?" Dagney was more and more intrigued, glad she had decided to get involved in this little drama. "Do go on."

"His name was Kise," Maggie said. "He was Eurasian. Lorn said he was the gentlest, sweetest human being she had ever known. They had made love only once, five years before he died. She had never been with anyone before that or since — sexually I mean, man or woman." Maggie's mouth twitched as she went on. "I can remember how hard she cried about his death. His cabin caught fire and he didn't make it out. Lorn was in unspeakable pain."

"She'd been in love with him?"

"Oh yes. She said it wasn't an ordinary kind of love. She made me promise I wouldn't tell anyone about him because, according to La, Kwo-am didn't want it known."

"When did this happen? The fire?"

"Nineteen fifty-eight," Maggie said. "After Kise died, Lorn told me everything. Like everyone else, I had believed that Amagyne had no father. I was quite shocked. Lorn said she had never told another soul about Kise."

Dagney was smiling. "Well, so much for virgin births."

163

"I don't know," Maggie said. "He may *not* have been an ordinary man. La told Lorn he was sent by Kwo-am, that he was a spirit — sometimes a deer, a bird, sometimes a man. Their child was a spirit-child."

"I see." Dagney cocked her head. "Did you believe this?"

"I believed it back then, but later I wasn't sure. Lorn said La told her Kise's existence must be kept secret. Lorn was worried that she had told me. I assured her I wouldn't speak of it to anyone."

"So La wanted the part about Kise left out, eh? And that disillusioned you?"

"No, not really." Maggie's face looked haggard. "When I was in my senior year of medical school, La revealed that there would be a Second Guide called the Catalyst, who, like Amagyne would be born of woman only. That's the part that bothered me." Maggie was tearing her napkin into minute squares.

"And?" Dagney said gently.

"I still feel guilty about what I did. There's a book called the *Fruit of She*." Maggie ran her fingers under the collar of her blouse. "It contains La's writings, messages from Kwo-am. We believed that if anyone tried to read it, it would self-destruct or something." Maggie paused. "It didn't."

"You read it."

"Yes." Maggie was breathing rapidly. "One day when La was away, I found the book in a wooden chest. The handwriting was pretty bad. About a quarter of the pages were written on." Maggie rolled the bits of napkin into a ball.

"My hands were shaking as I read it. I was frightened to be doing what I knew was absolutely forbidden. The words seemed like gems. Most of what I read had already been told to us by La, but a few things hadn't, something about Full Circle, something about a white horse. I don't remember the details. There was nothing about Kise. Of course I knew that not all the revealments were written, so that didn't really prove anything. But I was hoping to find some reference to him. Maybe my faith was a little shaky and I wanted to bolster it. I'm not sure. Then I got to the end, the part about the Catalyst. That's when everything crashed for me. I had never expected to find anything like that."

Dagney waited.

Maggie swallowed. There was a line of perspiration along her brow. "It said that the Catalyst would come to Circle Edge when the time was right. If she chose to stay, that would be a sign to proceed. If she triumphed in the Enactment of the Scourges of Zetka, that would be the next sign to proceed."

"Proceed with what?" Dagney was leaning forward eagerly.

Maggie seemed close to tears. "If the Catalyst triumphs in the Enactment of the Scourges, then she is to be sacrificed." She looked straight at Dagney. "It is her death that will bring on the New Page."

"Oh, great." Dagney whistled through her teeth. "Did they say how they plan to kill her?"

"No, just that it had to by the hand of a Kwo-amian."

"La is insane."

Maggie shook her head. "Maybe. I don't know."

"Has she ever actually done anything violent?"

"Never. Not that I know of. The death of the

Catalyst was the only violent allusion in the *Fruit of She*. After I read it, I left Circle Edge. I had planned to stay forever, practice medicine there. It took me a long time to adjust to the outer world."

Dagney signaled the waiter. "So once Jude does that scourges thing, then she dies."

"If she triumphs, yes."

"But no one knows this. The rest of the cult doesn't know."

Maggie lowered her eyes. "I should have told them."

"Well they have to find out eventually. Do you think they'd go along with it?"

Maggie nodded. "I'm sure La would explain it in a way that they'd accept." She shook her head.

"Any mention of Jude Alta in what you read? That she's the Catalyst?"

"No."

"They told Jude her father isn't really her father."

"Yes, of course. That's the revealment, *Born of woman only*."

"I wonder why they picked her." Dagney reached for her briefcase. "I'm going to call Jude's lover," she said.

"I should have told them." Maggie shook her head sorrowfully. "I hope it's not too late."

CHAPTER 17

Jude was back on the platform holding the rings. Minutes after her return to the pitch black room, her head had begun to feel strange again, and then the zetkap-filled images assaulted her.

For hours and hours it continued. Jude was beyond saturation. She was exhausted, drained, perpetually nauseated. Children's bloated bellies, people in cages, gay bashings, knifings, shootings, bombs. It did not stop though it seemed there couldn't possibly be more. And still it went on and on and on and on. *They've forgotten me,* Jude despaired.

*I've been here for years. This is my life now, my
eternity.*

She felt numb. She became dizzy and disoriented.
She tried to concentrate on the rings, holding onto
them with all her strength. She thought of the soft
floor beneath her, how wonderful it would be to let
herself slip down and lie on that soft warm quilted
floor and sleep and make the images go away and
maybe die. The left ring was moving. She had it by
just one finger. *I can't hold on,* she thought. *I have
to make it stop. I can't bear any more. No,* another
voice inside her said. *Don't let Zetka win.* "Amagyne,"
she called, but her voice was drowned out by death
screams filling the room, filling her mind. Jude forced
herself to tighten her finger on the ring. She moved
her hand, slowly, carefully. The screams continued,
continuing even after she had the ring securely again
in her sweaty grasp. Moaning aloud, she held fast to
the rings as a loud whoosh and flash of light came,
blinding her momentarily, then the rise of a
mushroom-shaped cloud, a pile of corpses, more
corpses, piles and piles of dead everywhere.

Then blackness. Silence. Jude could see nothing,
nothing at all. *Oh God!* It was absolutely silent. *I'm
deaf, blind and deaf.*

She was whimpering, crying softly, totally drained.

* * * * *

Amagyne pried Jude's fingers from the rings. She
and La carried her from the platform and laid her on
the soft floor. Her body was coated with sweat.

"Just rest now," Amagyne said.

I'm in heaven, Jude thought.

La wiped her brow with a cool cloth and gave her water. Jude rested, perhaps slept a little. They gave her broth, massaged her aching arms and legs. When she felt able, they helped her up and dressed her in a milk-white gown. La on one side, Amagyne on the other, they walked with her, supporting her body.

They were in the corridor and four Firstcomers were there. La and Amagyne helped Jude onto a fleece-covered cot and the women carried her outside. The waiting crowd hummed a beautiful melody, one Jude had never heard. She was carried through the mass of women all the way to the Amit. In the center of the Amit was a canopy. They placed Jude under it, the women of Circle Edge forming a wide circle around her. Amagyne stayed at Jude's side. She gave her more broth, and soon a thicker soup. Jude slept.

The next thing she knew, she was hearing La's voice and feeling cool fingers on her arm. Her head was heavy. She blinked her surroundings into focus.

La stood over her, smiling, but the smile seemed strange. Jude blinked more. To her left they had placed a table containing plastic bottles and tubes. To her right was Amagyne, her expression serene and calm, and beyond Amagyne a blur of people, the Kwo-amian vigil. Jude's mind began to replay the horrors from those endless twenty-four hours. She was too weak to speak.

La turned to the crowd. "Jude Alta has triumphed," she announced in her sure, deep voice.

The humming of that beautiful song came from the huge circle of women.

"She has absorbed into her mind the despicable

history of Zetka's evil. She had done this for all of us. And from her mind, the evil has permeated her blood. The store of zetkap energy flows through the body of Jude Alta, captured in her blood." La paused for a long time.

"We now shall drain the zetkap from her," she said finally, "if she chooses this."

"She must choose," a chorus of voices said.

"Shall we proceed?" La asked, looking down at Jude. "Shall we drain the zetkap from you?"

Jude's mind buzzed with hideous images. "Yes," she said weakly, nodding. "Take it away."

"Drain it," said the voices.

"Jude Alta has chosen to do this," La proclaimed, "to die and to be reborn as Laki-Seone who will usher in the New Page."

"She must die and be reborn," chanted the voices.

Amagyne held Jude's hand. There was soft singing in the background. Jude's head was very fuzzy. It was hard to stay awake. She felt a slight prick on her inner arm, saw a needle being inserted and the blood filling the syringe. *They're draining my blood,* she thought blandly. The woman with the needle was dressed entirely in white, her face covered with a white mask. Jude tried to sit up but was gently restrained. The woman attached a plastic tube to the needle and Jude could see her blood flowing through the tube and into the black iron bucket.

I'm going to die.

As the zetkap-filled blood was taken from her body, Jude's awareness grew dimmer and dimmer. *I'll be with Kwo-am.* And then all consciousness faded away.

* * * * *

The woman in white held the blood-filled iron bucket over her head. All eyes were on it.

"The Scourges of Zetka," said La waving her hand before the bucket. "Concentrated. Captured. Now to be destroyed."

Jude's form lay pale and motionless on the cot.

The women had built a fire. They placed a grate over it and atop the grate the woman in white put the iron bucket.

"Burn the zetkap," voices murmured. The flames lapped around the edges of the pot. "Burn! Burn!" Soon the blood began to boil. "Burn, zetkap, burn!"

Musicians played dark heavy notes, bassoons and basses. The boiling blood thickened. "Burn the zetkap! Burn it all!"

Miluna was at the front of the crowd, her eyes bright, staring at the fire. "Burn," she murmured. She glanced at Jude's still body. "Burn the zetkap!"

It burned long and hot until only dry black flakes were left in the iron pot. The woman in white scraped the flakes into a balsam wood box, and placed the cover on the box. She removed the grate from the fire and dropped the box into the flames.

"Burn!" the voices yelled.

The box caught quickly, causing a momentary flash in the already blazing fire. "Burn! Burn!" It burned until there was nothing left.

All eyes were on Jude. La stood before her, her fingers on Jude's forehead. "She will be reborn!"

Amagyne bent and stroked Jude's slack shoulder. The crowd waited breathlessly. Miluna's heart was

171

pounding. She thought of the shrikes, how they would always reawaken. She stared at Jude, waiting apprehensively for some movement, some sign of life.

CHAPTER 18

Toni dialed again and waited. The ringing went on and on. Still no answer. They're killing her, she thought frantically. She hung up and drummed her fingers anxiously on the desk. She considered calling Martha. Or the Doray sheriff. She picked up the phone and dialed Circle Edge once more.

* * * * *

The midday sun was hot on Miluna's back but her perspiration was not caused by the heat of the day.

173

Amagyne's hand still rested on Jude's motionless shoulder. All eyes were focused on Jude's face.

Another tense, deadly silent minute passed, then Miluna thought she saw Jude's eyelids flicker. She strained forward, staring intently at the tranquil face. No, there was no movement.

The sun beat down on the silent crowd. More minutes passed and then, finally, it happened, and there was no doubt this time: a little twitch of the lips. Then the eyelids fluttered. Miluna sighed deeply and smiled. The crush of women moved in closer. Jude opened her eyes.

Amagyne's hand was still upon her. "How do you feel?" she asked.

Jude blinked rapidly. "Fine," she said dreamily. She looked at the fire which was now just glowing ash.

Amagyne stroked her hand. "Are you ready to stand?"

Jude slowly moved her legs over the edge of the cot and Amagyne and La helped her to her feet. A roar rose from the crowd: "Laki-Seone!" The orchestra played and the cheering went on and on.

At last La raised her arms. There was total silence. "The blood we drained," the Sage declared, "contained from the mind of Laki-Seone the representation of all the zetkap in the history of the world."

Women nodded and murmured.

"We have destroyed it!" La proclaimed. Cheering followed. "The mind of Laki-Seone is clear," La said when she could be heard. "The blood that moves in her body is pure. She has been reborn." More cheers. "Laki-Seone's triumph over the Scourges of Zetka has

174

paved the way for the most important event since the first human being walked the face of the earth."

"Emergence!" a hundred voices shouted as one.

"Yes, the Ceremony of Emergence," La said. "One month from now."

She raised one of Jude's arms high into the air; Amagyne raised the other. The crowd went wild. Jude felt as if she would burst. She felt the spirit of Kwo-am wrap around her and raise her to new heights of exaltation. She swooned; Amagyne and La bolstered her. Jude felt their strength and power and the power of Kwo-am, and the power of Honore, Miluna, Starla, Joyce, Ella, Berryfire, and all the women there. The joyful cheering went on and on.

La stepped forward to speak again. "It is time to dance and feast and consummate the joy of this day."

Tables were carried to the flat ground of the Amit and tablecloths of brilliant hues laid upon them, and then trays and platters of food and pitchers and bottles of drink.

Jude still wore the white flowing robe as she rejoiced and feasted with the others. She felt free and fully alive, her mind clear and sharp, her body energized and strong. *Monama,* she thought repeatedly. She sat by Amagyne's side, feeling the powerful love between them.

At last the celebration came to an end. In her room in Sky Palace, events of the day flashed through her mind. The powerful sense of Kwo-am's closeness, the togetherness with her Kwo-amian sisters. She thought of the soft fleece, the blood burning, and of the little room and the wooden rings. She knew she had experienced terrible things in that room, the endless evils of Zetka. But she could not bring the memories clearly to mind. La had told her this would be. The images were blurred, the words a vague murmur of sounds that made no sense. She pictured Amagyne's beautiful face, and then she was asleep. Sweet dreams took her through the night.

* * * * *

When Jude awoke her first thought was of Amagyne. The thought shifted to a fantasy. She saw their bodies pressed together, felt the warmth of Amagyne's soft skin next to hers. Then Toni was there in her waking dream, and Jude felt confused.

The ringing telephone interrupted her reverie. It was Rosalie's nurse. "I'll come at once," Jude said.

She drove a jeep to the Mansion. At first Rosalie did not stir as Jude stroked her forehead. Finally her eyelids fluttered and when her eyes opened, they looked directly into Jude's.

"How . . . alive you look." The words were spoken softly, but Jude heard them clearly.

"Can I do anything for you, Rosalie?"

Rosalie nodded. Mrs. Clarkson was now near the bed.

"Do . . . what . . . I know you will do . . . the best. You are the best."

Jude's constricted throat would barely let her breathe. "Whatever I am, I owe much of it to you," she said, her voice breaking.

Rosalie's frail fingers squeezed Jude's hand. Jude watched the face relax, the eyes close again. She stayed another hour but Rosalie said no more nor did she open her eyes.

* * * * *

Martha was in the kitchen when Jude arrived at her house.

"I don't think she's going to make it, Martie." Martha put her hand on Jude's arm.

Jude talked for a little while about Rosalie, then she became silent. Martha got them coffee.

"We had a ceremony," Jude said, "the Enactment of the Scourges of Zetka. I triumphed."

Martha said nothing.

"There's something they told me, something real important, Martha, and I want to tell you about it. It's kind of a mind blower."

"I don't know how much more my mind could be blown."

"You look quite a bit like Dad, right?"

Martha tilted her head. "So?"

"And I don't."

"You look more like Mom."

"Yes, but also like . . . different, different from any of you."

"What are you getting at, Jude?"

"Your father isn't my father."

"Oh shit! Is that what they told you?"

"Yes."

"And you believe it. Jude, come on!"

Neither woman spoke for a while. At last Martha said, "Jude, I know in some ways you haven't been happy. I think you got real hurt by the world. By the real world. And now you've found something you think can heal the wound."

"It can heal all our wounds," Jude said.

"Is there any part of you that doubts it?"

"I have no reason to doubt it."

Martha played with a drop of coffee on the glistening wooden table. "So if Dad isn't your dad, who is?"

Jude looked solemn. "When Mom conceived me . . . she was chosen, Martha, chosen to give birth to me, and my destiny is to take part in a very important ceremony that —"

"What do you mean, chosen? For what? Who chose her?"

"Kwo-am. You'll understand more soon. You'll feel it too after the Ceremony of Emergence. The Ceremony will begin the New Page, the alteration of the world, Martha. It's as big as that. Zetka will wither and —"

"I can't stand to listen to this," Martha said sharply. "I never thought something like this could happen to you. Damn! I wish I could bring you back."

"Perhaps I can bring you forward."

"You've got an answer for everything. Did they teach you what to say? How to respond when people question their garbage?"

Jude felt very sad. "I love you no matter what," she said.

Martha's eyes were wet. "I know. Me, too, you know. I'll stick with you through this, Jude, but I just don't know what to do. With all your feminist and lesbian stuff, at least there was a certain sensibleness to it, but this . . . I feel powerless."

"You think they've brainwashed me."

"Yes, Jude, I do. That's exactly what I think.

They know you're vulnerable. They tell you things that make you feel needed, important."

"They knew I would come. They were waiting for me."

"They're waiting for anyone they think they can pull in. They want to expand their numbers. You told me yourself new recruits have to turn over all their money to them."

"They choose to, Martha."

"But it's not free choice if they're brainwashed. You're breaking Toni's heart, you know."

Jude felt the sinking sensation in her stomach. "She'll be OK." She hoped it was true. "I miss her. I wish she could share it with me."

"She's too sane." Martha bit her lip. "Shit. I don't want to attack you, Jude."

"I know. It's OK. So how did the meeting with Madsen go? The plans coming along all right?"

Martha's face brightened immediately. "Oh Jude, he showed me the blueprints. People will flock here from Denver and Boulder and even farther away. They'll come from Chicago. It will be Doray rather than Aspen. You wait."

Jude looked caringly at her sister. "It means so much to you, doesn't it?"

"It means everything to me. Doray's potential is unlimited, Jude, and I want to help it grow and develop. Who knows, maybe some day I'll run for mayor."

Jude raised her eyebrows.

"I'm serious. Do your Kwo-amian friends know about what's going to happen?"

"I don't know." Jude was thinking of the strange

juxtaposition of two worlds. "No one's ever said anything about it."

"They better think about it. Madsen's determined to get all the land he can when the Wright holdings go up for sale. That includes most of the Ladies' Farm, you know."

Jude nodded. *That won't happen,* she thought. She was sure of it.

The phone rang. Martha answered and then handed it to Jude. It was Mrs. Clarkson calling to let Jude know that Rosalie Wright had died.

CHAPTER 19

The funeral was solemn and grand. Most of Doray came and hundreds of people Jude did not know. Jude grieved deeply, her head lead heavy.

The morning after the burial, Jude and Toni drove together up into the mountains, to the place where Jude had gone after first meeting La. Jude talked about Rosalie for a long time and Toni listened. Finally Jude was silent.

After awhile Toni cleared her throat nervously. "Jude, there's something I have to tell you." She rubbed her palms over her jeans. "I know how raw you are because of Rosalie, but I have to tell you what I found out. It's about the Kwo-amians."

Jude looked at her with red-rimmed eyes.

Toni inhaled deeply. "Dagney Green went to New York and talked to Maggie Richards. It turns out that Maggie used to be a Kwo-amian. She was one of the first women who came out here with La."

"Really?" Jude said. "They told me one of the Firstcomers had left."

"She found out some things that totally disillusioned her about La, and about the whole religion. She found out La was lying about Amagyne having no father."

Jude looked scornfully at Toni.

"Lorn told her," Toni said. "She told Maggie about a man named Kise who lived near here, and who ended up dying in a fire. He was Lorn's lover, Jude. Amagyne is his daughter."

Jude was shaking her head vigorously. "No way."

"But that's only part of it. Maggie read that secret book, the *Fruit of She*, and —"

"No one reads that book," Jude cut in.

"Maggie did. She learned something terrible, Jude."

"That's the one thing that's forbidden."

"For the New Page to begin," Toni persisted, "the Catalyst has to be sacrificed. They're planning to murder you, Jude!"

"What?" Jude looked aghast at Toni. Then she smiled sadly and shook her head. "It's not going to work, Toni."

"That's what it said in the book."

"I know what you're trying to do, but it won't work."

182

"You think I'm lying. I was afraid of that."

"But I'm not angry about it," Jude said. "I understand your motive. I understand how desperate you feel. But in another month, you'll know what I know and everything will be beautiful. Your worries will be over."

"Jude, I didn't make it up. I swear. When Maggie found out Amagyne had a father, she got suspicious of La. She read the book and found out about the murder."

"Kwo-am is the spirit of life," Jude said. "Murder would never be a part of her plan."

"Get the book. Read it for yourself."

"Never."

"Why can't anyone read the book? Why do you think, Jude? It's forbidden because La has things to hide. I've never lied to you and I'm not lying now. I'm telling you exactly what Dagney told me."

"Then she's lying," Jude said, "or Maggie Richards is. Don't worry. Everything is going to work out for the best for both of us. After the Ceremony of Emergence, it will all change. Forget that nonsense about my being killed, hon. If Maggie Richards really said it, then it's because she wants to malign La for some reason. Don't believe such stupid lies, my love." She took Toni in her arms.

"I suppose it's possible that Maggie did lie," Toni said. She held Jude tightly. "I love you so damn much."

* * * * *

When they returned to Martha's house there was a message for Jude from Wesley Gliebman, Rosalie

Wright's lawyer. Could she come at two o'clock that afternoon to talk with Mr. Gliebman?

When Jude returned to the living room, Toni looked at her lovingly, then pulled her to the sofa and kissed her deeply. Aroused, Jude responded passionately.

Toni's hands found Jude's favorite spots. "It's been awhile," Toni said. "I don't know if I remember how."

"You remember," Jude assured her, brushing her tongue teasingly over Toni's lips. She led her to the guest bedroom.

Toni slowly undressed her, gently kissing each newly exposed area of Jude's skin, and Jude felt herself overcome by loving, erotic feelings. She fluttered her fingertips over Toni's smooth buttocks, as Toni planted flower-petal kisses along her neck. Deep and tender feelings completely filled Jude's heart. She drew her lover to herself tightly, trying to get her even closer, whispering heartfelt words of love.

The lovemaking intensified and Jude felt tingling wetness in her groin. She emitted a low gurgle of pleasure. Toni cupped her crotch, rubbing the slippery flesh rhythmically with the heel of her hand. Jude's back began to arch. Toni's fingers slid along the edges of Jude's opening. Jude's breathing grew rapid. As Toni continued stroking her in exactly the ways that pleased her most, Jude's excitement mounted. It was electric, rapturous, and growing, growing more, to a final bursting climax that seemed to last and last. She released a stifled gasp. Then, holding tightly onto Toni, she began to cry.

Toni stroked her wet cheek lovingly. "What is it, hon?"

But Jude could not explain. "Too many feelings," was all she said.

They stayed in the guest room until it was time for Jude's appointment with Rosalie's lawyer.

* * * * *

Wesley Gliebman took her into his private office. "Sit down, Miss Alta."

Jude had met Gliebman a number of times. He had always seemed rather uptight to her, as he did now. She took a deep leather chair across from his desk. Gliebman seated himself in the high-backed, oaken desk chair and cleared his throat.

"As you know, Mrs. Wright was a very wealthy woman. She left the major portion of her holdings to the Wright Foundation . . . a few parcels and some minor assets to distant relatives . . ."

Jude was having trouble listening. She had cried herself dry over the last couple of days and now felt the tears coming again.

". . . annual income of one hundred thousand dollars . . ."

She was thinking of Rosalie wearing the Mickey Mouse ears, wondering if she had saved them . . .

". . . and I or other attorneys and financial counselors of your choice are available for . . ."

The trip to Greece was another highlight. They had talked about returning there some day. Jude blinked the tears back. Rosalie loved snorkeling. Jude pictured her in the mask, pointing out a red-orange

185

starfish or a giant sea urchin attached to an underwater rock.

"Are you listening, Miss Alta?"

"I'm sorry. I'm having trouble —"

"Yes, you're probably in a state of shock. It will take some getting used to. Since the inheritance is in a trust fund, there will be no delay due to probate. I have the deeds here."

"Deeds?"

"To the Wright Estate."

"The Wright Estate."

"Yes. Didn't you understand what I said? You've inherited the Wright Estate and what is referred to as the Lake Valley, that is, all of the real estate surrounding the Estate, including Wright Lake. The parcel also includes most of the property on which the Ladies' Farm is located."

Jude's mouth hung open.

"And the annual one hundred thousand dollar income. You're a fortunate person, Miss Alta."

"She gave me the lake?" Jude's head was spinning.

"I'd be happy to discuss your financial planning with you. If you want to set up a meeting . . ."

"I . . . I think I'll . . . I want to go now, Mr. Gliebman. Thank you. I'll . . . maybe I'll contact you later."

"Yes, of course."

* * * * *

Toni and Davey were playing catch in front of the

house when Jude got back to Martna's. "So did she leave you a Ming vase?" Toni called.

Jude felt as if she were in a trance. She walked right past Toni. Toni came to her on the back porch. "What is it, love?"

Jude's head felt hazy. "She was very wealthy, you know. Very, very wealthy."

"Well, we won't hold that against her."

Jude bit her lip. "I need you to hold me, Toni."

Toni wrapped her loving arms around Jude. "My poor babe."

Jude clung to her and the tears came. Toni held her tightly.

"She left me the Estate."

"What?"

"And the lake. And the Circle Edge property. And a hundred thousand dollars a year."

"Oh, my God!"

"It's freaking me out."

"Oh Jude! She never gave you any idea she intended —"

"She never said a word. Toni, why does it scare me?"

"It scares me too."

"I don't know what to do. Do you want a new stereo?"

Toni laughed. "Well, I am sick of having just one speaker."

"I don't know what to do, Toni. Suddenly I have so much to deal with. Everything is changing."

"I know."

"I want to go for a ride," Jude said.

"All right."

"I mean a long ride. Let's take a tent along."

Toni seemed uncertain. "I guess I could stay a few more days. Randy can do some of the interviews without me. Let me give her a call."

* * * * *

They headed south on Highway 67 in Toni's rented car, and spent the first night at a wooded campground in Pike Forest.

"She and Ingrid are the only people I've loved who died." Jude stretched her hands over the campfire to warm them.

Jude talked about Rosalie until they had used up their pile of wood and the flames had dwindled to embers. Inside the tent, they zipped the two sleeping bags together and slept cuddled in each other's arms.

The next day they roamed the red peaks of the Valley of the Gods. Jude tried not to think of death or money or of being the Catalyst. She let the beauty of the surroundings fill her until she was at peace. Several times Toni tried to talk about what Maggie Richards had said, but Jude cut her short, saying the whole story was obviously Zetka-inspired.

They drove up Pike's Peak, then down and kept going south until they reached the Great Sand Dunes where they found a campground full of twisted scrub oaks and cacti, with a beautiful view of the dunes. Jude felt soothed and replenished by the beauty of Kwo-am's creations.

CHAPTER 20

Martha couldn't contain her excitement. "My sister, a millionaire!"

Jude and Toni had returned that afternoon and were sitting around Martha's dining room table.

"I think it's great," Martha exclaimed. "Of course it crossed my mind that she might leave you something big, but I didn't really believe it. I thought it would *all* go to the Foundation, like everybody said. You really had no idea?" she asked for the fifth time.

"None," Jude said.

Martha looked closely at her sister. "It's overwhelming, isn't it?" Jude nodded, and Martha smiled knowingly. "You'll adjust," she said. "I guarantee Madsen will pay top dollar for the property."

Jude stared at the table.

Martha's smile faded. "You are going to sell it to him, aren't you?"

"I don't know," Jude said.

"Of course you are. What else would you do with it?"

Jude shrugged. "Maybe I'll live at the Mansion," she said flatly.

Toni chuckled. "You'd never be able to find your shoes."

"You're kidding, aren't you, Jude?" Martha's smile was obviously forced.

"Maybe I'll donate it to some charity. Girl Scouts of America, maybe."

"Or some other worthy cause," Toni inserted. "If you're seriously thinking about giving the property away, may I suggest you talk with Gresh."

"Ah, yes," Jude responded. "The spa. The Feminist Fund."

Martha seemed close to tears. "Jude, you know how much the Lake Valley means to the town, how much everyone has been counting on it." Her voice had a pressured edge. "It's all people here have talked about for years, ever since the Foundation promised they'd sell it to us — to Madsen." Martha's eyes pierced Jude's. "You know how much it means to *me*."

"I know," Jude said. "Don't worry. We'll talk about it some more. I haven't made any decisions yet. I'm still trying to digest, all right?"

"Sure. All right. Will you talk to Madsen? Can I arrange a meeting?"

"I suppose." She looked at Martha, frowning. "We're not going to let this come between us, are we, Sis?"

"Of course not," Martha said immediately. She gave Jude's hand a squeeze. "You wouldn't let the Kwo-amians talk you into giving it to them, would you?"

Jude did not reply. "That reminds me," she said, looking at her watch. "Toni and I should get going. I'd like to get there in time for the sunset ceremony."

Toni pushed her chair back. "Now you really are sure they won't bar me at the gate."

Jude smiled. "Any friend of mine is a friend of theirs."

* * * * *

Doralee led the snake dance and Jude was one of the flutists. Toni danced with the others, holding her candle high. She sang along on the Catalyst song.

"I liked that," she said as she and Jude walked from the Amit to the Inner Garden where they were to meet La and Amagyne. "It creates a feeling of togetherness. I can see why you enjoy the rituals."

"I love it more each time," Jude said.

La and Amagyne were waiting at the entrance to

the Inner Garden. They each hugged Jude. "It's a great loss for you," Amagyne said lovingly. "A part of your heart will always be just for your Rosalie."

"She lives on in you," La said. "Praise Kwo-am."

"And us all." Jude took Toni's hand and brought her forward. "La, Amagyne, this is Toni Dilano."

"We welcome you to our home and our hearts," La said, placing her hands on Toni's shoulders. "I see the struggle in you. You feel drawn to us, feel yourself opening, and yet your mind tells you to beware."

Looking into La's intense eyes, Toni nodded.

"You danced with great spirit," Amagyne said. "It's good you have come."

"Thank you." Toni's voice was slightly hoarse. "Jude's told me quite a lot about both of you. I'm glad to meet you."

"Let us go in," Amagyne said.

Soon they were all in a pool seated on the contour seats discussing the ceremony that had just taken place and the talk Ella had given.

Toni seemed very comfortable. "What did Ella mean when she mentioned the *knife with no point?*"

"It is a story from the *Words of Kwo-am,*" Amagyne said. "There are stories for every situation."

"We talk about them all the time," Jude said, "at circle meetings. People get into all the possible meanings of them."

"The wisdom of the ages is in those stories," Amagyne said.

"I'd like to read some of them." Toni maneuvered herself downward a few inches until the water covered her shoulders.

"You will have a copy of *Words of Kwo-am* as a gift," La said. "I have already put one aside for you."

They talked of Kwo-amity and of Circle Edge and Rosalie and finally Jude told La and Amagyne about her inheritance. La seemed very pleased. "You will choose wisely," she said, patting Jude's arm.

No one spoke for several minutes, all seeming relaxed except for Toni who appeared to have grown tense. At last she spoke. "Could you tell me more about this Ceremony of Emergence?"

"I hope you will be here for it," La responded.

"Exactly what will happen?" Toni asked.

"The release of pure kwo-ami."

"But —"

"And the New Page leading to the Withering of Zetka shall begin."

"OK, but what specifically —"

"Come and witness," La said. "Twenty-six days from today."

"Maybe I will," Toni replied. "So Jude does the Ceremony and the New Page begins, and afterwards, is Jude . . . is she all right? Will she be the same?"

"We will all be changed."

"I mean . . ." Toni's jaw was tight. "Does Jude have to die for this to happen?" she blurted.

La's face darkened and so did Amagyne's. But it was Jude who showed the most dismay and displeasure. "Toni!" she rasped.

"The Ceremony of Emergence is a celebration of life and love, not of death," Amagyne said gently.

"Mmm-m-mm . . ." La hummed.

"Then she won't die."

"Of course not," Amagyne said.

193

Toni scrutinized Amagyne's face. "I'm glad to hear that." She relaxed visibly. "And I can be here for it? And our friends from Chicago?"

"We hope you all come."

La's humming continued. Jude could feel the vibrations entering her. The water was very warm. She noticed Toni's eyes beginning to droop. She felt quite content.

Later, in the sleeping hut, Toni stretched herself out on the bed. "I almost wish I weren't leaving tomorrow."

"Stay." Jude joined her on the bed.

"I wish I could. I really like it here, in a strange way. It's weird but pleasant, comfortable. I have to get back though. I want you to come with me, Jude."

"I know."

"Will you?"

Jude shook her head. "This is where I need to be. You're not still worried about what Maggie Richards said, are you?"

"If Amagyne was lying, she does it very well," Toni said. "It puzzles me about Maggie, though. Why would she make up something like that? I was tempted to ask La and Amagyne about her, tell them what she said about the *Fruit of She*. But Dagney said Maggie feels terribly guilty about reading the book, that she wouldn't want anyone to know she did it."

"Maybe she just *thinks* she did it," Jude said.

They lay silently for a while. "You know what I was thinking?" Toni rubbed her fingers along Jude's arm. "It could be that Amagyne doesn't know. La didn't deny it, it was Amagyne. She's not allowed to

194

read La's secret book either, right? Maybe she doesn't know you're supposed to die."

"Look, Toni," Jude said, irritated. "If Maggie Richards actually read the *Fruit of She,* which I highly doubt, and it really said anything about the Catalyst dying, then it was symbolic, like bleeding the zetkap out of me after the Scourges, like the shrikes dying and being reborn. Maybe they give me a sedative at the Ceremony and I sleep awhile and then am resurrected. Like the shrikes."

"Maggie didn't say it was symbolic. She said the Catalyst is sacrificed. She dies, not goes to sleep."

"Toni, don't you see how ridiculous that is? You see what it's like here. You've met La and Amagyne. Do you really think they're plotting my death? Why would Kwo-am want me dead? Why would La or Amagyne want me dead? It doesn't make any sense at all. Does it?"

"No," Toni said. She was quiet for a long time.

"Toni, I'm not going to die."

"Where does she keep her secret book?"

Jude's eyes flashed darkly for a moment, but then she smiled. "It floats in the clouds."

"Seriously, where?"

"Sunk deep in the juicy cunt of the great cosmic beyond."

"Jude! Where's your respect?"

"Crazy people can talk dirty."

"I love you so much."

"I know."

CHAPTER 21

The next morning, after she and Toni said their tearful goodbyes, Jude went to the Dome and sat by the pond. She felt her love for Toni very strongly.

After the Emergence, things will be different with Toni, Jude thought. *The truth of Kwo-am will be hers. She'll be a kwo-omni, and come and live here with me.*

Jude wondered if that ever really would be.

She began to imagine the Ceremony of Emergence. Eyes closed, she pictured thousands of women all around her, she and Amagyne and La in the center of the Amit. They were saying the magic words that would bring on the Emergence and the Withering of Zetka. Amagyne held a flower. She was dressed in white and bright blue. La was wearing a deep red gown. She held a knife.

Jude's eyes popped open. Her heart was pounding.

* * * * *

Fifteen minutes later, Jude and Amagyne sat facing each other at a small table in one of the parlors at Circle House. Each had a mug of tea before her.

"It's hard to begin," Jude said.

"I can see how you're struggling, Laki-Seone. I'm open to what you have to say."

Jude took a deep breath. "Do you know a woman named Maggie Richards?"

Amagyne nodded. "I knew her when I was a child. She was a Firstcomer. She left Circle Edge years ago and I have only the vaguest memories of her."

"Someone Toni knows talked to her recently. Was Maggie friends with your mother?"

"Oh yes, they were very close."

"Do you know why Maggie left?"

Amagyne hesitated momentarily. "My mother and Maggie loved each other," she said, "a very deep love. Lorn told me that she could not give all that Maggie wanted from her and so Maggie went away."

"Couldn't give what?" Jude asked.

"Lorn never felt the wish for physical love with anyone. We've talked about it. She thinks it has to do with her being my mother, the mother of the First Guide."

197

"I see." Jude was smiling. "So Lorn spurned Maggie and Maggie left Circle Edge."

"Apparently it was very painful for her. Do you want to tell me what Toni's friend heard from Maggie Richards?"

"She was bitter. She said nasty things about La." Jude drummed her fingers nervously on the table. "Did you know anyone named Kise?"

Amagyne narrowed her eyes. "Something comes . . . but only a glimmer. Who is she?"

Jude did not respond right away. "Did La do anything to get Maggie angry?"

"Lorn told me that Maggie blamed La for Lorn's choice to remain celibate. That angered Maggie."

"Yes, of course."

"It worries you, the things Maggie said to Toni's friend."

Jude smiled. "Not anymore. I just needed to understand." She leaned back comfortably and looked at Amagyne. "You haven't chosen to be celibate."

Amagyne smiled. "No."

Jude turned her head away, embarrassed. Amagyne sipped her tea. A long silence followed, which Jude finally broke.

"Martha wants me to meet with Jeffrey Madsen. He's a land developer. Now that I own the Lake Valley, Martha sees me as the one who can make her dreams come true. She wants me to sell Madsen the whole Lake Valley, including Circle Edge."

Amagyne's brow lifted.

"You wouldn't want me to do that, would you?"

"No, I wouldn't," Amagyne said.

"I'll think of something. Maybe I can work out some sort of compromise and make everyone happy."

Amagyne wished her luck.

* * * * *

That evening Jude went to Martha's house.

"I don't want Madsen to have the lake," she said when the two of them were alone. "Wait! Let me finish." She leaned closer to Martha. "I know how much it means to you to have your restaurant at a resort. I know that. Here's what I was thinking. You find a nice restaurant somewhere between here and Denver, or anywhere you want. Or build a new one if you prefer. You do that and I'll finance it for you. You can have your dream, and the lake and Lake Valley won't be overrun with tourists."

"Oh, Jude." Martha looked deeply pained. "You don't understand. It's Doray! It's this town. It's having the restaurant here that's important to me. This town is home for me. This is where my friends are, my life. You know that. This is where it has to happen."

"So build a great big restaurant here," Jude offered.

"And who will come to it? We need to attract more people. That's the whole idea of developing the lake and the ski slopes."

"Then it won't be Doray anymore."

"Yes it will. It will be the Doray of my dreams, full of people and activity. The town will be vibrant."

The intensity of Martha's desire moved Jude. "We'll work something out," she said.

* * * * *

Toni called the next afternoon. "I'm lonely for you. You like Amagyne better than you like me."

Jude laughed. "Baby."

"I'm going to kidnap you. I'm going to get a gang of dykes and we're going to come after you and rescue you. Then we'll de-program you."

"That's amusing," Jude said flatly. "Toni, I found out something important. I know why Maggie Richards made up that stuff about the *Fruit of She.* She was in love with Lorn. She left Circle Edge because Lorn rejected her. She directed her anger at La, blamed La for Lorn's celibacy. That's why she made up those stories. There's nothing to them, hon."

"Who told you that?"

"Amagyne."

"Oh, well then, it must be true."

"Toni, you met Amagyne. Do you really think she's a manipulative liar . . . and a murderer?"

"We can't be distracted by her charm. Yes, I think she could be lying to you. All for what she believes is the greater good."

"Maggie was a spurned lover. She left Circle Edge embittered."

"Jude, can you seriously tell me that you think you and Amagyne had no fathers and that the two of you are going to overthrow centuries of patriarchy by some ritual that will make good humanistic feminists out of everyone?"

Jude laughed. "I love how you put things, my love. It's worth a try, Toni. We haven't succeeded by protests or marches or lobbying or consciousness raising."

"We're succeeding. It takes time."

"How are the cats?"

"You're changing the subject."

"How's Pam? I miss her."

"She misses you too. Everyone does. It's time to come home now."

"I can't. I have to figure out what to do about the Estate and Lake Valley so my sister will be happy."

"That reminds me, Gresh wants to talk with you. She has some great ideas about what the Feminist Fund could do if it had a steady income. She's convinced Leslie's spa would be a perfect source. All they need is the Wright Estate and the lake."

"Oh, I see. Would they like my annual hundred thou, too?"

"Come on, Jude. Gresh is talking about serious projects that could really make a difference for women. You still care about that, don't you?"

Jude sighed heavily. "I feel pulled apart," she said. She had been stretched out on the easy chair in her room, but now she sat upright. "The Kwo-amians believe they're destined to have the Lake Valley. Martha so desperately wants her resort she drools every time we talk about it. And now my own true love wants it for a spa."

"I see what you mean," Toni said sympathetically. "Maybe you *should* just give it to the Girl Scouts."

"In a way it's so unimportant." Jude slipped her feet out of her slippers. "Everything's going to change soon anyway," she said, wishing she felt as certain about that as she sounded.

CHAPTER 22

Gresh called a couple of days later and spoke for
twenty minutes about the spa and the many projects
and organizations she'd like the Fund to be able to
support, including a non-sexist education program, an
organization of women artists, support for feminist
political candidates, various women's businesses, crisis
lines, shelters, women in the trades, day care,
different lobbyist groups, and even an international
peace institute.

Jude listened attentively. "They all sound

important," she said when Gresh paused. She had caught some of Gresh's enthusiasm, and even felt her old activist optimism coming back.

Before they said goodbye, Gresh made a futile attempt to get Jude to forego the Ceremony of Emergence. She ended up accepting Jude's invitation to come to Circle Edge for the Ceremony.

"September first," Jude said.

"I know. Your birthday."

"In the meantime, you've given me a lot to think about," Jude said.

* * * * *

After the talk with Gresh, Jude tried to take a nap but she couldn't sleep. When she went outside to go for a walk, Honore came to her.

"You look troubled, Laki-Seone. May I walk with you?"

Jude and her soul-sister walked along the path in the foothills and Honore listened empathically as Jude talked of her conflict. "I wish I could make everybody happy," she said. "I wish I'd inherited three estates and valleys."

"It's clear that there'll be some disappointment," Honore said.

"Maybe I could sell everything but the Circle Edge property and give the money from the sale to the Feminist Fund. Or maybe I could make a deal so the Fund gets a cut of the profits from the resort." Jude stopped walking. She shook her head. "No, none of those ideas would work."

"No, they wouldn't," Honore said.

"Because the Circle Edge property has to be part of the resort too — for the ski slopes. Damn! I have to think of something."

"You will," Honore assured her.

After they parted, Jude continued walking for nearly an hour, going over the different possibilities. Miluna caught up with her.

"La would like you to come to her, Laki-Seone. She's at the Inner Garden."

Jude found La alone in one of the pools. La poured Jude a glass of ice water from the pitcher next to her. Jude took off her shoes and rolled up her pants then hung her feet in the pond. She drank half the glass of water.

"You are troubled, Laki-Seone, and confused. I should have known that the pull of the outer world is still there for you. You have been so long out there and for such a little time with us."

As Jude looked at La and listened to her, she realized she still felt awed by her. She also loved her.

"I thought you would know what you have to do, but since you are confused, I will tell you. Come, get more than your feet wet. Come sit next to me."

Jude stripped and joined La in the pool. They both leaned back comfortably. Jude finished her glass of water and began to feel dreamily relaxed.

"The Full Circle is now to be," La said. "We knew the Lake Valley would come to us some day and now, since you have inherited it, we know when and through whom. I thought you would know this too, but I see you are being pulled by others from your past, people whom you care about but who do not understand."

"There's no way to please everyone." Jude looked

at the sky. The sun had set; the stars were coming out. She wondered if Kwo-am was watching her.

"There is only one way. The others from the outer world will understand this soon. I will say what partly you already know, Laki-Seone, that you must turn the Lake Valley and the Estate over to us, your Kwo-amian sisters, and from the edge we will move and the circle will be full."

Jude said nothing.

"It is our destiny," La added. "Meant to be."

The stars seemed to nod at Jude.

"Do not fret about the others," La said. "Your sister will soon come to know what now she keeps hidden from herself, the truths that you have allowed in. The worthy goals of your feminist friends will soon be met in other ways."

Jude laid her head back; her eyes were closed. "I am wealthy in so many ways," she said. She was quiet for a while. "I was thinking about a compromise." She turned and looked at La. "That I might give my spiritual wealth to Kwo-amity and my material wealth to my sister and the feminists."

La chuckled lovingly. "You delight me, Laki-Seone." She caressed Jude's cheek tenderly. Jude felt the love. "But don't you see," La said, "Full Circle *is* part of your spiritual wealth. I know that there are still some slivers of doubt in you. This is not unexpected." Her jaw suddenly jutted forward angrily. "It was part of Zetka's countermoves, you know, to have you stay so long in the outer world."

Jude's hand was resting on her knees. La placed her own hand over it, and they both were quiet for a long time. At last Jude said, "My friend, Gresh, is a truly good person. And a tireless activist. It will disappoint her." She took deep, slow breaths. "But she's also very resilient. She'll handle the disappointment OK. It's Martha I'm worried about." Jude looked at La. "Is that a revealment? That Martha will come to understand?"

"Yes it is, Laki-Seone."

Jude sighed. "There's one more thought I'm having." She felt her forehead perspiring. "Do you think Circle Edge could give me some money in exchange for the Lake Valley and the Estate? Pay me for them?"

La's brow descended. Then she shook her head. "You have no need of money, Laki-Seone."

"For the Feminist Fund."

"It is not needed."

Another silence followed, this one very long. "Yes, of course," Jude finally said. "Everything will change."

"That's right."

"They won't need money to fund those projects."

"It will be unnecessary."

Jude sank farther into the warm pool. La began to hum and the sounds filled Jude's ears and mind. She and La stayed silently in the water for a long time. "How are you feeling now, Laki-Seone?"

"At peace," Jude said. "Warm and safe and good."

* * * * *

Later that night, sitting on Martha's back porch, Jude no longer felt so good.

"I simply can't believe it! You aren't Jude anymore." Martha was on her feet, stomping back and forth across the porch. "You're a robot. A puppet. That charlatan says jump and you jump. I think you're so brainwashed, you can't think sanely anymore."

"It's my own decision," Jude said. "You know I never liked the idea of Doray being a resort town."

"La makes you think it's your own decision but it's not. She calls the shots for you now, it's obvious."

Jude felt miserable. "I know it's hard for you, Martha. I wish you could understand."

"Oh, I understand all right. They saw you coming, those fanatics. They're taking you for everything, Jude, mind and money." Martha was crying.

Jude went to her, but Martha pulled away, turned her back to Jude. "I've lost you and because of you I lost my future."

"Martie."

"Don't call me that! Don't call me anything. Go away. Please, just go."

"I'm sorry."

"You're sick. You're lost. Forget it. Goodbye. I don't know you anymore."

She'll get over it, Jude told herself numbly as she got in the car. *She'll come to understand. La told me so. She's my sister, she's Martie, of course she will.*

* * * * *

Another message from Jeffrey Madsen was waiting for Jude when she got back to Circle Edge. She called him and began to explain that she would not be selling him the property, but Madsen interrupted, insisting that she at least look at the drawings. As aversive as the prospect was, Jude figured she owed him that, considering that she was sending his pet project down the drain. She agreed to meet him the next day.

Madsen's office was a large rectangular room on the second floor of one of the few three-story buildings in Doray. He did most of his business out of Denver, he told Jude, but maintained this office for the Doray project. He laid a large drawing on the table in front of her. Jude barely looked at it or listened as he described the lodge, the restaurant, the condominiums, the ski slopes.

"I'm not selling, Mr. Madsen." Her tone left little room for argument. "I know you're disappointed. I'm sorry."

Madsen went to his desk and sat. "That sounds firm," he said.

Jude was still standing at the table. "It is. I've thought it over carefully. I don't want Doray to become a resort town. I don't want the lake developed. It's very firm. I've definitely made my decision."

Madsen shook his head. "A foolish decision. Especially in light of how good this town has been to you and your family. Dave Banks down at the gas station, for example, did your mother a very big favor years ago. He is one of the folks here who'd especially like the town to grow. Have a seat, Jude, let me tell you about how Dave saved your mother's reputation."

Jude remained standing, but felt uneasy.

"There was a Chinese fellow named Kise," Madsen continued, "who burned to death in his cabin thirty years ago. You might have heard about it.

208

Dave Bank's place was up the road from the cabin. He saw your mother leaving while the cabin was still in flames, Jude. She was wearing nothing but a blanket."

Jude sank weakly into the chair. "Kise?" she murmured.

"When Dave saw the Chinaman's charred remains, he figured it served him right, fooling around with a married woman. For your family's sake, Dave kept your mother's affair with Kise a secret. He only revealed it now because I told him you were reluctant to sell the property."

The sinking feeling in Jude's stomach brought her close to nausea. "I don't believe it," she said.

"You were born exactly nine months after the fire," Madsen continued. "No one in town except Dave Banks and me and your mother know your real ancestry, Jude. Think about it. I'm sure, for your sister's sake if nothing else, you'd like to keep it that way."

Jude was having trouble getting air. She staggered woozily to her feet and ran out the door.

CHAPTER 23

The moment she got to her room she dialed the phone. Her mother said she sounded awful. "Did you ever know a man named Kise?" Jude asked.

There was a dreadful silence on the line. Jude waited anxiously. When Claire spoke, her voice was hoarse. "Why do you ask?"

"Madsen told me you knew him years ago, before I was born. Did you?"

"What else did he tell you?"

"That you were with Kise in his cabin the day it burned."

Another long silence. "Jude, come home and see me."

* * * * *

Drained and frightened, Jude arrived in Chicago the next afternoon. She took a cab to her mother's apartment. Claire Alta looked terrible. She made them tea and they sat in Claire's neat little living room where Jude used to do her homework.

Jude looked at her mother. For the first time, she appeared old. "You knew Kise?"

"Yes."

Jude stared at the hot tea in her cup. "Madsen told me Kise is my father."

Claire's face contorted. She covered it with her hands and cried. Jude went to her, holding her mother while the sobbing continued, feeling sympathy and feeling afraid.

"The love . . . I felt . . ." The words came between sobs. "I still feel it . . . just to . . . to think of him." Jude stroked her mother's back. "He was so alive . . . so gentle, the gentlest person I ever knew . . . oh Lord . . . ohh . . . why did it have to be?"

Jude took a tissue from her pocket. Her mother held it to her eyes, then her nose. "Can you tell me what happened?" Jude asked softly.

Claire raised her head and looked at Jude with pain and sadness in her eyes. "I thought you would never learn of it. I thought it was all buried in the past." Claire took a deep breath. "I wish you could have known him." She swallowed. "The first time I ever saw him . . . I remember it so well . . . I was in the foothills. I knew that a young Chinese man had

211

come to Doray and built a cabin. People talked about it but I had never seen him. He was there for years before I ever saw him. I was out hunting that day . . . I never told you I used to hunt. That day . . . the day I met Kise . . . I had just shot a deer and I went to my kill . . . it was a doe. I was examining it and then I looked up and . . . and I saw . . . through the tree branches I saw his face . . . Kise's face. He had tears in his eyes. He never told me what the tears meant but I think they were for the deer. I never hunted again."

Claire wept and Jude waited, stroking her mother's back.

"I was drawn to him from the first moment. Like a magnet. He was a beautiful man — young, lean, with the smoothest skin I'd ever seen." Claire's eyes had a dreamy look. "He hardly seemed human." She sighed loudly. "That day, the first day, we sat on a rock near the river and we talked for a long, long time. He was so tender and sensitive. Such a loving person. So special. He seemed pure, but wise — a soft, deep wisdom. He never talked about himself. When I'd ask him questions he'd give these vague answers. *Where are you from? From the center of time moving always outward.* Things like that. And then he'd laugh. He was wonderful company, delightful. He talked about ideas and feelings but not events. It was odd but very pleasant."

She stared at the floor. "I tried to love Joe. I think I did for a while, early in the marriage. I thought he'd change. I thought he'd learn to be more . . . to show his caring more, to be more feeling, more sensitive. I thought he'd learn to give to me the

212

way I gave to him." She looked at Jude. "He never did. He is what he is. The little love he had to give he gave to Martha."

Jude nodded knowingly.

"Kise showed me his garden. He raised his own food — he was a vegetarian — and he carved beautiful wooden statues, of animals, mostly, deer and birds. Sometimes his carvings were of people."

Jude could see her mother's hand moving inside the pocket of her slacks.

"He gave me this."

Jude took the small wooden object. She had to look at it a while to figure out what it was — two people intertwined in each other's arms. It was beautiful. It reminded her of the carving she had found in the woods, the wolf and rabbit.

"After that first day, we would meet from time to time. I would go near his cabin and sometimes he would be there and we would talk."

Claire reached toward her tea, then stopped. "One day — it was a cold day . . . there was snow, lots of snow — Martha was maiking a snow fort at the neighbor's. Kathleen said she'd watch her for me. I went to see if I might spend a moment with Kise."

Claire was biting her lower lip. Her eyes caught Jude's.

"He lifted my spirits so. I would feel filled after being with him." She looked off into space. "His gentleness and goodness were overwhelming. I wanted to touch him, to lie with him, be held in his arms. I wanted to make love with him." Claire looked at her daughter again. "This is painful for you to hear."

"I'm doing OK with it," Jude said.

"I think he sensed my need . . . for the closeness, the caring. I think it was probably very clear to him how much I needed contact and . . . affection."

Jude nodded sadly.

"We walked and talked as usual, but this day — it was December third, nineteen fifty-eight . . ." Claire's hands were clasped together in her lap. ". . . instead of parting at the path near his cabin as we usually did, we kept walking, walking all the way up to his cabin. We went inside . . . and we . . . we were together." Claire looked at Jude, then away. "I never felt so connected with another human being before or since." A tear slipped down Claire's cheek.

Jude nodded, her lips pressed tightly together.

"We fell asleep in each other's arms." Claire sighed. "And then . . . when I awoke I was lying on the ground outside the cabin. My throat was raw. It took me a moment to clear my head and to realize what was happening. The cabin was on fire." Claire was gasping as she spoke. "I could see his . . . the roof had collapsed and I could see Kise's head and arm . . . under a beam . . . and . . . I went to him but . . ." Sobs stopped her words.

"He was dead," Jude said softly.

"Yes. The fire started from the kerosene stove, the firemen said. Kise must have awakened and . . . I'm sure this is how it happened . . . I was unconscious from the smoke so he wrapped me in the blanket and carried me outside . . ." She was pressing her hand to her mouth. "And then . . . and then he must have gone inside for Lexis, his dog, but . . . but he didn't make it back out."

"Oh, Mom, how terrible."

Claire took the carving from Jude's hand and, clutching it to her breast, sobbed pitifully. "He was the most precious being there ever was." She caught her breath. "I could barely eat or sleep for weeks. Joe insisted I go to the doctor. Of course that didn't help. He gave me some pills. It didn't help at all. I only came out of it when I realized . . ." She was looking directly into Jude's eyes. ". . . when I learned that I was pregnant."

Jude's heart sped up.

"Joe and I hadn't . . . we very rarely made love." Again Claire looked into Jude's eyes. "Only when I realized Kise's child was growing inside of me did some of the pain go away. He was so very special, Jude, like you are."

Jude was breathing rapidly through open lips. She didn't speak for a long time. She and her mother sat side by side, neither saying a word. Finally, Jude broke the silence. "Amagyne told me Joseph Alta was not my father."

Claire was frowning and nodding. "She senses things, doesn't she?"

"She told me I had no father at all."

"No father," Claire said sadly. "Oh, I'm so sorry, my angel."

They cried together. Jude felt overwhelmed with all the different feelings and thoughts. For a long time they sat together silently, and then Claire suggested they have some more tea.

In the kitchen, they talked some more. Jude listened to every scrap of memory Claire could retrieve about Kise. *Who was he?* Jude kept asking herself. *Was he sent by Kwo-am? Had he really fathered Amagyne? Was he really my father?*

"Will you be OK, Mom?" Jude asked as she was preparing to leave.

"I'll be fine."

"I could stay the night if you want."

"You go." She hugged her. "You look like him," were her final words to Jude.

* * * * *

Toni listened raptly as Jude told her everything that had happened since the meeting with Madsen.

"But it doesn't fit," Jude said, staring out the bedroom window. "La said I was born of woman only. If Kise is my father, she'd know it."

"She has her limits," Toni said.

"But Kwo-am doesn't." Jude was chewing rapidly on a wad of gum.

"After you told me —"

"Maybe Kwo-am doesn't reveal everything to La," Jude said.

"Maybe La doesn't reveal everything to the Kwo-amians. Jude, let me —"

"Another possibility is that my mother is wrong about Kise being my father. Maybe she's mistaken. Maybe when she realized she was pregnant, she just assumed it had to be Kise."

"Jude, there's something I've been trying to tell you. Dagney talked to Maggie again. She called her after I told her what Amagyne told you."

"Oh? And did Maggie finally admit she never read the *Fruit of She?*"

216

"Quite the contrary. She said it was true about Lorn and her, about their being in love and Lorn refusing to be lovers with her. But Maggie insists that had nothing to do with her discoveries about La. She swears she read the *Fruit of She* and found the passage about the Catalyst dying. I don't think she's lying, Jude."

"She hates La. She blames La for keeping Lorn from her. She's just being vengeful."

"You're very closed-minded sometimes."

"Maybe Kise *is* my father but he's not a real person, and that's why La says I was born of woman only."

Toni sighed. "Yeah, right."

"In La's dreams, Kwo-am appears in different forms. Maybe she actually takes on living, physical forms sometimes. Maybe Kise was Kwo-am personified. And through his physical manifestation, Kwo-am created Amagyne and me in our mothers' wombs."

"That must be it," Toni said flatly.

"In a sense, that would make me and Amagyne half-sisters."

"Two peas in a pod."

Even though she felt exhausted Jude couldn't stop thinking and talking. "It's uncanny how he sensed it somehow."

"Who?"

"Joe. My mother's ex-husband. Somehow he knew."

"I doubt it, Jude. He didn't treat you well but I doubt that it had anything to do with his *somehow sensing* that you weren't his child."

"You're so rational!"

217

"Thank you."

"I don't feel full of kwo-ami right now. I feel zetkap in me. Toni, can you believe everything that's happened in the last couple of months?"

"Barely."

They had gotten into bed and were sitting up, propped against pillows.

"It's more like a novel than real life."

Toni laughed. "Well I must admit your life has recently become more interesting than most."

"I mean, really! There I was, this basically kind of ordinary person just living my basically kind of ordinary life and suddenly I become a central figure in this fascinating women-centered religion . . ."

Toni was watching Jude closely.

". . . and I inherit a fortune. Shit! With all the different factions of my life vying for my property. Jesus! That should be enough, but then on top of all that, the man I thought was my father isn't."

"You're right. It's too much to believe."

"And I find out who my real father is from some capitalist who tries to blackmail me into selling him my property."

"Does that worry you? Madsen's threat to spill the beans about your mother?"

"That's the least of my worries," Jude said.

"Would the townspeople turn against Martha?"

"Not anyone she cares about. God, Toni, isn't all of this just unbelievable?"

"Yes. Someone must be making it up. Especially the part about you becoming a religious convert."

"How did it all get started?"

Toni shrugged. "For you apparently it started

thirty years ago when your mother was lucky enough to find a very loving man."

"I wish I could have known him," Jude said dreamily, barely able to keep her eyes open. She was trying to picture Kise when she drifted into sleep.

* * * * *

Jude remained in Chicago for three days. On the evening prior to her return to Circle Edge, Gresh had a dinner party. Dagney got Jude off alone on the back porch.

"Do you have any idea what's going on back here while you're out in the mountains communing with God?"

"What do you mean?" Jude asked.

"Toni and Becka," Dagney said.

"What?" Jude glared at her disdainfully.

"Hey, don't blame the messenger. I just thought you had the right to know. Take my advice, kiddo. If you value your relationship you better stay here and tend your own garden."

Jude felt disgust for Dagney, but also a hot rush of anxiety.

"It's real clear to anyone with an ounce of perception that Becka's still in love with Toni. So I guess with you staying in Colorado it's just natural that Becka would be spending nights at Toni's apartment — correction, your and Toni's apartment."

Jude's eyes were stinging.

"Hey, you two, soup's on," Pam said from the doorway.

Jude was not very talkative the rest of the

evening. When she and Toni got home, Toni asked her what was wrong.

"Sometimes I just hate all the changes," Jude said sadly. She was sitting on the rocking chair in their bedroom.

"I know what you mean," Toni said.

"I wonder if you and I are going to stay together."

"Of course we are."

"Everything's changing."

"Not everything. We're still a team." Toni looked closely at Jude. "Aren't we?"

"I guess. I feel so tired."

"Come on to bed."

"As soon as my head hits the pillow I'll be asleep," Jude said.

"That's fine."

Jude undressed and crawled under the covers, her back to Toni. Toni put her arm around her but Jude did not respond. Her breathing became slow and regular, although she was not asleep. She cried silently long into the night.

CHAPTER 24

On the flight back to Colorado Jude wondered whether she should tell Amagyne about Kise. Things should be revealed in their time, La had often said. *If La hasn't told Amagyne,* Jude thought, *then Amagyne probably isn't supposed to know.*

She called Madsen soon after she was back at Circle Edge and told him he was free to spread around whatever gossip he chose, but she was not selling. He tried again, half-heartedly it seemed, to convince her how embarrassing the truth about her parentage would be for Martha and for Joe Alta.

"They'll handle it," Jude said, and hung up the phone. *He knows he's lost,* she thought, feeling sure he'd say nothing.

That night Jude sat on a foam chair in one of the private lounges at Circle House with Amagyne across from her on the sofa. The backgammon game was set up between them, but neither was concentrating on it.

"I want to be close to you," Jude said.

Amagyne held out her hand and Jude took it and moved to the sofa. She could feel the warmth of Amagyne's hip against her own. Looking at Amagyne, she felt herself being drawn into the deep black eyes.

"I feel so valued by you," Jude said.

"You are a jewel," Amagyne replied. She moved her face closer to Jude's, pulling Jude further in with her eyes.

Jude felt herself being absorbed. "I'm loving you," she said.

"I know." Their faces were only inches apart.

"I mean —"

"I know what you mean." Amagyne said the words softly, her lips moving closer to Jude's.

The kiss was not like any kiss Jude had ever known. She felt instantly transported. She couldn't tell where she ended and Amagyne began or if there were any endings or beginnings at all. The merging was absolute, bodily boundaries gone. They floated somehow, Jude and Amagyne as one, to somewhere else in the room, or perhaps it was to another room, where a soft mat or cloud lay on the floor and they lay on the cloud unclothed and intertwined. Their bodies and souls moved, rhythmically, passion and

222

ecstasy coalescing, body and spirit one. Amagyne was a goddess and Jude a goddess too. The fluid of their mouths and vaginas was the soft mist and rain. Their smells were the oceans and mint and pine, their sounds the call of the mourning dove and wolf. Their caresses were a soft breeze bending the grass, building to a storm of bright, flashing lightning. And their tremblings and their orgasms were the tremors of the earth culminating in magnificent back-bending quakes.

* * * * *

Jude's head floated weightlessly. The night was still and quiet. She felt Amagyne's hand caressing her cheek. Through the skylight she could see tiny twinkling spots that were faraway stars. She was trembling.

Amagyne pulled the blanket up, covering Jude's shoulders. "I think it is confusion and uncertainty that makes you shiver," she said, "more than the cold."

"It feels so right to be with you," Jude said, "but also not right at all." Her tears made everything seem a blur. She sat up. Amagyne handed her her shirt. "I feel completely united with you, and yet . . ."

"It's all right," Amagyne said gently.

Jude took Amagyne's hand. "Inseparable. I feel blended with you. Cemented." Jude shook her head. "And yet . . ."

Amagyne listened caringly as Jude spoke about her complicated mix of feelings. When Jude had no more to say, Amagyne walked with her to Sky Palace and bade her goodnight with a gentle kiss on the forehead.

* * * * *

The next day Jude walked for hours in the woods. The sun grew hot so she took off her shirt and tied it around her waist. The sweat on her body felt good. She thought of Toni, their love, and of loving Amagyne. She thought of Kise and her mother and La. It was overwhelmingly confusing. When she thought of Martha, she began to cry.

Each time she had phoned Martha, Martha had hung up on her. Jude had written her a note: *Our love can overcome our differences. There must be a way for you and I to work this out. Please call me, Martie. I love you.* Martha had not responded.

Jude suddenly felt compelled to make things right between them. She hurried back to her room, showered, then drove to town. She parked in front of the cafe. The moment Martha saw her, she walked into the kitchen and out the back door.

"She barely even talks to *me*," Cal said. He and Jude were sitting on stools next to the grill. "After you told her you wouldn't sell to Madsen, she just sort of . . . deflated."

Jude felt profoundly sad.

"Madsen's leaving, you know," Cal said. "Closing down his Doray office. Apparently he's looking for another area for his ski resort. Martha blames you. She won't listen to reason."

"Did she read my note?"

"She wouldn't open it. I read it to her. No

224

reaction. She just stared. She's barely there half the time, Jude. She comes here to the cafe, but she just sits staring into space."

"She and I need a stretch talk."

"A what?"

Jude shook her head sadly. "I wish I could take away her pain."

* * * * *

Jude lay on her bed staring at the ceiling. At last she got up and phoned Toni.

"You sound down," Toni said.

"Too much is happening. Everything's a mess. Martha's totally rejected me and pretty soon you and I will probably end our relationship too."

"Don't say that, Jude."

"It'll just be me and the other Kwo-amians."

"Jude, what's going on?"

"My name isn't Jude."

"Oh shit."

"You and Becka will do fine without me."

There was a moment of silence. "Now where the hell is that coming from?"

"I guess I'm calling to say goodbye. Tell Pam goodbye for me, too, and Gresh, and everyone else. I know Pam won't want anything to do with me if I continue to be a religious kook, and Gresh won't since I won't be helping the Feminist Fund."

"Don't be ridiculous. They're your friends, Jude. They're both coming to Circle Edge for your birthday."

Jude switched the receiver to her other hand. "I didn't tell Amagyne about Kise and my mother."

"I thought you probably wouldn't. Jude . . ."
Toni's voice was full of sadness and tenderness. "I
love you so much. You know that, don't you?"

Jude felt her throat tighten. She bit on her lower
lip. "Sometimes I almost wish I hadn't found
Kwo-am," she said woefully. "My life was so much
less complicated before. No matter how many of us
become kwo-omnis, there will still be pain. Different
people needing different things. You needing Becka
when I'm gone."

"You think I've been with Becka? Sexually?"

"I know about it."

"Just what is it you think you know, Jude?"

"That she's in love with you still, that she spends
the night with you."

"Oh, I see." Toni let out a deep gush of air.
"Yes, she did sleep over a couple of times. So that's
what's bothering you? You think she and I are
sexually involved again?" Toni paused. "Have you
been with someone? I think maybe you have and
that's what this is all about."

"Dagney says Becka's in love with you."

Toni sighed audibly. "So, because she says so you
believe it." There was a long silence. "Do you have
anything more to say on this topic?" Toni asked.

"I made love with Amagyne."

The silence was heavy. "I thought you might
have," Toni said finally.

"Are you upset?"

"Yes."

"It wasn't because I don't love you."

"Mm-hm. And her?"

"Very different," Jude said. "Like a dream.

There's something unreal about everything at Circle Edge, but especially Amagyne. It's almost like she's on another dimension or something. She's a real person, but not really."

"Hm-m. So having sex with her is almost the same as having a sexual fantasy?"

"Yes."

"I'd like to be able to buy that."

"I truly love you," Jude said.

"I hope you do," Toni said tearily.

Neither spoke for a long time.

"It's scary," Jude said.

"We belong together."

"Yes."

"Come home, Jude."

"I can't."

"I need you."

Jude swallowed her tears. "I have to stay here, Toni. You know that. I have to see this whole thing through."

"I hate it!" Toni snapped. "I hate all of it. You know, sometimes I really wish I could just let you go. To your sappy Amagyne and your Kwo-amians and to your goddamn death if that's what you want."

Toni was sobbing. So was Jude.

"I'm sorry," Toni said after awhile. "I guess I've got my limits."

Jude couldn't speak.

"I'm not going anywhere, Jude. I can't desert you. As long as there's any hope, I'm hanging in. There is hope, isn't there?"

"Of course," Jude said tearfully. "We're a team, remember?"

"Yes, I remember." There was a pause. "I wonder what our lives will be like a year from now, five years from now."

Jude stood again and began to pace. "Our whole world will be different," she said, her vitality suddenly restored. "Especially by five years from now. Fewer and fewer people every day will feel the wish to be hurtful to other people. I imagine it to be not quite perfect but getting closer and closer. Violence and cruelty and oppression will be gone. You and I will be happy at our cabin at Circle Edge. Zetka's influence is going to wither and disappear. You'll believe it when you see it happening. You'll see it happening right after the Ceremony. You're still coming, aren't you?"

"Yes, of course. I'll be there six days from today. By the way, where does La keep her book?"

"There you go again. The *Fruit of She* is private."

"If you find it and read it and it says nothing about the Catalyst dying, then I'll become a Kwo-amian. Deal?"

"I can't do that, Toni."

"Maggie read it."

"She did not. If she had, La would know. We wouldn't be going ahead. Everything would have been ruined. Maggie did not read the *Fruit of She*. Can we talk about something else?"

"We have to talk about it eventually. Before your birthday. I'm not going to let them kill you."

Jude sat on the bed. "Toni, don't you realize that you're being influenced by Zetka? He's fighting back. He has control of Maggie and he's trying to control you. Don't let him, hon."

"I don't believe in Zetka."

"That doesn't matter. He can get you anyway."

"Yeah, right, the devil made me do it."

Jude laughed in spite of herself.

"It *is* ridiculous, isn't it?" Toni said hopefully.

"Your being so closed just doesn't bother me, Toni, because I know that in eleven more days it will all change. Oh, Toni, I love you so much. Are you angry about Amagyne?" Jude waited a long time for a response.

"I don't want to lose you to her," Toni said at last.

"Don't worry," Jude said. "Remember, we really are a team." She paused. "Right? We are, aren't we?"

"Of course," Toni said. "You sound better. Are you feeling better?"

"Yes. I wish you were here. I'd really like to hold you now."

They talked for a few more minutes then lovingly said goodbye. Afterwards Jude lay on her bed, holding her pillow, thinking about love and loyalty, wondering whether Becka was a threat, wondering how much room one person had in her heart to love others.

CHAPTER 25

Circle Edge was alive with women and more kept coming every day. The hills and woods were blanketed with their tents. Charcoal fires were everywhere. Rows of turquoise portajohns were set up near the Gate Building and in the woods east of the Amit. Excitement filled the air. Children played noisily. There was singing, dancing, stories being told, plans being made, for the New Page was at hand and Kwo-world soon would be.

Jude felt like a star. Many of the newcomers were overwhelmed by her and couldn't speak in her presence. Much of the time she was tingling with excitement. Occasionally she felt overwhelmed and would have to go off for a while and be alone. She and Amagyne were together frequently, though they did not make love, and neither spoke about the time that they had. Jude was not sure why. They would often hold hands and look deeply and lovingly into each other's eyes.

On Thursday, Toni arrived at Circle Edge. She embraced Jude tenderly. "You're trembling," she said. At her room in the Dome, where Jude now stayed, Jude clung to Toni but couldn't seem to get her close enough.

The next day, Pam, Gresh and Dagney came. Jude, Toni and Joyce helped them set up their tents in the city of tents that had grown at Circle Edge. Afterwards Jude took the Chicagoans on a tour. Gresh and Joyce wandered off at some point between Circle House and the stables. Jude wanted Dagney and Pam to come to the ceremony that was scheduled for two o'clock, but neither was interested, even when told they'd get a chance to see La. They all agreed to meet later at the Sky Palace Lounge.

Dagney and Pam headed for the Dome. The door to La's apartment was not locked.

"Anybody home?" Pam called.

No response.

"Nice place," Dagney said. She ran her fingers over an antique lamp table. "Very classy. The old gal obviously has a taste for fine things."

From La's living room window they could see most of Circle Edge and the rising mountains around it. A large crowd was gathered at the Amit.

Dagney began searching La's buffet drawers. She

231

and Pam went through the entire apartment, looking in closets, under sinks, checking all the books on the shelves. To no avail.

"I'm not surprised," Dagney said. She was sitting on La's easy chair and looking out over the mountains. "Things are a lot less free and open around here than Jude thinks." She pulled herself to her feet. "Well, time to start picking brains."

They went to the second floor of Ambrosia, and within ten minutes Dagney was engaged in a game of pool with a woman called Seabreeze who had lived at Circle Edge for thirty years. She got Seabreeze a soft drink from the machine and sat down with her to talk. Pam joined them.

Seabreeze spoke freely about Circle Edge, answering every question. She had known Ingrid Thorensen well. Ingrid had lived in neighboring Ridge Valley and had been a Kwo-amian for many years. She had been La's soul-sister. Dagney asked if Ingrid had ever brought a child to Circle Edge. Seabreeze recalled that she had. A young niece, twenty or twenty-five years ago, though Seabreeze could not remember the child's name.

"How come you're interested in Ingrid's niece?" she asked.

"More in Ingrid, really," Dagney said. "Because of the coincidence, Jude knowing Ingrid all those years and then Jude turning out to be the Catalyst."

"We were surprised when we learned the Catalyst had been born in Doray," Seabreeze said. "I think La must have chosen this place because the Catalyst would be born here."

Dagney mentioned that she had met Maggie

Richards and asked Seabreeze what had happened between Maggie and Lorn.

"I don't know exactly," Seabreeze said. "I know Maggie tried to get Lorn to run off with her. I think she hoped that if she could get Lorn away from La she'd have a chance with her."

"Were Lorn and La lovers?" Dagney asked.

"Some people think so. I don't know. They seemed more like mother and daughter." Seabreeze shrugged. "But who knows? It was their business. Maggie not only left Circle Edge, but Kwo-amity as well. I never understood that. She's the only Firstcomer that turned from us."

Pam watched Dagney, wondering if she would mention Maggie reading the *Fruit of She*. Dagney remained silent.

"Lorn missed her terribly. Some people thought Zetka was using Maggie somehow, as part of a countermove. I don't know. Is she happy in New York?"

"Seems to be," Dagney said.

They talked a short while more, then Dagney and Pam left. They asked around until they found Lorn. She was working in the Ambrosia kitchen.

"Laki-Seone's friends," Lorn said in a low operatic voice. "I heard you were here and hoped I would get to meet you." She was a tawny-skinned woman with short kinky hair and long thin fingers. She took them to a sitting room off the kitchen, and brought a tray of raw vegetables and spicy dip.

"Laki-Seone has talked about you, Pam." Lorn looked closely at Pam who sat across from her on a canvas chair. "She says you like to read Vonnegut and to repair and build things much more than you like teaching. And she says you quit smoking at least once a week. She also says she loves you very much."

Pam took a carrot slice and poked it into the dip. "I'm worried about her. Her name is Jude, you know. That's been her name for thirty years. It's hard to see her changing like this."

Lorn nodded understandingly.

"We'd like her to come back home."

"She has important things to do here," Lorn said gently. "She is the second spirit-child of Kwo-am. Do you understand what that means?"

"I understand what you're telling her it means. She's going to magically make the world a utopia, right? Because she's Kwo-am's spirit-child. That part means she had no father, right?"

"Born of woman only."

"Like Amagyne," Pam said.

"Yes," Lorn replied. Her expression was serene.

Pam looked at Dagney and got a nod. "What about Kise?" she said.

The muscles in Lorn's face seemed to collapse. Her chest rose and fell with her deep breathing.

"We know about him," Pam said. "Dagney talked with Maggie Richards."

Lorn was obviously struggling to control herself. Her lips and face twisted into a variety of strained expressions.

Dagney said, "She told me Kise was your lover and that he fathered Amagyne."

Lorn's long fingers were spread over her face. Suddenly she looked Dagney directly in the eyes, and then Pam. "He was not a man. Not in the sense you mean. He was Kwo-am. I am saddened to hear that

Maggie spoke of this, especially to people who would not understand."

"You think he wasn't human?"

"A nasty image has come to my mind," Lorn said, somewhat angrily. She had fully regained her composure. "I hesitate to say it to you."

"Go ahead, say it," Dagney said.

"Pearls before swine," Lorn said, looking Dagney firmly in the eye.

"Listen," Pam said plaintively. "We're not out to hurt you or anyone else. In fact, we'll keep our mouths shut about this if you can just help us get Jude out of here. Believe whatever you want about spirits and goddesses and magic, but we don't want Jude to be a part of it."

"She is the Catalyst," Lorn said firmly. "I did not make this be and I cannot unmake it, and would not want to." Her eyes were wet. "Maggie always possessed most of my heart," she said sadly.

"She didn't tell me about Kise for the fun of gossiping." Dagney's voice had softened. "She only told me because she was afraid for Jude."

"The outer world has damaged her," Lorn said. "She is lost."

"It was her integrity that made her speak," Dagney persisted. "She read the *Fruit of She*. She learned that the Catalyst has to die for the New Page to happen."

Lorn's fist came down with a crash on the wooden table. "It's what I feared," she hissed through clenched teeth. "Zetka has Maggie in his clutches. We were forewarned."

Dagney rolled her eyes. "This is hopeless," she said to Pam.

"If you would read it yourself, you'd see," Pam said gently to Lorn. "Something is wrong with La. For some reason she wants Jude dead."

Lorn stared straight ahead. "There are some among us who believe only Kwo-amians should be allowed into Circle Edge. There are some who say all others should be barred."

"You can't bar the truth."

"You are part of Zetka's countermove. He fears the New Page. It strikes terror in him for it means his end. He is using you. He used Maggie."

"Reading the *Fruit of She* would clear this up."

"No one reads the *Fruit of She*." Lorn's face showed sharp lines of anger. "It is Zetka's trick. Maggie did not read the *Fruit*. It is impossible. No one can read it while La still lives." She looked at Dagney. "What Maggie said to you was not Maggie speaking. She was possessed. She told you Zetka's lie."

Dagney shook her head. "Let's get out of here," she said to Pam.

"We didn't mean to upset you," Pam said. "We're worried about Jude, that's all."

"You are being used," were the last words Lorn said to them.

* * * * *

"That was sure a bust," Dagney said as they left Ambrosia.

They went to meet Jude and Toni in the lounge at Sky Palace.

Dagney took Jude aside. "How you doing, kiddo?" She smiled flirtatiously. "You know, there's

something about you that I find almost irresistible."
She chuckled teasingly. "But, that's not what I want
to talk with you about. It's La, the big cheese."

Jude had mixed feelings about Dagney. She found
her charming in some ways, but also a little
obnoxious and pushy. "What about La?"

"I'd like to meet her. Possible?"

"Not if you intend to harass her."

"Jude, honey, that's a strong word. I just want to
meet her, have a little talk with her. Maybe she'll
convert me. You don't think she'd be intimidated by
me, do you?"

"Hardly. It'd be like a gnat pestering a lion."

Dagney laughed heartily. "I think you're falling in
love with me. So how do I get to meet her?"

"I'll take you to her if you make some effort to
behave yourself. Deal?"

"Sealed with a kiss," Dagney said, taking Jude's
hand and pressing it to her lips.

An hour later, Jude introduced Dagney to La.
They were outside on a bench near the river. La held
both of Dagney's hands and looked her deeply in the
eyes. "You are curious, doubtful. No, it's more than
that, you're angry. Just a little afraid, I see. Yes. You
are learning about us, yet you don't feel at all drawn
to Kwo-amity." She released Dagney's hands and
patted her shoulder. "It is not important. You will
feel it after the Ceremony of Emergence."

Dagney cleared her throat. She seemed
uncharacteristically uncomfortable, but proceeded
nonetheless. "I've been wondering something," she
said, "about Jude and how you managed to get her
here and why. I've been having some real interesting
thoughts about that."

"I'm sure you have," La said quietly.

"They begin with Ingrid Thorensen. She was one of yours, right? Under your thumb, so to speak. And Ingrid managed to wend her way into the heart of Rosalie Wright, owner of the lake, et cetera, correct? Ingrid befriended the lonely widow and all that, gained her confidence. And interestingly, as close as those two were, Ingrid never happened to mention to Rosalie that she was part of this little fiefdom here." Dagney was looking pointedly at La. "She never mentioned to Rosalie where her real loyalties lay."

Jude was on her feet. "Dagney, come on, stop this, please."

"Hush, Laki-Seone, I do not need protection," La said. "Go now, leave your friend and me alone."

"I'd like her to hear," Dagney said. "Unless you're afraid I'll reveal something you wouldn't want Jude to know."

"As you like," La said.

Jude sat. Dagney continued. "So Ingrid befriends Rosalie. I would guess she hoped to become the heir herself but maybe that didn't seem possible or maybe Jude was the backup plan. In any case it seems pretty apparent that Ingrid helped convince Rosalie to leave the lake and the rest of the property to Jude. I'd guess Ingrid succeeded in the year nineteen-sixty-four, the year you announced the birth of the so-called Catalyst. Then, the way I figure it, as soon as Rosalie died, or was obviously about to, you could reel Jude in and then get her to give you the lake and the Wright Estate. You laid the groundwork for getting Jude by having Ingrid bring her here as a child."

"What are you talking about?" Jude protested. "I

238

never came here as a child. Dagney, why don't you —"

"Jude, they probably drugged you or something. You thought the visits were dreams. Remember those dreams you had as a kid, dreams about the *special place*. Don't look so shocked, I'm not a mind-reader. Toni told me about them. They weren't dreams, Jude. You were here. They were setting the stage for later. For now. To make you susceptible. It worked like a charm."

Dagney looked at La who was calmly scrutinizing her. "Now the part I'm wondering about is why Jude has to die. You already got her to agree to give you the Estate and the Lake Valley. Why do you want to kill her off? Does it have something to do with the fact that Kise is her father? That Amagyne and Jude have the same father?"

Jude was aghast.

La's eyes penetrated Dagney fiercely. "You know so little and yet you speak so much. And what you know, you twist so strangely."

"I shouldn't have brought her to you," Jude said.

"She is part of Zetka's plan, my Laki-Seone. I think her presence is one of the settlements. We will deal with it."

"She talked to Maggie Richards," Jude said, her face flushed from anger at Dagney. "I would have told you but I knew they were lies. I knew Maggie never read the *Fruit of She*." She looked beseechingly at La. "Was Kise Kwo-am?"

La smiled serenely. "Of course," she said.

Jude nodded. "I thought so."

"It is dangerous for Kwo-am's workings to be revealed when she has said this should not be," La said. "It worries me that Kise's name is spoken by those so deeply in the dark."

"Scares the shit out of you," Dagney said.

"Things should be known in their time, and some are not meant to be known at all."

"So you admit you knew about Kise, knew all along that he was Jude's father as well as Amagyne's."

"The things I know, I know in very different ways from you," La said gently. "I think in the end your eyes will be opened."

"I see quite clearly right now. It's Jude who's blind to what you really are."

La looked at Dagney pityingly.

"She's a fraud, Jude," Dagney said. "She's after your money and that stupid lake. Maybe now that I've brought things out in the open at least your life will be spared."

"I see no value to further conversation between us," La said. With great dignity, she rose from the bench. "Come, Laki-Seone, you and I should be together now."

They left Dagney and walked silently along the river. When they reached the cluster of fir trees, La spoke. "You are dealing with many changes and new awarenesses," she said. "Some are bound to be disturbing to you. There is a plan which we must follow in order to alter the direction the world is going. Unfortunately, we have enemies among us."

"I'm sorry Dagney is here," Jude said angrily.

"She says many upsetting things. How are they affecting you, Laki-Seone? What is in your heart?"

"I am not troubled," Jude said. "I understand about Kise, his being Kwo-am incarnate."

"This is a huge and powerful truth to take in."

"I've spoken with my mother about him."

"Yes," La said, nodding.

"Was his death part of the plan?" Jude asked.

"A countermove," La said. They were near the Inner Garden. "Zetka uses people, Laki-Seone, for his own ends. He tries to shake us from ours."

Jude nodded.

"Do you have trust in what I say and what Kwo-am reveals to me?"

"Complete trust," Jude said.

"There is more to come." La took Jude's hand. "It will come in its time."

"I trust you absolutely."

CHAPTER 26

Pam finally found La at Circle House speaking with a large group of women sitting and standing in a circle around her. Pam waited over an hour, listening to their talk. In spite of herself, she was impressed by some of the things La said. She seemed wise and loving. At last the group broke up and Pam had her chance.

"Excuse me. My name is Pam Holtz. I'm a good friend of Jude's from Chicago."

La took Pam's hands in hers. "I'm glad you are here. Come, let's sit over there where we can be alone." She led Pam to a little alcove along a windowless wall. "You wish to talk to me. What is it, Pam?"

"Uh, well . . ." Pam cleared her throat. "There's this rumor going around, you see . . . about Jude, you know, Laki-Seone." Pam was surprised by her own discomfort. "What they're saying is that the Catalyst has to die at the Ceremony of Emergence."

"Ah, and you are worried that this rumor might be true?" La inquired gently.

"I'm interested in rumor control," Pam said. "That book of yours, the *Fruit of She*. If I could read it, I could probably clear up all the talk that's going around."

La shook her head. "That cannot be done," she said calmly.

"But why?" Pam reached for her cigarettes then put the pack back in her pocket without taking one. "Why not?" She was edgy.

La looked at her warmly. "You needn't be worried. Close your eyes, Pam. It's all right, go ahead. Hum-mm-m. It is hard to accept things not immediately understandable to you. Humm-mm. You feel troubled. Hum-mmm. Yes, I understand."

Pam's eyes were closed. She began to relax. She realized she was beginning to feel hazy. She forced her eyes open. "What is that, like hypnosis or something?"

La smiled. "You can let go. You don't have to fight it."

"No, I don't want to let go." Pam blinked her eyes rapidly. "There's something else I've been wondering," she said hoarsely, "about Jude."

"Yes, you are filled with worries and wondering."

Pam spoke rapidly. "What if something . . . what if Jude has an attack of appendicitis or something and is in the hospital on her birthday? What if something like that happens?"

La smiled knowingly. "It will not."

"Right, I'm sure it won't," Pam said, "but, what if? What if something prevents her from doing the Ceremony?"

La rose. "Then Zetka will have won," she said, taking Pam's hands in hers. "You are a true friend to Laki-Seone. That is good. Allow yourself to let go, Pam. Let go of the worry." She released Pam's hands and slowly walked away.

* * * * *

The next day Dagney went to Corbette's Cafe. "I think we can get her back," she said to Martha.

Dagney had introduced herself and she and Martha had been talking for several minutes in the waitresses' booth. At first Martha had not been very warm or responsive, but now she was looking directly at Dagney with some life in her eyes.

They talked for half an hour more, Martha crying part of the time, for Dagney had told her about Maggie reading La's secret book, and what it said. Then they walked two blocks to the health food store where Martha's friend, Lace, worked. The three of them went next door to the coffee shop and talked.

An hour later Lace left. Dagney and Martha continued talking. Dagney told her she had visited Rosalie Wright's lawyer and he had confirmed Dagney's suspicion that Jude had become Rosalie's heir in 1964, the year the Catalyst's existence was announced.

She asked Martha many questions about Jude's relationship with Rosalie and about Ingrid Thorensen. "Did you know Ingrid was a Kwo-amian?" Dagney asked at one point.

Martha looked shocked.

"She and La were good buddies."

"I had no idea. I'm sure Rosalie didn't either."

Dagney signalled the waitress for a coffee refill. "I think Ingrid was La's source of information about Jude. I think La knew exactly when Jude was written into Rosalie's will and I think she helped make it happen. Through Ingrid."

"I'll be damned. So they planned it for years. They wanted Jude because she was their access to the Lake Valley."

"Yep. La seems very determined and very patient. She waited until Rosalie was close to death to recruit Jude. It probably took longer than she expected."

Martha was frowning pensively. "I wonder why La didn't get to Jude sooner."

"Too risky," Dagney asserted. "People who join cults tend to be the most vehement believers in the early months, then some of them snap out of it and split. Also it was important to keep Jude's involvement with Kwo-amity secret from Rosalie. I think La timed it just right."

Martha looked at her. "Jude's involvement wasn't a secret," she said. "Rosalie knew."

Dagney's eyes widened. "Really? Jude said she never told her."

"I told her."

"Ahh-h." Dagney seemed pleased. "Hoping she might help you convince Jude to get out."

Martha nodded. "I wonder if she tried. I'm surprised she didn't cut Jude out of the will after what I told her. She was very anti-religious."

"Interesting."

Martha sighed deeply. "I wish we could convince Jude of all this."

Dagney laughed. "And I wish every book I publish would sell a hundred thousand. Did you know the Edgers found gold on their property?"

"I had no idea. On their own land or the part that Jude now owns?"

"Good question. We should check that out. I bet you know what my guess is."

Martha nodded. "So that could be another reason they'd want Jude's inheritance." Her eyes suddenly teared. "But killing her . . . I knew Jude was in trouble but I never imagined it was as bad as this."

Dagney reached over the table and touched Martha's shoulder. "We'll take care of it," she said.

* * * * *

Jude had just gone into a lounge at Ambrosia when Joyce came up to her. "I've fallen in love," she declared. She pushed her fingers through her short, salt and pepper hair. "It's absolutely fantastic. I feel happy, wonderful, but I'm also worried. Her world is the outer world. Tell me, do you think there's any chance she would come here to stay?"

"Who?" Jude asked.

"Gresh."

"You're in love with Gresh?"

246

"Like never before. I might have to leave Circle Edge."

Jude smiled. "Well how about that? That was sure fast. And does she feel the same?"

"I'm sure of it. She says she knows that we have many differences, but that she loves me. I told her that after the Ceremony of Emergence maybe the barriers wouldn't seem so strong. But then I told her if that doesn't work out, I'll come live in Chicago."

"Really? You've been here a long time, Joyce."

"Ten years. I was married, you know. To a man, I mean. I always knew I was a lesbian."

"And a Kwo-amian?"

"I found that out ten years ago. I can be a Kwo-amian in Chicago. It's happening so fast." Her voice bubbled with excitement. "For me the New Page has already begun."

"Love does that," Jude said.

CHAPTER 27

Late Sunday morning, Jude jogged over to the river camp to visit Pam and Gresh. Gresh, especially, seemed to be enjoying Circle Edge. Neither she nor Pam were criticizing Kwo-amity, nor trying to influence Jude, although Dagney, of course, made frequent remarks.

Only Pam and Dagney were at the camp. "Dagney's got some good news," Pam said.

Jude took the lawn chair next to Pam.

"I visited your sister," Dagney said. "On your

behalf. It took a lot of work but I finally got her to agree to talk with you."

Jude looked at her incredulously. "Are you serious? How did you pull that off? That's terrific."

"I dug through the anger to the love," Dagney said.

Jude's eyes teared. "I know if she and I just talk, we can work things out. This is great, Dagney. Thanks. I really appreciate it."

"My pleasure," Dagney said. "Martha said the sooner the better."

Jude was on her feet. "I'll go right now."

"She wants me there too," Dagney said, pulling herself from her chair.

Jude's brow furrowed. "Oh, really? Why?"

"That's what she said."

"To mediate, maybe," Pam suggested.

* * * * *

Sarah was at the gate with a dozen other Edgers letting new arrivals in and occasionally letting women out. She greeted Jude warmly.

Jude told her she and Dagney were going out for a ride. "How are things? Have any crashers tried to come?"

"Some men in a pickup truck parked up the road and watched for a while. They didn't try to get in."

"You're ready for them if they try."

"The Guardian Edgers are here," Sarah said, gesturing to her comrades. Like Sarah, they wore belts with covered leather holsters.

"They have stun guns," Jude said to Dagney, "and tranquilizer guns and Mace."

249

"Laki-Seone," Sarah said uneasily, "La has told us that the Catalyst will leave the borders of Circle Edge only once before the Ceremony, and that she, La, will be with her."

"Oh?" Jude was slightly annoyed. "Well, something unexpected has come up, Sarah, and I have to go."

Clearly uncomfortable, Sarah suggested that Jude talk with La about it.

"This is great," Dagney said disgustedly.

"It's all right for us to go, Sarah," Jude said. "Take my word for it." She was beginning to feel angry.

"If only La had not said what she did, then surely I would, Laki-Seone." Sarah was squirming.

Jude backed off. "I'll clear this up with La," she said. "It should only take a few minutes."

"You're a prisoner," Dagney said.

"Don't be ridiculous. There's a good reason for it. I just wish La had told me. I'll meet you back at your camp." Jude was half running up the road.

"Jude, don't be dumb." Dagney caught up with her. "She's not going to let you go."

"Of course she will. If she's worried about me then we'll take some Guardians with us."

"I've got a better idea. Much less hassle." Dagney started toward the path near the river. "Come on. We'll take the back way out."

"The only way in or out is through the gate," Jude protested.

"Wrong. One of the Edgers showed me another exit."

Jude followed Dagney. They kept up a steady pace and were getting farther and farther away from the buildings and the camps.

"The Edgers use the path sometimes to get into the woods," Dagney said. "The entrance is hard to find, but Ella showed it to me. She's rather smitten with me, I believe."

"I wondered how long it would take you to score," Jude said snidely.

Dagney chuckled. "OK, this is where we turn in."

There was a barely discernible path. As they were pushing branches aside, Jude spotted Miluna in the distance, watching them. Jude started to wave, but decided not to. The narrow path took them along the foothills and through dense woods. When they finally emerged into a clearing Jude could see a foot bridge that crossed the river, and beyond that, the Wright Estate.

* * * * *

Pam was sitting outside her tent making tuneless dirge-like sounds on her harmonica when Gresh and Joyce arrived, hand in hand, all grins.

Toni trotted into the camp a few minutes later. "Where's my sweetie? Honore told me she was here."

"She's probably off walking on water somewhere," Gresh said. She looked at Joyce. "Oops."

Joyce punched her arm, then kissed her where she'd punched, then kissed her neck.

Toni rummaged through the cooler and came out with a can of Pepsi. "Seriously, where's Jude?"

"She went somewhere with Dagney," Pam said.

"I bet that scumbag is putting the make on her," Toni said.

"Nah." Gresh shook her head.

"Didn't you ever notice how she looks at her?"

"Dagney looks at every woman that way."

"I'm going to go look for her," Toni said after a while.

Pam put her hand on Toni's arm. "She's not at Circle Edge."

"What do you mean? Where is she?"

"Somewhere where La can't get her," Pam said guiltily.

Toni's eyes pierced Pam. "Tell me what's going on," she demanded.

"OK, OK, I will," Pam said nervously. "Now keep in mind the reason we did it, all right?" She moved back a little from Toni. "We figured we had to come up with some way to get Jude out of here. That's what you wanted too, remember," she said defensively. "Our plan worked real well, Toni. Jude's safe."

"Safe where?" Toni demanded.

Pam lit a cigarette and tossed the match into the fire pit. "In a cabin in the mountains. Dagney told her that her sister wanted to talk with her. She took Jude to Martha's cafe and then Martha drove them to this cabin way out in the mountains somewhere, supposedly so she and Jude could have a good place to talk. It worked just like we planned it, Toni. Dagney and Martha had already gotten the cabin ready. Nailed boards over the bedroom window and put a lock on the door."

"What?" Toni looked incredulously at Pam. "You bastards. How dare you!"

"Toni, come on. We saved her life. That's what counts."

Toni ran her fingers through her hair. She got up and paced for several seconds, then faced Pam. "Is she all alone there?"

"This friend of Martha's named Lace is staying with her. Jude's fine, Toni. Really. She's got TV, books, music. Plenty to eat. Martha's doing the cooking. She's safe now, Toni. This whole nightmare is almost over. We're just going to keep her there until September first comes and goes, just four more days."

Toni was calmer. "Hm-m, like protective custody," she said.

"You're not mad at us?" Pam asked tentatively.

"I wish you had told me sooner." Toni shook her head and sighed. "I'm sure Jude is plenty mad." She looked at Pam. "But like you said, what's important is that she's safe." She was nodding. "Yes, that's what counts. I think she should stay right where she is."

Pam scrutinized Toni.

"I want to be with her, though," Toni said. "I'll stay with her at the cabin until after Thursday comes and goes."

"I don't think you should go."

"Of course I'm going to go, Pam. I want to be with her."

"But, uh . . . well, I don't know where the cabin is."

Toni eyed her closely. "Well, then I'll have to find out from Dagney."

253

Pam looked very uncomfortable.

* * * * *

They found Dagney at the Dome.

"Congratulations," Toni said, smiling.

Dagney cocked her head. "Really?"

"Of course. This is what we came here for, right? To stop Jude from getting killed. I wouldn't have been able to do it the way you did, but I'm sure as hell glad it's done."

"Did you tell her whose cabin it is?" Dagney asked Pam.

"No," Pam said, "but she wants to go there to be with Jude."

"Toni," Dagney said, "there's this little part of me that just doesn't quite one-hundred-percent believe that you're as happy about what we did as you say."

"I think it was a pragmatic choice," Toni said, "under the circumstances."

"Exactly."

"I want to be with Jude."

"I'd hate to see our plan foiled. I think it's too risky to let you see her. She might talk you into letting her go. She can be very persuasive, you know, if you buy her premises."

"Like the right to self-determination," Toni snapped.

"See." Dagney looked at Pam. Pam looked down. "We'll take you to her at midnight, September first," Dagney said to Toni.

"Goddamn it, Dagney, who put you in charge?" Toni glared at her. "I insist you tell me where she is."

Dagney shook her head. "We didn't invite you or Gresh to participate because we didn't think you had the stomach for it. Right, Pam? And I still don't think you do."

"Come on," Toni said, her tone conciliatory. "I'm not going to let her go. You think I want her dead?"

"I think you have some ideas that would make it very hard for you to justify keeping her imprisoned."

"Of course it's hard. Isn't it hard for you?"

Dagney shrugged. "Not really. I've never been an idealist."

"You can blindfold me," Toni said.

Dagney shook her head. "No, Toni, I think it's better that you don't go to the cabin at all . . . until after September first."

The argument continued. Toni tried assurances, even threats. Dagney was adamant. Pam said nothing. At last, Toni left angrily, not saying goodbye to either of them.

CHAPTER 28

Toni found Amagyne at Circle House and asked to speak with her privately. Amagyne took Toni to a small alcove.

"Jude's been kidnapped," Toni said. "She's being held prisoner somewhere, until after September first. I don't know where."

Amagyne nodded. "Yes, it is what we suspected. Miluna saw her and Dagney leaving Circle Edge."

"They took her for her own protection, because they're convinced she's going to die at the Ceremony of Emergence."

The edges of Amagyne's mouth were tight as she listened.

"If we can prove she's not," Toni continued, "then they'll free her. The only way to prove this is by reading the *Fruit of She*."

Amagyne shook her head.

"La has to let me and Dagney read that book. If there's nothing in it about the Catalyst dying, then Jude will be freed."

"No," Amagyne said, still shaking her head. "That cannot be done, Toni."

"Why not? Dagney and I aren't Kwo-amians, so our reading the book shouldn't do any harm."

"No one reads the *Fruit of She*," Amagyne said.

"Don't be so damn rigid!" Toni was about to say more, but calmed herself.

"Were you part of the kidnapping?" Amagyne asked.

"No! I think what they did is disgusting. I want to free her. I'm asking for your help."

"Of course," Amagyne said. "Let us work together, but the *Fruit of She* cannot be read. Tell me what you know about the kidnapping."

Toni shook her head. "I've told you all I'm going to." She rose and left the room.

* * * * *

Martha was filling napkin holders when Toni arrived at the cafe. They went to the waitresses' booth. Martha seemed nervous.

"Pam told me what you guys did," Toni said. She smiled as brightly as she could. "I wish I'd had the nerve to do something like that myself. What a relief." She kept smiling. "I bet she's damn angry."

Martha eyed her skeptically. "Who?" she said. Her lips twitched.

"Jude," Toni said. "Now that you've saved her life, our next challenge will be to get her to forgive us. What do you think the chances are of getting her to give up Kwo-amity altogether?"

Martha's face took on a puzzled expression. "What are you talking about, Toni?"

"Hey, it's all right. I know all about it. The cabin, the lock on the bedroom door, your friend, Lace. It sounds like you planned it real well."

Martha let out her breath in a long sigh. Her eyes were teary. "Do you believe they were going to kill her?"

"I believe it enough to know that one way or another I was going to get her out of there." Toni smiled again. "But you and Dagney did it instead. So you're the heroes, I can live with that."

"Dagney was sure you wouldn't go for the idea."

"I wish I had thought of it. Of course I didn't have access to a cabin. Whose is it anyway?"

Martha cocked her head. "Didn't Dagney tell you?"

"She just said your friend, Lace, is involved."

Martha seemed deep in thought.

"I brought Jude's toothbrush and some clothes and stuff. Do you think she'll be glad to see me?"

"Did Dagney say you can see her?"

"Of course she did. She thought you'd give me a ride to the cabin or else give me directions how to get there."

"Dagney could have given them to you if she

wanted you to have them. Wait until September first passes, Toni. I'm sorry. I'm sure this is hard for you but Dagney and I discussed it. We don't think you'd deal well with seeing Jude locked up. I'm not either, I feel guilty as hell."

"I'll deal with it, Martha. I want to see her."

Martha shook her head.

Toni persisted but got no further than she had with Dagney. She thought about hiding somewhere near the cafe, then following Martha when she went to visit Jude.

Instead, she drove to the Doray Furniture Works. She found Joe Alta bent over a lathe. He turned off the motor when he saw her.

"I'm Jude's friend, Toni," Toni said. "Do you remember? We met once at Martha's house, a couple of years ago."

He nodded. "The professor," he said.

"I'm looking for Martha. I was supposed to meet her at her friend Lace's, but I forgot Lace's last name and I lost her address."

"She's the black one," Joe Alta said. "Nice enough girl, I guess. Hell, I don't know her name or address either. She works in that weird little store with all the bins of grain and the brown fruit. On Main Street. I bet they could tell you her address."

* * * * *

Lace's employer at the health food store told Toni that Lace was taking a few days off work, "to relax somewhere in the mountains," he said. He wasn't sure where but he knew Lace had a friend named Kelly O'Brien who owned a cabin outside of Wandry,

259

a town about fifteen miles from Doray. "Lace goes there sometimes," he said.

Toni found Kelly O'Brien on her lunch break at the lumber mill. She was very thin with straight blonde hair parted in the center. She was not at all talkative.

"Maybe they didn't tell you why they needed to borrow your cabin," Toni said. "They kidnapped someone and they have her locked up there in the bedroom. They nailed boards over the bedroom window. I'm sure they told you they'd repair any damage but did they mention the kidnapping?"

Kelly wrapped the remains of her sandwich in the aluminum foil she was using as a plate. She had eaten less than half of it.

"I apologize for spoiling your meal," Toni said, "but I take kidnapping very seriously." She paused. "And so do the police." She watched Kelly's face. It seemed to lose color.

"Your participation is like the driver of the getaway car in a burglary." Toni paused again. "In other words you will be considered an accessory when this comes to trial."

"They told me they were just playing a practical joke on someone." Kelly's voice was shaky.

"Some joke," Toni said.

* * * * *

Toni and Kelly stopped first at Circle Edge to get Gresh. Joyce came along also. Kelly remained wide-eyed the whole time and didn't say a word except to tell Toni the directions to the cabin.

260

When they arrived, Toni went alone to the cabin door. The other women waited outside. She knocked.

"Come on in, it's open," someone called.

A lanky black woman was stretched out in the easy chair near the chained bedroom door. She gasped at the sight of Toni.

"I've come to free her," Toni said, hands on hips, staring fiercely at Lace. "Move aside."

Lace straightened up in the chair. "I don't believe we've met."

"Toni Dilano."

"Toni!" Jude called from behind the bedroom door.

Lace's face held a hint of a smile.

Toni strode forward and unhooked the heavy chain. Jude was in her arms in an instant.

"I was thinking of letting her go anyway," Lace mumbled.

Gresh and Joyce came into the cabin and embraced Jude.

"Dagney told me Jude was suicidal," Lace went on, "but then Jude told me all about Kwo-amity, and I was seriously thinking of letting her go. Of course, Martha wouldn't have liked it," she added. "Hi, Kelly."

Tears streamed down Jude's cheeks as Toni held her again and told her how upset she had been, and how much she loved her.

CHAPTER 29

When they got to the main road, Toni suggested that Gresh head toward Denver rather than back to Circle Edge. "We could get a flight to Chicago, and you could rest up at home," she said to Jude.

Jude wasn't amused. "I'd like to see Dagney's face when she finds out I'm free."

"I wish you *were* free," Toni said sadly.

"I wish you people could give up that ridiculous idea about my dying," Jude responded.

When they got to Circle Edge, Toni and Jude went to Jude's room. Jude vented her anger at her

sister and Dagney, and said how glad she was that
Toni hadn't tried to usurp her right to make her own
choices. Toni admitted that she was tempted.

"You know what's weird?" Jude said. "I feel like
I can never forgive Dagney. She's a bulldozer, an
incorrigible controller. But for some reason, it feels
different with Martha. They both imprisoned me,
but . . ."

"You know Martha did it because she loves you."

Jude's eyes held tears. "She used to love me but I
don't know anymore. She was terrible at the cabin.
So cold to me." Jude let go of Toni's hand. "I think
I'll call her."

"Good luck," Toni said. "I'm going to go to the
camp. I want to see how Dagney's handling the
news."

As soon as Toni left, Jude phoned her sister. The
conversation was strained. They were both upset.

"I meant it when I said I want to help finance a
restaurant for you," Jude said at one point.

"I meant it when I said I'm not interested,"
Martha responded. "You just take care of your Circle
Edge friends. To hell with your family."

"Martha," Jude said angrily, "do you really think
I should do what *you* want with my inheritance,
rather than what *I* want?"

"I think you're lost," Martha said, also angry. "I
did what I could, but it's hopeless."

"You're writing me off pretty easily, *sister.*"

Martha was silent awhile. "I suppose it could be
seen that way."

"You said my inheritance would never come
between us."

Crying, Martha said, "I just can't accept you the way you are now. I'm not like Mom. I can't give that unconditional love. I loved you for who you were and you're no longer the Jude I loved. I don't love Laki-Seone, not one bit, and I never will!"

"I see," Jude said coolly. "Well, that's pretty clear."

"I don't think it is," Martha said, her voice choked. "I'm not saying you have to be what I want you to be for me to love you. You're a lesbian. I never had a problem with that. I think I'm pretty accepting, but Jude, the Kwo-amity stuff is too much. They've made you into somebody else. I've lost the sister I've always loved. Not only that, I've lost my dream for the life I've hoped for for years. Can't you understand my perspective?"

"Yes," Jude said quietly.

Neither spoke for a while.

"Come to Circle Edge on Thursday, Martha. Be here for it. See what happens."

"I'll think about it," Martha said.

"Mom's coming."

"I know."

"I'm not going to die."

Martha was crying miserably. So was Jude. "I love you, Martie," Jude said through her sobs, "and I always will."

After she hung up Jude sat for a long time, her thoughts shifting from Martha to Toni, and to Amagyne, and then to Dagney and Pam. The captivity in the cabin was already feeling like a dim memory. It had happened. Everyone knew why. And now it was over. Jude wanted to see Pam.

Three Guardian Edgers were waiting outside her

264

room, Sarah among them. "Amagyne said we have to take better precautions now," Sarah told her. "She wants us to watch over you."

They accompanied Jude to the camp, walking several paces behind her, their Mace and stun guns in their belts.

Dagney was the first to see Jude. "Congratulations," she said with a big smile. "Now you're free to choose." She tilted her head. "No hard feelings?"

Jude ignored her. Toni was on the hammock near Pam and Gresh. Jude started toward them.

"I see your bodyguards are near," Dagney said.

"And you know why better than anyone else," Jude replied. "Hi, people," she said to Toni and Gresh and Pam.

Pam looked everywhere but at Jude.

"I was just sitting here trying to figure out how you can tell for sure what's right and what's wrong," Gresh said to Jude. "Ethical dilemmas are very intriguing."

"It's wrong to use force except in self-defense," Jude said. "How's that for starters?"

"Limited," Gresh said. "What about using force to defend others? What about locking up check forgers? What about coercively preventing someone from committing suicide?"

"I'm neither a check forger nor suicidal," Jude said. "How come Pam won't look at me?"

"She thinks you're angry."

"And she thinks I'm suicidal."

"Well, not exactly," Gresh said. "What Pam actually thinks is that you're too irrational right now to make self-protective judgments. She does hope

265

though that when the moment actually comes, you'll have enough survival instinct left to tell the Kwo-amians to take a flying leap. She's assuming they're not going to shoot you or knife you or decapitate you. She's assuming you will be asked to do it by your own hand. And as doubtful as she is about your ability to judge rationally, she does retain some hope."

"I'm so glad to hear that. And does she regret her complicity in my kidnapping?"

"Well, she does take exception to characterizing your detainment as kidnapping. Since she defines the act as protecting a loved on, her main regret is that it didn't work. Nonetheless, fearing that you see it all quite differently, she chooses not to look at you."

"I see."

"Some of us think she wanted you rescued. After all, she did tattle. If it weren't for her, you'd still be doing cabin time."

"Do you think I should thank her?"

"You might consider that."

"She's still not looking at me."

"That's true."

"I can't stand this!" Pam shouted. Her head was buried in her hands.

"Oops, I think I heard her speak," Jude said.

"Come on, Pam. Face up to it, make up, and get it over with," Gresh said.

Pam sneaked a peek at Jude. Jude shrugged.

"I don't want to talk about it," Pam said.

"I think she wants you to beg her to let you forgive her," Gresh said.

Toni laughed. "You idiots."

Jude looked at Pam, waiting.

"Do you want to forgive me?" Pam asked quietly.

"Do you want to apologize or anything?" Jude returned.

"Apologize? Yeah, I'm sorry you got upset by what happened, the cabin and all. I'm sorry we had to do it."

Jude turned to Gresh. "Is that an apology?"

Gresh laughed. "Sort of."

"OK, I accept your sort-of apology. Step forward for your hug."

There was much laughter as they warmly embraced, but tears as well.

"Who are those women talking to Gresh?" Jude asked awhile later.

"People she knows from Chicago," Pam said. "A whole bunch of them came."

"So the Chicago lezzie feminists are here," Jude said. "I wonder why. Surely they're not Kwo-amians."

"This is a big women's event."

Jude nodded. "Unlike any other," she said.

* * * * *

The following day, Toni and Pam were sharing a bowl of popcorn at Ambrosia. "There's the Catalyst," Pam said, as Jude came in the side door.

Jude was flushed with excitement. "Look what Amagyne gave me!" she held out her hand. "This ring belonged to La's mother. La gave it to Amagyne to keep until it was time to give it to me. Isn't it beautiful?"

It was a large, perfectly circular ruby, set in silver.

"Very beautiful," Toni said.

"I get this wonderful feeling just looking at it. It seems to be so full of meaning . . . energy . . ." Jude was glowing. "Everything feels so right. Everything is going to work out right. Everything."

Pam looked out the window.

Toni looked at her watch. "We better get going. We have to go to town to buy stuff for the party. Want to come with us, Jude?"

Jude looked at the trio of Guardian Edgers who were sitting on the other side of the room watching them. "I have a date with Miluna. I'm giving her a flute lesson."

"You are coming to the party, aren't you?" Toni said.

"Of course. Little Chicago right here at Circle Edge. I wouldn't miss it."

Pam was staring at Jude.

"What?" Jude asked.

"I don't know." Her eyes were teary. "I have a weird feeling."

Jude put her arm around Pam's shoulders. "That's because you're such a weird person. Is it about me dying?"

Pam nodded.

"My great-grandmother lived to be ninety-six. I'm going to outdo her by at least four years."

"You'll be a wrinkled up toothless hag."

"I'll be very sexy."

"You probably will."

"See you at the party," Jude said.

* * * * *

The Chicago gathering was rollicking and rowdy.

Gresh and three women from the Lesbian Alliance were huddled on a blanket under a tree discussing the pros and cons of separatism. Leslie played bongos while others danced. The smell of marijuana was in the air. A group of five played poker at a card table near the tents, Dagney among them. Gresh and Toni were adding more sherbet to the bucket of punch when Joyce arrived.

"Have you seen Jude?" Toni asked her.

"No, Doralee told me she saw her . . . oh, maybe an hour or so ago. Don't you like calling her Laki-Seone?"

"Not really. Saw her where?"

"Leaving with La. They took a car. La was wearing her caramel-colored cape, Doralee said. She only wears that for very special occasions."

Toni frowned angrily. "You mean they left Circle Edge?"

"Yes." Joyce dipped a paper cup into the punch. "Laki-Seone was supposed to come to the party, wasn't she? Don't worry, Toni, she'll probably come later."

"I have to worry," Toni snapped. "Your people want to kill her."

CHAPTER 30

The blue of La's eyes was truly the same blue as the sky. Jude commented on it.

"Yes, the color surprised my mother. My grandfather was black."

"I didn't know that."

"I never knew him," La said. She scanned the mountainous vista. "This is a good place. You couldn't have chosen a better one."

Jude looked with deep affection at La, fingering the ruby ring.

La took in long breaths of the cool mountain air. The sun glistened on her snowy hair. "I didn't know I would grow this fond of you, Laki-Seone."

"I felt drawn to you from the beginning."

La looked deeply into Jude's eyes. "Your choice was always meant to be a difficult one, my child."

The words evoked an ominous feeling in Jude. She took the bottle of water La had brought and drank deeply from it. She offered it to La, but La shook her head.

"Kwo-am believes that your acceptance of her truths is full enough that you will not shirk from what is required of you at the Emergence . . ."

As La continued speaking, Jude's anxiety intensified. She took more water to soothe her dry mouth and throat. At one point, La began to hum and Jude immediately felt the calming effect. La talked of how Jude's spirit would be with Kwo-am. ". . . a reprieve from the physical world, a sojourn in the state of pure Monama. Hmm-mm." The edges of Jude's mouth twitched, but the humming entered her and soothed her.

"Artists will paint your image."

Jude could feel herself floating, joining Kwo-am, running through the woods, a deer; an eagle flying the skies. She felt light-headed. Her breathing was shallow.

At last, the humming stopped and soon after that Jude opened her eyes. She stared into the distance. Her face felt flushed. "It frightens me," she said.

La nodded. "Kwo-am trusts you to fulfill the Emergence despite your fear. I trust you also."

Jude wrapped her arms around herself. Her eyes

were stinging and she was shivering. "Is there no other way?" she asked, knowing what the answer would be.

"This is the only way," La said. "Your fear and doubt is part of it," she added sadly. "Zetka's countermove. You must struggle with it and you must choose."

Jude stared at a patch of thistle wedged between two large rocks. Both she and La were silent for a long time. Jude was feeling dazed, as if spinning through a surreal world. She realized that her whole body was trembling. "Continual Monama," she said. "It will be so glorious."

"Yes," La assured her. "You and Kwo-am will be one. Pure ecstasy."

Jude was swaying, her eyes closed. La's arm was around her. She rested her head on La's shoulder. She took deep breaths and she let herself dream.

* * * * *

When Jude and La returned to Circle Edge, Jude went to her room and lay down on her bed. La went to speak to Amagyne.

Amagyne's face was tense as she listened to the Sage. And then, for the first time ever, she questioned La. La answered her patiently, showing full understanding of Amagyne's distress. "I know this is difficult for you to accept," she said. "It was difficult for me as well."

"It's not that I have any doubt Kwo-am can perform miracles. My own birth is the greatest proof of that," Amagyne said. "And yet . . ." She looked silently out the window at the great mountains.

272

* * * * *

Jude felt warm arms encircle her. She opened her
eyes. "Oh, hello, hon." She yawned. "I fell asleep."

"I noticed. We missed you at the party."

Jude sat up, groggy. "I was dreaming about you.
You and Becka. I was watching you from above. I
was a sparrow and you were loving Becka."

"Dumb dream," Toni said. She pulled a pillow
behind her back.

Suddenly Jude felt woozy. The memory of what
La had told her came rushing back. She felt a sinking
fear, but immediately shook it off. The feeling of
excitement came then. "There will be another
miracle," she said.

Toni looked askance at her. "Don't tell me you're
with child."

Jude smiled. "This one will be even more
impressive. But I can't tell you. You'll have to wait
until tonight when La tells everyone."

"So many secrets," Toni said caustically. She was
tapping her hand nervously on her leg. "Want to
take a trip to Tahiti for a few days?"

"Later," Jude said. "What time is it?" She looked
out the window. "The meeting starts at dusk."

"There's plenty of time," Toni said. She began
stroking Jude's leg. "Your bodyguards are playing
cards in the hallway." Her hand wandered to Jude's
crotch.

"They won't bother us," Jude said.

Toni slowly moved her fingers. Jude felt herself
responding. *This could be the last time*, she thought,
for a long, long time. She pulled Toni on top of her

and kissed her deeply. Toni's shuddering response brought shudders to Jude. Their lovemaking was as intense and powerful as it had ever been. Thoughts suspended, Jude whirled in the world of timeless erotic sensations. Hot and flying, liquid and smooth and thunderous. Afterwards she felt both drained and full. She held Toni tightly to her and wouldn't let go.

* * * * *

As darkness came to Circle Edge, masses of women walked to the Amit. There was a cheery buzz in the air. Joyce and Gresh were hand-in-hand behind Toni and Pam. Dagney had gone ahead with Ella. Jude sat on a bench in the center of the Amit with La and Amagyne. Women were seated all along the Amit, far up the hills. Never before had so many people been there at one time.

Music began, the full Edge Orchestra playing first and then flutes taking over to play the *Coming of the Catalyst*. Voices joined in. Afterwards drums rolled and La stood up, tall and straight.

When the drums stopped, the silence was profound. When La broke it her voice sounded as if it came from the stars. "Kwo-am has brought us here!"

"We come from Kwo-am," a chorus of voices pealed.

"We have waited long. And now the Catalyst is here," La said.

The cheering voices and whistles and yells were deafening. The cheering did not stop. Jude felt dizzy. And still the outpouring continued until finally La raised her arms.

"Kwo-am brings us life and love."

The torches reflected flickering light on her caramel-colored cloak. Jude could see the pain in her face.

"Zetka demands cruel payment," La said. "Yet even in his cruelty Kwo-am finds the good." She paused. "Two days from now will be the thirtieth anniversary of Laki-Seone's birth, and the day of her greatest choice."

"She must choose," a score of voices called.

"There was a very great revealment made many years ago, a truth which only now am I able to share with you."

The waiting crowd was hushed.

"Hear this news for it is good news, though it is difficult."

The only sound was the soft brush of the wind. Thousands of eyes watched La in absolute silence. Toni was shivering and Pam put her arm around her.

La continued. "Zetka proclaims that no being living for thirty years in the world he helped form could possibly emerge unscathed enough to believe that Kwo-am's energy can ever truly prevail. So Zetka says. Is he right? Or is he wrong?"

"He is wrong!" hundreds of voices yelled, Jude's among them.

"Yet Zetka proclaims that our Catalyst's faith will fail her when the moment comes, the moment when Zetka's ultimate countermove must be enacted, when the price Laki-Seone must pay to begin the New Page . . ."

Total silence awaited La's next words. Even the wind was still.

275

". . . is her own earthly life."

The silence was unbroken, until at last there came some humming.

Toni was gripping Pam's hand so tightly Pam had to tap her to loosen it. "Oh God," Toni moaned, "I kept hoping it wasn't true."

"Kwo-am proclaims that the Catalyst will choose the New Page, that she has the faith and courage to fulfill the Emergence, to drink of the cup that will take her earthly body and free her limitless kwo-ami to free us all from Zetka's deadly grip."

"The woman's insane," Dagney hissed.

"If she fulfills Zetka's demand and dies, then Kwo-am's next move will be set into motion. Guided by Laki-Seone's energy, we will go forth and spread the truth, swelling our numbers. And when we are enough, we shall all converge our kwo-ami at the same moment, throughout the world, and through the Great Convergence, Laki-Seone shall rise from her tomb! She will come back to life!"

"Yes, we will make her live again!" a woman near the front screamed.

Dagney glared at the women all around her. "Are you idiots going to swallow this crap?"

". . . . and the growing numbers of kwo-omnis will eventually bring the complete expulsion of zetkap, and Kwo-world will be here!" La's arms were raised high in the air, the torchlight glittering on her white hair.

There was murmuring and whispering.

"What an arch manipulator," Pam snarled.

Toni could not speak. She stared at Jude who stood solemn and unblinking at La's side.

"I'd say it's time to bring in the cops," Dagney said to Gresh.

"Laki-Seone must choose!" La's voice boomed.

"She must choose," came the echo.

"Zetka is sure she will falter and fail," La said.

There were hisses from several enclaves around the Amit.

"God, is she setting it up. What a pro," Dagney said to Pam.

"Kwo-am is sure she will maintain the faith," La continued, "in Kwo-am and in all of us."

A flute began to play. La stood quietly, her arm solidly across Jude's shoulders. More flutes joined it. Women began to stand. Drums and other instruments played. Candles were lit and the snake dance began. Hundreds of women danced, winding around the Amit, but hundreds did not. Some walked quietly away. Others talked among themselves.

Jude danced alongside Amagyne, and when the dance ended, they went toward the Dome. They were surrounded and shielded by Guardian Edgers, the Firstcomers, and many other Kwo-amians. Toni could not get near Jude.

"It's murder," Pam said. "I don't care if ten thousand witnesses say she drank the poison freely. It's still murder."

"Let's hope she refuses to drink it," Gresh said.

"You saw her. You see what she's like. She's in their power." Pam's voice was gritty with anger. "She has no will, they've taken it from her. She'll drink the poison all right. And if we do nothing about it, then we're guilty of her murder too."

* * * * *

The campsites were buzzing with the heated discussion of circles of women. Great tension was in the air. At the Chicago women's camp, nearly a dozen people had gathered.

"My guess is that it's meant symbolically," Gresh's friend, Val, said. "Do you know about their Avowal Ritual? They kill a bird, but it's not really dead. They just sedate it, and when it comes to, they act as if it's an actual rebirth. I bet this will be the same."

"That's not the impression I got," Gresh said.

"Maybe everyone's supposed to believe it's real," Val offered hopefully, "even Jude, as a test of faith or something. She'll go to sleep and everyone will think she's dead and they'll put her in the tomb, only later they'll sneak her out and take her away somewhere and keep her drugged up until the Convergence, and then —"

"Wishful thinking," Pam said.

"I sure wouldn't count on it," Gresh added.

Toni arrived at the camp. "Guess where Jude is." She plopped down on the blanket next to Pam and Dagney.

"Where?" Dagney said. "Getting her head shaved?"

"She's with Theresa, their lawyer. She's making out her will."

"Fuck," Pam hissed.

"They wouldn't let me near her."

"You still think it's symbolic?" Dagney said to Val.

"We have less than forty-eight hours to get her out of here," Pam said.

278

"They guard her like hawks."

"Yeah, only she's the chicken."

"I say we go to the sheriff and tell him exactly what's going on at this nut house," Dagney said.

"What do you think the police would do if we told them?" Toni asked.

"Investigate, at the very least," Dagney responded. "There're enough women here upset about this impending murder to give the cops a good earful. If the sheriff gets enough witnesses saying there's a sacrificial death about to take place, I bet they'd stop it."

"The thought of it makes me sick," Gresh said. "Can you picture it? A bunch of hick cops with shotguns smashing their way in and busting heads and dragging people off."

"I don't think they'd even investigate," Pam said. "They'd say there's no crime, only talk. They'd say there's nothing they could act on. Besides, to me that's the absolute last resort. What else could we do to stop it?"

"Gather allies," Gresh suggested. "I think there are a lot of disgruntled people here now."

"Maybe it's really true though," Joyce said. Her voice was hoarse. "Maybe Laki-Seone really will be reborn and the New Page —"

"Stifle yourself," Dagney said, looking at Joyce disgustedly.

Pam shot a warning look at Dagney.

"I've got an idea," said Dagney. "We kidnap Lorn and threaten to kill her if La doesn't send Jude out of here and call off the Ceremony." Dagney suddenly grabbed a handful of her hair and pulled it. "Son of

279

a bitch! I can't believe what I just said." Gresh reached over and touched Dagney's shoulder. "I think I'm losing it," Dagney mumbled.

"What about letting everybody know that Amagyne and Jude had a father?" Pam suggested.

"I've already told dozens of them," Dagney said. "They think I'm Zetka's right-hand woman. All I've done by talking about it is make a bunch of enemies. We'd have to prove it."

"What are you talking about?" Joyce asked. "What father?"

"I wish Maggie were here," Gresh said. "Jude's mother is coming. Maybe if she told her story, and if we could get Maggie here, and if Jude would speak up too . . ."

Toni shook her head. "Jude believes Kise was Kwo-am incarnate."

"So does Lorn," Dagney said.

"Who's Kise?" Joyce asked.

"That's what they'd all end up believing. It didn't shake Jude's confidence in La." Toni sighed with exasperation. "Nor, apparently, has the fact that she has to die, and that they're making her will the Lake Valley over to them."

"Facts don't reach them," Gresh said.

"Hear ye, hear ye!" Two women walked into the camp. They were both tall and thin, and wearing cut-off blue jeans. "Hear ye, hear ye!" All eyes took them in.

"Sorry to interrupt. We're the human bulletin board making the rounds to spread the word."

"So, spread," Dagney said. "Did La part the waters of Wright Lake or get swallowed by a whale or what?"

Several other women who had been passing by stopped to listen. "That's Rosemary," Joyce whispered to Gresh, pointing to one of them. "She's the one I mentioned this morning."

"La's old friend from Brooklyn?" The woman Joyce indicated was standing a few yards away from them. She was gray-haired and wore a print blouse and polyester slacks.

One of the news-bringers was speaking. "We've been asked to let everyone know that, as of tonight, anyone who leaves the Circle Edge grounds will not be allowed back in."

There were a few sounds of protest and surprise.

"Why's that?" Pam asked indignantly.

"This will be in effect until after the Ceremony of Emergence," one of the announcers added. "It's a safety precaution. We have plenty of food if anyone runs short."

"Then I assume you're not letting any new arrivals in," Dagney said.

"Only those on the list," the woman answered. "Mainly Kwo-amians who haven't yet arrived. And a few others."

Joyce caught Rosemary's eye and beckoned her over. She introduced her to Gresh.

The announcers left and the women began buzzing among themselves about what they'd heard and how they felt about it.

Gresh gave Rosemary her chair, and sat on the cooler next to her. "Joyce tells me you knew La way back," Gresh said.

"Yes, she's certainly come a long way."

"So tell me about her. What was she like back in Brooklyn?"

Rosemary looked at Joyce. "You didn't tell her about . . ."

"No," Joyce said.

"About what?" Gresh pressed.

"I was going to tell you but . . ." Joyce seemed uncertain. "When I met Rosemary this morning at Ambrosia, we got to talking and she mentioned about knowing La back in New York. And then she said something about . . . she said she wondered what ever happened to La's son."

Gresh's head jerked back a good four inches. "La has a son?"

Dagney turned toward her. "What's this?"

"Of course I told her it was impossible," Joyce said. "I said she must have her confused with someone else."

Rosemary shook her head. "Oh, no. I'm not confused at all. I may be old but my brains aren't rattled yet. She had a son all right."

Dagney had pulled her chair next to Joyce. Pam joined them also, along with three or four other women from their group. Rosemary seemed uncomfortable to suddenly be the center of attention.

"Tell us about it," Gresh said.

Rosemary cleared her throat. "We lived next door to each other on Spruce Street. That was back in the mid-nineteen-forties. Her name was Lavender then. She had changed it from Alice Fenster. She and I were friends for a while. Our sons went to the same high school. Then later I heard from another friend, Laura, that Lavender had started some religious movement or something. When Laura got involved in the religion she and I sort of drifted apart and then she went off with Lavender out west along with some

282

other women. I guess by then Lavender had changed her name again. To La.

"I once mentioned La's son to Laura and she said La did *not* have a son. I didn't push it. So La wanted it to be a secret. It meant nothing to me. Anyway, years went by and I never really thought about La again." Rosemary looked around at the faces. All eyes were glued on her. "Until a few weeks ago," she said.

"I saw an article in some lesbian newspaper about Circle Edge and this big ceremony." Rosemary shrugged. "I had no plans. So . . . well, I came. All this stuff is really strange to me, I have to confess. I'm Presbyterian myself. I don't know why I'm here." She looked around the group as if to see if anyone had the answer. "I enjoyed seeing Laura again."

"You're absolutely sure he was her son," Dagney said.

"Oh, yes, of course. He was sixteen years old the last time I saw him. Charlie told me Kise didn't come to school anymore."

"What?" Toni nearly slipped from the rock she was sitting on. "What did you say?"

"Charlie, my son, he said that —"

"No, the name! What name did you say? La's son."

"Kise. His name was Kise."

"Holy shit!"

CHAPTER 31

Gresh was calm enough to make a suggestion. "I think we should take a walk over to Lorn's place. Do you mind, Rosemary? There's someone I think it's very important for you to meet."

Joyce led the way to Lorn's cabin, with Rosemary, Gresh, Toni, Pam and Dagney following. There was little conversation, though occasionally Dagney could be heard chuckling.

Lorn welcomed her guests warmly, although she seemed slightly cool towards Dagney.

When everyone was seated, Dagney began.

"There's been an interesting development. Rosemary knew La in Brooklyn. Like you did. But you never said anything about Kise being La's son."

Lorn looked disdainfully at Dagney. "How utterly absurd."

"Tell her, Rosemary," Dagney said.

Rosemary licked her lips nervously. "This is all very strange to me," she said. "I don't want to make trouble or anything."

"Not to worry," Dagney said. "Tell Lorn about Kise."

Lorn's jaw muscles were moving rhythmically.

"Well, he was a sweet boy," Rosemary began. "Very gentle. He was Oriental, you know. Part Chinese."

Lorn's jaw moved faster.

"And he was very artistic. I remember that. He did sculptures. A quiet-spoken boy. My husband and I used to wonder if he was . . . you know, well, it was my husband mostly. He thought Kise might be a fairy or whatever . . . gay, I guess they say nowadays." Rosemary was watching Lorn and seeming very uncomfortable.

"Anything more about Kise?" Gresh asked.

"Well, Lavender — La, that is — she worshipped the boy. I never did see a mother so devoted to her child, before or since. Maybe that's why he turned out, you know, gay, if he did." Rosemary was stumbling on her words. "Or maybe he died and that's why Lavender got involved with religion. Do you think maybe he died?"

"Yes," Lorn said. Her voice was very low. "He died." Her face was ashen. Suddenly she crumpled and sobbed. "It can't be," she murmured. "Kise

cannot be La's son. Kise was Kwo-am personified."
She held her face with both hands. "Her son! That
would mean La is Amagyne's —"

"Grandmother," Dagney said.

"And Jude's grandmother," Gresh added.

Dagney was gloating. "Which makes Jude the
daughter of the woman who seduced La's son, and
who was with him when he burned to death. La
probably holds Jude's mother responsible for his
death." She was looking directly at Lorn. "That could
make a loving mother like La quite crazy," she said.
Dagney smiled and leaned back on the sofa. "So La is
not just after the Lake Valley," she mused. "She's
been planning this for thirty years. She wants
revenge."

* * * * *

Lorn walked into the Meditation Room at the far
corner of the Dome. "I thought I'd find you here."

Amagyne and Jude were sitting before the fire.
Amagyne rose and went to her mother. "You're
crying," she said, wiping Lorn's tears.

"My soul is a lead weight."

The three sat on soft chairs in a little half-circle
in front of the dancing fire. "You love her very
much, don't you?" Lorn said.

Amagyne looked at Jude. "Very much."

"I mean La."

"I love them both. They are like blood to me,"
Amagyne said.

Jude's heart was pounding. She felt tension in the
air.

286

"And you know of *my* love for La," Lorn said.

"Yes," Amagyne replied.

Lorn took out a handkerchief and wiped her eyes. "For the first time ever, I find myself doubting her." She looked at Jude. "This settlement between Kwo-am and Zetka is not finding a good place within me. The dying and rebirth."

Amagyne nodded. "It's difficult, I know."

"It is very difficult for I have just learned something that is so unbelievable I feel like it must be a dream. You both must hear it." Tears streamed down her cheeks.

Amagyne encouraged her gently.

Lorn pressed her fist against her lips, then clasped her hands together. "I thought he was just created, magically, out of air. I never imagined that he was born like all the rest of us. Yet he was very much flesh and blood." She looked tearfully at Amagyne, her face distorted with pain. She took Amagyne's hand.

Jude could barely breathe.

"I thought you would never learn this," Lorn began, "for I believed it was supposed to be kept silent always, silent from everyone, even you. But now I must speak. This will be difficult for you, Amagyne."

Amagyne gripped her mother's hand tightly.

"It's about your father."

Amagyne's black eyes opened wide.

"You *did* have a father. A human father, at least a man who came to me in human form."

"What are you saying?" The words caught in Amagyne's throat.

"His name was Kise."

287

Jude sucked in her breath.

"But I was born of woman only, of you alone," Amagyne protested.

Lorn took her daughter in her arms. "Yes. Kwo-am came to La and revealed that that is how it must be told."

Amagyne's hands were tight fists.

"He died when you were five years old. You missed him terribly."

"I knew him?"

"Oh yes."

"I used to dream of a man with a soft voice," Amagyne said wistfully. "We'd walk in the woods. I dreamed about him often. He sang to me."

"It was not a dream. We visited him at his cabin. Many times."

"My father."

"Yes."

And mine, Jude thought, her face wet with tears.

"It was in nineteen fifty-three when La first took me to him." The reflection from the fire danced on Lorn's face. "I can still picture clearly that first moment, the first time I met him." Her eyes had become glazed. "I looked at him and my heart instantly filled with love. La had told me he was the spirit of Kwo-am, and that his essence was female. I had no doubt that this was so."

Amagyne didn't move a muscle as she listened.

"We melted together, he and I." Lorn's eyes remained hazy as she spoke. "We lay among soft down comforters and there were smooth fragrant creams and incense. We came to each other slowly. His skin was so soft. Oh, I can still feel the softness of his wonderful skin, the feel of his arms and his back, the delicious aromas of his neck where I buried my face, and of his chest where I rested my cheek."

Lorn seemed barely aware that Amagyne and Jude were in the room.

"I brought him to me, to enclose him within me. He entered me slowly, gently. I had always heard there would be pain, but there was none. I felt him within me, warm and smooth, creamy smooth along the inner walls of my being. Our movement was like rocking gently in a cradle, like rocking on the waves. Slow, rhythmic. We had merged and we moved as one, I, woman, and he, woman-spirit. And the waves continued and grew."

Lorn was staring into space. Amagyne's chest rose and fell. Jude was entranced.

"La told me that I was chosen for a special place in Kwo-amity and that this was a Mystery others were not to know. They were not to know who Kise was or that he and I had been together. We made love that one time and from it you were conceived." Lorn looked lovingly at Amagyne. "La told me the child would be called Amagyne and would be the First Guide." Lorn inhaled deeply. "She also told me that our love, mine and Kise's, would then be of the spirit alone, deep and lasting. I felt . . . I strongly wished to be with him again physically, but I accepted the way it had to be."

Lorn let go of Amagyne's hand and leaned back in her chair. Jude watched and listened wordlessly.

"La was very protective and caring of me through the pregnancy, and she was there with the midwife for your birth. We put you into warm spring water, Amagyne, as soon as you were born. As you know, there was a wonderful celebration."

Amagyne nodded.

"Several days after your birth, La and I took you to Kise, and he took you immediately to his heart."

A tear glided down each of Amagyne's cheeks.

"La and I cared for you, nurtured you. It was as if you had two mothers." Lorn smiled serenely. "From time to time we would take you to be with Kise. We would drive into the hilly woods until the road ended, Robb Road, then walk farther, to the other side of Deer Path, far beyond the usual berry-gathering and walking ground of the Edgers. That is where his cabin was. We called the visits our *special communes with the Kwo-am spirit.*"

"He held me on his knee."

"Many times. He played with you and he sang to you."

"Yes, I remember. There was a swing."

"He made it for you. Do you remember what you called him?"

"No," Amagyne said.

"Whisper. You called him *Whisper* because you knew you were not to speak of him to anyone."

"I don't remember that."

Lorn smiled wistfully. "Most of those memories are gone, I'm sure. The visits were not too frequent. Kise traveled a great deal, and he spent most of each winter away, in California where he worked on his carvings and sculptures."

Lorn looked immeasurably sad. "I never thought I would tell anyone about him, ever. Yet, when he died, I told Maggie, and now I am telling you."

Amagyne looked deathly pale. "How did he die?" she asked, her voice barely audible.

Jude's heart was pounding.

290

"In a fire," Lorn said, "when you were four years old. You and I were on our way to visit him when it happened. I saw the smoke and flames. I told you to go back to the car and wait for me. The cabin had collapsed. There was a woman there, a townswoman. She was sobbing and then she stumbled to her feet and ran away."

Tears flowed down Lorn's cheeks. Amagyne too was crying and so was Jude.

"As I got nearer, I could see him lying motionless at the edge of the burning timbers." Lorn's eyes were closed, her lower lip quivering. "I got closer and could see that he was . . . there was no life in him. Then I heard the fire engine coming and so I went back to where you were waiting and drove us home."

She wiped her eyes with the edge of her handkerchief. "We had made love only one time. He was my friend, he was the father of the only child I would ever have or want."

"I'm so sorry, Mother." Amagyne gripped Lorn's hand, weeping.

Jude felt the room spinning.

"I told Maggie what I had seen and, later, I told La. No one else." Lorn looked at Amagyne. "I thought he was Kwo-am, come to us in human form. I always believed that." She looked away. "Maybe I still do, I'm not sure." Her lip was quivering. She looked from Amagyne to Jude, then back to Amagyne. "Now I must tell you what I just learned."

"There's more?" Amagyne said numbly.

"I found out today who Kise's mother is."

Amagyne waited. Jude, too, her head straining forward.

"La," Lorn said. "Kise is her son."

Amagyne's mouth opened wide. Jude felt a tremor go through her body.

"No," Amagyne said. Her breathing came in loud rasping gasps. "I . . . I can't believe it. It couldn't be." Her facial muscles twitched. "Are you sure?"

Lorn nodded. She told Amagyne and Jude what Rosemary had told her. "She last saw him when he was sixteen years old. It was obviously Kise. La's son."

Amagyne was sagging in her chair. "What does it mean? Why? Why? I don't understand."

"She's our grandmother," Jude said.

Amagyne stared incredulously at her.

CHAPTER 32

It was nearly midnight when Amagyne left her mother and Jude and went to confront La. La did not deny that Kise was her son, and that he was the father of Amagyne and Laki-Seone.

"You should have told me," Amagyne said angrily. "It's not right that this was kept from me." She was trembling.

"I can see it seems that way to you," La said calmly. "Zetka is fighting fiercely now for his survival. He instills doubt, sending Rosemary, forcing disclosures when silence is needed. He has even infiltrated your heart, my Amagyne. Yet I was warned this could come and I was told what to do if it did. So, now I will speak. I will tell you everything and then we will tell the others, for this is how it must be."

Amagyne's hands held the arms of the chair.

"First, you should know that Kise was not an ordinary man. In a sense he was no man at all, a being beyond humanness." La folded her hands on her lap. She remained silent, eyes closed, until a peaceful look came over her face. Then she sighed. "He was the purest being who ever was born."

La's eyes narrowed. "When I was sixteen years old," she continued, "I was raped."

Amagyne gasped.

"It happened in a clinic in Brooklyn. I went there to be treated for my headaches." La touched her temples with her fingertips. "I would get very painful headaches sometimes. My mother heard that the doctor there, a Chinese man from Hong Kong, might be able to help me. He took me into the examining room. He closed the door."

"The doctor raped you and that's how Kise . . ."

La nodded. "When I found out that I was pregnant, I thought it was the end of the world. It was my fault, I believed. The pregnancy was my punishment."

La rubbed her temples.

"It was my burden, my destruction, my shame. I thought my life was over. I was ready to die and that is when Kwo-am came to me for the first time." La's voice was very low. "I had a dream and in the dream she appeared, though I didn't know it was she. I only understood dimly what the dream told me. She came

294

that one time, but never again until sixteen years later."

Amagyne took in deep lungfuls of air.

"From that life growing inside me, the dream seemed to say, would come the answer to all the pain. The word *Kwo-am* echoed in my mind. It was a new word, one I had never heard, but I knew its meaning. And the word *Zetka* was in the dream. I wrote the dream down."

La rose and walked past Amagyne to the far corner of the room. She moved more slowly than usual, as if her feet were very heavy. She got down on her knees and pulled back the rug, then lifted out a square section of flooring. She withdrew a green book.

La returned to her seat and laid the book on her lap. From among its pages she pulled out a sheet of notebook paper, yellowed with age. "I used to keep them in my dresser drawer," La said, "the dreams that I wrote out. And I used to keep this book in my wooden chest. But then I learned they needed to be hidden."

In a low voice, La began to read. "May fourteenth, nineteen-thirty-two," she began. "I dreamed I was in a beautiful hilly meadow full of wild flowers. Beneath a wild oak tree I gave birth to my child. I was not alone. There were birds and rabbits, squirrels, deer, wolves, and a black leopard. The animals chirped and pranced and chattered when the child appeared and I held it to my chest. They surrounded the baby and me and I could hear the echoing melodic words, *Kwo-am is with you and in you.* I heard the words in the air and trees around me. Then the beautiful black leopard approached us,

295

me and the child, coming close, stretching its neck. I could feel its warm breath as it bent and gently licked the baby's cheeks. *Through you it shall all begin,* the leopard said, looking into the child's eyes. Then from above and all around came the chant, *She who comes from you, born, choosing. Zetka defeated, withered and gone.* I listened to the words and I felt uplifting joy. *You are the Sage,* a voice said to me in the dream. *Through your child, Kwo-world shall arise. You know now, only you, only you are to know.*"

La's eyes were closed, the paper held loosely in her hand. "Then I could see her. My daughter. I pictured her standing there before the multitudes, grown to full womanhood, declaring the beginning of the time of pure kwo-ami, Kwo-world."

La folded the paper and slipped it back into the book. "That was the first dream. It was like no dream ever before. I knew it was more than a dream. It was a message, meant only for me. I could feel the powerful importance of the message."

La laid the book on the floor next to her. "When I awoke from that dream, I remember placing my hands on my abdomen. It was close to my time. Holding my hands here, like this . . ." She folded her fingers over her lean middle. ". . . I let the message take on its clarity. First the name, a new word that I had never before heard. Kwo-am. Named now and known now. Kwo-am, the powerful and good, God, the creator. Kwo-am coming to me to let me know that my child would be the one to defeat the dark one, Zetka, powerful and evil. Out of evil came good. From an act of violation sprang the perfect fruit."

La smiled, little lines crinkling about her eyes and mouth. "After the dream, I was a new person. So joyful, delighted now to be carrying a child. My daughter's name would be Amagyne, I knew, the word coming to me clearly out of a rainbow mist."

La's eyes welled with tears. She looked at Amagyne. "I had interpreted the dream to mean that the child I would bear would be the deliverer." Her lips pursed, La shook her head. "When the baby was born and they laid him on my middle and told me I had a healthy son, I felt myself tumbling, crashing down into a deep black abyss. I thought I had failed. I knew from the dream that the deliverer would be a woman. I thought I had failed, that Kwo-am had chosen me but I had failed. I looked at my helpless male baby and thought he was my failure.

"They called it post-partum depression, but they did not know what was happening to me. And yet the bleak heaviness did not last long." La smiled a dreamy smile.

"The child entered my heart. Failure or not, he filled my heart full. I loved my son with all of my being. Kwo-am, it seemed, had deserted me. Or perhaps the dream really had been merely a dream, I thought." La took a deep breath. "What a son he was! I have never loved anyone as much. Not my mother whom I loved relentlessly, nor you, my Amagyne, whom I love so deeply it eats my heart."

Amagyne bit her lip and tears slid from her eyes.

"He was an angel of a child. Yet I thought I had failed. There were times when I was sure the dream was only a dream and Kwo-am just a figment of my dreamy mind. I came to doubt that Kwo-am existed or that I was destined to help bring forth the destruction of Zetka. As the years passed, I became more and more convinced that none of it was real.

297

"Life was not easy for my son and me. We knew the degradation of poverty. Then the war came. Evil was winning. I searched everywhere for Kwo-am. The force of love and life was there and yet it eluded me. I sought it in all the religions I could find. I was wearing down. At last I took my child and went to an ashram in Pakistan. We stayed there for a year. An important year that replenished me. When it was time for us to leave, Ahlambrah Ti, one of my teachers, said some day I should send Kise to him and he would teach him.

"Kise and I returned to my mother's home in New York and I continued my search. Finally, years later, I learned what I was to do next." La's hands were folded and pressed against her chest. "The second dream came when Kise was sixteen years old. In it, Kise and I were walking along a deserted road in the country. We came to a fork. To the left the road was long, going far into the horizon where it disappeared into steep mountains. That was the road Kise was to travel. Along the other road the black leopard waited, calling me to come. With the leopard were many people, all women."

La sighed. "That was the second dream. At first, none of it was clear to me. It took time for my mind to be receptive to the messages. I was very confused during this time of my life. Sometimes I did not know what was real and what was not. Though at first I was unsure about the dream, gradually, it became clearer and I realized what my mission was: to begin living my calling as Sage, to be the medium, the one blessed and enabled to bring forth the word of Kwo-am. This meant that I would have to let Kise go and follow my destiny. Despite my bringing forth a son rather than a daughter, I understood that I was to proceed."

La's hands were tightly clenched in her lap. "Yet I did not want to part with my child. And I did not feel worthy of the calling." Eyes closed, she continued. "I was in torment. The dream recurred, over and over, and I knew I could not resist the message." She looked at Amagyne. "The next month, I sent Kise away."

"To Pakistan?"

"Yes, to my friend, Ahlambrah Ti. It was a wrenchingly painful separation. I told my son it was through women that I must work. He understood and yet he didn't. I had many dreams after Kise was gone, but they were upsetting to me. I was in great pain, missing Kise, trying to determine what I was supposed to do next. I met Carel then, and Laura, and Lorn and a few other women who seemed to understand.

"The dreams continued, and, little by little, it became clear what I was to do. I was to begin by traveling to the south tip of the United States and then continue by boat until I came upon land again. I did as the dream said. Carel had provided me with the boat. I sailed until I came to an island where I found a small cave high in the hills. Within the cave I found the carving, just as the dream had predicted."

"The leopard and the deer," Amagyne said, describing the carving which was kept at Circle House.

"Yes. When I found it, I knew a new dream would come, and that all would unfold." La rested her hands on the arms of the chair. "I was burning with fever as I lay there at the mouth of the cave clutching the carving. Kwo-am came to me then."

La seemed to relax as she continued. "Kwo-am spoke of her battles with Zetka, their many many struggles, including their struggle for the human soul. She spoke also of the many names by which she was known, and the confusions of humankind about her essence and her will.

"I returned home with my new understanding. I gathered the others and told them what I had learned. Laura, Carel, Estelle, Lorn, and the others, and later, Maggie and Brenda. They understood the significance of what was happening."

"You never told them about Kise?" Amagyne asked.

"No," La said. "I could not, yet I did not fully know why. The Firstcomers and I had become a close group. *We are an island in the wilderness,* we sometimes said." La smiled nostalgically. "One evening, after I had been back home for several months, I remember blinking my eyes and coming out of a daze, a strange state, as if I had been asleep. I realized I was sitting at my kitchen table, a pen in my hand, papers in front of me filled with writing." She looked at Amagyne. "That was my first trance writing."

"It must have been frightening."

"Exalting," La said, her face aglow. "I read what Kwo-am had written through my hand. *You who I have chosen, La, the Sage, blessed and enabled, I say this to you, hear it in your heart and let your hand put it on paper: In the beginning was free-flying Kwo-am, coming from nowhere, being everywhere . . .*

The words of Kwo-am, I knew, golden magic words written on pages of simple notebook paper. I knew there would be more words. I bought the book of blank pages."

Both La and Amagyne looked at the book sitting at La's feet.

"On the first page I wrote, *The Fruit of She.* On the next pages, I carefully pasted the notebook writings. The next time Kwo-am spoke through me and had me write, I wrote the words directly into the book. I knew that the words must not be seen by others, that I would tell others the messages as Kwo-am led me to, but that no one should look at the writings themselves."

Amagyne nodded.

"Over the next year, many messages came from Kwo-am, sometimes through dreams, sometimes through the trance writing. This was a painful year, Amagyne. Although my destiny was becoming clearer, I remained uncertain. I was poor, dreadfully lonely for Kise and terribly unsure about everything. Kwo-am had chosen me and yet Zetka tortured me. He made my mind play tricks on me. Sometimes strange thoughts came and strange impulses took over. Strange words would flow from my mouth. I was being tested, I knew. I understood that and still it was very trying.

"In the midst of this confusion," La continued, "my mother died."

Amagyne nodded sadly.

"Eventually the sharpness of my grief began to lessen. I was thirty-five years old by them. Your age. It was nineteen-fifty-one. Kwo-am and I were winning, I realized. It was all becoming clearer and clearer. I gathered the others and together we set off, and we came here, seventeen of us, to Circle Edge.

"Carel bought the little section of land near the river and we began to build our community. I continued to long for my son, a pain and longing I could share with no one. Then in nineteen-fifty-three, two years after our arrival at Circle Edge, I had a dream about Kise. Nearly four years had passed since I had seen him. In the dream Kise was revealed as the spirit and blood child of Kwo-am, which surely in some way I had already known. I learned that he would soon appear again, for it was time. This dream was not to be written, nor told."

"His existence was one of the Mysteries, wasn't it?" Amagyne said.

"It was. To be known only by me." La smiled a melancholy smile. "One day, soon after that dream, he came." The smile grew. "Kwo-am had sent him. He came to me in the woods, and our reunion was the most joyous moment of my life."

Amagyne smiled with her, her eyes full of tears.

"He would stay among the creatures of the hills and mountains and woods, he told me, for he was one of them. He built his cabin. We saw each other often though I spoke of this to no one. It had taken me so long to realize the full truth of Kwo-am's first visit, but at last I knew."

La was looking directly into Amagyne's eyes. "I understood then. Kise was the seed carrier. He *was* sent to me by Kwo-am. A human male, yet more god than man. I had not failed."

"Yes," Amagyne whispered.

"I will tell you the dream I had then, the dream through which I learned this."

La leaned and picked up the *Fruit of She*. She leafed through the pages and removed a loose sheet. She began to read. "There was a magnificent snow-white deer, and I knew the deer was Kwo-am. Mounted on the deer was a woman, young and pure and beautiful. The woman was Lorn. The deer turned into my son and he and Lorn went off together into the mountains. Then there were many many women gathered all around, celebrating, and in the center was a newborn baby cradled in Lorn's arms. The baby's name was Amagyne. And I could hear the chanting, *Born of woman only,* and I knew this was true. In the distance was the white deer."

La slipped the paper back into the book. "I understood how it was to be. That Kise's role in Kwo-amity, in union with Kwo-am, was to beget the First Guide. You, my Amagyne." She reached for Amagyne and grasped her hand. Tears streaked both their faces.

"But I knew I was not to let anyone know of this. Kise's part had to be hidden. As you said, it was one of the Mysteries which I had no choice but to obey. That Mystery was a Zetka countermove and I now know Zetka's reason." La shook her head sadly, her mouth revealing just a touch of anger. "He would send Rosemary Krepach here to Circle Edge to reveal that Kise was my son. It would result in doubt and dissention among the Kwo-amians. I know what Zetka's expectation is, that I will now be considered a fraud, and so Laki-Seone will not fulfill the Ceremony of Emergence, the New Page will not begin, and Zetka can continue to drive humans onward until they destroy themselves and the earth."

Amagyne let out a long breath. "We can't let that happen," she said.

"Perhaps there is still hope," La replied quietly.

"Lorn loved Kise," Amagyne said. "She told me she did."

"Lorn was a pure and lovely girl," La said. "A born kwo-z if ever there was. Yes, she loved him. The day I brought her to my son, she loved him instantly. I knew their child would be a female who would be the Amagyne I had mistakenly thought was supposed to come sooner."

Amagyne wiped at her tears.

"Your birth was hailed by all Kwo-amians. I had not failed. From me came Kise, from Kise, came you, Amagyne, the Guide.

"The years passed beautifully as you grew, my grandchild, though I could not tell you we were connected by blood. You were nurtured by my love and the love of your mother and, for a while, your father. You were nurtured and loved by all the Edgers and Kwo-amians everywhere. Yet I understood how it had to be with Kise. He was to remain away from the center. Zetka's demand. He had to remain at the edge, his place in Kwo-amity always to be silent." La shook her head. "At least, not to be revealed by me," she added.

"Kise was a loving presence in your life," La said. "It was beautiful to watch the two of you together."

Amagyne cried quietly as she listened to the stories.

"But then," La continued, "that woman from the

304

outer world entered his life." Lines of anger came to La's jaw and around her eyes. "I tried to stop him from seeing her. I sensed that no good would come of it."

"The fire," Amagyne said, her voice choked.

"I felt destroyed. Life's center was gone, taken from me. All else seemed hollow. The pain would not leave me. I was inconsolable. I waited for a sign from Kwo-am, a message, a dream. I waited in what must have been the closest thing to hell any devil or demon or Zetka himself could conjure up."

Amagyne placed her hand over La's but La seemed unaware.

"If it hadn't been for that woman, my son would not have died. I felt driven to go and confront her. I was afraid. If I faced Claire Alta, I was afraid what I would do to her. But by the time I pushed the doorbell at her house, I was calm. I knew at once the woman who answered the door was Claire Alta. Yet how could she have that glow in her face, that radiance? How dare she be happy! For a moment it seemed the rage would come again, but then, magically, it dissipated. I stood face to face with her, calmly, though not knowing what I would say. The words, I believe, came from Kwo-am, not from me. I told her I was a reporter for the *Colorado Springs Gazette*, that I was doing a feature article on the community called the Ladies' Farm and would like to ask her a few questions about it."

"You hadn't planned to say that?" Amagyne asked.

"It had never crossed my mind," La replied. "Claire Alta invited me in. She knew very little about Circle Edge, of course, and most of what she thought she knew was inaccurate. Then I asked her about herself. She spoke freely. She had just come from the doctor's, she explained, and had learned she was pregnant."

Smiling, La shook her head. "At that moment, my spirits lifted as high as hers. Yes, at that moment, I understood. The child in her was my son's child. A very special child. That's all I knew then. Only later did I learn more." La leaned back, her eyes closed. "It was five years after Laki-Seone's birth that I learned she was to be the Catalyst. I did not write the dream down, but I remember it clearly: Someone was moving amidst hills, snowy sunlit hills, a person and yet it wasn't a person. The figure seemed to be floating, and then coming near to a woman. They came together and there was a flash of blinding light." La squinted as she spoke. "But then darkness covered everything — complete, tar-black darkness. I could see nothing. I was frightened. I felt the terror of emptiness. Then the woman appeared again and her belly was large. A beautiful daughter was born to her. I watched the time passing in the child's life, the growing child happy and healthy and full of goodness. But then, in her fifth year, the movement and flow of her life stopped. I sensed the dark force of evil hovering near her. I saw her lying still and deathly ill in her little bed, growing weaker moment by moment. It seemed she would surely die.

"But then the force of Kwo-am arose, surrounding the child, breathing forth life. And the child opened her eyes and smiled." La opened her eyes and looked at Amagyne. "I felt the joy of Kwo-am's victory."

La folded her hands atop the book in her lap. "I

knew the dream meant that the child would recover. She would survive Zetka's visit."

"The scarlet fever," Amagyne said.

La nodded. "Later that day, I received confirmation that she was well. Ingrid told me. And that night, a trance came and I wrote." La leafed through the *Fruit of She*. "The words that came through my hand that day in nineteen-sixty-four were the words to the *Coming of the Catalyst*." She found the page and placed it in front of Amagyne.

Amagyne turned her eyes away.

"It is all right to look, my child," La reassured. She continued the story. "When the trance ended and I read the words I knew what Jude's part would be. Jude Alta, Kwo-am's second spirit and blood child, would be the Catalyst. Zetka's attempt to thwart Kwo-am's plan by making her die of fever had failed. Had he succeeded and we lost the Catalyst, hope for our future would have grown slim indeed. But with Kwo-am's help, the child survived. She had withstood the first obstacle of Zetka. This I understood. I knew that I alone was to know who the Catalyst was and how she came to be, that this was one of the Mysteries.

"To all of you, to all Kwo-amians, I knew that I was then to announce that the Catalyst existed and that some day she would come to us." La looked at Amagyne. "Read what comes next," she said.

Amagyne took the book. Her hands were shaking. She took deep breaths.

La reached over and pointed to the place in the book, the section following the *Coming of the Catalyst*. "Read it, Amagyne, it's all right."

Amagyne cleared her throat. She began to read

307

aloud. *"Zetka's second obstacle,"* she said in a shaky voice, *"will follow the Catalyst's coming to your gate. He will try to turn her from knowing the truth and choosing to be of you, of me. If he prevails, all will be lost, and those now involved in bringing great danger to the world will win."*

Amagyne's voice was stronger. *"If we prevail,"* she read, *"the Catalyst will be willing to submit to the Enactment of the Scourges of Zetka. From this ordeal she shall despise Zetka all the more and be all the more ready to fulfill the Ceremony of Emergence. If the Catalyst does not fail, then hope remains for the world. Now comes a Mystery for only you to know for now, La, the Sage, blessed and enabled . . ."*

Amagyne stopped. She looked at La.

"Go on," La said gently.

Amagyne read. *"At the Ceremony of Emergence, my spirit and blood child, the Catalyst, must sacrifice her earthly life. To choose life for all she must choose death for herself, death brought her by the hand of a Kwo-amian. Zetka will fight to turn her from this choice, using every means. She must choose. This is for you only to know until it is time to proclaim it to all."*

Amagyne stopped reading. She looked at La.

"When I learned she must die to bring on the New Page," La said, "as painful as it was, I had to accept it. I did and was at peace, though coming to know Laki-Seone as I now have makes it very difficult."

"It says nothing about her being reborn," Amagyne said. She began frantically to turn the pages of the book.

"It is not there, Amagyne."

"Then —"

"She *will* be reborn. That revealment came later, through a dream. It's not written. Turning evil into good," La said. "Laki-Seone's death will be used to create Kwo-world."

Amagyne rubbed her temples. La reached and touched her arm. "I watched the child closely through the years, the child called Jude. I kept track of her, mostly through Ingrid. Jude Alta's destiny was inevitable. I knew she would come to us someday and that her death and eventual rebirth would set free her full kwo-ami spirit which would begin the end of Zetka."

Amagyne nodded half-heartedly. La took the book from her, turned some pages, and read. *"From the Sage will come the Guides — the One Who is Formed, and the Catalyst, the One Who Chooses. From them will come the New Page."*

La looked up. "When I knew the time had come for her to be with us, I sent Miluna to her. Events from then unrolled until today. The time is close. The Ceremony of Emergence must take place the day after tomorrow. We must proceed as planned."

CHAPTER 33

At the camp Dagney was in a good mood. "Now that Jude knows everything, she won't be able to resist the obvious conclusion much longer."

"I'm not so sure," Gresh said, laying another log on the blazing fire. "I thought so too, but now I'm afraid she's believing La's explanations."

"Nope," Dagney said. "It's now come to the point where it's too much even for her to swallow. Look at her." She gestured toward Jude. "She's going over and over it in her head, I bet you. She'll have to end up realizing what a fraud La is."

"We'll see," Gresh said.

A few yards away Jude sat silently, fingers pressed against her forehead. Toni sat nearby. An hour earlier, Toni had found Jude leaving the Meditation Room after her talk with Lorn and Amagyne. They had sat together holding hands on the bench near the pond while Jude told Toni what she had learned from Lorn. "It wasn't supposed to be revealed," she had said. "So much is being revealed, I don't know what to think anymore."

Toni had insisted that Jude come with her to the camp for a while. Jude had gone reluctantly. Though she was there among her friends, she was apart from them, deep within herself. The voices around her were a blur, until she heard Amagyne's.

"Are you asleep, Laki-Seone?"

Jude thought it was a dream. *Come and join me,* she answered in her mind. Then she felt a soft touch on the sleeve of her jacket. She opened her eyes.

"Come, you're exhausted. Let's walk back to the Dome." Amagyne helped Jude to her feet.

Jude looked at Toni. "Will you come?"

The three walked through the grounds, five Guardian Edgers following close behind. Jude did not speak during the walk and barely said a word when she and Toni got to their room.

The next morning, she went off for a long, mostly silent walk with Miluna. When they did speak it was of the wildflowers, of the turning of the leaves as autumn approached. The little group of Guardian Edgers accompanying them remained at a distance.

At noon Jude brought some cheese and bread to her room. She told Amagyne the same thing she had told Toni, that she needed to be alone. Her mind was a jumble of contradictory possibilities and beliefs.

That afternoon Amagyne and Toni came for her. They waited while she splashed her face with cold water, then the three walked to the Amit among the hundreds of others.

When everyone was gathered, La raised her arms as she had so many times before. This time the atmosphere was subdued. There would be no music following this meeting, Jude suspected, no dancing.

"I now must tell you what could not be told before," La began. Every eye was on her. Jude sat to her left, between Amagyne and Toni. "Relentless Zetka pushes events forward," La said. "Yet it can be no other way." Her face looked worn and troubled.

"When I was sixteen years old," she began . . .

She told the story to the thousands of women, just as she had told it to Amagyne. Everyone listened intently, some murmuring occasionally or gasping. When La finished, there was stunned silence, then hushed, pressured conversations.

At last a tall, straight-backed woman rose. It was Laura, a Firstcomer. "Hear me!" she called.

Laura scanned the sea of faces. "Tomorrow is the day of the Ceremony of Emergence, the day we had all awaited. Despite what we have now learned from La, despite whatever uncertainties we may have, despite the difficulty of the choice Laki-Seone must make, let us celebrate our emergence tomorrow, either into the New Page, or onto the *next page*. In either case, life will go on. Let us proceed with the preparations for the Ceremony, and let us learn Laki-Seone's choice tomorrow, whatever it may be." Laura sat down.

"I agree," said a youthful Edger dressed all in blue. "Let there be a Ceremony. We must go on no matter what. Let us come together at dusk tomorrow, as planned, and what will be will be."

The crowd was buzzing. "Yes," a woman called out, "let the Ceremony take place."

"Hear, hear," others responded. There was applause and cheering.

"So it shall be," La said.

"So it shall be," dozens of voices echoed.

* * * * *

Jude, Toni, and Amagyne walked together back toward the compound. They were joined by Lorn and a group of other Kwo-amians, as well as Dagney, Pam, Gresh, and several other Chicago women.

With Amagyne in the lead, the women made their way to Circle Room, and seated themselves on chairs and sofas and on the floor. There was a heavy silence, which Amagyne finally broke. "Beliefs of mine that were always as solid as those mountains out there feel shaky today," she said.

Dagney grinned, trying to catch Toni's eye.

Amagyne's face was twisted in pain. "I cannot help wondering whether La's grief about her son could have made her susceptible to Zetka's influence."

"My sweet child," Lorn said. "How frightening to have those doubts."

"I have them too," Sarah said. "I'm afraid that the reason for Laki-Seone's death is to satisfy La's need for revenge rather than to bring on Kwo-world."

Pam whispered to Dagney. "She thinks the same thing we do. I'll be damned!"

313

"It's all going to come crashing down," Dagney whispered back.

"And then I think that perhaps Zetka is influencing *me*," Amagyne said, "giving me those thoughts. I do not know."

"I think you're now seeing things more objectively, Amagyne," Dagney said. "La made up the Ceremony of Emergence to meet her own needs, just as she made up everything else about Kwo-amity."

"No!" Berryfire protested. "That's not true." She leaned forward on her cushioned chair. "Maybe La's own needs did have something to do with the revelation that Laki-Seone must die. That may or may not be true. But even if it is, in no way does that discredit the other revelations."

"If the foundation goes, the whole structure goes," Pam said coolly.

Honore's hands were clasped tightly at her chest. "La didn't tell us about Kise because that was one of the Mysteries," she said. She was sitting on the sofa between Lorn and Sarah. Her voice quivered with emotion. "She wasn't free to talk about it and only did now because Zetka forced it out. And she wasn't free to talk about Laki-Seone's death and resurrection until now. La speaks the truth and always has." Honore glared at Amagyne. "I can't believe you could turn on her so easily."

Lorn put her hand on Honore's arm. "La has always acted for the good of all," she said, "yet I must admit that the revelation about the Catalyst dying troubles me greatly. Death comes from Zetka. Kwo-am has always had to accept this and never has she brought back to life, to continue living as a flesh and blood being, anyone whom death had taken. I fear for Laki-Seone. I feel doubt about her rebirth and yet . . . I don't know . . . I also feel hope that her rebirth *could* occur and the New Page could, indeed, begin."

"Lorn is torn," Dagney mumbled.

"No one who's met La could deny that she's a very special woman," Gresh said from her seat on the carpeted floor. "And Kwo-amity is a very appealing religion, as religions go. Like all religions, it's founded on the unprovable, perhaps the unknowable. Some people easily believe things that can't be proved or known. Others don't. We could speculate about why that is, but this is not the time.

"I think you would agree that the worst religions are those that inspire evil acts while claiming benevolent purposes. From what I know of Kwo-amity, it's never been guilty of that." Gresh paused. She looked from face to face. "Until now."

There was a moment of heavy silence. "You know she's right, Jude," Toni said.

Jude did not respond. She remained motionless, her arms resting leadenly on the arms of her stuffed chair.

"I believe in kwo-ami and in zetkap," Gresh continued, "though I call them by different names, and conceive of their source differently from the Kwo-amian view. I do not believe in magic. I do not believe that social change can come about by a ceremony, no matter how much we want it to, and I certainly don't believe that universal love and caring can be generated by ritual human sacrifice." She looked at Jude then, with tears in her eyes. "Nor that the dead can be returned to life."

Jude blinked back her own tears.

315

"This is myth," Gresh said. "This is fallacy. La is a human being and nothing more. She is subject to human failings and passions. Unconscious though I'm sure it is, her motivation for decreeing the death of Jude Alta — of Laki-Seone — seems, indeed, to be retaliation for the death of her son whom she loved beyond all others, beyond her love of humankind. La does not know this, I believe, and probably never will. But if you open your eyes, I think you can't help but see that it's true."

"You're too kind, Gresh," Dagney interjected. "La is fully conscious of what she's doing. This whole setup is a racket. La no more talks directly to God than I do. She's just another self-proclaimed prophet, with her own distorted motivations. La is a fraud and I think you all know it now. You must. Hey, but I can understand how difficult it is for you Kwo-amians to accept the truth. It's not easy to give up ideas that form the center of your life. It's not easy to see your hero deflated. I feel sorry for you, but wake up and smell the coffee, girls. A fraud is a fraud. She lied and she covers her lies with more lies. She's deceived you on a grand scale. She does not communicate with God or Kwo-am. There is no Kwo-am. La is Kwo-am and Kwo-am is a lie."

Joyce was leaning forward, eager to speak. "We each have to decide what we believe," she said the moment Dagney paused. "We're all struggling with it."

"Yes," Ella agreed. "It's hard to know *what* to believe."

"La is a self-centered manipulator." All eyes turned to Jude. "Deceptive and shrewd," Jude added.

"A user of other people." Many in the room looked shocked.

"Right on," Dagney crowed.

"Or is she?" Jude continued. "Maybe she's a deranged victim of a psychological aberration, a twisted woman, slightly mad. Sincere, perhaps, but delusional."

Several people nodded, including Gresh.

Jude's lip was trembling. "Or she could be more sane than anyone. She could be the one through whom Kwo-am, the creator of life and goodness, speaks to us."

"Kwo-am is with you, Laki-Seone," Honore affirmed.

"A wise woman," Jude continued, "full of love. Chosen, blessed, enabled. Knowing that sometimes choices are very difficult and that death is part of life. Knowing that miracles occur. La could be that."

"That she is," Berryfire said.

Jude's hands gripped the fabric of her chair. "Or maybe a mixture," she said. "Kwo-am's medium. Enabled. But also human. An enabled Sage but a driven human being. Driven by grief into rage, by rage to vengeance, and by guilt to self-deception." Jude shook her head, her throat and chest feeling tight with pain. "I have more questions than answers." She was blinking rapidly. "I think of La and partly I feel filled with love and trust. In some ways I feel it more now than ever, knowing how she has suffered . . . and knowing that she's . . ."

"That she's your grandmother," Honore said lovingly.

"Jude, don't be blind!" Pam said.

317

"Is it all a sham?" Jude was looking straight into Pam's eyes. "Or is it all true? Is it a delusion? Or is it finally the full reality? If I die tomorrow, will it mean nothing but the end of one more human life? Or will I be born again and bring forth the New Page, the Withering of Zetka, Kwo-world?"

"You're not going to die." Toni leaned forward on her chair. "We can't let her, can we?" She looked from Pam to Gresh to Dagney.

"Hell no," Dagney said. "The sane among us have to stand together." She looked pointedly at Ella. "What about you? Your eyes have been opened, haven't they?"

Ella's hands were clasped together. "To tell the truth," she said softly, "I do have great doubt now about La. And I know I'm not the only Kwo-amian at Circle Edge who does." She looked at Sarah.

"I don't think there should be any Ceremony of Emergence," Sarah said, her eyes filled with tears. "I think our Sage is not what we thought she was and it tears me apart to admit that. Amagyne, you are as human as the rest of us, and so is Laki-Seone. The miracle that made everything believable to me was that you were born of woman only. Now I know there was no miracle at all."

"You don't know that," Honore said angrily. "La tells us Kise was sent by Kwo-am. I believe her. To me, nothing has changed. But believe what you will." She glowered at Sarah. "In any case, Laura spoke wisely today. The Ceremony of Emergence must take place no matter what." She looked at Jude. "Whether you participate in it or not."

318

"Yes," Lorn said. "We should proceed as agreed. What Laki-Seone does is up to her. She must choose."

"Yes, she must choose," echoed Berryfire and Honore.

"This *choose* shit is making me sick," Dagney said. She turned to Toni. "Let's get Jude the hell out of this crazy place."

Jude was feeling profoundly sad. "I'm not ready to leave," she said.

"That's irrelevant." Dagney looked around. "Anybody here who doesn't want to be a party to this murder, will you help us get Jude out of here?"

Sarah sat up straight. "I'll help," she said. She fingered the leather holster strapped to her belt.

A Guardian Edger who stood near the door put her hand on *her* holster. "You're not taking her anywhere," she said. "You heard her. She doesn't want to go."

Toni looked at Dagney. "We can't force her."

"The cops can," Dagney said.

"Listen." Amagyne spoke firmly. "All of you." She looked from face to face. "It is not for some to decide for the others. Each of us must decide for herself. That is our way, the Kwo-amian way." She looked at Gresh, then Pam. "And the feminist way," she added. "Each of us and each woman at Circle Edge must decide. At dusk tomorrow there will be a ceremony at the Amit. Each woman must decide what she will do, whether she will participate or not. Each woman must determine her own action, but none must determine that of others."

319

"Well spoken, Amagyne," Honore said.

Gresh started to protest, but Lorn spoke over her. "As always," she said, "Amagyne speaks wisely." As she rose Honore helped her. "Let us go our separate ways now, and think about all of this, talk together if we wish."

"Come on, Jude," Toni said.

Amagyne took Jude's hand. "I will be present tomorrow night no matter what you choose, Laki-Seone. Perhaps you will be there at my side to fulfill the Ceremony, perhaps not."

"I will be there," Jude said. Toni started to speak, but Jude went on. "I'm not sure what I'll do, but I will be there."

"There are preparations, then," Amagyne said.

Honore gave Jude a warm hug. "I wish you well, soul-sister."

"Choose from the heart," Berryfire said to Jude.

Amagyne again had Jude's hand in hers. "As you know," she said, "according to the revealments, you are to spend the twenty-four hours before the Ceremony with Kwo-amians only, meditating, resting, cleansing yourself, hearing the *Words of Kwo-am*, eating fruit and drinking spring water. This is how it is to be. Are you agreeable to it?"

"Yes," Jude said.

"How about spending some time with me first?" Toni proposed. "I'd like to be with you. Let's go somewhere we can be alone for a while."

Jude was staring at the plush carpet. She looked at Toni, her eyes red and moist. "I don't want to hurt you," she said. "I understand what this is doing to you."

Her crying stopped the words. Toni leaned over and embraced her.

"I love you, Toni, but I can't . . . I need to be alone with my thoughts now, to mull everything over and feel and think. I need to do it on my own." She looked out the window. "There are three or four hours of daylight left and then the preparations begin. I want to spend that time by myself."

Toni looked away. "I see," she said.

"There's a place in the mountains where we went once together, Toni. That's where I want to be. I want to go there and look at the sky and think and meditate and . . . and, I guess, see what I feel."

Toni looked at Jude. "Goodbye then, *Laki-Seone*," she said angrily. Tears streaked her face. Sobs choked her. "Goodbye, my love," she murmured and she turned from Jude and ran out of the room.

* * * * *

Three carloads of Guardian Edgers accompanied Jude up Rim Canyon Road to the place in the mountains where she had gone three times before, once alone, once with Toni, once with La. The Guardians remained at the cars while Jude climbed higher. She sat alone on the cliff and looked at the sky whose color was the same as La's eyes.

CHAPTER 34

Dagney and Gresh walked along the river, deep in conversation. "For almost forty years, La's been sitting pretty here at Circle Edge," Dagney said. "She'll probably become a bag lady now that her empire is falling apart."

Gresh shook her head. "I bet she emerges on top somehow."

Dagney shrugged. "You could be right. She's a pro."

"I think she really believes Jude will be reborn."

"See what I mean," Dagney said, laughing. "She's

even got you fooled." Dagney picked up a large stone from the path and tossed it into the bushes.

"Maybe so." Gresh shoved her hands into her pockets. "It seems strange that she'd still feel the need for revenge, though. After thirty years."

"Thirty years and nine months, to be exact." They came to a bench and Dagney sat, gesturing for Gresh to do the same.

"You have to understand La," Dagney continued. "She was pathologically attached to the boy, remember. When he died, that energy transformed into pathological hatred for the one she held responsible. She's completely obsessed with it."

"She seems so calm."

"Yes, she is. She's a very controlled woman, and very patient. She's been planning the perfect revenge for all these years. She made sure Jude would feel drawn to Circle Edge by having her brought here as a kid. I bet Jude was thoroughly love-bombed by the Kwo-amians on those visits."

"We don't know for sure that Ingrid brought her here. Remember Pam found out Ingrid actually did have a niece about Jude's age?"

Dagney nodded. "Sure. That's why La chose that as the cover story. No, those weren't dreams Jude had about this *special place*. It was part of the plan."

"Could be," Gresh said. She bent over and picked a wildflower. "It was a lucky coincidence for La that Jude turned out to be a lesbian, don't you think?"

"It wouldn't have mattered," Dagney responded. "La would have proceeded regardless. Some of the Kwo-amians are straight, you know. About ten percent. Some say even more, but that the others are in the closet." She leaned back and laughed.

323

"Joyce says it wasn't coincidence at all, Jude being a lesbian, that it was Kwo-am's doing." Gresh suddenly looked pointedly at Dagney. "Do you believe in God?"

"Sure," Dagney said. "Always have. I've got my own ways of thinking about it though. I'm not too hot on organized religion, as you might have surmised." Her eyes narrowed then and the edge of her lip curled. "I was raised Catholic. It didn't take me too long to figure out what a crock those phonies were selling."

Gresh nodded. "Maybe that anger is what's fueling your total rejection of Kwo-amity."

Dagney looked askance at her.

Gresh buried the toe of her Reebok in the deep grass. "There's something about this place," she said. "It gets to a person."

"Oh, boy. We better get you out of here."

Gresh smiled. "Don't worry," she said. "I'm not convinced yet." She stared up the river. "But I have to admit I'm not as sure as you are that there's nothing to Kwo-amity." She caught Dagney's expression and laughed. "You think that's ridiculous, don't you? You think you've got everything all figured out."

"Obviously," Dagney said.

"Well, I'm just not so sure, that's all."

"I can't believe this."

"La doesn't seem like a charlatan."

"Like I said, the woman's a pro," Dagney said, still looking sharply at Gresh. "You worry me, Gresh."

Gresh laughed again. "Mostly, I agree with you," she said. "Even though part of me can't help wondering. Anyway, you do make a pretty convincing case against La, I'll grant you that."

Dagney smiled proudly. "Do you think I could convince them?" She gestured toward the four Guardian Edgers downriver from them.

"No," Gresh said. "Do you think you can convince Jude?"

"I don't have to," Dagney said. "I'll bet you anything Jude is busy convincing herself right now. It's a damn big leap of faith to believe you can die and be reborn. I think the fear of death will jar her to her senses. She'll find a way to justify refusing to die."

"I hope you're right," Gresh said.

* * * * *

It was nearly dusk when Jude returned to Circle Edge. Amagyne was waiting for her at the gate. "The musicians are in the Dome garden," she said. "The preparations begin with you and me in the spring pool. Are you ready?"

Jude took a deep breath. "I'm ready," she said.

She drank cool spring water while sitting in the pool. Time drifted by. She ate fruit and was bathed by Kwo-amians, and sung to. She heard hypnotic humming. A little later, she sat in the sauna, sweating, feeling the cleansing. She showered in cold water and afterwards received a leisurely deep massage. Dressed then in a thick blue robe and stretched out in one of the moss-like chairs, she listened to readings from the *Words of Kwo-am*.

At midnight Jude and Amagyne went upstairs to

their beds to sleep. Alone in her room Jude thought sadly of Toni, and felt a longing for her. She thought of Rosalie and the feeling of loneliness grew. She had often said that there were four women in her life. *There are more now,* she thought, *many more.* She thought of Kwo-world and Monama and the blue of La's eyes.

In the morning, La and Amagyne and Honore came to her. They and a band of Edgers took her along the river path that led to the Inner Garden.

* * * * *

"They're isolating her," Toni said. "They won't let anyone near her."

Dagney was hunched over the grill. "You want a hamburger, Toni?"

"She's lost," Toni said. "We've lost her."

"She'll see the light," Dagney said.

"There's still hope, Toni," Gresh said. "Isn't it kind of early for hamburgers, Dag?"

"They're reinforcing the brainwashing," Toni stated angrily. She poured a cup of coffee.

Pam returned from the showers with a towel draped over her shoulder. "The debate rages on," she announced, tossing her towel over her tent. "I've identified five categories. Want to hear?"

"Sure," Gresh said. "Categories of what?"

"Peoples' reactions, the Kwo-amians. Where's Joyce?"

"With her people," Gresh said.

Pam looked askance at Gresh. Gresh said nothing and Pam went on. "First there are the *La-ites.*

They're the ones still totally loyal to La. They believe everything she said is true, including the stuff about Jude having to die. The second faction believes La made that up. They think her other revealments were true but not the one about Jude having to die. I'm calling them the *Neo-Kwo-amians.* They're pissed at La for lying. A lot of them have already left Circle Edge or are packing up to go."

"They're quitting Kwo-amity?" Gresh said.

"No, just quitting La. They feel betrayed by her. They're talking about waiting for the new Sage."

"How'd you learn all this?" Dagney asked. She flipped her meat pattie.

"I listen. This place is buzzing. There are little groups talking and arguing all over the place. Most of them don't mind my listening. The *Harmonics* also think the revealment about Jude dying is false, but they see La as vulnerable like everyone else, and they forgive her. They don't think it's an intentional lie. And they still believe all the other revealments."

Toni sat silently, staring at the fire. Each minute that passed was bringing Jude closer to death.

"Then there's group four, the *Waverers,*" Pam continued. "They don't believe the idea to kill the Catalyst came from Kwo-am either, but for them this casts doubt on *all* La's revealments. They're not sure La ever did receive messages from Kwo-am, but they're not sure she didn't either."

To Toni the conversation seemed absurd. "I should have left her locked in the cabin," she said. "It's too late now."

"No, it's not," Gresh said. "I've been thinking about it, Toni. Jude's very sane. I think she'll only go so far with this. When they give her that poison, I think she'll dump it on the ground." She put her arm around Toni's shoulder.

"There's one more faction," Pam said. "Number five, the *Erstwhiles*. They're not in doubt like the *Waverers*. The *Erstwhiles* are sure that La never communicated with Kwo-am. Some think La made it up intentionally; others think she was delusional and actually believes it herself." Pam frowned. "I probably need two separate names for these groups."

"Let's gather the *Erstwhiles* and storm the barricades," Dagney suggested.

"I wouldn't be surprised if they're already plotting something," Pam said. "They seemed to get kind of quiet when I came around — this one group, at least. I sat there with them, filing my nails and acting innocent, but they finally asked me to leave."

"The revolutionary underground," Dagney said. "We need to connect with them."

"There were only five of them," Pam said.

"I bet there are hundreds. You know, the first group, the *La-ites*, they're using force to keep us away from Jude, or the threat of force, at least — all those damn bodyguards. I think we're justified in using force to get at her. We and the other non-Kwo-amians, and the *Erstwhiles* could join together."

"And do what?" Gresh said. "Attack the *La-ites*? Shall we use weapons? Fight our way to Jude and drag her out of here? Is that what you're suggesting?"

Dagney shrugged. "You got any other ideas?"

Gresh looked over her shoulder at the group of Guardian Edgers. "No," she said.

"I wonder which category Jude's in," Pam said. "That's what really matters."

* * * * *

The noon sun came and went and the preparations continued. A small Avowal Ritual took place with Jude writing out her doubts on red paper, having them burned, welcoming the rebirth of the shrike. She bathed and saunaed and ate and drank. She listened to more music and stories and lulling humming. From time to time she grew groggy and dozed. The time passed quickly. Amagyne was always at her side and La came several times to visit.

As the sun sank lower and lower everything grew quiet in the Inner Garden. Jude had been floating dreamily in the pool, her eyes sometimes half open, sometimes closed. The music had stopped, she realized. The other Kwo-amians were gone, it seemed, though there was still humming coming from somewhere. She let her eyes close again. She felt good, very good, vibrantly refreshed and alive, yet very peaceful. She dozed.

Amagyne told her it was time to go, that the sun would soon be gone. She asked Jude if she felt at peace, and Jude answered that she truly did. They walked slowly to the Dome, surrounded by Edgers who hummed to them. Then they were in Amagyne's apartment.

Amagyne held Jude close and kissed her tenderly. The kissing grew more passionate. Jude was tremendously aroused, even more than she had been the other time with Amagyne. They went together to Amagyne's bedroom and lay on the soft feather bed.

329

Jude floated and soared. The two became one, bodies and spirits fully merged. Never had Jude felt so ecstatically happy and complete.

Still holding her tenderly, Amagyne told Jude it was time to dress. She kissed each of Jude's eyelids, then helped her up. Jude donned the silver suit Amagyne laid out for her, a one-piece flowing garment that shone brightly under the night sky as they walked to the Amit.

The immense crowd made a path for Jude, cheering as she came. The atmosphere was alive with the energy of thousands of women. Jude walked as in a dream, knowing, yet not knowing where she was and what was taking place. She reached the platform that had been erected in the center of the Amit and walked up the ten stairs to the summit. The mass of women spread out below looked like waves on the sea. The cool night air caressed Jude's cheeks. She stood on the platform, Amagyne at her side, and sensed what was going on around her, more with her heart than her eyes or ears.

People were moving down below, making patterns with their movements. There was speaking, different voices, one at a time, saying words Jude could not decipher. They seemed to be talking in some strange language, or perhaps in code. Jude felt light-headed, as if she were moving beyond her body.

The patterned movement, beams of moving colored light, music and drum beats, circled her below. Above, Jude felt the pull, the calling. Amagyne was speaking now, but Jude could not make out the words. Amagyne handed her something, pressed it into her palm. It was cool to the touch, hard, a goblet perhaps. Am I to drink from it, Jude wondered. Yes, that's what I'm to do. She held the goblet out at arm's length. The only sound was a single flute. Jude wondered if she were playing it, then realized, no, she was standing at the peak of the earth, about to drink cool, magical spring water.

She brought the container to her lips. Ah yes, it was cool and sweet. Nectar that would take her to the calling that she heard so clearly now. She downed it all, drank until the glass was empty.

On the platform was the fleece-covered cot, like the one that had been at the bleeding after the Scourges. It was soft. She lay her head back on the soft pillow. Soft and floaty. Very floaty. She felt herself floating away, floating away, floating until she was gone.

Toni was crying. "It really happened."

"As it was meant to," Dagney said.

"Do you feel it the way I do?" Pam asked.

"The tingling?" Dagney said. "Yes, that, but the lightness too, the openness. I feel so full of . . . I don't know, of love, I guess, loving feelings."

"I feel it," Toni said.

"We are kwo-omnis," Dagney said, raising her hand, palm open, and bringing it to her chest. "The New Page has begun."

"Laki-Seone is in us all." Toni breathed in deeply.

"Gone for now but soon to return," Gresh said. "I didn't know it would feel like this. I never felt so at peace."

"We are free to be as we always should have been," Dagney said. She rolled up a pair of jeans and put them in her backpack. "Things will be very different in Chicago now."

"Everywhere," Gresh said. "Women are going forth. Soon it will reach every corner of the earth."

Toni was silent, the tears still on her cheeks.

"You miss her," Pam said softly.

"Terribly."

"Do you feel angry?"

Toni shook her head. "I feel grateful, grateful to Laki-Seone and grateful for our future. I know she'll be with us again soon, but seeing her in the tomb . . . it . . . it's very difficult."

"I know," Dagney said, "but it won't be long. The future has begun." She was smiling broadly. "Let's hit the road, sisters."

The exodus from Circle Edge was joyful. On the drive to the Denver airport, the Chicago women took turns reading aloud from the Words of Kwo-am.

Their plane took them eastward. Outside, in the sky, along the airplane's wing, flew Laki-Seone, drifting, flying, floating . . . Monama, pure Monama.

Then someone was touching her shoulder. "Wake up, Laki-Seone. It is time."

Jude opened her eyes. Amagyne stood before her outside the pool. She reached her hand to Jude. "It's almost dark. We must get dressed and go to the Amit. The Ceremony of Emergence is about to begin."

CHAPTER 35

At the Amit, a maze of rope had been laid on the ground in half-moon curves and arcs. Its outside rim was a full circle. The two ends of the rope met in the center of the maze. Women had taken places along the rope, picking it up and holding onto it so that they were all linked together. The women on the perimeter, forming the circle that enclosed the others, were dressed entirely in white and each held a lighted torch.

Jude and Amagyne and a group of about twenty other Kwo-amians walked solemnly across the empty

333

grounds of Circle Edge toward the Amit. The circle of light in the distance was large and beckoning. The breeze rippled Jude's rose-colored pantaloons and her purple wide-sleeved jacket. *This is not a dream,* she thought, fingering her ruby ring.

As they left the path and stepped onto the periphery of the huge Amit, thousands of eyes were on them. There was not a sound. Jude and Amagyne entered the labyrinth along the path left for them. The hush gave way to humming, thousands of throats humming a low chant as Jude and Amagyne continued through the multitude of women until they reached the center of the maze.

Spotlights from the edges of the Amit shone on the place where the ends of the rope lay on the ground. Jude stooped immediately and picked them up, one end in each hand. At that moment the humming turned to cheers. The circle was complete. The Ceremony of Emergence had begun.

Jude wrapped the ropes around her wrist and tied the ends together. Music rose from different areas within the maze of women, spotlights illuminating one group of musicians, then another. Flutes played the beginning notes of the *Coming of the Catalyst* and the singing began.

Scanning the faces, Jude spotted Toni twenty feet up the sloping Amit to her right. She was solemn and still. Not far from her were Honore and Miluna, singing, and near them, silent, were Gresh and Dagney and Pam. And then Jude's eyes fell on Martha. *She came,* Jude thought. *And Mom.* Claire Alta stood next to Martha, holding the rope with both hands, looking straight at Jude. Jude's eyes filled with tears. *They're all here,* she thought, as the final verse was sung.

"*. . . she must choose. She must choose.*"

Into the silence that followed, Amagyne's voice came. She spoke of the meaning of this day and of this moment, for all of them at Circle Edge, and for all the world. Soft flute sounds and bells and a marimba accompanied her words. The crowd listened silently as Amagyne spoke, her voice clear and sure. Jude listened to the heartening words, feeling very calm.

"*. . .* and tonight is the climax of their terrible struggle. Tonight, the Catalyst, accepted by both Kwo-am and Zetka as the symbol of that struggle, must choose."

A spotlight shone brightly on Jude. She could no longer see the people surrounding her, but then one figure emerged. La. Coming towards her, dressed in a long white cloak.

The Sage moved slowly, with great dignity, until she was next to Jude. Held aloft in La's ancient hands was a white ceramic flask. It glistened in the light.

"The poison," Gresh whispered to Dagney.

Musicians began to play somber, eerie tones, interspersed with light, cheery refrains.

"Look at Toni," Dagney said. "She's in shock."

The music ended.

"The time is now," La's voice called. She was holding the flask high over her head.

Jude stood next to her, arrow straight, chin high.

La lowered the flask and from it poured clear liquid into a tiny cup. As drums softly played in the background, she spoke. "Laki-Seone, you have been chosen, and now you must make the greatest choice ever made." She looked deeply into Jude's eyes. "Kwo-am is loving you. We all love you." Tears came from her sky blue eyes, clear liquid, the same color as the liquid in the cup. "I love you," La whispered as she held out the cup to Jude.

"And I love you," Jude said to La. Only those very close to the center could hear it. Jude looked over the crowd she could barely see. "Are you there?" she called.

A moment's silence and then many voices responded: "We are here!" "Yes, we're here!" "Yes, Laki-Seone, yes!"

The spotlights moved and Jude could see again.

"Toni!" Jude called. "Are you with me?"

"I'm here, Jude," Toni called from the gently sloping hill to Jude's right.

"I feel you with me."

"I'm near you, but I don't think I'm with you, Jude."

"You will be soon," Jude said with great certainty. "I love you deeply, my love."

"And I love you," Toni murmured, but the words were choked and inaudible.

"Mother?" Jude called.

"Here, Jude, I'm here," Claire Alta responded.

Jude followed the sound, her eyes floating over the faces until she found that very familiar one. "I've made my decision, Mom."

"Yes, Jude," Claire said in a choked voice. Her face was distorted with pain. "I need you in my life," she added, but Jude did not hear.

"I love you, Mother. I feel full of love."

336

Claire nodded. Her eyes were full of tears.

"Martie?"

"Yes, Jude."

"I'm not afraid."

Words caught in Martha's throat.

"Are things OK with us?"

"Very OK," Martha said. "But Jude, *I'm* afraid. Jude, I don't want —"

"Martie, I'm not afraid of death. I don't feel fear of it, truly I don't."

"Oh God." Martha's face muscles collapsed, then so did the rest of her. Claire bent to her as did other women around them. They put her head between her knees. They rubbed her wrists.

La remained holding the cup in her outstretched hand.

"Rosalie Wright," Jude said sadly. "You are here in spirit. I feel you with me."

Jude looked at Amagyne. "You are here." She looked at La. "And you." She smiled lovingly at them, then looked at the cup. Slowly she reached her hand toward it and La let it go.

In the center of that huge gathering of women surrounded by huge mountains, Jude Alta stood, her feet solidly on the ground, holding the cup of poison in front of her with both hands. "I had a dream." Her voice was strong and resonant.

"Ahh-hh."

"I dreamed that I died. And out of my death sprang overriding joy and peace. The force of Zetka withered and disappeared," Jude crooned.

"Kwo-am is with you," several voices called.

"Oh my God, she's going to do it!" Toni cried. "Jude!" she screamed.

337

The spotlights were on Jude again; she could hear Toni but could not see her. Toni stumbled toward the center, trying to push her way through. Both of her arms were seized; she was encircled by Edgers.

"But dreams are not reality," Jude called, looking in Toni's direction. "There is no good choice but to respect reality."

Jude's mother began to smile.

"My dream was just a dream. It moved me and made me happy but it was just a dream." Jude's hands were steady on the cup. The rope remained secure around her waist.

"I know that it was just a dream. In reality," Jude continued, "what we call Zetka is very powerful. Zetkap influences us all. That is real."

Toni tried to free her arms, but the strong hands held her firmly.

"Zetka even influences La."

There were murmurings. Jude could hear Amagyne's heavy breathing next to her. "Sometimes Zetka comes disguised as Kwo-am, zetkap as kwo-ami."

"Mom, we can't let her die." Martha was sobbing.

"She's not going to die," Claire said.

"Inside me there is wisdom," Jude declared.

"In us all," someone responded.

"Yes, in us all. My wisdom, my judgement, my mind tempered by my heart which is full of love . . . they all tell me that my death . . . to free goodness . . ."

Toni was still being held by women on either side. Had they not been there, she would have crumpled to the ground.

338

". . . that this is not Kwo-am. This comes from Zetka."

"Yes, that's right!" The shouted words came from Toni.

"I will die . . . I know I must. I accept that . . . but I do not accept that this is my time."

A slow large smile crossed Martha's face.

"I have a choice. I will not always have this choice, but I do now. And I choose not to die!" Jude's face was aflame with emotion.

The hush was palpable. Dagney broke it. "Hallelujah!"

"I choose not to believe that my death or anyone's death is the road to goodness."

"She's not such a loony after all," Dagney whispered to Gresh.

"For that is not the Kwo-am I know," Jude's clear voice continued. "It's hard to know what truth is. I'm learning more day by day. But always I must go within myself for the answers. I must use my own judgement. I must think and weigh, balance feeling with knowledge. I do that now and as I do, it leads me to choose what I know Kwo-am is. I choose what I have learned Kwo-am means."

She held out her arms. "I choose LIFE!"

There were a few isolated cheers, and then more.

"I choose to believe that my death is not what you need, not what anyone needs. What's needed for the New Page you have already begun, all of you, my Kwo-amian friends, and my seeing-is-believing friends who view La's teachings about Kwo-am as a fantasy. I say the New Page has already begun and that we will bring it forward together."

A few uncertain affirmations followed. Toni was jumping up and down. Martha was sobbing happily.

"I thank La for teaching us so much," Jude continued. "I forgive La whom I have grown to love deeply . . . I forgive her for not being perfect, for not being invulnerable."

Slowly Jude lowered the cup. Slowly, as ten thousand eyes watched, she poured the poison drop by drop onto the ground. "To life!" she shouted.

"To life!" a number of voices repeated.

"To Kwo-am!"

"Kwo-ami!" "Life!" "To us all!"

The pandemonium that followed lasted for many minutes. Jude and Amagyne and La stood without moving in the center of it.

At last La raised her arms. Trumpets blared. The spotlight shone on La and soon all eyes were upon her.

"Laki-Seone has made her choice," La's deep strong voice called. "She is the One Who Chooses. She was placed amid the moves and countermoves of forces greater than us all. And she has chosen."

La's hands were at her sides, her voice lower. "Yet Zetka demands sacrifice for the New Page to be possible."

Pam was watching La closely, aware that one of her hands had disappeared into the pocket of her ivory cloak. "Son of a bitch, she's going to kill her!" Pam rasped.

"Zetka requires death!" La said.

Pam tried to run forward but was restrained after no more than five or six feet.

"And death she shall have!" La proclaimed.

Jude stared at La.

"Stop her! Don't let her do it!" Pam bellowed.

No one moved.

From her pocket La pulled an object that glistened in the spotlight.

"She has a knife!" Pam screamed, struggling to escape. Again she was restrained. "She's going to kill Jude!"

Different women from different parts of the Amit moved forward. Others went into action instantly, preventing them from reaching the center. There was scuffling. Pam was on the ground. Dagney struggled with two Kwo-amians, trying to free her arms from their grip. People had let go of the rope; they tripped over it and over each other. Claire was jostled by women pushing and shoving all around her. Several dozen Guardian Edgers had formed a protective circle around La and Jude and Amagyne.

La said something to one of the Guardian Edgers who immediately passed the word to others. Moments later a half dozen trumpets sounded and the chaos at the Amit ended as suddenly as it had begun. People who had fallen pulled themselves to their feet or were helped up by others. Everyone looked toward the center, toward La.

La's right hand was upraised. All eyes were upon it. The spotlight shone on her. La held the white flask.

Jude's hands flew to her chest.

Thousands watched, spellbound, as La uncorked the flask. Jude wanted to grab it from her but she could not move. La put the flask to her lips.

A groan escaped from Jude.

La tilted back her head and drank.

Moaning and crying came from the crowd.

"For me there will be no rebirth," La said, dropping the flask onto the ground. "You will carry on our work," she said, her voice weak.

She reached out to Amagyne. Amagyne supported her. Jude too moved forward and held her.

"The *Fruit of She* is an open book now," La said. Her voice was barely audible.

Jude and Amagyne helped her to the fleece-covered cot. Jude's face was shiny wet with tears, her breath coming in gasps.

"I love you," La said to Amagyne, "and you," to Jude. "Kwo-am is with you," were the last words she said.

She lay motionless then, except for her sky-blue eyes which moved slowly back and forth between Amagyne and Jude. The breeze rippled the edges of her frost-white hair. There was a slight smile on her lips.

The smile remained even after La's eyes had flickered and closed and her breathing stopped.

CHAPTER 36

Jude had six Firstcomers carry the cot to the Inner Garden and lay La's body near the waterfall beneath arches of flowers. The following day would be the Ritual of Death and Farewell.

Amagyne sat on a canvas chair at La's left, Lorn at her right. Jude stayed with them, doing what she could to comfort them, especially Amagyne whose pain seemed to have no bounds. After the Ceremony, Jude had briefly spoken with Toni, her mother and Martha, and her Chicago friends, then returned to the

Inner Garden to be with Amagyne. She sent Honore to fetch the *Fruit of She*.

On the grounds of Circle Edge and in the buildings, different groups gathered to talk or just sit silently together. Reactions to the Ceremony of Emergence were as intense as they were varied. Some were angry at Jude, some at La; some were confused, frightened, dismayed. Some went off to be alone. Others held each other. Some could not stop talking; others sank into deep silence. Many were grieving openly. Many seemed stunned.

Toni was with her group at Circle House in one of the small gathering rooms. Claire and Martha were with them.

"I wonder if she's a *Harmonic Kwo-amian* now," Pam said, "on her way up to *Erstwhile*, hopefully."

"Who?" Joyce asked. She had brought a tray of snacks and was passing it around.

"Jude. She could be a *Waverer* at this point." Pam took a handful of crackers.

"I highly doubt that she's wavering," Gresh said. "She doesn't seem a bit unsure about anything. Didn't you notice that aura of self-confidence about her after the Ceremony?"

"You thought so too?" Toni said. "I agree. She seemed so decisive, completely sure of herself."

"Maybe she intends to be the new Sage," Dagney suggested, chuckling.

"Jude is done with Kwo-amity," Martha said. "That's obvious."

"I wouldn't count on it," Gresh said.

The group continued talking until Honore came and invited them to go upstairs to the auditorium.

"Laki-Seone wants you present for the reading of the *Fruit of She*," Honore said.

"Looks like Jude's calling the shots now," Dagney said.

"Eat your heart out," Pam retorted, giving her a friendly poke ·

* * * * *

Every seat in Circle House Auditorium was occupied, and women crowded the aisles. A section in front had been reserved for Jude's family and Chicago friends. Jude sat alone on the stage, a microphone on the table in front of her.

"I'm ready to begin," she said. Her voice was strong and low-pitched. The hall became silent. Jude held up a book. "This is the *Fruit of She*. I've asked you to come because I want to read part of it to you. I know you're still in shock about what happened tonight, but I thought some of you might find the words helpful. For your grief and for your uncertainty."

Jude opened the book to a marked place. "This was written this morning," she said. She began to read: *"If the Catalyst chooses not to fulfill the Ceremony of Emergence, then Zetka's victory is total . . ."* Jude looked up momentarily, her face serious, almost severe. *". . . unless the Sage provides Zetka with a sacrifice. At the Ceremony of Emergence, a Kwo-amian believer must die if there is to be any hope for the New Page. Such is Zetka's countermove. She who the Sage chooses to sacrifice must be killed by the Sage's own hand. This Zetka requires, sure the*

Sage will not comply." Jude looked up. "So it is written," she said solemnly. "But Zetka was wrong about La."

Jude continued reading. *"If the Sage does sacrifice a Kwo-amian, then at the moment of the victim's death, a child will be conceived somewhere, of woman only, and will be the New Guide. This is my countermove. The New Guide will be born in the late spring in a hut that will be constructed for the birthing on the shore of Crescent Lake which will contain the victim's kwo-ami along with the kwo-ami of others who have died. As soon as she is born, the New Guide will be bathed in water from the lake, and trees will be planted around the lake. The New guide will live with her mother and others in what has been known as the Wright Mansion. Kwo-amians will live in dwellings they will build within the Full Circle. Full Circle must be purified in preparation for the coming of the New Guide. The lake and Full Circle land must be used only by Kwo-amians and those few trusted others whom the wise Kwo-amians might welcome."*

"La wants control even from the grave," Dagney whispered to Pam.

Jude read on, her voice maintaining its steadiness and low resonance. *"If Laki-Seone chooses not to fulfill the Ceremony of Emergence, this means she was unable fully to transcend zetkapian doubt, but is to be forgiven, for the choice was too difficult for her."* Jude's voice faltered almost imperceptibly. *"Yet,"* she continued, *"the One Who Chooses has the opportunity to do the next best thing, to complete the Full Circle and pave the way for the New Guide by passing on*

346

the Lake Valley to the Kwo-amians. *She shall always walk tall among them.*"

Jude closed the book. "That is all," she said. "I thought it best to share this with you now, while people are all still here at Circle Edge. Please tell the others."

Jude stood and left the stage. Amagyne came to her side immediately, and they were quickly surrounded by many Guardian Edgers. Toni watched Jude leaving through a rear door, followed by a troop of Edgers.

"I guess it's goodbye, Jude!" Dagney said to Toni. She put her arm around Toni's shoulder. "At least she's alive."

* * * * *

That night at two a.m. the grounds of Circle Edge were deserted. Toni couldn't sleep. She had been unsuccessful in her attempts to find Jude, though Miluna had arrived at midnight with the message that Jude would come to the camp in the morning to be with Toni. Toni slipped out of her sleeping bag and pulled on her sweatpants. She took her jacket, which had been serving as her pillow, and crawled out of the tent. Pam did not stir.

The night air was cold, the clear sky a mass of stars. In a few camps women still sat around fires. Toni walked the path that took her to the Dome. She was tempted to go in and try to find Jude, but did not. She kept walking until she came to the clearing, then sat on a bench and looked at the mountains and the beautiful starry sky. She could see several women

347

walking along the river path. Across the clearing was the rocky hillside that housed the Inner Garden. Toni wondered if Jude was there with La in an all-night vigil.

A half hour passed as Toni sat thinking about all that had happened in the last few months, wondering if Jude would ever come home. Sudden movement caught her eye. She looked up, toward the cliffs, and saw something white moving in the night. She blinked and stared. It was a horse, a white horse, trotting toward the cliff. She could dimly distinguish the muffled sound of hoofbeats. The horse reached the entrance to the Inner Garden, and stopped. Toni sat up straight on the bench and stared intently. The horse remained standing motionless as if waiting. Toni wondered if there were wild horses in the area. Mustangs maybe. The horse still did not move.

After a few more minutes, Toni could see someone coming out of the Inner Garden tunnel.

She sprang to her feet, her heart pounding, her mouth wide open. The figure that had emerged from the crevice in the mountain walked slowly toward the horse, her head high, her white hair glowing in the starlight. *"Oh my God, oh no, it can't be!"* Toni's hands were pressed against her mouth. The woman mounted the horse in one graceful sweep, the white of her flowing cloak merging with the whiteness of the horse.

Toni blinked rapidly, breathing in gasps. She could hear the soft sound of hooves striking earth. She stared dumbfounded as horse and rider glided smoothly away, becoming smaller and smaller, until they disappeared into the woods. Toni's feet were rooted to the ground, her mind numb. She had no idea how long she stood there. Finally she saw three people running toward the Inner Garden entrance. Toni began to run also. By the time she reached the crevice she could barely breathe. She leaned against the cliff to catch her breath.

The tunnel was lit with torches. She could hear voices. A half dozen women were in the bamboo hallway. "What happened?" Toni croaked.

"Did you see it too?" a woman asked, gazing wide-eyed at Toni.

"La," Toni said. "Where is she?"

The Edger's eyes were glazed. "She's gone. Kwo-am came for her and took her away."

CHAPTER 37

"There are so many versions of reality, aren't there?" Jude's smile took in the four she had asked to come — Toni, Amagyne, Martha, and Gresh. It was noontime, the day after La's body had disappeared. "*My* version, what *I* believe to be reality is important to all of you, I know."

"Centrally important," Amagyne said, "and to more than just us."

Jude smiled lovingly at Amagyne. "I wanted to tell you all at once, what I believe and what I will do. I want you to understand."

Toni squirmed in her chair. Gresh laid her hand comfortingly on Toni's arm.

"It's very clear to me. It starts with my values. I deeply believe and always have that caring and respect, non-violence, sensitivity, compassion — the Kwo-amian ways —"

"Those are also feminist values," Gresh interrupted, "humanist too."

"I know," Jude said. "I want to promote these values and, because of Rosalie, I'm in a good position to do so."

"Not just because of Rosalie," Amagyne said.

"I'm very sure about where I stand," Jude continued. "More sure than I've ever been." She looked at Martha. "I know I've disappointed you, Martie, by refusing to sell to a developer."

"I'm coming to terms with it," Martha said. Much of her old vitality had returned. "I know it's your inheritance and your choice. I'm just glad you're still alive. I've been talking with Gresh, though. She has some good points, Jude, about the spa and —"

"Yes," Jude interrupted, "the Feminist Fund is important, and Gresh advocates it very well." She smiled warmly at Gresh who returned the smile. "And La has revealed that —"

"You know, some people are saying she didn't really die," Gresh said. "That the stuff she drank just put her to sleep."

"She died," Amagyne responded. "I was with her . . . her remains for several hours." Amagyne's lip was quivering. "There is no doubt about it. She was also examined by a physician."

"A Kwo-amian physician," Gresh rejoined.

"So many versions," Jude said softly.

351

"Obviously the whole horse thing was staged," Martha stated. She turned to Toni. "You said yourself you couldn't be sure it was La. Anybody could have put on the cloak and a wig."

"Go on, Laki-Seone," Amagyne said. "You wanted to say something about La."

"Yes." Jude looked across the room at a painting of the winged dancer, then back at her friends. "La has revealed that the New Guide will do what I failed to do: bring forth Kwo-world. My part now is to provide the setting, the Estate and Lake Valley, so that the circle will be complete."

"Full Circle," Amagyne said. "So it was revealed."

Jude looked from face to face. "If I believe in Kwo-am, then surely this is exactly what I must do. My choice is quite obvious."

Toni nodded sadly. Gresh looked at the floor.

"I believe very deeply in what I understand Kwo-amity to mean," Jude said. "I do believe in Kwo-am . . ." Her eyes caught Amagyne's.

Toni glared at Jude and Amagyne.

". . . as a spiritual force, which many people call God. And I believe in Zetka . . . as a symbol for evil." Jude inhaled deeply. "I believe in their meaning," she said, "but, Amagyne . . ."

There was deep pain in Amagyne's eyes.

"And Toni . . . Martie, Gresh, the truth is — I do not, I cannot truly believe in them literally in the way La talks of them."

Gresh's eyes were dancing. Toni looked flustered. Amagyne's jaw was rigid. Martha was jiggling on her chair.

"I found that out the last time I went alone up

352

into the mountains and made myself really think clearly. I wanted to believe God communicates with La as she said, and that my father was sent by God, by Kwo-am, and . . . and all the rest. But I can't. I don't."

The silence in the room was electric.

"I believe La was sincere in all she said and did," Jude continued, "yet I do not believe God spoke to her, or that I was chosen, or that I can save the world. Despite the feelings I got when I convinced myself all this was true, I know in my most honest and rational self that the feelings do not mean that what I wish were so — in fact, is. The feelings are genuine but they do not reflect reality."

She looked at Amagyne sadly. Amagyne stared back, her face expressionless.

"I think La loved me," Jude continued, "loved Jude, the person. But she also hated me. Unconsciously. Wanted me dead . . . as revenge for the death of her son. This is what I believe. And I believe that La's choice to die was well-considered. She believed it to be Kwo-am-inspired, I'm sure."

The group appeared stunned.

Jude continued. "I believe there is potential for the world to progress toward the values of feminism and of Kwo-amity. But I don't believe it can happen through . . . magic." She gazed apologetically at Amagyne. Then her eyes went to Gresh. "These values may never be fully achieved, and probably won't," she said, "but I believe the Feminist Fund is a step in the right direction."

Gresh looked quietly pleased. No one said a word.

Finally Jude spoke again. "So now you know

353

what I believe. On the basis of these beliefs, I've made my decision. I'm giving the Estate and the Lake Valley to the Feminist Fund."

She looked at Toni with tears in her eyes. "I'm done," she said. "I'm ready to go home, hon."

Toni flew out of her chair and dashed toward Jude. At the same moment, Jude rose and plunged toward Toni. They met in the middle in a crush of arms and tear-wet faces, and stood clasped together, crying and laughing. Their words were muffled by kisses and joyful exclamations. Toni said something about the cats being lonely for them. Jude said something about what a long summer it had been. "Thank you, love, for being so patient with me," she said tearfully. They clung to each other tightly, joyfully.

EPILOGUE

On a sunny spring day of the year following Jude's sojourn with the Kwo-amians, she took a phone call from Wesley Gliebman. It seemed there was to be yet another twist.

In Rosalie Wright's original will, the lawyer explained, Jude was to inherit the entire Wright fortune, with the exception of a few million dollars worth of assets set aside for the Wright Foundation. "But she changed it just weeks before she died," Gliebman told Jude. "I don't know why. There were some stipulations in the new will of which I was not allowed to inform you until nine months after Mrs. Wright's demise. It might be rather shocking, Miss Alta. Perhaps the telephone is not . . ."

Jude told him to go ahead.

Gliebman proceeded to tell her that, according to Mrs. Wright's will, if, during the nine-month period following Mrs. Wright's death, Jude had not sold or given or made the property she had acquired from Mrs. Wright available to the Kwo-amians or any other religious group, and had not sold all or any portion of said property to a for-profit organization, then Jude would inherit the full Wright holdings, with the minor exceptions previously mentioned.

Gliebman was in the middle of listing what the holdings consisted of when Jude fainted.

Toni found her on the floor.

When she was conscious again, Jude called the lawyer back. She wrote while she listened.

"You own practically the whole town of Doray," Toni said after Jude had hung up and Toni read over the list. "Not to mention a ton of stocks and bonds. You're a multi-multi-millionaire, my love. You're not going to faint again, are you?"

"Oh, Toni, now I've got more decisions to make."

"You'll handle it, sweetie. You're a lot better at making decisions than you used to be."

Jude knew that was true. After all, she was the One Who Chooses. She was the Catalyst. And so it was revealed.

WOMENWORD MAGAZINE
September, 1999

by Nikki Xavier

VALLEY OF THE WOMEN: A SHANGRI-LA IN COLORADO?

The entire town of New Page, Colorado has been taken over by an influx of feminists, most of them lesbians.

Over the past ten years, Kwo-femazon, an all-women, non-profit corporation, has acquired much of the town's real estate and most of its businesses; Kwo-femazon members hold the majority of the town's civic offices.

There have been a variety of reactions to the takeover, from lauding New Page as a "20th Century utopia," to denouncing it as a "refuge for pinko perverts." Spokeswomen for Kwo-femazon, Inc., refer to the town as an "experimental community," the first of many they hope to create.

Kwo-femazon was incorporated in 1990. New Page Mayor, Martha Alta Corbette, calls the organization "a feminist/spiritual/humanist community-corporation."

This past September 1, the Kwo-femazonians held a ceremony to commemorate the death, ten years ago, of La, the revered Sage of the esoteric religion, Kwo-amity, practiced by many of the members of Kwo-femazon. The ceremony took place at Crescent Lake in a huge private compound called Full Circle, owned by Kwo-femazon and located on the outskirts of New Page. Thousands of women linked arms under the stars and paid homage to the memory of the departed leader.

Adherents of the religion claim that soon after La's death in 1989, their goddess, Kwo-am, appeared in the form of a white horse and took the Sage away with her. The body of the beloved prophet has never been found.

Kwo-femazon's goal and purpose as stated in its charter is "to develop a community where opportunity for the fulfillment of each member's needs is maximized." Most New Page residents interviewed believe the organization is accomplishing its goals. The few who seem less enthusiastic are not members of Kwo-femazon.

Many long-term Dorayites, apparently not happy with the changes, moved out of New Page over the last ten years, selling their property to Kwo-femazon, Inc. Kwo-femazonians were elected to the town council and the school board. Kwo-femazonian teachers began filling the vacancies left by departing Dorayites. Kwo-femazonians bought out the businesses of the departing old-timers and opened their own new businesses. The Kwo-femazon-dominated town council changed the town's name and the Kwo-femazonian majority changed its character.

The community strives to meet members' needs for "safety, health, meaningful work, comfort, leisure, recreation, companionship, belongingness, individuality, respect, and involvement in social change." All of these needs are defined in some detail in the charter.

How did this unusual organization come to be? Grace "Gresh" Greshow, a member of the Kwo-femazon Board of Directors says, "Kwo-femazon happened when three essential ingredients merged: feminism, Kwo-amity, and Jude Alta's immense fortune."

When Jude inherited the Wright fortune, she used it to create Kwo-femazon. "About a dozen of us began developing the concept," Jude says. This group included Jude's lover, Toni, a sociology professor; Amagyne, Jude's half-sister and a Kwo-amian from birth; Gresh, a coordinator of the Edgewise Feminist Fund which is a grant organization originally based in Chicago; Lorn, Amagyne's mother, who was one of the first members of the religion; and several other Kwo-amian and non-Kwo-amian feminists. Jude also mentions an old acquaintance of hers named Dagney Green, owner of the women's publishing house, *Out and Out Press,* who got a sizable grant from the Fund, but who "rarely comes near the place."

Once the group was clear on the direction they wanted to go, they brought in consultants to help them work out the details. The written product of their work is the charter and by-laws of Kwo-femazon. The living product is the community of New Page, Colorado.

Most of Jude's family is with her at New Page. Her mother, Claire Alta operates a word-processing business. Jude's sister, Mayor Martha Corbette, runs the town's largest restaurant with her husband, Calvin. Jude's other sister, Amagyne, like Jude, serves on the board of Kwo-femazon, "a full-time occupation for anyone," Jude says.

"New Page can comfortably accommodate up to 5000 year-round residents," Gresh explains. "We now have 3800. About half of us live within Full Circle and the rest in town or nearby."

In addition to the social contact with other Kwo-femazonians, the use of Kwo-femazon-owned facilities, and the right to employment, members of Kwo-femazon, unlike the affiliates, have voting rights and the right to hold office.

Kwo-femazonians also have some obligations. According to the Kwo-femazon charter, all members must agree to attempt to meet their needs, physical and emotional, in ways that respect others' attempts to meet their needs; make sincere efforts to avoid inflicting harm or pain on others; strive for open and honest communication; and work toward social change. They also agree to try to resolve conflicts by using the "Steps to Peaceful Co-existence" (P.C.), an individualized mediation system developed by Kwo-femazon.

Another important component of Kwo-femazon is the Edgewise Feminist Fund, a grant organization which funds projects that promote feminist and humanist principles. One of the Fund's primary beneficiaries is the well-known Wright Peace Institute, which has made significant contributions toward world peace.

Toni Dilano received a Fund grant to support her research project on the role of women in religion. "I would have had trouble getting it financed elsewhere," she says. Toni also has a part-time faculty position at the University of Colorado.

New Page has one public school, Wright Elementary and High School. Like everything else at New Page, the school has changed radically since Kwo-femazon. "Flexibility, sensitivity, individual attention and learning by doing," are the key guidelines used at Wright, according to Pam Holtz, a teacher at the school.

The first child born at Full Circle since the inception of Kwo-femazon is an angelic-looking girl called Lana. Her birth was jubilantly celebrated by the inhabitants. "She was born in a little hut on the shores of Crescent Lake," her mother explains. "We planted trees around the lake to commemorate her arrival."

The Kwo-femazonians who call New Page home believe it to be a "dream come true," as Kwo-femazonian, Lace Washington, a Doray native, put it. "No rape, violence, racism, or sexism, and plenty of good company. It's a satisfying life."

359

Jude Alta concurs, describing the sense of "fulfillment and completeness" she feels at New Page, feelings that she used to think were unattainable. "It's a good start," Jude concludes.

A few of the publications of
THE NAIAD PRESS, INC.
P.O. Box 10543 • Tallahassee, Florida 32302
Phone (904) 539-5965
Mail orders welcome. Please include 15% postage.

PLEASURES by Robbi Sommers. 204 pp. Unprecedented
eroticism.   ISBN 0-941483-49-5 $8.95

EDGEWISE by Camarin Grae. 372 pp. Spellbinding
adventure.   ISBN 0-941483-19-3   9.95

FATAL REUNION by Claire McNab. 216 pp. 2nd Det. Inspec.
Carol Ashton mystery.   ISBN 0-941483-40-1   8.95

KEEP TO ME STRANGER by Sarah Aldridge. 372 pp. Romance
set in a department store dynasty.   ISBN 0-941483-38-X   9.95

HEARTSCAPE by Sue Gambill. 204 pp. American lesbian in
Portugal.   ISBN 0-941483-33-9   8.95

IN THE BLOOD by Lauren Wright Douglas. 252 pp. Lesbian
science fiction adventure fantasy   ISBN 0-941483-22-3   8.95

THE BEE'S KISS by Shirley Verel. 216 pp. Delicate, delicious
romance.   ISBN 0-941483-36-3   8.95

RAGING MOTHER MOUNTAIN by Pat Emmerson. 264 pp.
Furosa Firechild's adventures in Wonderland. ISBN 0-941483-35-5   8.95

IN EVERY PORT by Karin Kallmaker. 228 pp. Jessica's sexy,
adventuresome travels.   ISBN 0-941483-37-7   8.95

OF LOVE AND GLORY by Evelyn Kennedy. 192 pp. Exciting
WWII romance.   ISBN 0-941483-32-0   8.95

CLICKING STONES by Nancy Tyler Glenn. 288 pp. Love
transcending time.   ISBN 0-941483-31-2   8.95

SURVIVING SISTERS by Gail Pass. 252 pp. Powerful love
story.   ISBN 0-941483-16-9   8.95

SOUTH OF THE LINE by Catherine Ennis. 216 pp. Civil War
adventure.   ISBN 0-941483-29-0   8.95

WOMAN PLUS WOMAN by Dolores Klaich. 300 pp. Supurb
Lesbian overview.   ISBN 0-941483-28-2   9.95

SLOW DANCING AT MISS POLLY'S by Sheila Ortiz Taylor.
96 pp. Lesbian Poetry   ISBN 0-941483-30-4   7.95

DOUBLE DAUGHTER by Vicki P. McConnell. 216 pp. A Nyla
Wade Mystery, third in the series.   ISBN 0-941483-26-6   8.95

HEAVY GILT by Delores Klaich. 192 pp. Lesbian detective/
disappearing homophobes/upper class gay society.
                                          ISBN 0-941483-25-8   8.95

THE FINER GRAIN by Denise Ohio. 216 pp. Brilliant young college lesbian novel. ISBN 0-941483-11-8   8.95

THE AMAZON TRAIL by Lee Lynch. 216 pp. Life, travel & lore of famous lesbian author. ISBN 0-941483-27-4   8.95

HIGH CONTRAST by Jessie Lattimore. 264 pp. Women of the Crystal Palace. ISBN 0-941483-17-7   8.95

OCTOBER OBSESSION by Meredith More. Josie's rich, secret Lesbian life. ISBN 0-941483-18-5   8.95

LESBIAN CROSSROADS by Ruth Baetz. 276 pp. Contemporary Lesbian lives. ISBN 0-941483-21-5   9.95

BEFORE STONEWALL: THE MAKING OF A GAY AND LESBIAN COMMUNITY by Andrea Weiss & Greta Schiller. 96 pp., 25 illus. ISBN 0-941483-20-7   7.95

WE WALK THE BACK OF THE TIGER by Patricia A. Murphy. 192 pp. Romantic Lesbian novel/beginning women's movement. ISBN 0-941483-13-4   8.95

SUNDAY'S CHILD by Joyce Bright. 216 pp. Lesbian athletics, at last the novel about sports. ISBN 0-941483-12-6   8.95

OSTEN'S BAY by Zenobia N. Vole. 204 pp. Sizzling adventure romance set on Bonaire. ISBN 0-941483-15-0   8.95

LESSONS IN MURDER by Claire McNab. 216 pp. 1st Det. Inspec. Carol Ashton mystery — erotic tension!. ISBN 0-941483-14-2   8.95

YELLOWTHROAT by Penny Hayes. 240 pp. Margarita, bandit, kidnaps Julia. ISBN 0-941483-10-X   8.95

SAPPHISTRY: THE BOOK OF LESBIAN SEXUALITY by Pat Califia. 3d edition, revised. 208 pp. ISBN 0-941483-24-X   8.95

CHERISHED LOVE by Evelyn Kennedy. 192 pp. Erotic Lesbian love story. ISBN 0-941483-08-8   8.95

LAST SEPTEMBER by Helen R. Hull. 208 pp. Six stories & a glorious novella. ISBN 0-941483-09-6   8.95

THE SECRET IN THE BIRD by Camarin Grae. 312 pp. Striking, psychological suspense novel. ISBN 0-941483-05-3   8.95

TO THE LIGHTNING by Catherine Ennis. 208 pp. Romantic Lesbian 'Robinson Crusoe' adventure. ISBN 0-941483-06-1   8.95

THE OTHER SIDE OF VENUS by Shirley Verel. 224 pp. Luminous, romantic love story. ISBN 0-941483-07-X   8.95

DREAMS AND SWORDS by Katherine V. Forrest. 192 pp. Romantic, erotic, imaginative stories. ISBN 0-941483-03-7   8.95

MEMORY BOARD by Jane Rule. 336 pp. Memorable novel about an aging Lesbian couple. ISBN 0-941483-02-9   8.95

THE ALWAYS ANONYMOUS BEAST by Lauren Wright
Douglas. 224 pp. A Caitlin Reese mystery. First in a series.
ISBN 0-941483-04-5   **8.95**

SEARCHING FOR SPRING by Patricia A. Murphy. 224 pp.
Novel about the recovery of love.   ISBN 0-941483-00-2   **8.95**

DUSTY'S QUEEN OF HEARTS DINER by Lee Lynch. 240 pp.
Romantic blue-collar novel.   ISBN 0-941483-01-0   **8.95**

PARENTS MATTER by Ann Muller. 240 pp. Parents'
relationships with Lesbian daughters and gay sons.
ISBN 0-930044-91-6   **9.95**

THE PEARLS by Shelley Smith. 176 pp. Passion and fun in
the Caribbean sun.   ISBN 0-930044-93-2   **7.95**

MAGDALENA by Sarah Aldridge. 352 pp. Epic Lesbian novel
set on three continents.   ISBN 0-930044-99-1   **8.95**

THE BLACK AND WHITE OF IT by Ann Allen Shockley.
144 pp. Short stories.   ISBN 0-930044-96-7   **7.95**

SAY JESUS AND COME TO ME by Ann Allen Shockley. 288
pp. Contemporary romance.   ISBN 0-930044-98-3   **8.95**

LOVING HER by Ann Allen Shockley. 192 pp. Romantic love
story.   ISBN 0-930044-97-5   **7.95**

MURDER AT THE NIGHTWOOD BAR by Katherine V.
Forrest. 240 pp. A Kate Delafield mystery. Second in a series.
ISBN 0-930044-92-4   **8.95**

ZOE'S BOOK by Gail Pass. 224 pp. Passionate, obsessive love
story.   ISBN 0-930044-95-9   **7.95**

WINGED DANCER by Camarin Grae. 228 pp. Erotic Lesbian
adventure story.   ISBN 0-930044-88-6   **8.95**

PAZ by Camarin Grae. 336 pp. Romantic Lesbian adventurer
with the power to change the world.   ISBN 0-930044-89-4   **8.95**

SOUL SNATCHER by Camarin Grae. 224 pp. A puzzle, an
adventure, a mystery — Lesbian romance.   ISBN 0-930044-90-8   **8.95**

THE LOVE OF GOOD WOMEN by Isabel Miller. 224 pp.
Long-awaited new novel by the author of the beloved *Patience
and Sarah*.   ISBN 0-930044-81-9   **8.95**

THE HOUSE AT PELHAM FALLS by Brenda Weathers. 240
pp. Suspenseful Lesbian ghost story.   ISBN 0-930044-79-7   **7.95**

HOME IN YOUR HANDS by Lee Lynch. 240 pp. More stories
from the author of *Old Dyke Tales*.   ISBN 0-930044-80-0   **7.95**

EACH HAND A MAP by Anita Skeen. 112 pp. Real-life poems
that touch us all.   ISBN 0-930044-82-7   **6.95**

SURPLUS by Sylvia Stevenson. 342 pp. A classic early Lesbian
novel.   ISBN 0-930044-78-9   **7.95**

PEMBROKE PARK by Michelle Martin. 256 pp. Derring-do and daring romance in Regency England.   ISBN 0-930044-77-0   7.95

THE LONG TRAIL by Penny Hayes. 248 pp. Vivid adventures of two women in love in the old west.   ISBN 0-930044-76-2   8.95

HORIZON OF THE HEART by Shelley Smith. 192 pp. Hot romance in summertime New England.   ISBN 0-930044-75-4   7.95

AN EMERGENCE OF GREEN by Katherine V. Forrest. 288 pp. Powerful novel of sexual discovery.   ISBN 0-930044-69-X   8.95

THE LESBIAN PERIODICALS INDEX edited by Claire Potter. 432 pp. Author & subject index.   ISBN 0-930044-74-6   29.95

DESERT OF THE HEART by Jane Rule. 224 pp. A classic; basis for the movie *Desert Hearts*.   ISBN 0-930044-73-8   7.95

SPRING FORWARD/FALL BACK by Sheila Ortiz Taylor. 288 pp. Literary novel of timeless love.   ISBN 0-930044-70-3   7.95

FOR KEEPS by Elisabeth Nonas. 144 pp. Contemporary novel about losing and finding love.   ISBN 0-930044-71-1   7.95

TORCHLIGHT TO VALHALLA by Gale Wilhelm. 128 pp. Classic novel by a great Lesbian writer.   ISBN 0-930044-68-1   7.95

LESBIAN NUNS: BREAKING SILENCE edited by Rosemary Curb and Nancy Manahan. 432 pp. Unprecedented autobiographies of religious life.   ISBN 0-930044-62-2   9.95

THE SWASHBUCKLER by Lee Lynch. 288 pp. Colorful novel set in Greenwich Village in the sixties.   ISBN 0-930044-66-5   8.95

MISFORTUNE'S FRIEND by Sarah Aldridge. 320 pp. Historical Lesbian novel set on two continents.   ISBN 0-930044-67-3   7.95

A STUDIO OF ONE'S OWN by Ann Stokes. Edited by Dolores Klaich. 128 pp. Autobiography.   ISBN 0-930044-64-9   7.95

SEX VARIANT WOMEN IN LITERATURE by Jeannette Howard Foster. 448 pp. Literary history.   ISBN 0-930044-65-7   8.95

A HOT-EYED MODERATE by Jane Rule. 252 pp. Hard-hitting essays on gay life; writing; art.   ISBN 0-930044-57-6   7.95

INLAND PASSAGE AND OTHER STORIES by Jane Rule. 288 pp. Wide-ranging new collection.   ISBN 0-930044-56-8   7.95

WE TOO ARE DRIFTING by Gale Wilhelm. 128 pp. Timeless Lesbian novel, a masterpiece.   ISBN 0-930044-61-4   6.95

AMATEUR CITY by Katherine V. Forrest. 224 pp. A Kate Delafield mystery. First in a series.   ISBN 0-930044-55-X   7.95

THE SOPHIE HOROWITZ STORY by Sarah Schulman. 176 pp. Engaging novel of madcap intrigue.   ISBN 0-930044-54-1   7.95

THE BURNTON WIDOWS by Vickie P. McConnell. 272 pp. A Nyla Wade mystery, second in the series.   ISBN 0-930044-52-5   7.95

OLD DYKE TALES by Lee Lynch. 224 pp. Extraordinary
stories of our diverse Lesbian lives.   ISBN 0-930044-51-7   8.95

DAUGHTERS OF A CORAL DAWN by Katherine V. Forrest.
240 pp. Novel set in a Lesbian new world.   ISBN 0-930044-50-9   7.95

THE PRICE OF SALT by Claire Morgan. 288 pp. A milestone
novel, a beloved classic.   ISBN 0-930044-49-5   8.95

AGAINST THE SEASON by Jane Rule. 224 pp. Luminous,
complex novel of interrelationships.   ISBN 0-930044-48-7   8.95

LOVERS IN THE PRESENT AFTERNOON by Kathleen
Fleming. 288 pp. A novel about recovery and growth.
                                              ISBN 0-930044-46-0   8.95

TOOTHPICK HOUSE by Lee Lynch. 264 pp. Love between
two Lesbians of different classes.   ISBN 0-930044-45-2   7.95

MADAME AURORA by Sarah Aldridge. 256 pp. Historical
novel featuring a charismatic "seer."   ISBN 0-930044-44-4   7.95

CURIOUS WINE by Katherine V. Forrest. 176 pp. Passionate
Lesbian love story, a best-seller.   ISBN 0-930044-43-6   8.95

BLACK LESBIAN IN WHITE AMERICA by Anita Cornwell.
141 pp. Stories, essays, autobiography.   ISBN 0-930044-41-X   7.50

CONTRACT WITH THE WORLD by Jane Rule. 340 pp.
Powerful, panoramic novel of gay life.   ISBN 0-930044-28-2   7.95

MRS. PORTER'S LETTER by Vicki P. McConnell. 224 pp.
The first Nyla Wade mystery.   ISBN 0-930044-29-0   7.95

TO THE CLEVELAND STATION by Carol Anne Douglas.
192 pp. Interracial Lesbian love story.   ISBN 0-930044-27-4   6.95

THE NESTING PLACE by Sarah Aldridge. 224 pp. A
three-woman triangle—love conquers all!   ISBN 0-930044-26-6   7.95

THIS IS NOT FOR YOU by Jane Rule. 284 pp. A letter to a
beloved is also an intricate novel.   ISBN 0-930044-25-8   8.95

FAULTLINE by Sheila Ortiz Taylor. 140 pp. Warm, funny,
literate story of a startling family.   ISBN 0-930044-24-X   6.95

THE LESBIAN IN LITERATURE by Barbara Grier. 3d ed.
Foreword by Maida Tilchen. 240 pp. Comprehensive bibliography.
Literary ratings; rare photos.   ISBN 0-930044-23-1   7.95

ANNA'S COUNTRY by Elizabeth Lang. 208 pp. A woman
finds her Lesbian identity.   ISBN 0-930044-19-3   6.95

PRISM by Valerie Taylor. 158 pp. A love affair between two
women in their sixties.   ISBN 0-930044-18-5   6.95

BLACK LESBIANS: AN ANNOTATED BIBLIOGRAPHY
compiled by J. R. Roberts. Foreword by Barbara Smith. 112 pp.
Award-winning bibliography.   ISBN 0-930044-21-5   5.95

THE MARQUISE AND THE NOVICE by Victoria Ramstetter.
108 pp. A Lesbian Gothic novel. ISBN 0-930044-16-9 6.95

OUTLANDER by Jane Rule. 207 pp. Short stories and essays
by one of our finest writers. ISBN 0-930044-17-7 8.95

ALL TRUE LOVERS by Sarah Aldridge. 292 pp. Romantic
novel set in the 1930s and 1940s. ISBN 0-930044-10-X 7.95

A WOMAN APPEARED TO ME by Renee Vivien. 65 pp. A
classic; translated by Jeannette H. Foster. ISBN 0-930044-06-1 5.00

CYTHEREA'S BREATH by Sarah Aldridge. 240 pp. Romantic
novel about women's entrance into medicine.
ISBN 0-930044-02-9 6.95

TOTTIE by Sarah Aldridge. 181 pp. Lesbian romance in the
turmoil of the sixties. ISBN 0-930044-01-0 6.95

THE LATECOMER by Sarah Aldridge. 107 pp. A delicate love
story. ISBN 0-930044-00-2 6.95

ODD GIRL OUT by Ann Bannon. ISBN 0-930044-83-5 5.95

I AM A WOMAN by Ann Bannon. ISBN 0-930044-84-3 5.95

WOMEN IN THE SHADOWS by Ann Bannon.
ISBN 0-930044-85-1 5.95

JOURNEY TO A WOMAN by Ann Bannon.
ISBN 0-930044-86-X 5.95

BEEBO BRINKER by Ann Bannon. ISBN 0-930044-87-8 5.95
Legendary novels written in the fifties and sixties,
set in the gay mecca of Greenwich Village.

VOLUTE BOOKS

JOURNEY TO FULFILLMENT Early classics by Valerie 3.95

A WORLD WITHOUT MEN Taylor: The Erika Frohmann 3.95

RETURN TO LESBOS series. 3.95

These are just a few of the many Naiad Press titles — we are the oldest and
largest lesbian/feminist publishing company in the world. Please request a
complete catalog. We offer personal service; we encourage and welcome
direct mail orders from individuals who have limited access to bookstores
carrying our publications.